Of Ecstasy and Ash

———

A Novel By

Jeanne Renee

OF ECSTASY

AND

ASH

A NOVEL BY

JEANNE RENEE

*For the ones who know what it is to long for more. I see you. I am you.
And for Jeremy, who doesn't let go.*

Author's Note

Dear Reader,

As you embark on this journey, there is something you must know. This is not a tale of triumph, not in the way some might hope. But it is a story of longing, grace, and reclamation much like my own.

Since every lived experience of chronic illness and disability is unique, I can only offer my own transmuted through this retelling of the tragically beautiful ballet *Giselle*. I cannot speak for the chronically ill community; I can only write what I know. And while it is vital to have joyful representations of chronic illness and disability, I believe there is value in exploring the messy, vulnerable aspects of those identities as well.

I needed such honesty. Perhaps you do too. Which is why I wrote the bones of this book at the height of my illness when there was no diagnosis, no treatment plan, no peace. Rest assured, I will write books about chronically ill characters living their best, most vital and sexy life soon, but at the time of telling this story, I was not there yet. My grief, shame, anger, and fear about the state of my body were still too present.

And while many of our symptoms overlap, Eliška's much more

acute illness stems from a congenital heart defect, while mine originate from the ongoing management of Hashimoto's thyroiditis, IBS (irritable bowel syndrome), vestibular and ocular migraines, ME/CFS (chronic fatigue syndrome), shingles, and the agoraphobia I developed as a result. Like Eliška, I spent many years longing for a body and life that felt out of reach. So I allowed her to feel the internalized ableism I am still excavating from within myself.

I cannot regret telling this side of my journey with chronic illness, because I know many of you will understand it intimately. I hope you feel seen and validated. And I hope you, like Eliška, learn that you are worthy of the biggest life you can imagine.

~ Jeanne Renee

CONTENT WARNING

This book contains descriptions of intimate partner violence, chronic illness, ableism, sudden death, homophobia, pregnancy loss, suicidal ideation, mild gore, sexism, and open-door consensual sex. Please read with care, my dears.

Their cheeks had the satin frost-glow of the moon;
    Their eyes the fire of Sirius.
    They circled, and droned a monotonous tune,
    Abandoned to love delirious.

~George Meredith, *Phantasy* (1861)

Death is nothing at all. I have only slipped away into the next room.

I am I, and you are you.

~Henry Scott Holland, *The King of Terrors* (1909)

ACT ONE

Before

One

Eliška

When the soft knock came at the door, the day was still pale and new. Thin enough to crack. Eliška startled, pricking her finger on the needle. She frowned as the bead of blood welled up, dark and stinging. Pressing the small wound to her mouth, Eliška set down her embroidery. It wouldn't do to stain the creamy linen. The offending salt and copper disappeared on her tongue and the ache eased.

It was too early for visitors. Morning mists still ringed the castle above the village of Hrozno, which was only just beginning to wake. She glanced to the back of the small cottage where her mother still lay abed, an unusual sight. Cloaked in the flickering glow of an oil lamp, the older woman stirred but did not wake, her black-and-silver braid resting limp on the pillow like a slumbering snake.

Please don't wake up, thought Eliška. Not yet. She so rarely had mornings to herself without her mother whipping about, forceful as a gale, and was greedy for quiet. Perhaps if she remained silent, the untimely guest would go away. She held her breath.

Instead, the insistent rasp of a whisper slithered under the door.

"Eliška," called the voice, and her name rose into the room like a ribbon of smoke.

She knew that voice. Allowing herself exactly one steeling blink and a resigned sigh, Eliška pulled her shawl tighter, crossed the polished wood floor in her stockinged feet, and eased open the door.

Radek Varga loomed in the doorway. Shadowy and expectant, he stood with a dead hare hanging from one big hand as the damp morning air curled around them. Bright blood dripped from the creature's mouth onto the threshold. A bad sign. Mamička wouldn't like the mess, although she overlooked almost everything when it came to Radek and his gifts. Eliška kept her face carefully blank as she took a breath through her mouth. The tanner's acrid stench was as relentless as his attention.

"Good morning, Eliška," Radek said in a breath of mist and handed her the hare. "For you and your mother."

The light from the kitchen hearth lit the tall man's ruddy beard and made his autumn eyes shine. He reminded Eliška of a dead fox she'd stumbled across once in the woods. Even as it moldered in the underbrush, its snarling lips decaying around sharp teeth, the creature's tail had flamed a brilliant, beautiful red.

"*Ďakujem*, Radek. You should not spoil us so," she said, her voice low and flat. The animal's pelt was soft against her hands, the flesh still tender and pliant. She and Mamička would eat well tonight, even if the stew tasted of obligation. Eliška twisted her face into a smile and moved to close the door.

But Radek, anticipating her reserve, rested his big hands, hard and tawny as the leathers he made, on the lintel to keep Eliška from shutting him out. She bit the inside of her cheeks in annoyance, but resisting would only prolong the exchange.

"A moment," he whispered, leaning closer. "After chapel yesterday, I overheard Pán Nagy and Pán Takacs speaking of the harvest. I believe the reaping is nearly at hand." The tanner smiled at this news, clearly pleased with himself for being the bearer of it.

"Nagy could not keep himself from bragging about his expectations for this year's vintage. The way he carried on, it had best be the finest year ever. Worthy of a festival to remember, or he will have to humble himself next year."

Though Eliška had already heard this news from her mother two days ago, she couldn't keep the corners of her mouth from betraying her as they twitched with earnest excitement. The harvest festival. Anticipation bloomed in her head like an intoxicating fog. The harvest festival was a bright spot in her restricted existence, and she looked forward to the revelry every year. And year after year she was relegated to the outskirts to watch the dancers; Mamička declaring her too ill to participate. Determination for this year to be different hardened in her palm like a stone.

Misreading her response, Radek pounced on the opportunity of her smile. "Shall I lead you in a dance then?" His amber eyes drifted across her face before dropping to her lips. His own mouth tightened in response. "A gentle one to be sure."

Eliška's pleasure drained away, and she sank her teeth into her bottom lip without thinking. The notorious blue tint of her fingers and lips had deepened, the dizzy spells were becoming more frequent, and her swollen feet now made her boots feel unbearably tight. Even those accustomed to such things about her appearance had noticed the changes of late. Her neighbors' worried stares could not lie. Nor could her mother's constant hovering.

"Of course Isha will be honored to dance with you, Radek."

The brass voice clanged against Eliška's back before she could answer for herself. Radek's eyes darted over her shoulder, and they turned together as Eliška's mother came forward.

Wrapped in an intricately embroidered shawl, the bright patterns fell over Mamička's straight shoulders like a cascade of spring violets, wood sorrel, and ransoms. Unlike Eliška, whose uncovered maple hair escaped its braid in tangles around her winged ears, her mother's crisp white cap was securely in place as always.

"That is, if Isha hasn't taken a chill from standing on the threshold at this hour." Mamička's reproach was clear, but Eliška knew it was for show. Her mother wasn't angry at Radek for the early call, but at her for not inviting him in to sit by the fire.

"*Dobrý den,* Pani Ciernikova," Radek said, giving the widow her formal name and a small bow. "Forgive me for the early intrusion. Hunting was fortunate this morning and I thought you would enjoy the extra game."

His assumption of their need hung in the air like a winged beast, circling and unwanted. Eliška scowled at the imagined thing, hating it for its vile truth, though she could not suppress the way her mouth watered at the thought of the hare's roasted flesh.

Despite her thinness, Mamička always moved like a strong wind and took the hare still clutched in Eliška's hands. "How could I be cross with the bearer of such gifts? Come warm yourself, *syn,*" said Mamička, her softness for Radek alone.

Radek smiled, sharp and hungry, at the familial greeting but made no move to enter the house. Another drop of the hare's blood smacked the floor in a scarlet sunburst, drawing Eliška's attention. She felt Radek's liquid eyes on her, begging, but she said nothing. Nothing to reproach. Nothing to invite. Nothing, for Eliška knew Radek's pride would only stretch so far. When her gaze stayed fixed on the floor, no invitation forthcoming, his heavy boots backed out of the doorway. Her breath loosened as both his wanting and his smell drifted away.

"My thanks, Pani Ciernikova, but I cannot accept," said Radek. "There is much to be done at the tannery."

Eliška met his eyes then for the briefest moment and dipped in a perfunctory curtsey.

"*Dovidenia,*" he said and was gone as suddenly as he'd arrived. Eliška could not make herself regret it, though she knew her mother would try.

Mamička closed the door with a huff and thrust the hare back into Eliška's hands, her careful manners no longer on display.

"Headstrong girl." Her eyes gleamed crow-black in the fire-light. "Why do you persist in this foolishness, Isha? Radek Varga is a strong, patient man who can feed you. Care for you. Who *does* care for you in spite of...everything," she said, gesturing vaguely to Eliška and her many deficiencies.

She could not contradict her mother. There was wisdom in her words. But neither could Eliška encourage Radek's advances without playing traitor to her own soul. He was coarse and without imagination. He did not listen to her. Not even the promise of more meat and fine leathers was enough to tempt her into having his hand. In silent rebellion, Eliška pressed the soft wool of her shawl to her nose, ridding herself of his scent.

Exasperated, her mother snatched the carcass back from Eliška's numb fingers and hung it in a corner of the tiny kitchen to be dressed, and started banging around to prepare the morning meal. "I know you have preferences, child. I am not blind. But what will you do without a husband when I am gone? Go to a convent? Barter your embroidery for crumbs? Or perhaps trading poultices and tonics for scraps as Babička Olga does would suit you?" Mamička goaded over her shoulder.

Eliška fisted her small, cold hands at her sides. She knew better than to rise to such baiting, but the last comment struck its mark. She met her mother's blunt stare, matching her for once.

"Babička Olga is the greatest healer in the valley. There is no shame in how she lives. Why can I not work to earn my own keep and live simply as she does?" Eliška moved closer to the fire as she spoke. Summer still lay across the valley, green and dense, but each morning the darkness thickened as the shadow of autumn crept closer, chilling her bones. Standing at the open door in the damp air had been a mistake, but she would never admit it.

Her mother set a blackened pot on the bricked stove and faced Eliška. The corners of her wide mouth crimped with annoyance.

"You would ask me this? Your mother who cares for you?" The questions stained the space between them, dark and disastrous as spilled ink. They both carried scars from this familiar battle, a miller's wheel of hurts to which there was no end.

Bitter words scratched at the back of Eliška's teeth, eager to get out, but she clenched her jaw against them. There were better ways to use her limited energy.

Probably taking Eliška's silence as victory, Mamička rinsed her hands in the wash basin before grabbing a loaf of bread and the jar of butter from the shelf. As she worked, the set of her shoulders softened against Eliška's silence.

"I know you have longings, Isha. I do. It is normal when one is young. But you must be practical, yes? Think of me and the soul of your blessed departed father if not for yourself." Putting the buttered bread on the table, her mother added more softly, "You would grow used to the smell in time."

Eliška sighed, the fight draining from her completely. Her mother meant to be kind. She knew this, but resented the familiar lie all the same. Mamička knew perfectly well it was not only Radek's smell and dogged persistence that set Eliška's teeth on edge. They simply were not a match, and she couldn't explain how the tanner himself didn't see it. Sometimes she wondered if it was because she didn't accept him that Radek would not relent. A fox on the heels of a hare.

Determined not to argue anymore, Eliška took a deep breath, grabbed a rag, and dipped it into a bucket. Cold water stung her fingertips, echoing the dull ache in her head. She'd had another restless night of dreams: strange, fleeting wisps of a faceless foreboding just out of reach, like a tune half remembered. Eliška rung out the rag. She would try a different topic.

"Radek heard the harvest will begin soon. Pán Nagy expects a good vintage." She said this both to distract her mother and gauge her reaction. Eliška envied many things, but she did not long for the grueling task of harvesting the grapes. She'd seen enough of her fellow villagers' blistered hands and bent backs to know she was, for once, fortunate in her inability to work the fields. Her weak heart spared her this, even as it snatched away so much else.

She'd never forget the sight of little Vladimir being carried into Babička Olga's surgery after an accident in the fields. The cloth covering the stumps of his fingers was bright as her favorite scarlet thread. His screams had squeezed her bowels, young as she was then. He'd had no more than ten name days and now at nearly sixteen, the twisted, pink flesh of his loss made her heart ache. But the festival that came after the grapes were harvested and crushed? That was something else altogether.

Momentarily placated, Mamička sniffed and moved her attention back to the hare. "Yes. The grapes are fine and should make a good vintage, God willing. I'm not surprised Martin has finally started bragging about it, though I still say the grapes in the north corner are too small yet. He'd be wise to give them more time."

Eliška mopped the blood from the floor, her body tense with listening. She did not care for the intricacies of wine making as her mother did, but knew the survival of the estate—and therefore their village—depended on it.

"Your father always knew just when to begin. Baron Pálffy himself said he never had a better harvest master than your father. Though Martin Nagy does a fair job," she said stiffly, "he is not my Ján."

Ján Ciernik. Eliška had three clear memories of her father: a warm, calloused hand on her shoulder, the tangy perfume of crushed grapes imbedded in his clothes, a pair of merry brown eyes behind a pale ring of pipe smoke blown for her amusement. More out of habit than need, Eliška pressed her finger into a hollow between her ribs, just above her left breast.

Beat, beat. Beat, beat. Beat, beat.

So sang the heart she'd inherited from her father—a heart that only carried him through his twenty-fifth year. She thought about this more often as her twenty-first name day approached in the fall.

"I wish I remembered him more." Eliška dropped her hand

and stood, the blood now nothing but a damp patch in the dim light. She wanted to stay angry with her mother for siding with Radek, but couldn't quite muster the energy.

Her mother pursed her lips. It was nearly a smile. "As do I. At least we still have each other, Isha," she said and yanked at the hare's pelt.

The hide came away with a wet sucking sound as Eliška went back to her embroidery.

Two

Albin

The crystal goblet shattered against the stone wall with little more than a soft, brittle *clink*. Albin sighed with disappointment. He'd expected something grander when he'd heaved the fine object across the room, but his father hadn't even blinked. Clearly this was not the first time someone had thrown crystal in the presence of Baron Milan Pálffy von Erdod.

"Was that necessary?" the baron commented over the rim of his own faceted glass. His black mustache sagged as if bored. "Fits of passion are quite unmanly."

His nostrils flared in frustration, Albin renewed his pacing, though his steps were muffled by the thick, massive rug covering the floor. "Perhaps such displays wouldn't be necessary if you bothered to listen, Vater."

The baron sighed. Again. "Albin, *mein Sohn*, I've been listening to your incessant babble about this since you were in knee socks and your nurse read you too many adventure tales. Feminine things, those novels. It is time you attended to your duties," the baron said before sipping his claret, thoroughly nonplussed by his only child's agitation.

Clenching his teeth, Albin watched his father admire the

crimson liquid through the sparkling facets as if the wine was an enormous ruby before turning away in disgust. The man admired little else these days. Hardly a fortnight had passed since Albin's middle of the night return from Vienna, but that proved plenty of time to become reacquainted with his father's familiar edges. Drink and solitude had only sharpened them since they'd last been together at a social event.

"You know," the baron said, shifting the goblet so it caught the light. "Your Onkel Moritz gave your mother and I this set as a wedding gift, I believe. Shame it's incomplete now. She was quite fond of it."

Albin raked a hand through his pale hair, too familiar with his father's games and jabs to react further. Clearly even a rash display of ardor would not shake the baron out of his cold placidity. *Fine*, Albin thought and, changing tactics, feigned a contrite expression. Albin didn't revel in this calculated duplicity, but had used it often enough to know it could be effective.

"You make a fine point, Vater. Forgive me the outburst, but I am passionate about this. I'm not asking leave forever. Plenty of gentlemen tour the Continent before settling down. Some might even call it customary. If you would give me but one year to go east, I shall gladly—"

"You have had your year," said the baron with more steel in his voice than Albin had anticipated.

Albin watched as the older man pushed out of the velvet chair and stretched slowly to his full, considerable height. "Three, in fact. I had hoped attending university in Vienna and giving you time for your dalliances, would free you from this...obsession." He gestured to the large wood and glass hutch that held Albin's extensive collection of Oriental artifacts—jade, porcelain, literati paintings—and nearly spilled his wine. "But I can see that, if anything, receiving a proper education has only made this mania worse."

Still hoping to pacify his father, Albin held his expression steady and remained silent. Those shelves held Albin's most prized possessions; treasures that fascinated him and stoked a longing in him to *get away* that no one, certainly not his father, understood. To the baron they were his son's trinkets, of no more importance than a bag of glass marbles.

The count, moving with the languid speed of someone who can never be considered late, set down his goblet on the ornate sideboard and drummed his fingers against the polished wood.

"I know you are still young and wish to have your way, Albin, but I will not be swayed. An alliance with the Carinthian province must be made to stabilize the region before the whole goddamned empire dissolves into revolt." His father's half-drunk gaze flashed with sincerity. "The peasants are steeped in this nationalism. The situation can hardly merit waiting a month let alone a year. We must do our part or face the emperor's displeasure. You know this." The baron adjusted his cravat and inhaled sharply. "Which is why the lady and her family will be here in roughly a week's time and shall stay for the harvest festivities. It will give the two of you a chance to become reacquainted with one another. Once the vintage is secured, we will see to a proper wedding shortly thereafter. Before Michaelmas."

Before Michaelmas.

Anger rolled through Albin's chest, billowing and black as a thunderhead, as his fate was laid before him in stone. Michaelmas was little more than a month away. He wanted to throw another glass. To bare his teeth and howl. At least trapped beasts are at liberty to thrash against their cages.

"And if I refuse? Surely there is some other unwed noble welp available?"

His father gave a prosaic laugh and waved him off. "Come now. Don't be soft. You, *mein Sohn*, are the only 'welp' with a claim on this estate, which unfortunately needs your bride-to-be's dowry." The baron approached Albin now and clapped him on the back, his long, lean fingers heavy with intent. "You would not want to be blamed for the downfall of our estate, after all. Nor explain to the emperor why we could not suppress a regional revolt."

Albin held his breath as the baron leaned in close, his breath thick with wine. "Think of the wellbeing of our tenants if you haven't the sense to think of your own." The baron gestured with his free hand. "They cannot run from their responsibilities."

Albin faced his father and took stock of the man who was supposed to have loved him more than any other. Many considered the old baron handsome. His dark hair was still full and shot through with silver; his green eyes bright as the jade carvings Albin had fallen in love with as a child. The color of jungles and seas, places Albin had dreamed of since boyhood and would likely never see if he married now for political gain and took control of the estate as his father intended. Then the children would start arriving in the world and if there was one thing Albin had no intention of doing, it was being an absent father.

"I see," Albin said, his voice flat as he pulled away and crossed to the other side of the large, sumptuous room. His mind spun as wildly as the patterns on the enormous rug under their feet. Nauseous with despair, Albin measured the weight of his next words carefully. "Then I'd like to use my remaining week of freedom to get reacquainted with the park and grounds. Visit the tenants, perhaps. Enjoy a bit of sport. Watch the harvest." He spoke with as much confident nonchalance as he could muster, praying his father wouldn't sense his desperation.

Albin examined his own fairer, heavier-boned countenance in the polished glass of the display hutch in front of him, and awaited his father's reply. His mother's amber eyes stared back at him, wide and panicked as a cornered hare's. He swallowed hard; missing her tasted like a mouth full of ash, but he kept his voice as light as possible.

"If I'm to sacrifice myself on the altar of the estate to keep the region from breaking into open revolt, then perhaps I should spend some time getting reacquainted with my lands. As you said,

I've been away a long time." *Or at least get out of this damned stone prison while I can*, Albin thought as he watched his father's reflection over his shoulder. The baron pursed his lips in thought before smoothing out his well-groomed mustache. Albin knew he'd won this small victory before the older man spoke.

"Take a few trustworthy men with you," the baron said. "I've been informed the harvest shall begin shortly. Make yourself familiar with the workings of it if you must. But for Christ's sake stay on the estate and be back to take your place as my heir after the festival. We shall introduce your bride to her new tenants shortly thereafter."

Albin blinked. It was not enough time, and he most certainly didn't want a company of guards trotting after him. "I'd prefer to go alone. To travel quietly as to avoid notice. I have the rest of my life to be lord of the castle, after all. I could stay in the old crofter's cottage. Surely you don't think the tenants will molest your newly returned lord?"

The baron picked up his abandoned drink and finished the claret in a gulp only to choke gently and cough wine onto the rug. Albin winced. That rug was Persian, the workmanship priceless. Clearing his throat, the baron stepped on the stain without noticing. Albin took a deep, steadying breath through his nose. It would not do to complain.

"Christ," the baron swore softly before pinning Albin with an irritated gaze. "If I allow you this last lark—to carouse among the tenants and trapes across the land like a vagabond—do you swear to hold to your engagement and take over the workings of the estate? No more of this going east nonsense?"

Hope flickered in his belly. It wasn't much, but Albin was desperate enough to accept the crumbs his father offered and gave a single, decisive nod. "No guards. And I'll not be interfered with or followed until the festival."

The baron rolled his eyes, but Albin knew he'd gained ground in the negotiations.

"Fine. But I insist you take at least one reliable man and send word immediately if you need assistance. Final offer." With this last statement, his father pinned him under a green stare which made Albin feel far younger and smaller than he was.

Albin cleared his throat. "You won't announce my presence? Or interfere?"

The baron's face flashed, clearly annoyed at being pressed, but nodded after the briefest pause. "I give you my word on your mother's grave."

Albin's heart squeezed. He hated when his father swore in this manner, but knew it was the one promise he could trust. For all the baron's aloof coldness, loving her had been the one thing the two men had in common.

"*Danke*, Vater. I shall depart in the morning."

Returning to the sideboard, the baron refilled his wine and raised the glass to Albin. "Try not to do anything stupid, boy. We're all counting on you."

THREE

ELIŠKA

"Have you nothing better to do besides bother an old woman, little bird?"

Olga Prochazkova bit out the same greeting she had since Eliška started visiting the healer a decade ago. The other village children had whispered behind sticky fingers that the ancient woman was Ježibaba herself come to spy for her evil sister, Baba Yaga, who liked to simmer children in her soup pot. The bolder, crueler children even threw stones over the healer's fence and dared one another to make faces at her during mass. But Eliška —small, thin, perpetually out of breath—had poked her nose over the babička's gate with a mouth full of hope and nothing to lose. If the old woman really was Ježibaba, then perhaps she could make her well.

Eliška supposed another child might have been run off by the salty greeting, but not her. Babička Olga's frank words and kind hands had drawn her in, soothing as a salve. She could not have loved the old woman more if she had been her own blood. To this day, the ritualized exchange gave Eliška immense comfort. She gave her usual answer.

"*Nie*, Babička."

Nearly toothless gums flashed pink with delight at the familiar response, and Olga beckoned to her young friend from inside the mouth of the tiny white cottage, the black roof pitched like a pointed hat. Eliška eagerly pushed open the gate, but paused as a sharp *creak* cut across the air. She frowned, looking toward the sound. Orange rust caked the hinges. Had they been in such a condition at her last visit? Eliška couldn't remember and glanced around the front yard of her mentor's cottage carefully. The windows were as filmy as the old woman's eyes, the front step scattered with leaves. Hungry vines grew up the fence posts and weeds poked up in the garden. Eliška frowned. Her friend's tidiness was slipping. It wouldn't do.

Radek could fix this.

The thought swooped down on her like a crow, loud and unwelcome. Eliška jerked away from it. She would owe him nothing else. She would fix it herself.

"Must you always be underfoot?" came Olga's traditional second demand.

"*Áno*, Babička," Eliška answered, closing the gate behind her. Eliška ignored her tingling fingers and admired her old friend. And Olga was indeed old. No longer bothering to tie it up, the last wisps of the village matriarch's hair fell in a snowy braid down her hunched back. Solid as a boulder through the middle, the woman's strong arms and legs had carried her through more than seventy years, if rumors were to be believed. And rumors were plentiful as field mice in the small village of Hrozno. Eliška would know.

Babička Olga clicked her tongue. "If you must stay, then I shall find a use for you, bird." Olga tossed the false insult over her shoulder as she waddled through the dark mouth of her cottage. Her white braid swung behind her, free as a mare's tail.

Eliška crossed the little yard and thanked the Blessed Virgin she lived down the lane from Babička. The old woman had served as the village midwife and healer since Eliška's mother was a girl. Having never married herself, Olga had delivered every babe in the

Little Carpathian hills within half a day's journey—except for the youngest Molnar girl who famously shot out onto the bed clothes before Olga could get there—and most of their parents as well. Life and death hung across Babička's shoulders as surely as her black shawl, scaring off some while drawing in others.

She poulticed wounds, stitched torn flesh, brewed teas, tended to births, and removed teeth; all skills Eliška was learning as well. But she performed other services too. Things even Eliška knew little about and spoke of less. Every household in the village attended mass without fail, but the old ways ran deep as the Tatra Mountains were high, and she knew Olga's door was often filled in the night by a desperate soul in need of her cunning. Some villagers called it witchcraft, others harmless superstition. Babička Olga ignored both and set out a crust of bread for the škriatok in the stove as faithfully as she prayed to her rosary. To Babička, faith was faith.

Determined to help the beloved woman, Eliška ducked inside the dim cottage and was greeted by the familiar musk of leaf and root. Dried herbs hung in bunches from laundry lines along the walls and woven baskets clustered in every corner. What would have served as kitchen in another house was a surgery here, the large wooden table embedded with the memory of every life saved —or lost—on it. The planks had been scrubbed clean, but she avoided touching them anyway. Just because the blood wasn't visible didn't mean it wasn't there. If she focused hard enough, she could almost smell it, metallic and salty. A small fire blazed in the hearth and the windows, though dirty, were unshuttered and let in just enough light.

"Grind this," said Olga, holding out a familiar mortar and pestle to Eliška.

She took it and settled herself into a favorite chair by the window as they both set about their tasks. Eliška knew Olga wouldn't speak first, but bided her time anyway. She was in no hurry to return home with its air of unmet expectations despite the unfinished embroidery work awaiting her attention. Content to pummel the herbs she'd been given, Eliška waited as long as possible before the words overtook her.

"Radek called again this morning," Eliška said, trying to sound unaffected. "He brought a hare this time. Mamička was...herself." Her head ached less now, and the gentle crush of brittle leaves satisfied some small restlessness in her. Made her feel useful. Today she could do this small thing and was gratified by it.

Babička Olga's white eyebrows lifted in mock surprise, her milky eyes full of understanding. "As rose the sun, *áno*? No doubt he will be back on the morrow and the day after until you give the lad a firm answer. Yes or no. You know this, bird." She clicked her tongue again and went back to her herbs. "The question is not will he come back, but what will you do when he does?"

Eliška shot a glance at the healer and added more leaves to her pestle. What indeed, she thought and inhaled the pleasant scent of thyme and bay. Her body might be weak—there was no denying it. Even now she tightened her grip around the pestle to fight off the numbness in her fingertips. A husband would be useful. But by God in heaven her mind wasn't weak and she would not marry against her will. Not even for her mother.

"There is nothing to do." Eliška sighed. "Mamička wishes me to marry Radek. She is not wrong to want it," she said, pressing harder with the pestle. "But I do not want him and there is no other man who will have me. No way to make her see I wish to keep what little freedom I have."

Babička Olga wiped her herb-stained fingers and hummed tunelessly as she often did while thinking. Eliška peeked at her sideways. Waited as Babička pounded away at the herbs in her own mortar.

"Your *matka* and *otec* married under such a match. They loved well. Warm and steady as a hot stove in winter." She offered Eliška a snaggled smile. "They grew you in that love. Have you no faith in such a thing?"

Eliška stiffened. She hadn't expected this response from Olga Prochazkova, the proudest old maid in the Hrozno, having shunned many a suitor in her day if the stories were true.

"I know many do well with such arrangements," she said, trying to keep the exasperation from her voice. "I do not think myself above comfort or companionship." Her hands stilled as she gazed out the dusty front window. The sky burned blue above the red castle, which peaked over the top of the green woods. Beyond it all lay a world she would never see. Soon the birch and chestnut trees would dress themselves in gold and crimson as autumn faded into winter, taking another year of her life with them. Her twenty-first name day was only a few moons away and she knew little of what lay beyond. Each day held enough struggle—she couldn't afford to think further than the present.

But an unnamed yearning rose in Eliška's chest, and she felt her cheeks grow hot with feeling as she faced her wise friend, willing the old healer to understand. "I know what I am, Babička, and invalids shouldn't be choosy. But time seems to go so fast and I only—"

Babička was watching her now with sad, shrewd eyes.

Eliška licked her dry lips and didn't need a looking glass to know they were too dark. "I would have real love with a man of my choosing. Or be left alone for as long as I have."

Olga's tender smile flattened. She nodded and reached out for Eliška, wrapping a gnarled hand around her wrist. "I too was a girl like you. Once. Long ago. And I am alone as I wanted. But your mother only wishes what all mothers wish: for you to be safe."

Eliška's fervor ebbed, and she took a shaky breath, embarrassed by her passion. "I know. They both mean well I suppose. But safe is not a life."

"Then stop hiding, little bird," she said, raising a bushy eyebrow. "State your intentions and do not waver. But do not be surprised by the wrath that follows. Your mother's or young Radek's. Their wills are strong too and will not be easily set aside."

Then, like a dog hearing what others cannot, Babička Olga cocked her owlish head and turned sharply to the stove. There was no need for a proper fire now, but bones as old as the healer's required extra warmth, so the cook fire smoldered day and night.

Eliška knew this look and sat up straighter, following the healer's gaze. Flanked by plastered brick and stone, orange coals flickered among the ash. Olga leaned forward and muttered to the fire, "I'm listening, Dedko. What have you to say?"

The hairs on Eliška's arms bristled as she held her breath. Nothing happened, but Babička continued to stare into the tired flames and whisper encouragement to it as if the coals lived. They waited, the silence thickening. Then with a loud *snap*, sparks flew from the mouth of the stove, scattering themselves across the floor. Eliška leapt up and hurried to stamp them out. More than one cottage had been scorched to the ground by such an event.

"Careful, bird. Good. Now move away slowly," Olga commanded when the last vagrant spark faded. "Do not smudge them."

Eliška obeyed, slapping at her singed stockings as she went. When she stepped clear of the blotted embers, a distinct path of ash pointed to the door, the arrow-shaped tip clear and sharp. Her heart stuttered as she met Babička's wide stare. There were many things about the old ways her teacher would not speak of, but this sign was obvious even to Eliška.

"A stranger is coming," said Eliška.

Olga nodded, her wrinkled mouth pursed. "Yes, and one whose arrival is worth foretelling to us. We must keep watch." A darkness fell over her face. "We do not yet know if this bodes for good or for misfortune."

Eliška, brimming with awe and dread, turned to search the empty road outside as she pondered what it all meant.

FOUR
ALBIN

"This is quite possibly your worst idea ever, sir. And after the debacle in Paris, that's saying quite a lot," said Miroslav Medved, shouldering his over-stuffed satchel.

Albin chuckled indulgently at his valet and dearest friend's distress. When the baron had insisted Albin take a man with him, he knew Miro was the only choice. Anyone else would have either infuriated him with their nagging and hovering or worse, bored him to death. Albin would be damned before he'd tolerate either. Still, it behooved them to be cautious. If his father kept his word and didn't have them trailed through the village, he and Miro would be exposed to the usual dangers of the road and peasant life, not to mention the discovery of their true identities. They would have to be canny. At his core, Albin knew this undertaking was foolish, but between his impending nuptials and dashed travel plans, he couldn't seem to make himself care.

"Worst ever? If memory serves, you rather enjoyed yourself in Paris," Albin teased as he tightened the saddle bag onto the mule. The homely beast twitched its ears and gave an irritated stomp sending a stray pebble skittering across the vast stable floor. The wicked, old Billy goat in the stall closest to them bleated its displeasure.

Miroslav scurried out of range of both beasts. "I'm surprised you remember anything of that holiday with the amount of brandy you imbibed; and then there was the bottle smashed over your head." Miroslav glanced at the mule carrying their meager supplies. "I still don't see why we can't take a proper horse," he said, pushing up his cap. "Villagers do have horses."

Freed from their confines, Miroslav's black curls fell across his freckled forehead. Despite being several years older and blessed with an abundance of caution, there was an effervescence to his friend's presence which always cheered Albin and had since their first meeting. When Albin was no more than two years old, Miroslav, the carriage master's six-year-old son, rescued the little lord from a water trough. Albin remembered nothing of this, but had heard his mother retell it so often he could picture a spindly young Miroslav, all dark hair and elbows, running through the grounds with Albin's fat, wailing, blonde self in his arms. The two took a liking to each other, and young Miroslav began carting younger Albin around whenever possible much to the household's shock. Both fathers tried to curb the boys' familiarity, but the late baroness indulged the young friends. They'd hardly spent a day apart in the last twenty years.

"Because," said Albin, ignoring the entirely true comments about brandy and brawling, "we are supposed to be poor brothers traveling in search of work during the harvest. And in case you haven't noticed—" Albin gestured to the stalls full of champion-bred horses behind him. "Peasants do not have mounts such as those. Do you want to upend our ruse before it even begins?"

"Yes."

Albin swung at him.

Miroslav easily dodged the playful blow. "Here you are worried about horses when we could not favor each other less as brothers. We're completely unconvincing."

It was true. The men couldn't have been less alike in appearance, but Albin wasn't concerned. "People see what they want to see. No one will care if we keep our heads down and work the harvest."

"Easy for you to say, sir. And what am I to do while you are off playing pauper?" asked Miroslav, adjusting the opposite saddle bag.

"Play pauper along with me, of course." Albin loaded the last of the supplies and led the mule out into the wide yard. With the sun content to hide behind a scrim of low clouds, the morning held tight to its dewy chill. Didn't matter to Albin, though. Oppressive heat or punishing rain—it made little difference. He welcomed both as long as he remained outside the towering red and gray stone walls he both loved and loathed. Besides, he and Miroslav needed the sweat and grime of the road to complete their disguises if they were to remain hidden in plain sight.

Close behind him, Miroslav made a derisive noise. "A joy to be sure. My heart palpitates with anticipation. But in earnest, Bini. Don't you worry the people will recognize you? Not now perhaps, but after you return as the heir to the estate with your fiancée. Don't you think—"

Albin held up a hand to stop him. It wasn't as if he hadn't considered the consequences of the deception. He had. Albin had mulled over the situation last night, each possibility worn smooth with examination, but only one constant remained, smooth and hard as a river pebble: it didn't matter. Not enough to hide in his quarters and squander what little time he had left to live as he chose. Free and unrecognized.

"They won't know me now," he replied, shaking his head. "I was a child in knee pants the last time I spent more than a day in the village. Father made sure of that." Albin swung around to face his friend and smiled through his doubt. "Even if some old crone recognizes me, what of it?"

Miro raised a black brow. "And after you're presented?"

Albin knew his friend made a valid point, but he shrugged away the implications. "What would they say, precisely?"

His friend shrugged. "Nothing, I suppose. To your face. But it won't do you any good for your tenants to think you a buffoon. Which they will, mark my word."

Albin glared at Miroslav and lifted his chin. He could play the part of a haughty nobleman when necessary—he was born to it, after all. "The only buffoon I see is the one who insists on wearing such a gaudy hat for traveling. Did I not mention we are supposed to be peasants?"

Miroslav touched the stylish black velvet cap on his head and scowled anew at his lord. "This is my plainest one. You would not send me into the vineyard hatless, would you? Oh, gracious lord." Miroslav smiled a ghastly, toothsome smile then and bowed to Albin, who immediately smacked the offending hat off his friend's head.

"Here," said Albin, snatching the wide brimmed hat of a field hand from the nearest stable boy. "This shall do nicely." He plopped the field hat on Miroslav's head and handed the velvet one to the boy with a wink.

"Why thank you, sir. If anyone can make this atrocity look dashing, it is I." Miroslav secured the ridiculous item atop his dark curls and strode across the yard like a king.

Albin, chuckling, grabbed the stoic mule's reins. "Come now, Linus. We can't let him out all alone. He might find himself set upon by a marauder on the road for such a hat."

The mule did not seem particularly amused with Albin's joke, but flicked his ears without care and followed his lead rope. Unlike Linus and Miroslav, Albin was eager to get on with the adventure —even if it was only down the great hill along the winding, wooded road to his own village. It was likely the last unaccompanied one he'd have for some time. Possibly ever.

Miroslav was waiting for them at the end of the vast interior yard, whistling. His tall, lean figure and easy smile belied the strength and sharp wit beneath. Both of which had gotten Albin's ass out of a bind on more than one occasion. Albin pulled his own hat lower as the late summer sun finally pierced the veil of clouds, and vowed not to lead his friend into mischief. He wasn't after trouble. Not this time. Just freedom. Like any kenneled dog, he only wanted to spend his remaining time as a bachelor basking in the sun at the end of his chain.

As they approached the massive walls at the edge of the courtyard, stone-faced guards labored to open the gate. They did so without comment or expression. Miroslav nodded to each, but Albin stiffened and walked silently, head high. He knew his father's staff wouldn't dare breach protocol, but Albin could imagine what the servants thought about seeing him dressed so plainly. The only thing that traveled faster than fire through a castle was gossip, and he knew himself to be a favorite topic. He didn't blame them. Truly. His behavior must seem ungrateful at best and mad at worst. That didn't mean he was going to subject himself to anyone else's derision. His father's would suffice. Albin let the doors close behind them with a satisfying bang as his shoulders fell with relief. He was out.

⁂

More than a decade had passed since Albin and Miroslav had played in these woods, but the cool green light and heady scent of moss and pine pricked his senses, setting off a ripple of memories. On the rare occasion when the baron had let his heir and only child off the castle grounds, Albin was always accompanied by a host of guards. He'd hated it even then, preferring in some ways to stay home where at least he could run wild with the facade of freedom. The one time he and Miroslav had tricked the guards and ran off, Miroslav—not Albin—had been whipped upon the boys' return. Vater had forced him to watch.

Albin swallowed against the tightness in his throat. Even now the memory of the welts, red and furious across Miroslav's stripped back, soured his stomach with shame. Miroslav hadn't cried until after it was over, but it had taken two of his father's men to hold Albin in place while he thrashed and cried for his friend. The whole escapade had been Albin's idea. But his father achieved his aim in the end. Albin never ran from his guards again.

He prayed this foray into a wooded escapade would make up for the last one they'd taken all those years ago. At least his impending marriage would mean more distance from his father. The old baron had made it clear he wished to retire from running the estate, and the regional politics it involved. For Albin, this meant freedom in degrees to manage the land and people as he saw fit. He didn't think the baron was cruel to his tenants—time would soon tell—but easing the weight of his father's yoke couldn't be a bad thing. Though it pained him to think on it, even he could admit that a respected baroness like his mother was sorely needed.

But not yet, Albin thought decisively and pushed his contemplation aside.

"Christ, it's good to take in some fresh air." Albin's voice sounded forced even to his own ears, despite the truth of the statement. It *was* good to be out of doors by themselves. He stretched his arms wide and made a show of breathing deeply as they continued to plod down the winding road to the village.

"Correct me if I'm mistaken, sir, but I do believe there was air to be found on the grounds of the castle," said Miroslav. "Not to mention hot baths, feathered beds, and that exquisite game hen Cook makes drenched in plum sauce."

Albin glanced at Miro who was now leading Linus. Both beast and man seemed amusingly content with the arrangement, even if Miro liked to complain like a child at times. "It won't work, so you can stop torturing your own stomach now. Besides, who can enjoy the bracing air with everyone stalking around, watching a man?"

Miroslav cut him a hard look. "You think too much of it, sir. People must do their jobs after all."

"Spoken like a man who is not watched," Albin shot back, one fair eyebrow raised and started whistling aggressively. Miroslav shook his head, to which Albin cleared his throat and continued.

His spirited tune carried them along as they moved deeper under the wooded canopy, where the light dimmed. The air quieted and Albin stopped whistling, struck with the sudden sense of holiness he sometimes felt when entering an empty chapel or grove of trees. The road down to the village often brimmed with activity as laborers and goods moved to and fro, but on this late August morning, the men were unusually alone. A stillness enveloped the misty little hollow and Albin wondered angrily if his father had placed spies along the road. The idea smothered his mood.

"Your father's going to put me on the rack if we're set upon, you know," said Miroslav in a low voice, as if also sensing the change in the air.

"I can always count on you to be jolly, can't I?" replied Albin. He wanted to ignore his companion's comment for the sarcastic jab it was, but both men understood what the baron was capable of if something were to happen to his only heir.

Unease settled over Albin. Nothing seemed out of place and yet the dim light and sudden coolness felt unnatural. "Besides, Vater doesn't have a rack. Anymore. Torture went quite out of fashion, and you know how he likes to stay *á la mode*," Albin said, scanning the trees, the road ahead, the shadows, unable to shake the sense they were being watched.

The underbrush rustled off to their left and both men tensed, whirling to face the sound. Albin peered into the foliage, his fingers curling around the smooth hilt of the dagger in his belt. The hair on his neck bristled as the mule stomped and snorted. Otherwise, the road was silent. Not even the trees moved. It was as if an invisible blanket of snow had fallen across the hollow, silencing the world. Seconds ticked by. When nothing happened, Miroslav straightened, sheathing a dagger Albin hadn't seen him draw.

Miroslav glanced at Albin. "You're skittish as a colt, sir."

"Me?" quipped Albin, as he straightened up and took hold of Linus' lead rope. "I believe you're the one who actually drew his weapon at what was probably a squirrel."

"Someone must defend your honor," said Miroslav as he started walking. "Even if you are intent on this charade."

Ignoring Miro, Albin clicked his tongue at Linus to start moving, but the mule remained planted, ears pricked. "Come now, Linus. Don't be stubborn." Albin pulled on the lead rope to no avail. Linus' nostrils flared.

Miroslav doubled back. "Trouble with your ass again, my lord?"

"He's as stubborn as you." Albin redoubled his grip on the beast's halter.

"Perhaps he needs incentive. Sweets always get you moving," said Miroslav as he pulled a small crab apple from his pocket.

Albin, who was well aware of his own penchant for sweets, shot Miro a vengeful look. "Daggers. Apples. What else are you hiding from me?"

Miroslav had no time to answer before a violent gust of wind roared down from the canopy at them. Linus leaped forward with a startled bray, jerking the lead from Albin's hands.

"Damn it!" Albin hollered before shutting his mouth against the flurry of leaves and dirt hurtling around them.

"Come on!" came Miro's voice as both men took off running after the mule.

The gust rushed through the arbor of trees, expelling mule and men like a cough, debris flying, and then disappeared into the meadow, melting back into nothingness. Gritty and startled, the men kept running after Linus. Miroslav's long stride eventually caught up as the mule slowed to a trot and he caught hold of the lead. All three stood panting in the grass, companions in their surprise. Feeling nearly as spooked as the damn mule, Albin swiped at the leaves in his hair and glanced back at the hollow. The trees were still once again, the sky clear. Only the smallest breeze rolled around in the grass at the mouth of the tunnel.

It sounded like laughter.

FIVE

ELIŠKA

The fairy ring stood out against the bright grass like a large, pale scar. A bite mark on the earth. It was new. Eliška was sure of it. Only yesterday afternoon she'd walked this path back from Babička Olga's instead of taking the high street home. She'd wanted to be alone to mull over the fire's odd prediction. Travelers often came through Hrozno on their way to the castle, but how often was their arrival foretold? And why to her and Babička? She found no answers along the lonely path but had enjoyed the quiet anyway.

She often took the small track behind the houses. Skirting the edge of the woods, the thin dirt trail was a good place for admiring the unruly grass and bright wildflowers that dotted the undergrowth among the trees. It was infrequently used, which meant fewer people and their stares. Better to keep company with the birds, squirrels, and hares who knew nothing of pity and gossip.

Surely, she would have noticed the wide circle of withered grass kissing the path right behind her own garden fence. Wouldn't she? Eliška was always searching for new patterns and colors to put into her embroidery and prided herself on noticing what others did not. Paying close attention now she looked around the bright, unremarkable afternoon. Nothing seemed out of place. Still, the arrival of the ring so close on the heels of the stove's prediction felt significant. Her heart gave a small, startled jump as if expecting someone to leap out of her. But she was alone as usual.

Picking her way toward the eerily perfect circle, Eliška moved with exaggerated care that for once wasn't the result of her weakness. Babička Olga had warned her about crossing circles or disrespecting signs of Them—the old ones. Eliška didn't really believe in the river vodnik or forest leshy but tried to heed the old woman's advice in strange matters.

As she crept up next to the ring of withered grass, a memory welled up and trickled into another and another until a deep, long-forgotten remembering roared through her, too powerful and vivid to push down. She must have been very young, but now recalled the day vividly.

The grass had been the tender green of spring then, barely thrusting through the snow-softened ground, and the circle of white capped mushrooms had been just her size: a hoop planted to lure her into another world, or a protective cove for secrets. She hadn't known not to cross such otherworldly stamps then and sat in the center of the circle for a long time, delighted by the ants scurrying across her feet and the spicy scent of wet earth.

Watching a group of tiny brown sparrows flit through the shafts of warm afternoon light was the last thing Eliška remembered before the wind rose. It had been rustling the treetops, but suddenly swept over the glen in a violent whoosh, stealing her new cap. Eliška darted after it just in time to hear her mother scream. She'd frozen in place and turned, sensing even then what such an animal sound meant.

Her father had been in the ground more than a week before Eliška remembered her lost cap. When she'd snuck out the back gate to go looking for it, the fairy ring was gone; sucked back into the other world from whence it came. But the scrap of fabric remained. Clinging to some brambles just inside the tree line, the white cap waved to her, beckoning, a dingy and obstinate flag. She'd snatched it from the shadowy grasp of the woods and run back to the cottage, spurred by the childish certainty that if she slowed or turned around, Baba Yaga herself would appear and gobble her down whole.

Babička Olga and many other women came to the house daily then, mostly to clean and cook. Eliška was often shooed out of doors. She wasn't sorry for it. She hated the sight of her mother's once busy hands now limp. Her sharp voice silenced. It had been more frightening than death to her child-self: seeing her mother alive but not. Eliška could still picture an equally ancient version of Babička Olga feeding her fresh rolls, their tops gleaming with butter, and then fitting a basket over her tender arm.

"Go pick flowers for a garland, little bird. Your matka needs joy now," Olga said, and closed the door on Eliška.

Years passed before Eliška had wondered about her mother's state of mind in the months following her father's death. Now Eliška worried about the sinking weight of such melancholy every time her heart pained her, or her breath ran short and tight. With a blue-tipped finger pressed to her chest, she wondered now, *what will Mamička do when I die?*

Pushing those particular ghosts aside, Eliška knelt beside the odd ring, her errand forgotten. She longed to trace the perfect shape with her fingers, learn its mysteries. Discover if such things really were made by groups of Vila cursed to dance in death and never find peace. But to cross over was an invitation for disaster. Eliška understood this now as surely as she knew she would die before her mother—maybe even before Babička. Staring at the pale disk, a delicate fury twisted open inside her as long-rusted hinges swung free.

Angry tears welled up, spilling over her lashes. It wasn't fair: her half-dead heart, her grieved mother, her weaknesses. She longed for a different, fuller life more than anyone she knew, and it was as if this very longing had damned her to a lesser existence.

Fisting her bloodless fingertips, Eliška gritted her teeth against the smallness of her life, no more than a flash of light in a world of wonders.

With her jaw clenched against the tears, Eliška filled her lungs with air until they burned. Then she let go of her fists and her breath all at once and stomped through the ring, leaping at the last step lest a beast from within grab ahold and drag her down.

Chest heaving, she stood there seething in the sunshine, waiting for disaster to strike. Half hoping for it. At least then she would be the architect of her own demise. But whatever demons inhabited the ring, earth was not their element. Whirling to face the thin place, Eliška cursed herself and wondered if it was her turn to die—or if she had doomed another.

As Eliška stood there nauseous with emotion, the wind rose like a great bird taking flight, lifting the loose strands of hair around her face and pulling at her skirts. She steeled herself against it and waited for the blow to come, hardening her heart. But no cry came, no herald of grief. Trembling and curious, she opened her eyes and there, across the meadow at the edge of the trees, were two figures. No more than dark specks along the road into the village. They moved steadily down the path with a mule in tow, though they didn't hurry. Eliška squinted and, with practiced ease, crouched behind a tree, watching until she could see them more clearly.

They were men and looked of an age with her, though vastly different in appearance from each other. The first was tall and lean with curling black hair and a crisp face. The second was shorter, broad of shoulder, and fair as a wheat field. And while the tall man's shoulders drooped, the shorter man strode forward like a giant. Eliška heard their chatter, but was unable to make out what was said. Then they rounded the bend toward the village and disappeared behind the trees. Eliška twisted her mouth in thought. People didn't often visit Hrozno, and the few who did were either familiar merchants or guests of the Baron who simply passed through. But she'd never seen these men before. She was sure of it. Some catlike sense twitched deep inside, and she felt both wary and intrigued.

"Strangers," she said aloud, remembering the prediction at Babička Olga's.

As she spoke, the wind rose again. Panic at what she'd done in a moment of despair swirled through her as if the wind had entered her veins. She had to tell Babička Olga. But whether she would speak about what she'd done to the fairy ring or the men's arrival, she didn't yet know.

⁂

Eliška came through the door so fast, the fat gray cat startled and spat at her feet from under Babička's chair. "He's here. The stranger. I just saw two men on their way into the village. He must be one of them. Or both," she blurted all at once before taking a breath.

Babička's head snapped up from the book she was examining, a great magnifying glass clutched in one hand. "Perhaps. And perhaps not. The fire told of a single visitor. One is not a stranger." She went back to her reading. The cat gave another angry meow from behind her mistress's ankles.

Eliška hadn't considered this in her haste. "But I've never seen either of them," she protested. "And they're about my age. They look like common folk. They cannot have been here before, can they?" Eliška stooped to cajole the offended cat. It hissed again, yellow eyes wide.

"That is one idea, bird. Sit and tell me of it," Babička said as she set the book and magnifying glass in her lap. The old chair creaked ominously under her movement.

For once, Eliška had no desire to rest, but sat out of habit. Each breath grew shallower than the one before and there was much to say.

In out, in out, in out.

"Perhaps one of them came here as a child?" Eliška asked before an alarming possibility came to mind. "Could the embers be wrong?"

The old healer reached down to pet the startled cat. "Signs do not lie. But it is always possible to read them incorrectly," she said, rubbing the beast's ears. "I think another answer is more likely. One we have not yet discovered."

The cat, having forgiven Eliška her intrusion, eased out from under her mistress' chair and rubbed its back against her ankles. Eliška scratched its head and thought on this. Perhaps Babička Olga was right about there being another answer, but the men's appearance immediately after her fitful march through the forbidden ring sat in her mouth like a sore. She couldn't put aside the idea she'd called them somehow, as she had the whirlwind at her father's death. Chewing a corner of her lip, she opened her mouth to confess.

"Aha!"

Eliška startled as her teacher looked up from the book in her lap a second time, the magnifying glass once again close to her nearly-blind eye. It bulged above her gummy, joyful smile. "I have found it."

Eliška swallowed her words. "What have you found?"

Babička lowered the glass and pinned Eliška with her milky stare. "A banishing recipe."

Eliška raised her eyebrows. The healer almost never referred to her 'special recipes' as she called them. Outside these walls, they were forbidden. Eliška waited a heartbeat. Then two. And took a breath.

"Who are we banishing, Babička?"

The old woman closed the thin, loose-leafed leather book and fitted it back inside its hiding spot among the carved-out pages of a larger volume.

"Not who. What." Babička's eyes darted around the cottage as if trying to track a flash of light. "I sense something new in the woods. Something—unnatural to this place. I would have it gone. The škriatok does not like the smell of it," the old woman said, and gestured to the stove as if someone were standing by it. No one was.

Eliška was so surprised Babička had answered her question directly, she sat there dumbly unable to form words, let alone respond to such statements. Then her mind unfroze and questions spilled out. "What is it? Can I help? How will we do it? When?"

A rasping laugh escaped the old woman's mouth like a puff of smoke. "Calm yourself, bird. There is no more work to be done tonight." She gestured to a ceramic bowl on the table with a damp cloth draped over it. "The dough is not yet ready."

Eliška sat back down, the weight of her friend's words settling in. She'd spoken of her house spirit—škriatok—as if he were real. Again. Eliška pushed that particular oddity aside for now. "Do you know what it is, Babička? Please tell me. I'm not a child anymore and I want to learn what you know."

The old woman pinched her wrinkled lips and sighed. "You may not be a child anymore, but you pester like one." She waved in the direction of the woods. "It is only the hunch of an old woman. Remember that. People are often wrong. Signs speak truth."

Eliška swallowed her rising unease and, with all thought of the strangers pushed aside, rose to peek in at the dough. The soft tan mound was heavily flecked with herbs and smelled strongly. "Rosemary, thyme, sage, wild garlic." Eliška leaned closer, sniffing. "Vinegar? In bread?"

"I have no looking glass and my black candles are gone. Too risky to make again." Babička shrugged. "And dedko škriatok is too old to leave the stove now, so he cannot help me."

Eliška kept her face in check, though she wondered what had

caused the change in Babička. She'd never spoken so freely about her house spirit or her cunning work. Why was the old woman sharing her knowledge so suddenly? One possibility gripped Eliška's heart like no breathing fit ever could. Fear pooled in her stomach.

"Babička." The words cut her tongue. "Is something amiss? Are you ill?"

The healer gave a loud, snorting chuckle. This time, the cat darted under Eliška's skirts, indignant at the ruckus.

"Oh, child. I feel old as the sun. My teeth are gone. I can hardly see and my bones ache. But no. I am well, and certain to live as many more moons as the Good Lord should see fit to keep me here," she said with a chuckle and crossed herself.

The tightness in Eliška's chest loosened, relief seeping out. Like most truly old women, Babička Olga was skilled in telling half-truths and evading questions she didn't like—but she never lied. Accepting this, Eliška then wondered how Olga could plan a banishing spell in one breath and speak of the Good Lord in another. She knew such talk was dangerous and felt grateful for her friend's confidence. Not for the first time she wondered if Babička Olga and Father Timotej had more in common than she'd been led to believe. The cat chose that moment to purr loudly, bringing her blasphemous mind back to her body.

"I pray it is so," Eliška said and smiled. But Babička Olga didn't smile back. Only stared at her. Into her. The foretold travelers, her reckless disregard for the fairy ring—everything darted back through Eliška's mind like quarrelling birds. She scratched the easily offended cat's head and said nothing.

"As do I," said the healer and hoisted herself out of her chair. "Now come help with what can be tended to now. These cobwebs are getting too thick even for my liking."

Six

Albin

The unlocked door to the crofter's cottage swung open with a bang, nearly flying off its sagging hinges. Even through the darkened doorway, Albin could see dust falling from the thatched roof as the dank, musty smell of long disuse rolled out to meet them like a fog.

"Appears...quaint," ventured Albin, stepping back from the now open structure which was to be their quarters for the week. Made of ancient stone and thatch desperately in need of white-washing and restacking, the crofter's cottage squatted in a scant meadow off the main road just a short walk outside the village boundaries. Though tiny and rundown, the place boasted a rickety corral for Linus, a decrepit water pump, and a latrine that was functional if ripe. Its windows were shuttered, its chimney sturdy, and a wide swath of woodland was close enough to hunt small game in. It was perfect.

Miroslav swore with great creativity in several languages.

Albin shot him a glare, but there was no heat behind it. "It could be worse, you know," he said with a shrug and strode inside.

The place was dark, dusty, foul smelling—and completely private. Albin adored it.

"The things I do for you," Miroslav grumbled from behind him as he dumped both their satchels on the floor with an air of humbug.

Albin knew his friend's objections were partially for show and once they'd settled in, Miroslav would come around. He always did and usually enjoyed Albin's escapades more than he'd admit. Besides, Albin thought, the whole thing was an adventure. What did he care where he laid his head for a while, so long as it was his choice? He could think of worse places to be.

Determined to enjoy himself, Albin surveyed their lodgings for the duration of the harvest: thick walls of plastered stone squatted over a packed earth floor that needed to be swept of mouse droppings. The shutters would keep out any rain, mostly, and the small fireplace would do for simple cooking and heating. As his eyes adjusted to the dim light, he saw chamber pots neatly stored under rustic wooden beds, and off by the stove stood a large wooden table with a narrow wooden bench. Scarred and dusty, everything was badly in need of a good scrubbing, but it would suffice.

"Hardly worse than the room you found for us in Paris," Albin chided, stretched his arms wide as if to embrace the endless possibilities the bare room offered.

Miroslav scoffed. "A fair bit worse. At least those stables were free from vermin and contained fresh straw," he said, bending to inspect the hay-stuffed mattresses on each cot. "Which I cannot assure here. I fear we shall be devoured by fleas before the night is out."

Albin waved this off, though he was none too keen to test the moldering mattresses either. From the look of them, fleas would be the least of their biting inhabitants. "A small matter. We shall procure some fresh straw for the ground and sleep there." Striding across the room, he unfastened his belt and laid it across the table. His dagger clanged against the wood. The polished jade hilt glowed eerily in the dim light of the colorless abode. Father had insisted he bring some form of protection. Albin didn't disagree, but being seen with such a fine blade was out of the question. He would keep it at hand in the night and when hunting, but dared not carry it openly.

"A small matter he says." Miroslav's mock irritation was approaching real annoyance as he forced open one of the shuttered windows. A long bar of light struck the opposite wall. "I still don't see why you chose to exile us here, sir." He probed one dark corner for a broom and went to work on the floor. "Why not Bratislava for some real entertainment?"

Albin smiled at his valet. He was well acquainted with Miroslav's taste for luxuries—he also knew his friend to be a better shot than himself and a decent cook when pressed. They'd be fine. He ignored Miroslav's grumbling accordingly.

"You know precisely why and are starting to sound like an old nursemaid. Quiet yourself, man. Here—" Albin took the broom from Miroslav. "I packed a snare. Will you have a go at it after feeding Linus? The dried meat will run out sooner than we should like and I'd rather not spend too much time in the market."

Miroslav scowled even as he started rummaging through the bag. "We're to be thoroughly domesticated then, are we? Fine. And what shall you do while I'm out?"

"Clean—yes, I am capable—and then find the village water well, I think. Perhaps I shall ask after the harvest master." Albin swept at the mouse droppings and tried to imagine tricking one of his father's most important tenants. Soon to be *his* important tenant. It was a risky, ungentlemanly thing to do. He knew this and tried to brush it off anyway. But the guilt had other ideas and burrowed deeper.

"It need not be the end, you know." Miroslav's voice broke in, his tone suddenly serious as if reading Albin's thoughts.

Dust and bits of straw hung in a sliver of sunshine like a gold chain strung between them. Though Albin's thoughts were muddled about many things, on this he was perfectly resolved.

"Yes, it does," Albin said, starting to sweep. "You know, the only thing my mother ever really wanted was for me to inherit and give her gads of fat grandchildren. Even though she can't see any of it, I fully intend to do so. Marrying puts an end to many things." He leaned gently on the broom and pushed down the bitterness welling in his mouth. "Which includes going to the Orient. In spite of what you may think—what everyone thinks—I wish to be a good husband. I will not fail my mother. And I certainly won't be bested by my goddamned father."

A darkness crossed Miroslav's face with startling speed as his already deep brown eyes went black. Albin knew nearly every expression on his friend's face, but something about Miroslav's dejection felt sharper. Deeper. More like anger than sadness.

"Are you angry with me?" Albin said, feeling more concerned than he wanted to sound.

Miroslav blinked and mastered his expression, his voice cool. "Of course not, sir."

Albin guessed at the meaning of this sudden formality and spoke to it.

"There's no need to fret, Miro. You know I shall always keep you on. Where and when I am fortunate enough to travel, so shall you." Albin clapped his friend on the arm, but Miroslav stiffened. His unusual silence pushed forward a new and unwelcome idea. A possibility he hadn't considered stumbled into the light with stunning clarity. Albin was surprised to feel his own heart sink at the idea of it. He stepped back.

"Unless you would prefer a new situation once I marry? To be employed elsewhere?"

Miroslav's eyes widened as he came back to himself and straightened to his full height. "No. That is not—no, sir." Miroslav shook himself out of his discomfort. "Besides, who else could you possibly trust to keep you out of mischief?" he asked, mirth returning to his voice.

Albin smiled, more certain of his footing as the sudden fear of losing his friend loosened. "Right. For a moment there I feared you were going to abandon me to those people," he said, gesturing toward the castle on the hill.

"You mean to your kin and hearth, sir?"

Albin stepped over the comment as surely as if the words lay at his feet. He pointed to the door. "Were you planning to set off before dark or not? We wouldn't want to be outwitted by hares."

Miroslav squinted down at Albin and shifted the snare to his shoulder. "Is that a challenge, sir?"

"Obviously. Plus, you eat more than I do."

Miroslav raised one black eyebrow in disdain. "As well I should, Your Excellency—since I do all of the work and am not disposed to become portly round the middle like some." With that, Miroslav spun around and closed the door behind him with a bang that shook another cloud of dust from the thatch ceiling.

Albin's laugh boomed off the walls as he rolled up his sleeves and went to work on the cottage.

⸎

The morning slipped by quiet as a shadow. After Albin set the cottage to rights and had a shoddy midday meal of dried venison and apples—it would be some time before Miroslav returned with any game to cook—Albin decided to explore the village. They'd need more water soon and he wasn't inclined to drink from the decrepit pump nearby. He'd be damned before he spent this week ill with the shits. Albin was here to do what pleased him and right now, poking around town to fetch a bucket of cool water sounded like paradise.

As he stepped outside, the afternoon sunshine lay dense and warm on his back. He'd actually enjoyed the time spent tidying the cottage, but was eager to be about again. Miroslav might bemoan the necessity of hunting, but Albin knew better. Miro enjoyed the woods and would likely dawdle away the afternoon. Albin didn't expect him back until dark bearing either a field-dressed kill or his own shame.

Albin flexed his hands. There was a sore, well-used feel to them, and he savored it the way his father did a fine claret. He clenched them, memorizing the tender flex of muscle. Too soon he would have little other than quills and bank notes to set his hands to. He would give them real work while he could and strode down the road happily, the song of gravel under his feet a joy to hear.

Despite the rustling leaves and blanket of yellow and white wildflowers kissing the edges of the deeply rutted road, Albin's mind wandered to his jade collection, homesick for it in a childish way. But as he wandered down the main road into the village, the sun was ripe and helped focus his attention. People were busy going about their days, but each one noted his passing without fail. A few young men nodded companionably. A few old men frowned, pipes held tight in their remaining teeth. Children pointed openly and called to their mothers. Albin smiled at each one and tipped his hat with a flourish, winking at more than a few wrinkled babkas and eating up their surprised smiles.

He may have been there to fill his canteens with as much water as he could carry, but filling his eyes with the sights of the village was no small pleasure. The only difference was Albin realized he was accustomed to seeing the village from above. Now, as he walked along the sloping street lined with brightly colored houses, dark pitched roofs, and jagged fences, he imagined himself shrunken down, doll-like, suddenly wandering through a toy town. He loved everything about it and smiled gaily as he saun-tered toward the large stone well, which had just come into sight. He passed a gaggle of young women going the opposite direction, water splashing in their wake like laughter.

And all at once then she was there, standing in front of him as if dropped from the sky.

Albin didn't move—couldn't move. The girl was so close the heat from her body pressed against him like sunshine. He dared not approach, though he could have lifted a hand and touched her. She appeared just as startled as himself and stared back, frozen. Albin took in the shards of gold in her green eyes, the stamp of each freckle across her high cheekbones, the fragile length of neck under her strong jaw. The deep, almost bruised color of her mouth. Propriety screamed for him to step back; to avert his stare. He could not. Albin filled his eyes with her and was rewarded with a faint crinkle of awareness around the girl's eyes. He was pleased and wanted to move even closer. But reason finally grabbed hold, and he stepped back as her smell—lavender, sweat, recklessness— invaded his senses.

I mustn't. The thought shouted inside his head. He didn't want to listen.

The girl, however, held his gaze far longer than was customary and did not step back. Intrigued, Albin flexed his dimples and earned a wide smile in return, which revealed a charmingly twisted eyetooth. Desire to taste her mouth seized him like an angry fist. He imagined the bite of that tooth upon his own lips and clenched his hands, wanting. But a sharp call from the group of girls stole her gaze and she hurried past him, only to be carried away by her companions. Albin watched them float down the street, a clutch of petticoats and aprons.

With his heart pounding in his ears, Albin considered following her. Blessedly his sanity took over and he stayed put before filling his own water containers. Moving without thought, he started back down the road toward the cottage, his head swinging side to side, searching for the girl and then chastising himself for doing so. A girl wasn't part of the plan, he reminded himself. There was no time. Which had never stopped Albin's flirtatious nature before, but this was different. He was practically a married man. And though he hated being a pawn for political gain, he knew his father was right—the stability of the region *did* hang on a peaceful alliance. The marriage was non-negotiable, as his father put it. Lives were at stake.

Albin hated when his father was right. The thought made his steps slow, his gait clumsy as if under a weight far greater than the water. Albin shook his head to clear it of such heavy thoughts and looked back once more for the girl, but in vain. *Pity*, he thought, her striking presence once again flooding his head. He smiled at the ghost of her bold stare and smacked squarely into Miroslav.

His friend's unexpected appearance broke open the daydream, spilling its contents of tangled limbs and pretty freckles onto the road along with a slosh of water.

"Christ. Are you trying to scare the piss from me?" Albin snapped, only to chuckle at his half-soaked shoes.

Miroslav frowned. "I thought you would be pleased to know hunting proved a success." He held up a pair of hares with one hand and a dusty bottle in the other. "And I fetched wine from the old cave. Damn fortunate our boyhood cache is still intact after all this time." Miroslav's voice remained light, but his black eyes were wounded. "Though I suppose there is a chance it has gone sour."

Albin shook his head again before glancing over his shoulder down the main lane. "Forgive me. I was just—distracted," he said, forcing a smile. "You succeeded more quickly than expected. Well done, good man. Any other news?"

With Miro's good humor restored, he fell in alongside Albin. "I inquired with a lad along the road about where to find the harvest master. We should go speak with him on the morrow."

Albin strode along the damp road only half listening. The crops, wild game, merchants, and the tenants who worked the land were vital to the estate's survival—he knew this, but found his thoughts drifting back to the girl, a ship to a siren's call. Her unpainted mouth, the color of wild cherries tinged with frost, her dappled eyes, her bold grin.

"You're ignoring me."

Albin snapped back to the present.

Miroslav had stopped walking several paces back and was

frowning. "On my honor, why do you even ask for this information if you aren't going to attend to it?"

"I'm sorry, Miro. Truly, I was listening to you. I just—will there not be abundant time for talk of the estate later?" said Albin, setting down the water canisters. His shoulders had started to burn.

Miroslav glared at him.

"Fine," Albin relented. "You were talking about the harvest master. Go on. I swear I'm listening now."

Miroslav rolled his eyes and tossed the wine bottle. Albin caught it smoothly.

"God's bones. You do realize you're going to inherit all of this soon, yes? Perhaps you should pay its workings some mind."

Albin swiped his thumb across the dusty bottle. His family crest stared back at him like an inescapable eye, the stylized lions and rearing hart stark against the white and blue background. "How could I forget," he murmured.

SEVEN
ELIŠKA

The edge of the hard chair bit into the back of her legs, but Eliška was not about to give Alena Tothova the satisfaction of seeing her squirm. Eliška wouldn't be surprised if her neighbor had given her the most uncomfortable chair in the house out of spite. Thinking on it, a smiling Alena *had* made a show of offering this seat to Eliška when she filed into the Torthova's large front room behind her mother and the rest of the women on the street. It was their weekly embroidery day—nearly as unavoidable as mass. Eliška curled her lip in annoyance.

What began as a one-time event for Pani Tothova to show off her newly redecorated sitting room, had continued as a simple way for the street's women to exchange news and gossip under the guise of sewing. Normally, no one paid her much attention and more time dedicated to her thread craft was welcome. But this unspoken battle with Alena over Radek's affections was ridiculous. With a deep, steadying breath, Eliška ignored her bruising thighs and placed another stitch. She would not give anyone the satisfaction of seeing her squirm.

She enjoyed the feel of the needle in her hand as it pressed through the flaxen cloth. The swift give of penetration followed by the whisper of thread passing from one side to another eased some undefinable ache inside. She had never told anyone this as she suspected it to be another one of her oddities. When a person was not-so-quietly known as The Invalid, she took care not to mention anything else that might be considered odd.

Nonetheless, the quiet rhythm of the work calmed her. Though her limitations were numerous, Eliška was good at making ordinary things beautiful with her embroidery, mimicking the world around her in color and design, from the deep blue of shadows to the bright burgundy of crushed grapes. It brought her no small pleasure. And if mothers with broods of children were willing to buy her impressive work instead of struggling with their own, so much the better.

Leaning closer to the patch of crisp linen stretched within her embroidery hoop, Eliška pictured the exact curve of a violet and placed her stitch. Deft and focused, this was her element, and the hum of conversations filled the room like smoke, deepening her sense of ease. She let out her breath and aimed her needle.

"Of course, I shall never be as good as Eliška," said Alena, her voice a hammer.

The words struck Eliška with such force, she misplaced her stitch. She sucked in her cheeks. Now the point of the petal would need to be picked out leaving the cloth imperfect.

"But I haven't as much leisure time to practice, of course," Alena added, her intent clear.

Eliška imagined the satisfaction of jabbing her needle into stupid Alena's wrist, then blinked against the violent thought. Instead, Eliška raised her eyes, face carefully blank. Her haughty neighbor smiled, white teeth bared, and thrust out a pointy chin.

No, Eliška thought caustically, *you'll never gain any skill unless vicious, idle words magick into a talent.* But Eliška only pressed her lips into their own watery smile and let the comment pass. Nothing would give Alena greater pleasure than seeing her upset.

Eliška bent back over her work, letting the comments drift back into the hum of conversation.

It was no secret Alena desired Radek. Or at least desired his profitable tannery business. She'd been trailing him for years, quietly tormenting Eliška every time he showed her favor instead of Alena. The game was tiresome. She had no interest in Radek and Alena knew it—which made Radek's tenacity all the more troublesome. She had tried diverting Radek's attention elsewhere more times than she cared to count, specifically at the eager Alena. After all, if he called off his own pursuit, even her mother couldn't blame her. But every attempt had failed. Radek persisted. Alena spit her venom. Around and around it went.

She'd felt jangly and restless since seeing the stranger near the well. His appearance right in front of her had been nothing short of shocking—like a bolt of energy surging through her. He was so handsome, fair and broad shouldered with mischievous eyes that had held her own, unrepentant. And then he'd smiled and sent an arrow of heat into her belly. Even now, her muscles tightened at the memory.

Biting at her lip to keep from smiling, Eliška pressed down her curiosity and focused on the rhythmic thrust and shiver of needle and thread. *In out, in out, in out* went the tools, more dependable than her own heart. Her shoulders relaxed once again as she fell into the work of her hands. She could master herself and would not let such troublesome and unfamiliar thoughts disturb her.

Alena's mother, a stringy woman with dark eyes and a high brow, cleared her throat, attempting to command the room. Eliška paused her stitch, knowing from experience whatever Pani Tothova was about to say amounted to little more than spiteful gossip. Eliška often resented such talk, having been the topic of it herself, but her interest piqued anyway. The edges of the village pinched her heart, tight as an old shoe, and any news from outside was welcome.

"Get on with it, Edita," said Mamička, practical as always. "What news does the well bring today?"

Eliška's lips twitched. Her practical mother approved of gossip even less than she did, but knew how to put information to use when necessary.

"Well," Pani Tothova began, the overly formal lace edging on her headscarf quivering as she preened. "There is word the vintage shall begin any day now and—"

"That is not news." Mamičks's strong voice countered. "Pán Nagy and I spoke of this already. It will begin two days hence if the weather holds. Perhaps even on the morrow."

Her mother went back to sewing, her face still. Eliška held the insides of her cheeks tight between her teeth to keep from smiling.

"And," Pani Tothova continued as if Mamička hadn't spoken, "there is word the young master has returned from university and means to marry an Austrian noble lady whom he became reacquainted with in Vienna. A political match, of course," she said, sniffing as if this were somehow unexpected.

Eliška couldn't help but roll her eyes. What had the social climbing Tothova family expected? To marry Alena off to their lord's only heir?

"I do not suppose nobles marry for any other reason." The words were out of Eliška's mouth before she could check her tongue.

Maria, a tired, sweet young woman with too many children, chuckled at the observation and Pani Tothova pinched her lips into a sour expression confirming Eliška's suspicions. Maria quickly covered her mouth in embarrassment and then smiled at Pani Tothova as if to soften the blow of her laughter.

"Forgive me, Pani Tothova, but what Eliška says is true. Only last night I overheard my husband say to Pán Kovac the political unrest is spreading around the empire. Perhaps a strong alliance with a powerful Austrian family would be a good thing for the village?" Then Maria leaned forward, her plump, pretty face eager as a pouncing cat's. "Though I do wonder what she will be like. Do you think our young lord will love her?"

"I'm sure love has little to do with such matches," said Mamiccka. "Though I do hope she will be as good to the castle staff as our late mistress was. Pán Nagy's nephew only just began as footman for the baron and it would be a shame to see the household go down under a new mistress."

"Do you think she'll arrive for the festival?" Alena asked, drawing the room's attention back to herself. "If the harvest really is to start—"

"It is," Mamička and Pani Tothova said in unison.

Alena huffed at being interrupted. "Then perhaps the couple will be announced at the festival?" finished Alena. "Imagine the gowns she'll have..."

"Hmm," murmured Eliška noncommittally. Though her imagination was piqued by the idea of a dashing bridegroom and mysterious bride dancing in their finery among them, the notion of a forced union for any reason chafed.

"Though it is a pity they will be forced to wed," Eliška muttered.

Every eye in the room flew to her. Mamička held the only unsurprised expression. "A pity? I suppose the fortunes of entire regions are less important than the feelings of two young nobles?" Mamička asked quietly, though there was no mistaking the challenge in her voice. "Love is a blessing. The Lord knows I loved your father. But so is survival. And as ours depends on theirs, I hope for nothing more than an advantageous match."

Eliška bristled. Though she could not refute the truth in such harsh words, no one—not even a noble lady—should be matched without a choice. She thought of the way her mother simpered around Radek and her stomach soured. She didn't think such a match would sit easy on her soul even if her neck were draped with jewels, her body adorned with satin. She straightened her shoulders. She took in the glances of these women she'd known her whole life and couldn't help pitying them for a change. "Perhaps they are not so different from us. They have hearts, no?"

Alena sniggered. "What does a heart encased in gold know of love? I should think all their comforts and pleasures make up for much."

"I don't know," came Maria's soft voice. "I think it might be lonely up there for all its beauty." She gestured over her shoulder.

Whatever other opinions existed, they went unsaid as the women returned to their work, mouths unusually still. In the quiet, Eliška looked through the room's wide front window edged with delicate lace curtains. The castle was just visible above the trees, a dark pink gash against the sky. Her chest tightened at the sight. She imagined her heart to be the exact same shade of stone.

⚜

"Such a smile does not sit well with my bones."

Eliška's head lifted from her needlework to find Babička Olga staring at her, eyes squinted. After spending the afternoon with the other women, and not accomplishing enough her work, she'd retreated to Babička Olga's where she would be both comforted by the presence of another body and left alone to embroider.

"I'm not smiling," Eliška said, her face falling intentionally blank.

She'd been thinking about the boy on the street again, and might actually have been smiling, but made certain she wasn't now. After pondering on it more, she'd decided the two strangers must be laborers here for the grape harvest. It didn't happen every year, but had on occasion when word of a nearing harvest traveled between villages. Such men were viewed with open suspicion, being unknown, and no one save an already married man could be a worse object of infatuation.

Eliška knew even a penniless nobody from their village would be preferable to a man without roots. But as she trained her eyes onto the tight, perfect stitches swirling under her hands, she wondered what such a life would be like: new woods, mountains, vineyards, farms. The feel of a strong back and easy breath. Roaming in total freedom among new people. The longing she kept carefully banked in her heart flared at the idea of such freedom.

"See?" Babička Olga's voice crashed into Eliška's thoughts. "You are not here. Something makes you smile. What is this about?"

She never lied to Babička Olga. Not about anything important, anyway. And on the few occasions she had tried, there was no point. Olga had an even better nose for untruths than her mother.

Eliška anchored the needle gently in the flaxen cloth and met her old friend's veiled eyes. "I saw one of the strangers up close today. By the well. He smiled at me." She didn't mean to sound defiant, but heard the challenge in her voice nonetheless.

Olga raised a wiry white eyebrow. "Did he now?" She stood and shuffled over to the bench Eliška sat on and eased herself down. Neglected dust puffed into the air around them as if the old woman had exhaled woodsmoke.

Eliška coughed and batted at the air with a smile. "I will sweep for you later," she said and felt a stab of guilt she hadn't done so already. She was so concerned with completing the new cap she'd forgotten the chores.

Babička Olga waved her offer, and the dust, aside. "Dust is no matter. Smiles, though"— her old eyes flashed at Eliška—"can matter a great deal."

Eliška flushed but sat tall. "It was nothing, Babička. Just a polite smile from a stranger. For all we know he'll be gone tomorrow. Or after the harvest at the latest, and we'll never see them again. You said yourself, we might not have read the ashes correctly."

The healer took hold of her cold fingers and patted them. Olga's warm, dry skin was thin as new ice in some places and rough as bark in others. They always comforted Eliška.

"That, little bird, is what I am afraid of." Babička Olga put a bony knuckle under Eliška's chin and lifted her face until they were practically nose to nose. Eliška wondered what the woman's milky eyes saw.

"Eliška?" Babička Olga rarely used her real name and the sound of it on her wrinkled lips was not entirely welcome. Eliška resisted the urge to squirm out from under her friend's hands.

"You are beautiful and kind and sharp of mind. A treasure to an old woman. But do you think you are the first pretty girl this young man has smiled at on his travels? His coming, if indeed he is the right one, was not foretold by mistake."

Eliška winced. She too had wondered this very thing, but resented the assumption of her gullibility. She leaned away and looked back at her embroidery. "I'm not a fool. It was just a smile."

Babička Olga squeezed her hand and stood. "True. A smile can be just a smile," she said, and moved back to her own work by the hearth, easing down into a chair as weathered as herself.

Eliška watched from the corner of her eye as the woman poked the fire, which flared up in irritation. "And an ember can be just an ember."

With the message received, Eliška stabbed her needle through the cloth and was careful not to smile again.

Eight

Albin

"I've never seen anything like it. It's a wonder we didn't spot it from the ramparts. The thing damn near glows," Miro whispered, and Albin found himself swallowing down a jagged chuckle as they stood on the immaculate front step of the harvest master's house.

The object in question was the large cottage itself, which had been painted an alarming shade of pink. Most of the cottages were painted in cheerful colors—blues, yellows, greens—and boasted tidy porches and lace trimmed windows, but the harvester master's abode bore more resemblance to an elaborate Parisian confection than a humble village dwelling.

"I for one am glad to be seeking employment from a man of such fine taste," Albin added gamely, determined to enjoy himself.

"You would be," shot Miroslav, craning his neck to take in the multiple layers of lace curtains on the windows. "Truly, it looks like something from a Parisian courtesan's boudoir."

Albin snorted. Either Martin Nagy had an interest in vibrant colors, or he was rather indulgent of his wife. Albin wasn't sure which would be the more interesting truth about the notoriously stern vineyard master. "Where would one even procure such a color of paint?" he muttered to Miro, who was reaching up to knock on the door. "Quite impressive, really. Perhaps we should inquire and repaint the crofters' cottage while we're here? A matching pair would quite suit, I think."

Now it was Miro's turn to bite back a laugh just as the large, polished door of the Nagy household opened. The figure in the doorway was completely incongruent with the frilly exterior. The vineyard master—if this was him—was a tall, reedy man with pinprick eyes, and an expression devoid of humor. Though neatly dressed and respectable in his dark mustache and white shirt, his eyes held the harried look of someone perpetually in a hurry.

"Áno?" the gruff man said by way of greeting in a startling deep voice.

"*Dobrý den*. Please forgive us for intruding, but we are looking for Pán Nagy. We were told this was his residence?" Albin spoke quickly in his most genial voice. The tall man in the doorway oozed annoyance.

His dark eyes pressed into them. "Who would be asking?"

Miroslav dipped his head in deference. "My name is Otokar, and this is my brother Lajos. We're in search of work and were told the village's harvest would begin any day now." Miro employed his most earnest expression, going along with the game. "Could he use extra help?"

Nagy's eyes drifted from Miro to Albin and back, his mouth twisting in suspicion. Albin, always inclined to smile, did his best to match Miro's wide-eyed expression of earnest hope. It worked.

The man looked them over for another moment before giving a single sharp nod. "Do you have any experience?"

"Yes," Albin lied. "Though it has been a few years since we worked a vintage."

Nagy scowled.

"But our backs are strong and we're fast learners. You won't be disappointed." Albin rushed before catching his gaffe. The harvest master had yet to introduce himself.

Miroslav went very still next to Albin as Pán Nagy ran a hand over his face just as the wail of an infant erupted from behind him. He winced. "Fine. Come to the eastern fields at sunup ready to work. You'll get paid at the end of the day depending on whether or not you're of any use."

Then he snapped the door shut in their faces before either man could say thank you. More crying erupted from inside as a toddler's wail was added to the cacophony of sounds. Albin noted Miroslav's alarmed expression.

"Don't look so upset, Miro. I don't think the babe will be in the fields tomorrow."

Miroslav shot him a vicious glance as they retreated down the front steps and back onto the rustic street. "And more the shame," Miro said. "I'd rather change wet nappies and play with a few babes than break my back for that *arschloch*."

Albin let out the laugh he'd been biting back as they careened down the street toward the center of the village. There was an energy moving through the air this morning and Albin wanted to drink it in. He could practically feel it fizzing around them like champagne bubbles pushing everyone into motion. It was intoxicating.

"Come now, chap," Albin said. "It's not like you to be so morose. Think of the clout we will have once it's discovered we helped harvest the grapes to the most fabulous vintage the estate has ever seen."

Miro continued to scowl, but Albin could see the corner of his mouth twitching. A good sign. Miro glanced back at the vivid pink house and glared down his long nose at Albin. "If that man doesn't kill us both in the process of harvesting your precious grapes, I might have to do the job myself before the week is out."

Albin smiled, sniffed the air for the scent of fresh bread, and ignored his friend. This was going to be fun.

"I think this might be the most delicious thing I've ever put in my mouth," Albin moaned before taking another enormous bite of the circular pastry filled with plum jam in his hand. It was flaky, salty, sweet, and rich all at once and he was going to need another despite the pastry being nearly the size of his face.

Miroslav mumbled his agreement through his own mouthful of buttery pastry. The fact that Miro didn't even crack a scandalous joke at Albin's expense only proved his theory: this was indeed one of the best things he'd ever eaten. That they had been living on dried venison, apples, hard cheese, and stale bread for twenty-four hours was entirely beside the point.

From their resting spot near the well, Albin considered the cart where they had bought the delectable treat. Clearly the pretty redhead selling the *koláč* was a better cook than the one employed by his father in the castle. Albin was determined to hire her. But first, another pastry and some persuasive flirting seemed in order.

Having licked a spot of jam off his thumb, Albin dusted the crumbs from his hands and stood up. "I want another."

"We haven't the coin for another. Not until we get paid by Nagy on the morrow anyway, since someone insisted we 'embrace our adopted station' and not bring much ready money. Do you recall hearing anyone say such a ludicrous thing, sir?" Miroslav asked as he rose to brush at his own trousers.

Albin ignored the jab and made sure there was no remaining jam on his face before raising an eyebrow at Miro. "Who said anything about coin? Did you not see the fetching vendor? I will work my charm and make it worth her while in the end. Watch and be impressed, man."

Miro's face fell. "Oh no."

"Oh yes."

"Sir, are you truly planning to swindle a poor village girl for another pastry?"

Albin stopped, offended. "Of course not! You act like I'm going to steal it. I'm simply going to convince her to give us pastries now and will reward her tenfold upon the occasion of my inheritance. And," he added before Miro could protest, "I plan to offer her a position in the kitchen. I find I can no longer live without these pastries."

Miroslav scoffed. "And what makes you think she'd want to? Are we not here so you can run away from the castle?"

But Albin was determined and ignored his friend's taunting. "Watch and learn, man," he said and headed for the cart.

The line of customers had dwindled, so he felt less guilty about striding up to the side of the stall as the plump red-haired girl hurriedly passed out pastries and collected her coins. She hadn't noticed him yet, though an old man in line eyed him warily. Albin tipped his head to the man and was happy to wait and watch. The girl was young—too young really for such flirtations—but there was no bite behind Albin's smile so he flashed it with confidence when she finally caught sight of him. Her round cheeks were flushed and there was a smudge of jam on the collar of her blouse, but she smiled back and held up a finger for him to wait as she finished her last exchange.

Wiping her hands on her apron, she gave him her attention. "Would you have another, sir?"

Albin flexed his dimples. This was going to be easier than he thought. "I just had to give my compliments to the cook. That was the best *koláč* I have ever eaten. I'm sure no finer pastry could be found in the emperor's kitchen," he gushed and then bowed deeply.

She flushed an even darker shade of pink, her pale eyes sparkling. "Why thank you, sir. It is an old family recipe. I've been making them since I could reach the table."

He feigned shock. "You made them? But you're so young! I

thought such fine cooking was surely the work of a babka," he teased before hunching over and pretending to gum his teeth.

This elicited a smile from the girl who, young as she was, apparently knew when she was being flirted with. And to Albin's surprise, she leaned onto the stall's counter in order to put her own ample charms on display. "Just me. Were you in need of anything else?"

Though he truly had no intention of acting on his flirtations, Albin couldn't possibly resist such an entertaining turn of events. He leaned in as if preparing to share a secret. "Well then I must confess—yes. You see, I was telling the truth when I said that pastry was the most delicious thing I've ever eaten *and* that I must tell this revelation to the angel who created such a confection." Then he leaned away, hands spread in dramatic contrition. "But alas, we haven't anymore coin until the morrow when our day's wages have been paid."

At his revelation, the pretty pastry seller cocked a ruddy eyebrow at him and leaned back into her stall. Clearly, she was as bright as she was industrious.

"I know what you are thinking, miss, and you're right on all but one account," Albin said hurriedly, unwilling to admit defeat so soon.

Now it was the girl's turn to fix him with an appraising stare. She crossed her arms. Apparently, being flirted with was one thing and being swindled was quite another. "And what would that be, sir? You seem to be the one entirely in want."

Albin gave her the full force of his smile. He liked her spirit and considered for one mad moment telling her the truth. But he settled on a half-truth instead. "You're wrong in thinking I'm trying to get something for free. I'm simply stating the truth of the matter: I haven't enough coin to pay for two more pastries now. But," he said, leaning closer. She didn't pull away. "I would reward you handsomely later for your generosity. Very handsomely."

She chewed at the side of her mouth in thought and stared

straight at him as if to discern his intentions. He liked her all the more for her canniness and thought such spirit would serve her well in the castle kitchens. He must remember to get her name before he left.

Albin could practically taste his second pastry when a shadow fell across her pink face and she straightened up, her puckered smile no longer mischievous.

"Dasa? Is there a problem?"

The voice came from behind him. Turning, Albin was confronted with the owner of the voice and his stomach dropped. Big and ruddy-haired with a leather vest despite the heat, the man staring down at him was a large, bearded copy of the girl. The resemblance was startling.

"No, brother. Just a customer offering his compliments."

Damn, Albin thought. And he'd been so close, but knew he didn't have it in him to talk his way through a surly brother, too. With a large, deliberate step away from the cart, Albin dipped his head in acknowledgement and winked at the girl. "Until tomorrow and another batch of your delicious offerings, Mistress Dasa," he said and sauntered around the man who seemed to be the source of a biting smell, and toward Miroslav who was doubled over with laughter.

NINE
ELIŠKA

Mamička didn't approve of her foraging at night.

"You should be abed early, Isha. There is much work to be done for the harvest tomorrow," her mother grumbled, but made no move to stop her. When Babička Olga called, Eliška went. Even the night before a harvest. Not even her mother would defy the old healer.

"Yes, Mamička. I promise not to stay too late," she said as a faint rapping sounded at the door. Saved from further conversation, Eliška grabbed her warmest cloak and hurried to answer it.

"Good evening, Babička. *Vitaj.*" Eliška swung the door wide and offered her arm to the healer.

"*Dobrý večer.*" Babička Olga took her help, though she didn't really need it, and nodded to her mother. "Agata."

Babička greeted everyone by their first name since she had been there when most had received them.

Mamička inclined her head in deference, offering the old woman the respect she deserved. "And a good evening to you, Olga. I did not realize the full moon had come so quickly. There is much preparation needed for the harvest on the morrow. I hope you and Eliška will be well and make haste."

Babička nodded, but offered nothing more and turned to Eliška. "Come, bird. You shall make us late."

"Yes, Babička," she said, hiding her smile. She wasn't the only one anxious to get out from under her mother's watch and into the night.

Eliška knew she was only allowed to accompany the old woman to keep an eye on her. Olga was too valuable to the village to lose and no one else chose to accompany her into the woodlands and meadows at night. Eliška often smiled at this, since more than once Olga had steadied her breathing or guided her around a troublesome root. The old woman might not see well by day, but her eyes carried them through the moonlit forest with a near second sight. No matter the reason, Eliška savored her momentary freedoms: the sharp blue air, the swollen moon, the tug of the lusty wind on her petticoats. Only then did she feel truly well. Olga must have known how she cherished these nights, because she never mentioned the mishaps to her mother.

Thinking on this, gratitude buoyed Eliška up as she stood alongside the grandmother of her heart. "Of course, Babička," she said and fastened her cloak.

"*Bud'te opatrní*," Mamička admonished as she reluctantly handed over a large basket for gathering.

The land was generous this time of year, overflowing with plants and fungus for the healer to use in her remedies—both common and not so—throughout the year. There was much to be done.

"Do not fret, Agata. Your girl is safe. They shall guide us," answered Babička Olga, patiently.

Eliška held her breath as her mother threaded her arms, eyes wary in the flickering candlelight. She did not approve of talk about the old ways and refused to consider that even though their village was Catholic to its bones, the marrow of that bone held something older still. Beliefs and traditions as old as the mountains themselves.

"I still don't see why you can't gather during the day," Mamička grumbled.

Babička made a dismissive noise in her throat and touched Mother's cheek. "I have been working under the moon and stars since before you were at your own mother's breast, Agata."

Framed by the doorway, Mamička frowned but said nothing more, her eyes tender. Eliška took advantage of the pause and steered the healer out the door and into the narrow front garden.

"We must go now if we are to be back soon," Eliška called to her mother. Catching a glimpse of the sky, she saw the stars were winking at her.

"Dávaj si pozor," her mother called as Eliška closed the gate behind them.

"We always are." Eliška tossed the promise over her shoulder and headed into the night.

⁘

They reached the edge of the village quickly. Leaving the dirt road at the customary place, the women waded into the long grass made silver with moonlight. Stars blinked overhead as the wind skimmed across the meadow, beckoning them forward, deeper into the wild places. Eliška knew she must save her energy, and so let Babička Olga direct their words along with their feet. When the old woman remained silent, she did as well. Now was such a time, as she listened to the methodical swish of their skirts and breathed in the scents of leaf and mud, sap and bark. The night air was damp against her face, which she tilted up to the stars.

A sudden breeze rose, whipping Eliška's always errant hair into her eyes. Olga stopped and she mimicked the healer, but was confused. They usually paused closer to the tree line to begin gathering. Then without warning, a shiver burst through her body. As a deeper, colder chill settled on her skin, Eliška peered over the old woman's shoulder...and saw it. She sucked in a shocked breath as hair bristled down her back.

Just ahead of them, suspended in midair, was a glimmering patch in the darkness, opaque and agitated as a reflection in water. Roughly the shape of a human, the specter hovered just off the ground. Not daring to breathe, she leaned close to Babička and whispered, "Is that—"

The healer reached back, silencing her with the sharp, unexpected grip of her hand. Babička's unclipped fingernails bit into her forearm, and she did not move again, riveted in place. Blood beat hard in Eliška's ears as she stood rooted, waiting, but for what she didn't know. Finally, after what felt an eternity, the pearlized shadow drifted skyward and disappeared among the trees. The frothing air fell still as a quieted sea.

Eliška filled her lungs and trembled, suddenly slick with sweat under her bodice. She'd sensed odd things in the woods before— nameless, unnatural presences better suited for children's tales than real life. Especially on these nights. And although Babička talked of Them as fact, not fancy, she had never quite believed. Until now.

Without speaking, Babička Olga released her stinging grip, reached into her basket, and drew out a dark loaf of bread from under a kerchief. Understanding lit inside Eliška. Of course: the banishing spell. She watched as Babička stooped and placed it on the ground.

"They're hungry," the old woman whispered and stepped around the offering. "I pray bread is enough. We cannot risk using flames so close to the vineyard."

Babička's words plucked at her fear like a gluttonous insect, biting hard only to circle back around for another taste. She forced herself to move, giving the bread a wide berth as if touching it would make her too eligible for consumption by the white shadow.

Hunching deeper into her cloak, she walked closer to the old woman. She was not above seeking comfort.

They stopped just shy of their usual grounds in a place dense with vegetation and reeking of tree rot and mushrooms. Eliška's breath steamed gently as her heart rate slowed. The stars clustered and flowed like a stream over the pitch sky, while the moon cast its ashy shadow across the ground. Still shaken by the ghostly apparition, she kneeled in the grass and took a pair of small, cold shears from the basket. Her hands trembled, but not from weakness.

"Are you going to tell me what that was or force me to ask Father Timotej?" Eliška asked after a time. She spoke quietly, but without whispering so Olga would hear her as she clipped at the feathery stalks of tansy. She saw more than heard the old woman's grunt, her round shoulders quivering. Then her dusty voice drifted toward Eliška.

"Timotej always was a good boy and he's a better priest than most. Honest. Merciful. But full of answers. Too many answers."

Eliška sliced into another pale stalk, carefully avoiding her own fingers. "What good are questions without answers?" she asked. After what she'd just seen, Eliška had little patience for her friend's meandering answers.

The old woman gave her a jack-o-lantern smile, all tooth and eye. "That's the spirit, bird. Hold fast to it." She went back to gathering. "I do not have better questions or answers than our sweet priest. Only different ones."

Eliška lost her grip on the shears and dropped the tool. Her fingers were starting to tingle. She fumbled for the handle in the loosened earth. "Am I to guess then?" she asked, her fear sharpening into irritation. "Or should I go down to the riverbank and ask the old vodník? I suppose you will tell me he too is real?"

If Babička took offense at Eliška's harsh words, she didn't show it. "It's been said before, child. You must listen." Then she tilted her head in the direction of the river and gave a loud sniff. Eliška quieted, straining her senses to find the trim river where it lay like a black snake at the bottom of the valley. She could almost hear it hiss.

Babička coughed. "You would do well to avoid the vodník. He is in no mood for charity these days and it would break my old heart to see you stolen and forced into one of his teapots."

Eliška, having no idea how to respond to this, blew a strand of hair from her face and went back to work, her blood humming with frustration and fear. Why didn't Olga ever speak plainly she wondered, chewing the corner of her lip? Could it be that her friend's fence wasn't the only thing falling into disrepair? She wouldn't be the first toothless elder Eliška had seen grow forgetful and frail.

She cut a glance at her companion. Just visible in the bright moonlight, Babička Olga's knotty hands moved with assurance. Her gaze was steady. *Nie.* Olga was no feeble crone. Her body might be slowing, but her mind remained scythe-sharp. Besides, she'd seen the white shadow too. If the healer was mad, then she was too.

They gathered in silence for several minutes before it came to her. Don't seek answers, seek better questions. Sitting back on her haunches to rest, Eliška kneaded the idea like a bit of leftover dough.

"Why are they hungry?"

"Aha," Babička Olga whispered, her voice a rasp of excitement. "Now we begin. Many creatures dwell here. Most remain hidden. Especially those behind the veil. It matters not what we call them, though you already know their names."

Eliška's mind whirled, unable to process all Babička was telling her. She tried again. "What do these ones want?" Her voice came out in pieces.

Babička looked around and then cocked her head, listening. Eliška listened too, though for what she didn't know. The normal sounds of the night forest murmured around them. Then the old woman nodded in apparent satisfaction and returned her attention to Eliška.

"Revenge."

Eliška balked at the blunt reply. "Revenge? For what?"

Olga didn't answer.

For the second time that night, gooseflesh rose along the back of her neck. She peered into the slashes of shadow all around and swallowed. Her weak pulse started to thrum. "Are we in danger?"

The old woman went back to work, rending root from earth like flesh from bone. "We are not what they seek. Not tonight."

Eliška took a deep, almost gasping breath as if her body craved the air. Because it did. She needed to slow her racing heart. "I don't understand."

"May you never," said Olga before taking pity and facing her. Moonlight slipped over the woman's time-scored face like rivulets through rock. "I know not why they have come, but I cannot keep them at bay forever. Bread is a poor substitute for souls."

A shudder of fear rustled Eliška's bones. "What kind of creature seeks souls?"

She didn't expect Babička Olga to answer. But she did.

"Víla." The word slid from the old woman's mouth like an oath.

Eliška recoiled. Babička had long spoken of the old ones as if they existed outside the tales desperate mothers told to frighten wayward children into obedience: Don't put your hand in the stove or the škriatok will bite you. Don't play by yourself near the river or the vodník will pull you under. Don't cross a fairy ring in the grass or a host of víla—the vengeful spirits of betrayed lovers— will carry you away in a dance.

Eliška's stomach sank, her breath shallow as a winter grave.

TEN
ALBIN

"**A**re you trying to cut off your fingers, or are you just stupid?"

The vineyard master's words boxed Albin's ears, shining a light on his ineptitude. Albin smiled. After a fitful night's sleep, he and Miro, along with most of the village, arrived in the sloping vineyard just after dawn under the quietude of fatigue and excitement. Many hours later, the whole day was bright with sunshine, sweat, and song. He was dirty, tired, hungry—and felt gloriously alive.

Albin tipped his head up to the tall shadow of the fierce man above him and shaded his eyes. "Neither, sir. Only green I fear," Albin replied and offered up his harvesting shears. "Would you show me how it's best done? I would learn from a master."

Pán Nagy scowled at the flattery. But he snatched up the shears and stooped to instruct Albin while muttering curses that left Miroslav, who was crouched on the other side of the vine, choking with laughter.

"There. Do it right or I shall kick both your arses out of the fields and send you to help cook with the old women and cripples," he said and spat on the ground at Albin's feet. "If the grapes are not collected at the fairest time, the vintage shall go to piss and it will be my neck on the block, see? And do not think for a second I won't take you and every other louse here down with me."

Miroslav coughed loudly and shut up just as Albin succeeded in making a perfect cut.

"No, sir. Or yes, sir," Albin said, holding up the unmarred grapes to the man. "*Ďakujem.* We will prove useful yet, I dare say. You won't regret hiring us."

The harvest master scowled but made no further objection to Albin's technique. With a last disdainful sniff, Pán Nagy moved down the row to spur along another harvester.

"Christ almighty he's wound tight as a new pocket watch," muttered Miroslav, leaning his face close to the row of twisting vines between them. "When you're presented to the village as Baron Pálffy you shall likely give that unpleasant man a heart attack. I almost feel sorry for him. Almost," he said, brushing sweat from his dirty brow with the back of his hand.

Albin did the same, rolling his neck to ease the ache of being stooped over all morning. He took another clump of the indigo fruit in hand and admired it, his thumb delicate across the tight skin. "Hopefully not. I need the man. Perhaps he'll just shit himself from the shock and then we'll all get a laugh? Though I hope he comes away knowing I meant no harm. He proves a good foreman, does he not?"

Miroslav gave an inarticulate grunt. "Speaking of shit, what is that stench? Smells as if we've both pissed ourselves and I do not recall getting drunk last night," he complained as a pungent whiff of ammonia enveloped them.

Albin shuffled along, this time kicking up a clod of mud that splattered the precious fruit. He'd noticed the smell too, and it was getting worse. "I cannot tell, though it's not the foreman at least."

Miroslav shrugged, his long limbs akimbo so close to the ground. "Perhaps, but the man's a pretentious dandy as well. I don't care what station Nagy was born to, he's as arrogant and driving as the duchess you tried to seduce last fall."

Albin snorted. "So says the pot to the kettle," he said and breathed deeply despite the stink before making another cut.

Miroslav scowled at Albin from under the wide brim of his hat.

Albin knew that look well, having been on the receiving end of his friend's exasperation many times. "I seem to recall you being rather fond of Lady Hortensia's daughters on the dance floor. Plain girls, perhaps, but good fun at a ball." Albin clipped another clump of grapes. "They even made your giant feet appear deft."

Now it was Miroslav's turn to give a barking laugh, which earned a derisive grunt and vicious curse from behind them. Albin whirled expecting to see Pán Nagy again ready to box their ears for sniggering.

It wasn't the harvest master, but the big, red-headed fellow from the square. The brother. Albin steeled his face against the surprise, but wasn't sure it was enough. The man leveled a fierce stare at Albin before his glance skated over to Miroslav, darkening further. "You're in the crofter cottage down by the river," he said, without preamble.

His tone left no room for questions. Albin watched as the man severed the neck of the grapes perfectly, his eyes darting between Albin and Miroslav. As he moved, Albin had the alarming realization the stench was coming from the man. And he had clearly heard their complaints.

"Yes. That's us." Albin smiled, hoping to charm the reeking harvester. It wouldn't have been the first time he'd lulled someone into agreement with his cheerful wiles. "We've only just arrived and were fortunate enough to find work." He gestured to the rolling fields of vines around them with the forest and hills rising sharply beyond. "Beautiful valley you have here." Albin smiled best he could while breathing through his mouth and wondering about the man's smell. He didn't appear any dirtier than Miroslav or himself, but being downwind from the man was enough to make Albin's eyes water.

The man would not be put at ease. His frown deepened, reddened, giving him the overall appearance of a monstrously large fox. "You speak well for traveling harvesters. Particularly for ones too poor to pay honest girls for their wares."

Albin held his smile in place like a shield, his tongue a lance. He dared not shoot a glance at Miroslav, though he anticipated his friend's tension. "My thanks. Our mother married beneath her and taught us as she had been. She was a lady." *At least there was truth in that*, Albin thought. "As to your second accusation, I can only beg pardon. The girl is a damned fine baker and though you do not know me, I am good for the coin."

The red harvester curled his mouth in consideration, but appeared unmoved. "Strangers do not come here often unless they are merchants or on their way to the castle. Where did you say you were from?"

There was nothing prying in the question, but Albin felt the suspicion rolling off the man and chose his answer carefully. "I didn't. Our village is near Zilina, though we have been traveling for some time and seen much of the empire." Albin gave Miroslav a just-play-along glance before addressing the unpleasant man. "My brother and I were on our way to Bratislava in search of work when we turned into your valley." Albin took hold of the vine in front of him. Heavy orbs of dark fruit hung invitingly between the bright leaves. "To our good fortune."

The man gave Albin another hostile glance, but moved away without speaking. As he strode along the row of vine, a chunk of damp, moldering earth flew up and hit Albin in the face. He startled backward, nearly falling. A smattering of laughter erupted from the row of harvesters next to them.

Before Albin could move, Miroslav stretched up from his crouched position and leaned over the vine, menacing as a cobra. His long arm snaked toward the stinking harvester who, turning to face them, had finally cracked a grin. But Albin was faster and clamped onto Miroslav's sleeve, staying his hand. Miro met his stare, dark eyes lit with rage.

"Don't," Albin hissed.

Livid, Miroslav shook off Albin as he turned back to the man. "I would have your name, sir." Miroslav's voice slid out like silk, belying the deadly steel of its intent.

The man watched them with mock innocence, a bemused smile on his mouth. "My apologies. Did your lady mother never tell you harvesting was rough work?"

Albin pushed Miro back once more before wiping his face, laughing overly loud. "Of course. No harm done." Albin extended his hand to the stranger. No matter how much he wanted to blacken the man's eyes, Albin would not let this ruffian ruin his time.

"Your name," Miroslav ground out through clenched teeth, his anger undaunted.

Across the vine from Albin, Miroslav vibrated with restrained anger. But Albin knew his friend wouldn't openly defy his command. This week was too important. If a little dirt and humiliation were the price, so be it. Until he was announced as heir, he was not yet above such things.

The big harvester ignored Albin's outstretched hand, took the measure of Miroslav, and looked back at Albin. "Radek Varga," he ground out in a deep, rasping voice.

Albin just smiled pleasantly up at him. He'd run afoul of more than a few hulking men in his time, and they generally came in two varieties: gentle giants who always seemed mildly embarrassed by their stature, and intimidators who enjoyed towering over people. It wasn't difficult to see which kind of man Radek Varga was.

"Varga?" mumbled Miroslav. "That explains a bit."

Catching the insult, Radek's eyes flashed, but Albin stepped in his path. "Do not mind my brother. He's a bit protective."

The village tanner, as they now knew him to be, apparently

thought better of beating Miroslav and begrudgingly shook Albin's outstretched hand only to come away with a palm full of mud. Radek shook out his palm in disgust as the nearby harvesters turned their laughter on one of their own.

"My apologies," Albin quipped, flinging the mud from his own hand and trying not to smile. "You were right. Dirty work indeed."

⁂

Dirty wasn't the half of it. Not only were he and Miroslav blistered and filthy, the work gave new meaning to the phrase back-breaking. Albin tried to straighten all the way upright only to find he couldn't. Not without spasms racing up and down his back anyway. Miroslav was no better off, gritting his teeth against cramped and knotted shoulders. As the day had worn on, many harvesters rotated out to rest, but Albin had been determined to push himself. Stubborn to the core, Miroslav stayed with him in the fields until the shadows ran long across the ground and a bell rang for the evening meal. Workers were dismissed by the seemingly omnipresent—and apparently tireless—Pán Nagy whose rangy legs hadn't stopped moving up and down the rows all day.

"It appears we are no better off than a pair of old women," said Albin, laughing at himself as they trudged out of the fields and toward the village square where a meal was to be served.

Irritated, Miroslav snorted and swung his long arms to stretch them. "Speak for yourself," he said before leaning close. "For the record, sir, this had better be the best goddamned wine your land has ever produced, and I shall expect more than my fair share of it."

Albin chuckled as he rolled his neck gingerly and took a long swig of water from the canteen they'd brought from the cottage. As the younger and older harvesters had tired, they took to ferrying water back and forth for those left in the fields. Albin tipped the brim of his hat back to let the breeze steal across his sweaty brow, the sky a bright bowl above him. Sore and more fulfilled than he'd been in some time, he heaved a contented sigh.

"You look damn pleased with yourselves for a pair of tittering dandies with nothing to gain from the vintage."

Albin turned toward the deep voice and found Radek standing nearby. Just then the breeze changed, and the man's smell wafted in Albin's direction. Albin blinked and felt glad for his own filthiness—at least the sour smell of his tired body would wash away. He took an obvious breath through his mouth and the tanner rolled his eyes.

"On the contrary," Albin said with genuine glee. "We are taken with this vineyard and would feel quite bereft if the crop was to fail." He glanced at Miroslav then and pulled his hat down over his face. "What do you say, brother? Shall we travel this way next year for the harvest? It would be a shame not to taste the fruits of our labor after all. Even if the company is less than keen." Albin kept his gaze on the ground as the red man approached, his shadow looming as he moved closer.

"I do not think it would be in your best interest to return this way," the foul-smelling man scoffed.

"Then it is our good fortune your opinion does not matter," said Miroslav.

Albin's head snapped up as the two taller men stepped toward each other. He scrambled between them once again. Verbal jabs were one thing; a beating quite another. Albin knew Miroslav could hold his own in a fist fight, but for some reason he knew in his gut that this tanner was out for more than a bit of blood. Perhaps flirting with the pretty cart girl had been a worse insult than he had anticipated.

"That's enough!" came the reedy voice of Pán Nagy. The harvest master pushed through the small crowd of villagers who'd gathered to see what was amiss. The man's long face was scrunched tight as a fist with weariness and irritation. Albin stepped up to meet him.

"It was my fault, Pán Nagy. I poked fun at the tanner, but I meant no harm."

"I don't care two shits who started it," the man bellowed, and stared up at Radek without concern. "There'll be no brawling in my vineyard. None. You fight, you lose your pay. If a single grape is damaged it will be your head, you hear?" He poked a long, dirty finger in Albin's face, his eyes livid. "Fortunately, you two asses kept up so I won't throw you out, but you've been warned. Shut your traps and work." Then he pointed at the tanner. "You know better, Varga." Then he stormed off as quickly as he'd intervened and waved a hand at the gathered harvesters who fled like mice. "What are you waiting for? Food's ready," Pán Nagy shouted behind him without looking back to see if he'd been listened to.

Radek shot a glare at Albin and Miroslav before heading toward the village square. Others fell in line behind him, casting suspicious glances over their shoulders.

Miroslav spat on the ground where the tanner had stood and crossed and recrossed his arms angrily. "Shame your father did away with the rack after all," he said in a low voice. "I'd pay to watch that bastard beg for mercy."

Albin let out a low, unconcerned whistle. He'd enjoy making the tanner pay in time, but wasn't concerned now. He was too busy thinking about the exceptional old foreman and wondered what his father paid the man. Probably too little. "Uh huh," he said to himself and knew his first order of business would be to give the man a raise.

ELEVEN
ELIŠKA

The long tables placed in the town square groaned under the weight of too much food and the fatty, sweet smells had even Eliška's timid stomach growling. Pillows of potato dough topped with sheep cheese and bacon, cabbage-filled pirogy with chewy edges, steaming pots of bean and vegetable soup, links of spicey sausages, and delicate pastry filled with plum jam all sat growing cold in the approaching sunset, as those either too young or too old to work the fields waited for the harvesters to return. When the announcement had come the night before that the grapes were ready, each house had flown into action. For Eliška, that meant helping her mother since early this morning after the strange night with Babička Olga.

Now seated in the shade of the church, Eliška watched as a small, sticky hand reached out from under a table toward a tempting array of treats. The sweet, fried dough balls were still too hot to eat, but that didn't stop the babes from trying. At least until old Pani Kis slapped away the roaming hand. Shocked giggles erupted from under the table. Eliška smiled. She remembered doing the same thing as a child: sneaking to grab the fried dumplings in her bare hands only to skitter away to gobble them down in peace, some babička's voice slapping the air behind her. Singed fingers and tongues had seemed a small price to pay for the rare sweets. Even now, far from a child, she liked to eat the clouds of dough too hot. Still withstood the scolding for doing so. Still didn't care.

With nearly all the men, women, and older youths in the fields, it fell to the grandmothers—and Eliška—to guard and serve the meal and tend any who were injured in the fields. This meant unwatched children roamed the village, fleeing supervision like great clumps of birds flocking from one adventure to the next. She didn't mind being with the babes or cooking. The sting lay in the lack of choice.

Still tired and unsettled from her encounter with the white shadow the night before, Eliška stretched and tapped her fingers against the lingering numbness in their tips. She glanced west. The road to the fields was still empty; the workers were late returning home. But in the days ahead, nothing would matter more than the crop. Each row of grapes had to be harvested at the optimal time or the vintage would be less than ideal and would not fetch the correct amount at market. If the wine failed, they all failed.

Eliška twisted her mouth at the idea, anxious. It didn't happen often, but one hungry winter was enough to mark the memory, and she had no desire to repeat the long-ago experience. Especially not with rumblings of rebellion on the wind and an unproven young lord about to install himself in the castle. Always relegated to the company of women, she didn't hear much about the world outside Hrozno, but unrest had been on the lips of every traveling merchant since last summer. The men had started to whisper amongst themselves, shoulders hunched and tense, bracing for an invisible blow. She didn't know if they would be the shield or the spear and it added to the simmering unnerve she'd felt all summer.

"There you are, Eliška." Pani Kis broke in as she swatted away yet another greedy, chubby-fingered hand. "The little beasts shall eat everything before the harvesters are fed. Come."

Eliška yawned and stretched again. After such an eventful night and busy morning, fatigue pulled at every fiber of her being; she was not up for minding a gaggle of small children. But she was loath to admit such a thing. She would not fail at such a small task.

"*Prídem.* I'm coming," she said and forced her wobbling legs to stand. It was a good thing she had a plan. With her hands deep in the pockets of her apron, Eliška let out a stabbing whistle. Little heads snapped to attention as she seemed to magick tiny flaxen dolls into being from her pockets. With fistfuls of the mini playthings, she strode toward the pack of toddling humans now darting toward her. Children fled their hiding places to take hold of the toys, squealing with desire. Her heart fluttered and spots momentarily dotted her vision, but Eliška could not have felt more satisfied had she been the Pied Piper himself.

"For you, and you, and you. *Áno*, Tereza, you too." She placed a doll in each child's hand before they darted off to play, their greedy stomachs momentarily forgotten.

Pleased with herself, Eliška lifted a hand to shield her eyes. Mamička had appeared in the village square, a sure sign the workers were on their way. Backlit by the late afternoon sun, the older woman was tired, but clearly satisfied. And she was smiling at Eliška. A real, rare smile. Eliška smiled back at her mother, allowing the moment to seep through her, warming as a hot drink. She felt it ease her breath. Perhaps it even reddened her lips.

"When did you find time to make such things?" her mother asked with an amused shake of her head. Though her face was damp and smudged with dirt and sweat, she strode forward with such energy Eliška nearly sighed with envy. Not for the first time, Eliška silently chided herself for being jealous of an aging widow who had no choice but to work hard.

Instead, she quirked an eyebrow. "I have my ways," Eliška answered back, her voice mischievous. She wanted to bristle at the insinuation under her mother's surprise, but couldn't. Between the sickness and stubbornness, she knew there was little she did that truly pleased her mother, but the small vanity of her sewing warmed both their hearts. Just then, it was enough.

"Where is everyone? There might not be any food left if Pani Kis can't keep little Jakub from eating his weight in sisky," she whispered, gesturing towards a little boy shoving yet another ball of sweet dough into his mouth, an expression of pure bliss on his freckled face.

Mamička chuckled. "The workers will arrive shortly. Pán Nagy fears the rains will come and delay optimal timing," she said, examining a now tepid plate of schnitzel.

Eliška watched her mother move to wash her hands and was struck with a pang of pity. It was no secret she had helped direct the harvest long ago with Eliška's father. They had seen several successful vintages together, side by side. Then he died and the position was given to a new man, her mother forgotten. It was the way of things. Though Pán Nagy had proved a good foreman, she knew her mother still longed for the position, but could only hope to counsel Pán Nagy when he had an ear for a woman's input. He was a fairer man than many, and valued her mother's opinion on such matters, but it was not the same and everyone knew it.

Eliška reached out and grasped one of her mother's cold hands, still damp from the wash basin. Matka stilled and smiled at Eliška, gesturing toward the tables.

"A fine meal to be sure."

Then a familiar shadow passed behind her mother's eyes— something Eliška had seen before. A sadness. A haunting. She was never sure what to make of it. Then it was gone, and Mamička squeezed her hand as the first heralding shouts reached their ears.

"We'd best get ready," her mother said, and the tender moment fell away.

All heads turned toward the road, as the harvesters trickled around the bend, a drizzle of sweat, hunger, and fatigue. Several of the older children saw them and began running toward their parents, the flaxen dolls abandoned in the square to be crushed underfoot. A massacre of tiny bodies.

"Take this," Mamička said, as she thrust a huge ladle into Eliška's hands. "You can serve the *kapustnica*. You won't have to lift any platters then."

Her mother's words jabbed like needles, but she fisted her tingling fingers around the scarred handle and moved into position behind one of the long tables. Grandmothers and aunties too old for the fields flanked her as she stepped back into the role she could never leave behind. Sick.

Greetings were exchanged and brows mopped as the harvesters washed up and filed down the line of tables, the new pungent smell of sweat mixing with the more pleasant scents of food. Eliška nodded her head and smiled at each familiar face. She would serve their food and play with their children, but she would not allow them to see her shame. Her perfectly clean hands. Her shallow breaths. Her longing. No, those were for herself alone, if nothing else in this life ever was.

Her smile froze in place when Radek's scent reached her nose just before his large shadow fell over her. She lifted her chin, unwilling to be cowed. Taller and broader than most of the men in the village, he practically glowed in front of her, his cheeks ruddy with color and his hair a shock of flame. She knew he was handsome in a rough way. Strong. Persistent and proper. For what felt like the hundredth time, Eliška knew she should be pleased by Radek's interest, but it was like trying to light a wet hearth. No matter how much flint she used, a fire would never catch.

"Eliška," Radek greeted in a low voice, his bowl outstretched.

"*Ahoj*, Radek. It's good to see you unharmed," Eliška said, ladling his soup. She had no wish to be unkind; could not afford to be in truth. But neither did she want to encourage him. The back of her neck prickled as if being watched. She suspected it was her mother.

"It was a fortunate day," he said before lowering his voice

further. "You look well." His words were formal, but he did nothing to mask their tenderness. He should be moving on, but lingered.

Eliška offered a small smile and put the ladle back in the soup so he wouldn't see her hand tremble. "Thank you," she said softly, but gave him nothing more.

Radek met her silent resistance with his own, their unspoken impasse a near-tangible web entangling them. They remained frozen and silent until the man behind Radek cleared his throat at the delay in his meal. Radek threw a vicious glance at the man, held it a heartbeat too long, and then moved along the line.

She released a breath and turned her attention back to the next outstretched bowl, her energy waning. Before she knew, her fingers had loosened, the ladle dropped from her hand. Soup splashed on the woman in front of her.

"Isha?" came her mother's arrow voice almost immediately.

"I'm fine, Mamička. My hand slipped," she said, cursing herself for the mishap. She couldn't afford public blunders. They revealed too much. And if she wanted her mother to believe she could dance at the harvest festival, let alone live without a husband and learn Babička Olga's healing craft, then she needed to prove it.

"Forgive me," she said to the woman. "I'd be happy to wash your apron for you," she offered and gave her a second helping and her best smile.

The woman, who Eliška recognized as one of Pani Kis's daughters-in-law, wiped at the splatters on her apron. "No harm done. I can't get much dirtier in truth," she said kindly and moved on. But her mother was at Eliška's shoulder, her hand on the ladle. "Young Draha will take your place. Her new babe is a good sleeper and shouldn't fuss. Take him and sit in the shade."

Eliška tightened her grip and filled another bowl, refusing to acknowledge her mother. She anticipated her mother's firm grip; expected her hand to be forced. She was prepared for that. Something worse happened.

"Please." Mamička's voice had lost its command and taken on a note of open pleading instead. "Please, Isha. Just rest."

One simple word and Eliška was undone. She blew out a resigned sigh and stepped back on shaking knees, handing off the already small task she'd been given. Frustrated tears stung her eyes, but she blinked them away, unwilling to be any more piteous than she already was.

Taking the tiny, swaddled infant from a young woman, Eliška shuffled back to her shady nook against the church. Sliding to the ground, she nestled the tiny boy into the crook of her arms and let the earth under her and the wall at her back do the work for her. Relief flooded her body at the rest, but she'd be damned before she let them see it. Carefully, Eliška faced away from the line of hungry harvesters and gulped air into her burning lungs.

⁂

The dishes had been collected and the remaining food distributed for the next day before Draha came to retrieve her son, miraculously still limp and solid against Eliška's chest. Part of her was sad to relinquish the warm child even though her arms had fallen asleep under his weight and her backside ached from being on the ground so long. He'd been a sweet presence, and she enjoyed the smell of his delicate head.

Draha smiled through her exhaustion as she eased the babe out of Eliška's arms. "Thank you," she whispered as she nestled the child close. The baby squirmed slightly at the movement, but drifted back to sleep, his tiny mouth rooting toward his mother's scent.

Eliška smiled as the woman moved away, though it cost her to admit her mother had been right. Stretching her numb limbs and pushing herself off the ground, she held on to the church wall a moment to be sure of her footing before stepping toward the dwindling crowd. There was no doubt her mother was still there and Eliška wished to go home. Tomorrow would be another taxing day. Though the sun was still visible above the treetops, twilight would be on them soon, and she couldn't shake the shiver she'd pressed down since seeing the white shadow.

She was still thinking about the specter in the woods when she saw the blonde stranger among the lingering harvesters, his presence as startling as a needle prick. Even from this distance, Eliška recognized him, her weariness forgotten. He hadn't seen her, but every move he made sent an agitating ripple through the air. She could almost feel it.

Smiling, he jostled his tall companion and joked with a few of the other men. Though sweat and dust streaked his face and his honeyed hair stood out in a wild tangle, the stranger's dishevelment only added to his charm. And she wasn't the only one to notice.

Alena stepped in front of her, eyes trained in the same direction. Eliška bristled. Though she had no official claim on the stranger, his arrival had been foretold in front of her—not haughty Alena—and she couldn't help thinking he was meant for her somehow. Even now she warmed at the memory of their encounter at the well. Though they hadn't spoken, she remembered the way he looked at her. *Only* at her despite the press of people around them. Or how he'd leaned in, his eyes following her as she smiled and moved off with her companions, carried away by the current of convention.

Perhaps he would glance her way again, she thought, and trembled at the possibility. Biting a healthy flush into her lips, Eliška separated herself from the crowd to be more visible.

She knew the moment he saw her. He paused mid-sentence, staring like a man enchanted. Satisfaction surged from low in her belly, a delicious permeating heat. She smiled just as Alena turned toward Eliška, following the stranger's gaze. She held his gaze, despite their audience. A derisive noise and the swish of skirts reached Eliška's ears, but she didn't care. The blonde stranger was coming toward her. Panic flooded her chest, blood thundered in her ears, but she held her ground as he ate up the space between them with intention.

He stopped just out of arm's reach, the fingers of one hand drumming against his leg. He shifted his weight and she realized the most astonishing thing—he was nervous. A pleased smile tugged at her lips, but she remained quiet. Smiling at this handsome stranger was one thing—speaking first was another. She fixed her eyes boldly on him and waited.

His easy expression faltered as he opened his mouth to speak, stopped himself, and then blurted, "I saw you. Near the well."

Eliška raised an eyebrow at him. "Perhaps it was I who saw you."

He gave a small laugh, the sound as golden as himself and she felt absurdly pleased for having inspired it.

"Yes, perhaps it was." His fingers continued the steady rhythm against his thigh. "You weren't in the fields today."

Her breath caught as two opposing thoughts took hold. First, he'd looked for her. Second, what had he thought of her absence?

"No," she said. "I was needed here." If her body had been like any other body, the blood might have rushed to her cheeks at the half-truth, staining them a tempting pink. But not hers. She bit her lower lip again.

If the stranger noticed anything odd about this, he didn't show it. "I can't tell you how glad I am to find you here. For a while there, I was afraid I had imagined you."

Eliška's heart flip-flopped. "Well, then. Now you don't have to be afraid."

The edges of his full lips quirked up at her ridiculous comment. "At least not of you being a dream. What is your name?"

"Eliška Ciernikova. And yours, sir?"

"Eliška Ciernikova," he repeated, drawing the syllables out as if tasting each one. "My name is of little import compared to such loveliness."

Warmth stole up her neck. She knew such pretty words meant nothing, but couldn't stop herself. "That seems unfair. What am I to call you?"

"I would answer to anything you wished to call me."

The brazenness of his words sent another jolt of wonderful heat into her belly, but this one held a hint of a warning, too. Was he in jest? Uneasy, she stepped back.

"Forgive me," he said, stretching a hand toward her as if to stay her retreat. "I tease too much sometimes." Then he crossed his arms, uncrossed them, and crossed them again. "My friends call me Lajos. Lajos Cerveny."

Lajos. Eliška rolled the name around in her brain, examining it. Lajos. "Are we to be friends then?"

"If a man such as myself could be so lucky."

"And what sort of man is that?" she asked.

Lajos paused. Drummed his fingers again. "A traveler."

Eliška was more than a little frightened by such an answer. Questions crowded forward, jostling for prominence, but only one was necessary. "Will you be staying for the harvest festival, Traveler Friend Lajos?" she asked, daring to use his given name.

He flashed a true smile then, a boyish grin full of pleasure. "Yes, Beautiful Eliška Full of Questions. I believe I shall."

She nodded and bit the insides of her cheeks to keep from grinning. He stepped closer and her breath snagged in her throat.

"Our driving harvest master, Pán Nagy, says the rest of the grapes need another day or more on the vine. May I call on you in my idleness?"

Before she could move, he took hold of her hand, gently, fingertips and palms scarcely touching, and pressed his lips to it. Eliška's mouth went dry when he looked up through lashes the color of honey and let go.

Several moments ticked by as her mind formed an answer, but

her mouth refused to speak. With her breath held tight against her heart, she nodded. Then, she darted her eyes meaningfully down the lane, and whispered, "The yellow cottage with the bed of iris."

He followed her glance, dimples flexed. "Until tomorrow then."

"Tomorrow." She breathed the words like a prayer and turned away, hoping to appear unaffected to anyone who'd been watching them. And, of course, people had been.

It wasn't Eliška's first kiss. Radek had snuck a kiss to her cheek more than once, and many summers ago, Viktor Juhasz had kissed her after mass behind the church on a dare. It had been the kiss of a child—brief, airy, more rite of passage than affection. This kiss was no less fleeting. No less innocent, and yet her blood raced, and her head spun from something other than her weakness. Pressing her other hand to the memory of his touch, Eliška dared to imagine herself dancing with Lajos at the harvest festival, full of wine and mirth, weightless as a soul.

TWELVE

ALBIN

With his belly pleasantly full and his mind brimming with tomorrow's possibilities, Albin followed Miroslav's lead as they headed to the cottage for the night. Their shadows stretched thin and long across the road as they waved polite farewells to their fellow harvesters and strode along in weary silence. Albin felt pleased as a fat cat with a mouse at the day's work and hummed contentedly. No sooner had they rounded the bend on the road than Miroslav grabbed him by the arm and held fast, pulling his face close.

"Hey!" Albin protested, but Miroslav didn't move, his dark eyes fierce under furrowed eyebrows.

"Quiet. I have oft wondered about the condition of your sanity, but am now utterly certain: you are barking mad, Bini. Have you no shame? Which is an unnecessary question because the answer is most assuredly *no*. Are you seriously considering seducing that child?"

Albin pulled out of Miroslav's grasp. "I am quite sane, and have no villainous plans for anyone besides the stinking tanner. What kind of man do you take me for?" Albin ground out, insulted. He was genuinely hurt—and discomforted—by the accusation of seduction, and did not care for the feeling at all.

"I merely smiled at her and exchanged a word. A conversation which the *young woman* freely participated in. Last I checked that was perfectly genteel behavior."

Miroslav glowered. "Genteel my ass. She is a country innocent whom you will be lord over very soon. What will happen to her if you two become acquainted and you disappear only to reappear as her lord? Do you think she—any of these people—your people, I might add, will take kindly to such low behavior?"

Albin strode away and back again, flustered. He couldn't argue against the cold rationale of his closest ally, but that didn't stop the frustration simmering under his skin. Did the man have no heart? No sentiment for fate or romance? Surely the pleasant thrumming of his blood meant something? He just needed to make Miro understand.

"This is all based on your assumption that I intend to harm the young lady, which I do not. And, if we were to become acquainted, who is to say they will even care?" he said. "Am I not, as you are so fond of reminding me, soon to be the master of this estate? May I not exercise my remaining freedom with a harmless flirtation?" Strung tight with conviction, Albin took it even farther. "Must I swear that I mean the beauty no ill intent? Because I will, readily."

Miroslav shook his head in frustration and wiped a dirty hand across his dirtier face. "I do not mean to paint you as a villain, sir. But I thought this was to be an unencumbered time." Miroslav flung his arms out. "A time to do as we may. To get reacquainted with your lands. To—" Miroslav stopped himself. "To spend time together as we once did as lads before you take a wife."

Albin's annoyance softened, deflated. Of course, he thought. Miroslav only wanted what was best for him, as he always did, and saw the girl as an hindrance. Touched, Albin smiled brilliantly and clapped Miroslav on the arm.

"As do I, man. Don't fret. There are still good times to be

had," said Albin in his most reassuring tone. "I admit it, I admire the girl's elfish beauty, but flirting was a mere lark, Miro. Nothing more. I am a romantic at heart, but you are right to caution me."

Irritation ebbed out of Miroslav's face. The mood softened.

"Perhaps I spoke too harshly, sir. I know you are here to enjoy your freedom and would never intentionally harm—"

"No, no," protested Albin. "I often lose my head in these matters and depend on you to find it for me."

Miroslav gave a small, pleased shrug and cleared his throat. "Well then," he said and redirected their course for the cottage. "Shall we?"

Albin fell in beside him as the leaves rattled in the treetops like coins in a jar.

⁓⊶⊷⁓

Albin realized with a wave of trepidation and delight that he was solidly drunk. The wobbling walls had been his first clue. After returning to the cottage exhausted and in better spirits, they made a roaring fire in the stove before setting themselves to the task of drinking all the wine. Too soon they were sniggering about childish escapades until Miroslav produced another bottle—this one containing brandy—from under his moldering cot.

"Devious cad!" Albin had shouted with surprise. It was usually he who led Miroslav astray, and little could have pleased him more than to see his friend lean into the moments he always held himself against. They worked well this way: Albin pulling Miroslav forward while his friend tempered his own rashness. Albin raised an empty cup to his friend's genius.

"I shall take that as a compliment coming from you, sir," Miroslav said, uncorking the amber liquid with a flourish. "Damn," he muttered as the tiniest bit spilled on the earthen floor.

Albin flung himself forward and feigned lapping it up from the ground before laughing at Miroslav's predictable disgust.

"Beast," Miroslav muttered as he poured the alcohol with exaggerated care. Albin chuckled as he crawled across the floor with the playful lumber of a bear, his cup caught between his teeth.

Even drunk, Miroslav rolled his eyes at Albin's antics.

Laughing at himself, Albin sat contentedly on the floor, his battered metal cup outstretched. His entire body felt warm and slightly numb, his edges pleasantly blurred. "I should fine you for pilfering my father's good stashes," he said, carefully enunciating each word. "But since you didn't keep the goods for your greedy self, I'm inclined to overlook it."

"Ha!" Miroslav laughed at him and filled Albin's cup. "I'm afraid your time here will make 'overlooking' anything more difficult."

Albin inhaled the spicy scent of the liquor and frowned. "This smells like an off year to me. And what do you mean 'difficult to overlook'? Blast your riddles, man."

Miroslav filled his own cup then, his high brow furrowed to match Albin's. "I fear people will doubt your word after this. Don't you?"

Irritated once again at the sudden shift, Albin sampled his cup and wiped his mouth with his hand. "You worry too much. All will be forgotten, in time. You'll see. Once the village realizes all the plans I have for them—improving the harvest, opening more trade, bringing in books, better arming them against thieves—"

"Like ourselves?" said Miroslav with an exaggerated attempt to sip like a gentleman.

Albin reared back in mock indignation. "We are not thieves! And my father's stuffed coffers do not count," he said, laughing into his cup.

Miroslav chuckled, but the hollow ring of the sound troubled Albin. *Damn his practical hide,* thought Albin, staring at the shining contents of his cup. He knew if he did not quell Miroslav's fears now, they would plague them as surely as hungry dogs after a hare for the duration of their time. Albin would not have it.

"I'm serious, Miro," he said, twisting the simple cup between his blistered hands. "You know how much I hate that I must be here. Be reduced to this for excitement," he slurred, gesturing wildly around the cottage. "Wedded and shackled to the fate of this land is not a choice I would make for myself." He stared into the fire then and felt such sadness and hope waring inside, he thought his head would split. "You saw how it was today—there is some good I could do here. It will be my official reason for being in hiding. But I can't do any of it alone, so for the love of all that's holy will you shut up and enjoy yourself?"

Miroslav twisted his mouth in consideration. "The girl?"

Albin slumped back against the wall, nearly spilling his drink. "The girl is simply that. A girl. A charming one to be sure, but I see your point. I will keep my distance."

As soon as the words left his mouth Albin knew them to be a lie. He had to be careful with this one. Something in Miroslav's expression warned him this flirtation would not be tolerated as usual. And yet—maybe because of it—Albin could not remember ever feeling such desire. Instant, demanding want. He trailed his finger around the rim of the cup, thinking of her. Eliška. Yes, he would have to take care with this one.

"I'm in earnest, Bini."

Albin snapped back to the tiny room, his face wide open. "As am I. She is tempting, to be sure and I do not care to be denied. But I see your wisdom." Albin shifted and enjoyed how the hearth fire seemed to sway along with him. He took another sip. "You worry too much. Like a babička."

"And you not enough," Miro said, putting down his cup and staggering to his feet. "Now, if you'll excuse me, I must go take a piss in the woods like the peasant I was born to be."

Albin laughed and hoisted himself up as well. "That is a hell of an idea, lad. But you're mistaken. I, by some sick twist of the stars, was born to be a wandering peasant and you lord of the castle."

Albin stumbled across the room and clamped onto his taller friend's arm, leaning on him for support. "If this were a fairytale, we could switch places and be happy," he said, and smiled up into Miroslav's shadowed face.

Albin's vision blurred gently as Miroslav looked down at him, jaw locked, pupils dilated, and pulled out of his grasp.

"I want nothing of your castle, sir," Miro said, the air between them suddenly sharp, and swung open the door, leaving Albin unsteady in the dark.

Thirteen

Eliška

Eliška was no stranger to odd dreams. They often fretted and scratched at her sleep like Babička Olga's old cat at the garden door, persistent but harmless. Other nights, the dreams slid through her mind like a dank mist, their presence more feeling than memory. And every once in a while, the dreams roared in like a squall that rattled her teeth and slapped her awake, wet and shivering, as if she'd just come in from a storm. It had been one of those nights.

Damp with sweat, Eliška blinked her eyes open and forced herself to breathe through her nose. *Not real, not real, not real*, her heart seemed to say with each erratic beat. Her stomach wobbled as half-remembered images drifted further and further away: the gathering moon—fat as a prize ewe, a jewel bright as blood, a toothless mouth agape with grief, a white shadow hurtling toward her. She didn't understand what the dream meant, if anything, but she knew such images would haunt her if she allowed them to. She would not.

Eliška inhaled again to rid herself of the specters, but fear still pressed on her chest, heavy as a pail of milk. Just a dream, she reminded herself. They weren't supposed to make sense. Mamička often said dreams were just our fears taunting us. Nothing more than her own bluster and fuss twisted up and thrust upon her as a reminder to pray more. As if every single day wasn't already strung together with whispered pleas for breath. For strength. Her entire life was a paperchain of prayers. Babička Olga told her the world had much to tell if a person was canny enough to listen. More and more often she found herself wishing the old woman wasn't always right.

A gentle clatter came from across the cottage. Eliška wiped her face and sat up carefully, the old bed creaking under her. She squinted at the too-bright light which told her she'd overslept.

"Finally awake, Isha? Are you unwell?" Mamička stuck her head around the lime-washed stone of the stove and surveyed Eliška with a frown. "You were thrashing again. I nearly fetched Olga, but then you quieted so I thought perhaps sleep was best."

"I'm fine," Eliška said, not at all sure if she was. "Just tired after yesterday."

Mother was already dressed, her hair secured under her best cap. Eliška saw her mother's good apron laid out on the table, the fringe of colors bright as wildflowers against dark soil. Eliška had embroidered yellow crocuses around the edges, her stitches small and more even than anyone else in the village. Even in her groggy state, a small ember of pride crackled knowing her mother had the finest apron in Hrozno. Clearly, Mamička was going out. And despite the churning in her head and stomach, a tiny thrill shot through her.

"Hmmm. I expect that's true for the whole village. Did you not sleep well?"

"A bad dream is all. I can't remember it now. Where are you going?" Feeling steadier, Eliška slid out from under the covers. The air was cool and helped dry the sweat from her neck and under-arms. She was grateful. If the sweat beaded on her face, Mamička might not leave.

"To market first. We're running low on salt. Then to see Pán

Nagy to discuss the continuation of the harvest. That wife of his may be pleasant to look at, but the woman hasn't the sense to help her husband with such things with all those babes about."

Wiping her hands restlessly, Mamička left the rest of her thought unspoken as she turned back to Eliška. With her hands planted on narrow hips, her arms poked out like stunted wings. As soon as Eliška saw the resemblance, she couldn't unsee it. Her mother as a dark, thin bird. Flightless, but fierce. So unlike Eliška herself.

"I've set a bowl of porridge out for you, and the kettle is ready for tea. There's still a bit of honey left as well. Will you be able to weed the cabbages later?"

"Yes," Eliška said without thought and picked up the wooden comb. "Pani Molnarova also wanted the new bonnets for her granddaughters done by Michaelmas. I'll work on them if it gets too hot." Slowly, she combed the tangles and damp patches from her hair and let the muddy truths out into the morning air. Nerves bubbled in Eliška's heart, scalding and savory, as other possibilities formed. Delicious, dangerous alternatives to the mundane tasks laid before her.

She bit her tongue against the ready lie. As much as she resented her mother's meddling and overprotection, she'd never been one for deliberate falsehood. *Well*, she thought as she worked her hair into a bun at the nape of her neck, if Lajos didn't come for her, she would indeed pass the morning as she said, content in the garden or working her embroidery. *Or nearly content*, she told herself. Even as the word formed in her mind, Eliška knew she was fooling herself. She was not content. Glancing at the sliver of light peeking through the curtains, she felt the familiar restlessness at her core stretch and flex, waking up even as she did. If she had ever been content, she certainly wasn't now.

Eliška turned back and found her mother watching her with a tight expression. She pretended not to notice and proceeded to get dressed.

"Well then," her mother said. "I saw Maria in her garden this morn with the new babe if you should need anything." She straightened her apron, avoiding Eliška's eyes. The meaning behind her unsaid words filled the room, thick and acrid as smoke. *If you should need anything—if you should become ill.*

Eliška bristled. She hated her mother's words, but not as much as she hated the necessity of them. Eliška decided she would not 'need anything' today, no matter how her head ached or her breath rasped. She would not be weak or coddled or stopped from doing what she wished. Not today—not ever again if she had anything to do with it.

Putting on her own day dress and work apron, she nodded at her mother. "I'm sure Maria has more than enough to do today. I shall be fine," she said, determined to be so and then added, "Should I expect you at midday?" She hoped her voice sounded neutral, though her pulse thrummed at her throat. If Mamička heard the anticipation and suspected.

"Not today. I've loaded an extra basket of bread and cheese to take with me. I expect to be back by dusk. A simple soup would be plenty for dinner if you can manage it." Mamička turned then and eyed her carefully, as if reassuring herself of something.

Eliška rallied all the cheerfulness she could. "I shall have supper ready," she said, moving forward to kiss her mother's cheek. "I am fine. Truly. If I have need of you, I will send Maria's eldest boy to the fields or have Babička Olga tend me. Now go before you are late."

Warmth finally dispelled the worry in her mother's eyes, and she took Eliška's face in her wiry hands. Eliška smiled and hoped her lips were pink enough. Her mother's eyes tightened and then released, apparently satisfied. She returned the kiss. "Very well. Take care of yourself until I return," she said and gathered her things.

"I always do," Eliška whispered and walked to the door. She watched her mother slip through their small yard and out into the street, waving just a little so Mamička would not find fault in her eagerness. Then, Eliška slid into the dim house and closed the door. The click of the latch against her back sounded of freedom.

⤬

Eliška tended the garden early, taking advantage of the cool morning air. The deep cold made her bones ache, and the heat left her struggling to breathe, so these mild late-summer days were some of her favorites. And although she wouldn't have admitted it, she had no wish to be caught sweating and disheveled if Lajos happened to stop by. Despite the fatigue and numbness in her hands, she weeded their kitchen garden behind the cottage quickly. While she cleaned and fussed over the herbs and vegetables she and mother would preserve for the winter, a warbler sang in the mellow warmth and bees buzzed merrily through the wildflowers over the fence.

They were comforting sounds, the kind that eased the tightness in her chest, and before long, Eliška was humming along. She didn't have a voice for singing, but the rhythm came naturally to her. Music of all kinds rolled through her when she listened, and although she couldn't match the notes with her voice, her muscles always knew what came next, her feet which step to take. If she could. In a moment of fancy, she lifted her arms over her head in a delicate arch and closed her eyes. A breeze rose and she let it rush through her fingers as if they were leaves, her arms branches, her body a trunk.

Babička Olga told her a story once about creatures called dryads, tree spirits in the shape of women, and Eliška had felt sorry for them. After all, what could be more trapped than a tree? Now she imagined being strong, tall, and able to dance on every breeze. She changed her mind. To be a tree would be a great gift. A sudden shiver ran through her at the thought. After seeing the white shadow in the woods—the vila—perhaps Babička was right about other things. Part of Eliška reasoned that if she believed in a Father God in the sky and a resurrected Christ, then surely the earth could be full of wonders too.

Just as she was pretending her toes were roots planted deep in the earth, a loud *tsk* broke her reverie. Eliška's eyes flew open, her arms dropped, afraid she'd been caught by Lajos. But it was only her neighbor, sour old Pani Nemeth, staring over their shared fence with a pinched expression. The childish excuse died in her mouth even as her cheeks went pink.

"*Dobré ráno*. Good morning." Eliška smiled in greeting to the woman, unwilling to let her dower neighbor ruin her mood. The older woman just scowled and shook her head before ducking back into her own bed of cabbages. Eliška just hoped her neighbor wouldn't notice if she left the house, or speak to her mother about it if she did. She turned her attention back to the birds and the sound of her own breath.

When the weeding was done, she went inside to clean herself and rest, no longer able to push away the fatigue weighing down her limbs. But her mind buzzed with a frantic energy her body could only long for, so she tried to settle into her embroidery. It was no use. Every footstep on the path or rustle of the trees sent her eyes darting toward the door, her breath cut short. Waiting. Hoping. It didn't take long for Eliška to give up because she refused to make needless mistakes in her patterns. Annoyed with herself for being so impressionable, since she had never lost her head over a young man before, she settled in with a book of herbal remedies she'd borrowed from Babička.

It was just past noon when he finally came. Unlike the early morning calls of Radek, this time when a soft knock at the door broke the quiet, Eliška's heart jumped and fluttered with expectation. She all but tossed the book aside and walked to the door. Cursing herself for being such a fool, she swallowed back a cough, her mouth suddenly dry.

"Who is it?" Her voice sounded thin, and she winced. He must not know of her weakness. Not yet. Let him have an opinion of her aside from her illness first.

"A lost traveler," whispered the longed-after voice.

Eliška smiled to herself in the dim cabin, triumph thrilling through her as she opened the door with trembling hands and caught her breath. Lajos stood framed in the dark doorway, tousled and golden as a shaft of wheat. He flashed his dimples and swept into an unnecessary bow. She was grateful because it gave her a moment to breathe before having to speak.

"Aha," she said, playing along, and shielded her eyes as if struggling to see. "Is it Lajos, the traveler? I had quite forgotten about him."

Lajos's lips quirked as he picked up her lead. "Yes, I was afraid you would forget me as I am entirely unworthy of your affections. Shall I go then, good lady?" He took a step back as if to leave, but she saw the gleam in his eyes. She noticed the way his throat moved as he swallowed.

Even as Eliška savored the word 'affection,' she kept tight control over her expression. No matter how recklessly her thoughts leaned toward this boy, Babička Olga's warning still held firm. She was determined to keep her wits about her.

"Are you so easily sent away?" She stepped forward in challenge, leaving the cool confines of the house for the bright step.

Lajos met her at the joint between shadow and sunlight. He made no move to touch her, but she sensed he too was keeping himself under tight control. The space between them hummed with something she couldn't name, and a muscle tightened low in her belly.

"Not so easily. In fact, I am beginning to believe nothing short of your harshest rebuke could drive me off." His expression softened. The corners of his mouth tightened as the constant flirtation was replaced with something far more appealing and terrifying. Sincerity.

Eliška closed her eyes for a moment and breathed as her heart limped on. Here they were already. Just beyond the shallows and wading deeper. She wanted to plunge in; to let the maddening, restless current of feelings inside her take hold. Sweep her away. But Eliška held herself in check. For the moment, and found his steady gaze when she opened her eyes. "Then I hope you do not grow weary of staying. I'm afraid I do not have the heart to send you away."

At that, he did not smile or try to charm her, but went very still, his amber eyes bright. Then they drifted over her shoulder into the dim house.

"Is your family in?"

Eliška shook her head. "No. My mother is out for the day to consult on the rest of the harvest. She's very knowledgeable and often confers with Pán Nagy."

Lajos nodded. If he thought it odd for a woman to do such a thing, he didn't show it. Eliška's attention sparked higher.

"And your father? Siblings?"

She dropped her eyes in hesitation. It had been so long since she'd answered such a question. "No. My father died when I was very young. It is only Mamička and I."

She longed to invite him inside. To watch as he took in her home and feel the intimacy of such a thing. But she balked. Already, someone would have seen him call on her. She would wager her best needles that someone—possibly several someones up and down the street—were watching them right now. To go inside with a strange young man would be beyond reckless. "I can bring you some water here on the steps, but..."

His face lit with understanding. "Of course. I see." He moved his glance from side to side, as if the brilliant iris beds her home was known for held the answer to some deep question. "Perhaps a walk?" he suggested, golden head popping up. "Surely there would be no rebuke for a stroll in broad daylight? I am at your service wherever you lead."

The possibility of the day unfolded before her and Eliška's excitement with it. But to accept his offer now would mean confronting her mother later and Radek soon after, and her tight chest and weary limbs told her she did not have the energy for both pleasure and obligation. As usual, she must choose carefully.

"A stroll would be fine, but I am not quite free." Then she leaned in, a breath away, and whispered, "Down in the meadow, past the grove of birch, there is an old tree stump with several large stones just next to it. Meet me in one hour."

She leaned away, exhilarated by her forwardness. Would he think her rash? Wanton? If Lajos thought anything at all, it was carefully buried in his heart, for he made no reply at all save for a long look from under his buttery lashes and a quick nod.

"Thank you for your directions, miss," he hollered suddenly for any onlookers. "I shall certainly find my way now." He bowed to her and backed out of the yard, closing the gate behind him and, with a wink, Lajos strode toward the village square with purpose.

Eliška bit the inside of her cheek to keep from smiling. It wasn't until she tasted the copper tang of blood that she remembered to go back inside. Behind her, the irises trembled.

FOURTEEN
ALBIN

Albin couldn't remember the last time he'd felt so anxious. Not the nervous sort that leaves one sweating or frightened, though he felt those things too, but the delicious agony of anticipation. When your heart clenches and your palms sweat because you cannot wait

to see what happens next. That kind. Albin wiped his hands on his trousers and took a deep, steadying breath. He searched the deserted clearing just inside the mouth of the woods as if doing so would make Eliška appear as she first had by the well: instantaneous and luminous.

The stump hadn't been difficult to find. Covered in brilliant lichen and a few brave mushrooms, what was left of a once-mighty oak squatted large and imposing as a giant toad among the undergrowth. The only oddity in an otherwise quiet and unremarkable meadow. It was a clever place to meet, both hidden and accessible, though closer to the crofter's cottage than Albin would have liked. Giving Miroslav the slip had proven a challenge.

Miroslav's loyalty to Albin ran deep; he didn't often leave his lord's side when they were off adventuring. But so did Miro's appetite for comfort. Albin felt a twinge of guilt at sending

Miroslav into town for more supplies—ones he could have bought while out himself. It turned out game wasn't as plentiful in the woods as Albin had hoped, and their bread and cheese were gone. Plus, they'd apparently drunk all the wine and half a bottle of brandy, waking up with mighty headaches. Like a gentleman, Miro had taken up the more difficult task believing Albin too sick to accompany him. Albin's conscience pinched over the deception—he was going to owe Miroslav his own castle by the time this adventure was over, he thought, rubbing a hand over his bristled jaw. And their time would be over soon. Too soon. But not yet.

Albin shook his head against the guilt and lingering intoxication. All around the sun slanted across the ground in wide white swaths, but he felt cool in the shade of the birch grove. The oddly mercurial winds of the valley were gentle this morning and foretold of more harvesting tomorrow. He enjoyed the thought. It would be a great vintage, and he was glad to have put his hands to the vines as something other than the lord. He may just scandalize himself every year and work the fields alongside his tenants while his body still allowed it. Even if he didn't enjoy the work, which he did, the mere idea of his father's outrage at the indiscretion was fodder enough. Smiling to himself, Albin flexed his sore, blistered hands and savored the usefulness of them.

"You look pleased as a cat who's caught a fat mouse."

His eyes flew toward the sound of her teasing voice. He went from smiling to grinning like the drunken fool he was. "Only because I was imaging the loveliest visitor," he said, not bothering to hide his pleasure.

She stepped from around the curve of a large elm and into a ribbon of sunshine. Her soft brown hair, too-wide mouth, freckles, and deeply shadowed eyes glowed as if the light originated from within her. Overwhelmed by the sight of her, Albin felt the smile fall from his face, breath robbed from his throat. God help him, he was a fool for beauty. He nearly fell to his knees.

"Are you well?" she said, moving into the shade and seemingly back to earth.

Ashamed to find himself so flustered, he cleared his throat. "Yes, quite. I am just a fool in the presence of your beauty."

To her credit, Eliška smirked at him, disbelieving his flattery. "Do you always say such things to girls you hardly know?"

He started to throw the banter back her way, but found himself nervously drumming his fingers against his thigh, troubled. Before he could stop it, the truth slipped out. "Yes. I'm afraid so."

Eliška's eyebrows shot up.

He watched as the weight of his honesty settled around her, heavy as wet wool. But she didn't sag under it or turn away, instead boldly holding his stare.

Albin stepped forward, hands lifted as if he might spook her. "Which is why I do not expect you to believe me. Not one word." He moved closer. "But if you give me the chance, I will prove my sincerity instead of merely professing it." He inched nearer.

Her eyes widened at his approach, but not with displeasure it seemed. The thought emboldened him. "If I were your champion, what would you have me do to prove my affection genuine?"

Amusement danced across her face, and her plum mouth twisted as if seriously considering the possibilities. He waited, loving that he didn't know what she might say.

"Such a serious matter requires some thought," she teased, and put a hand to her chin. Then her face lit with an idea and Albin found himself smiling in anticipation.

"Feats of strength." She said this with a straight face, though Albin could see the mischief in her eyes.

He took an intentional step back and gave a comically deep bow. He could not think with the scent of her skin curling into his pores like hooks. Warming to the game, he scanned the ground for something suitable to lift. Near the stump sat a trio of stones. Dusty and gnarled, they appeared exceedingly heavy. Straightening up, he pointed dramatically to the stones.

"Aha! A challenge for the fair maiden's favor," he said and strode around the largest stone as if circling his prey. He tossed a glance at his lady.

Smiling now, Eliška moved closer and curled up on the stump, her arms crossed over her chest. She was breathing hard, and a sheen of sweat dappled her nose and chin, but she seemed happy. Albin felt gratified that she had hurried to meet him and imagined kissing the sweat away. With a sharp inhale against such a dangerous thought, he bent to grip the stone.

"Shall we put a wager on it?" Eliška said suddenly, her voice cheerful despite its tender rasp.

Albin glanced up at her, delighted. "Does the lady often wager on things?"

She wrinkled her nose at his accusation, but held her head high. Albin couldn't have been more pleased with her willingness to play along. Perhaps, his heart hoped, he'd finally met his match.

"Why of course not," she said, her voice thick with mock offense. "But there will never be a better day to start, will there?"

She raised her eyebrows at the stone while Albin pushed at it.

"The lady speaks true. Though I am wounded, madam, that you have so little faith in me," he teased. "All right. What would the lady like to wager?"

Eliška pursed her lips in thought and Albin lost his breath. Then another wide smile sliced across her pale face.

"I bet you a dance at the festival you cannot lift the largest stone."

A rasping chuckle escaped him. "The lady bets against her champion? I shall never recover my pride."

She laughed then, bright and loud. "Don't worry, friend Lajos. I am hoping you fail."

Albin ran a hand through his hair at the sounds of his false name. It still caught him off guard, though he did his best to hide it. He rubbed his hands together in anticipation as his voice turned serious. "And what do I get if I succeed?"

The mischievous expression on her face fell away. He watched her swallow hard, pull her hands into her lap.

He straightened up. "Please don't misunderstand me. I meant no offence. I would never—"

"To see me again, here at noon the next time you are free from harvesting." Her voice did not quake as she spoke, but Albin suspected the request cost her much. Even he knew flirting was one thing, a genuine admission of desire quite another.

Warmth spread through his chest as if he'd downed a tumbler of brandy. Albin bowed again, this time in sincerity. "Your servant," he said and bent to grip the rock.

Though many men of his station grew feeble and fat with leisure, Albin had always prided himself on maintaining his strength and thought he could at least move the damn thing. He was wrong. He heaved and tugged, making a grand scene for Eliška's entertainment, but could not budge the stone and bloodied both his palms in the trying. When he finally relented, he found her doubled over, shaking with laughter, her face glowing. It nearly knocked him over. At least he'd accomplished this and closed the space between them.

"I have been vanquished, my lady. It seems we are destined for a dance," he said and knelt at her feet. "But perhaps you will give your champion a boon and choose a more manageable task so that I may see you again as well?"

She startled at his closeness. Then her mirth disappeared as she grabbed his hands and turned them to the sky, surprising them both. Albin's mouth went dry with lust even as he followed her gaze to the shallow cuts along his palms. A newly broken blister oozed.

"You're injured," she whispered and pursed her dark lips in displeasure.

"Hardly," he said, curling his fingers in. "Mere scratches."

Her soft brow creased. "You should have stopped. I did not mean for you to harm yourself for my entertainment."

"Of course you didn't. It was my own doing." He watched her closely, taking in every line and curve of her face. "I wanted to make you laugh. And I succeeded, yes? The victory and fault are mine alone."

She sank her teeth into her bottom lip and frowned, her face somber with some unnamed concern. Albin's confidence soured at his apparent misstep, the source of which he couldn't quite detect. Was she upset with herself or him? Did she truly care about his wellbeing or was she annoyed at his carelessness? She would not have been the first. He did not yet know her mind and mustn't waste what little time they had together.

Cautiously, he folded one of her small, cool hands into his. "Shall we sit and talk a while? Will you tell me of yourself?" He was afraid she might bolt away and melt into the woods, more startled doe than girl. She didn't.

Looking up from their hands, Eliška straightened, her turtle-shell gaze open and searching. "Alright. But I wish for you to tell me a story from your travels. A true one."

Albin cleared his throat, trying to contain his smile. There were so many, and not nearly enough. His heart bellowed with wanting more. But what could he possibly tell her that wouldn't reveal himself completely? Then he let the joy of retelling take hold and laced their fingers tighter. "Have you ever been chased by a bear?"

Fifteen

Eliška

A flock of small birds darted across the meadow in front of her, their backs bright with sunlight. She watched them dip and bend in unison across the tall grass and wondered, not for the first time, how separate creatures could be so in tune. Tired and content, she closed her eyes and imagined herself cresting over a breeze, the sun on her back only to be pulled along by the being next to her. She wasn't sure if such a connection to another soul was a source of comfort or terror.

"I've lost your attention."

Lajos's voice cut into her thoughts, and she turned toward the sound as a compass needle swings north. Eliška didn't know exactly how long they'd been in the meadow—an hour or so perhaps—but she was already accustomed to the rhythm of his voice, the pleasant weight of his nearness, and was loath to leave either. Her eyes found their mark and drank the sight of him dry.

They had been trading stories, carefully revealing themselves one small detail at a time. He loved riding and boxing matches, she spoke of her embroidery and training as a healer. Both knew what it was to lose a parent and be an only child. The unmanageable weight of such things. Both enjoyed sweet cakes, dances, the sunset over the Little Carpatians. Eliška did not say much of her knowledge was gleaned secondhand; the product of imagination. Everything about Lajos was wild and shimmering and joyful—a firebird in flight. She did not want to weigh him down with too much truth.

Sitting just out of reach behind her, Lajos's grin was teasing, his tawny eyes mischievous. A breeze ruffled his fair hair, and she was tempted to press her finger into his dimpled cheek. Instead, she fisted her hands in her lap, numb fingertips stinging.

Never was on her lips, but she bit back the confession. The intensity of her attraction to him, even in this quiet moment, frightened her. So she threw her own cheeky smile at him before spinning around in the grass to face him. Their knees nearly touched, but not quite, and the energy of their not-touching vibrated between them.

"Then win it back," Eliška challenged and sucked in a small breath, startled by her own boldness. Unable to hold his gaze, she stared at the ground between them, her neck hot with anticipation.

Lajos said nothing, didn't move at all, and unease crept over her like a shadow. Only the stillness of the meadow reached her ears and she feared she'd finally offended him. Did he think her foolish or forward? With panic squeezing her chest, Eliška braved a glance at Lajos to explain, only to find him staring over her shoulder, his face a pale mask. A new kind of dread seeped through her. Had they been discovered?

"What is it?" she whispered, her voice tight, and followed his gaze.

She saw nothing out of place. Light danced between the shadows of the trees as they twisted and creaked in a sudden gust of wind that had Eliška shielding her face, but that was all.

"Lajos?" Eliška laid a gentle hand on his arm, but his eyes stayed fixed on the trees, searching. "What did you see? Are we being watched?"

He shot her a dazed look. "Did you not see it?" Lajos breathed as he got to his feet.

She scrambled after him. Lajos's amber eyes had gone dark, the line of his mouth tense. Shivers crept up her arms and she brushed at them as if flinging away spiders. She knew of only one thing in these woods capable of causing such alarm, but had not thought the white shadow visible by day. Had the banishing spell not worked? Was something else afoot which Babička had not told her about?

"I see only the trees in the wind," she said. "What was it? Tell me." Carefully, Eliška took his hand. He startled, but then pulled his gaze down to hers. A nervous smile fluttering over his lips.

"I thought..." He squinted into the tangle of green woods, thick with summer undergrowth and wildflowers before clearing his throat. "You will think me a great fool, but I could have sworn —" Lajos stopped and he shook himself. "It was nothing. I've had too much sun perhaps. Or being with you has made me fanciful," he said with a forced lightness and tucked a loose strand of hair behind her ear.

Eliška frowned. She wanted to press him, to know what he thought he saw, but didn't know how to ask. Would he think her ignorant if she spoke about the víla as more than old superstitions? Would Babička Olga want her to reveal such information?

Then her mind spun in a new direction as Lajos trailed his thumb across her skin, moving from her wrist to the center of her palm and back again. Heat and energy raced up Eliška's arms and coiled in her belly. She gave a sharp inhale at the sensation, burning at her lack of control. Gathering her nerve, she lifted her eyes to Lajos.

Whatever had drawn his attention to the trees no longer held sway, because he was staring at her mouth. Self-conscious of their dark tint, Eliška sucked in her lips, hiding them. Lajos released his breath in a soft groan.

"Damn it all," he said and took a deliberate step away from

her. "You will make a cad of me yet, my lovely Eliška." His voice was light again as he raised her hand to his mouth and planted a formal kiss on her knuckles.

She enjoyed the tender feel of his lips on her skin, but her shoulders sagged with disappointment. Being near him caused a delicious heat to expand through her belly and his distance snuffed it out. She wanted the feeling back. A new-found recklessness gripped her, and she raised his hand to her own lips, planting a kiss. "Would that be such a tragedy, Traveler Lajos?"

Lajos tipped his head back and laughed. "You know, my dear? I can think of few things I would like more than to find out," he said and tucked her arm through his.

Eliška shivered at the feel of the tight muscles under his worn shirt. If he was similarly affected by her nearness, he did a better job of hiding it.

"But I fear the shadows are lengthening and I would scarce stand a chance at wooing you if your mother was angry, no?"

Eliška's stomach sank, all tingling warmth forgotten. Mamička. She had not cared about the time, but Lajos was right. She would never hear the end of her mother's chastisement if she was caught. Knowing her mother would likely overlook such an indiscretion if she was with Radek sent a wave of anger surging through her, buoying her up.

Reluctantly, Eliška freed herself from Lajos's grasp. "You're right. I must go." The rush of strength she gained from her frustration was already waning. She needed to hurry. Fainting would be worse than getting caught. He couldn't know. Not yet.

He didn't try to stop her, but his face fell as she moved away and her belly warmed with satisfaction.

"May I see you back?" Lajos asked.

How pleasant it would be to let him escort her home under the late afternoon sun, their fingers brushing as they strolled through the woods. But the meadow grass had grown dark with shadows, and she was already late.

"Another time. Or have you already forgotten our wager?" Her breath was becoming shallower—forced—but she smiled as she edged away.

Lajos grinned at her and placed a hand over his heart. "I could no sooner forget my own beating heart," he said and bowed deeply. "*Dovidenia,* Eliška. Until we meet again."

Eliška rolled her eyes at this flattery and felt a fool for believing a word of it. But believe him she did, as she hurried through the trees, walking too fast, not noticing the translucent fingertips dangling above her from the branches.

Sixteen

Albin

Albin wanted her so much it physically pained him. Not for the first time tonight he had to adjust himself like a boy of fourteen, his balls tight with need. Her scent, sweet and acrid with lavender and sweat, filled his memory and made his mouth dry. Thinking of Eliška was like feeling himself rise to a girl for the very first time. The confusion and lust nothing short of blinding. Consuming. Every time he saw her, he had to clasp his hands behind him to hide their trembling. It shamed him to admit it, but shame didn't stop it from being true. He trembled with desire, especially now that he knew she was not only beautiful, but bold, curious, playful, and accomplished.

Even now, lying on a mattress of hay in the dark cottage, wrapped in the smell of woodsmoke and listening to Miroslav snore after his own busy day of hunting and errands, Albin's mind was full of Eliška. E-l-i-š-k-a. He rolled her name around in his mouth like a hard sweet, wanting even more. She had listened to his stories and told a few of her own. He was pleased and a bit surprised at how alike they were in mind and taste. But Albin knew people well enough to sense when they were dancing around their own secret and Eliška most certainly was. He suspected it had to do with her oddly colored lips and fingertips. Why she was absent from the fields when other girls her age labored alongside their families. He was not blind to nor bothered by these peculiarities. Quite the contrary—they intrigued him.

He imagined tracing the delicate column of her neck with his fingertips as her quick pulse fluttered at his touch. Kissing the cluster of freckles across her cheeks, down to that dark, mysterious mouth. Tasting the damp creases of her arms and legs. Hearing her voice rasp and—

A brief fart sounded from across the room, breaking into Albin's fantasy. Miroslav, still dead asleep, rolled over and settled deeper into his bed emitting a soft snore. Albin wiped a hand over his face and gave a silent chuckle. Miroslav always could bring him back to his senses, even in his sleep.

It needled Albin that his most trusted companion disapproved of his growing attachment to the girl. Because of it, they'd spent the evening under a cloud of tense disquiet. Albin didn't think Miro knew about his meeting with Eliška, but he clearly sensed something sour about Albin's story about getting turned around in the woods. Miroslav rarely approved of much Albin did, but his irritation with this particular flirtation was different. Miroslav usually just rolled his eyes at Albin's occasional escapade and warned him to be cautious, which Albin always was.

Albin didn't hold with forcing women to do anything, let alone intimacies, nor with planting bastards across the continent. He didn't consider himself a moralist, but he did have a conscience and never intended to cause harm. Unlike many young men of his station, Albin had never been with a woman in service or one who hadn't returned his attentions. It didn't take charm or courage to corner a governess or barmaid, behavior he had no tolerance for.

His father was a cold man, and hadn't offered much useful information to his son—he was usually too busy entertaining wealthy guests or attending to the affairs of the estate. Or drinking. But Albin could give him this one grace: he had loved Albin's mother and did not tolerate or encourage indiscretion. Which made his insistence on a political marriage for his son all the more infuriating. If anyone could understand marrying for love, it should have been his father.

And yet here was Albin, fantasizing about an innocent girl from his own village while engaged to be married. Perhaps he truly was the scoundrel Miroslav accused him of being. It wasn't as if his fiancée was unpleasant. Quite the contrary. She was beautiful, well-educated, wealthy, and kind. She even had spunk enough to smack away his roving hand once when they were barely more than children forced to attend the same grand event. They'd laughed about it years later at yet another dreadful dinner where they'd been seated next to each other.

Though she made a charming companion, Albin shuddered at the endless string of boring state and social affairs stretched out in front of him. Even on the edge of sleep, his throat tightened. In fact, his fiancée was everything a man such as himself should want. But Albin knew in his heart he wouldn't be a good husband to her. It wasn't himself who deserved better, but her.

The unfairness of it all settled like a stone in his gut, but Albin refused to succumb to reality. Not yet, he thought defiantly and rolled onto his side. He pictured Eliška again: pale skin flecked with copper, forest eyes, sharp smile, frozen fingertips. Her bold stare and slightly winged ears. The way she chided him for flirting too much. The obvious pride she took in her intricate craftmanship. Her clever, hungry mind. The way she listened as if what he said truly mattered.

Holding Eliška in his mind, Albin's empty hands drifted lower, pleasing himself on her image. The ecstasy came fast, and he had to stifle a groan at his release. But even as he spilled himself into the hay, a sharp sadness took hold. There were so few days left. With unshed tears burning his throat and the sound of Miro's ruffled breathing nearby, Albin drifted to sleep and dreamed of jade dragons, towering savannah beasts, and a girl with frosted lips.

Seventeen

Eliška

The two women had not spoken of the white shadow since that night. Nor did they now as they waded through the grass, all silver and shivering in the twilight. Eliška was tired. A bone-deep kind of tired that clung to her limbs and dragged at her mind. And she'd been distracted all evening thinking about Lajos. Only after Mamička scolded her for nearly burning the bread had she attempted to push their afternoon in the meadow from her mind. Despite that, when Babička had called once again, Eliška jumped at the chance to go out. She would not willingly miss a night to speak freely with the old woman, her weary body be damned.

When Eliška had commented on the lack of bread in the basket as they set out under a waning moon and a high breeze, Olga had simply snapped her fingers under Eliška's nose and started down the familiar road toward the woods without a word. She wanted to question her mentor about what Lajos thought he'd seen in the meadow, but there was no way to explain without exposing herself. So she stayed quiet and fell into step beside the healer.

The forest felt different now. Though Eliška knew each bend

of grass and whirl of bark like her own skin, she'd never look at this place the same way. Knowledge did that, she supposed. Changed the familiar. The white shadow—víla or not—had stained the woods forever. She wasn't sure if she loved or hated this fact, but felt the surety of it deep in her gut. Then the wind rose. Eliška didn't want to see the shadow again. Not exactly. But there was no denying the moment of excitement that swept through her before the breeze settled quietly around their feet like a contented cat and Babička Olga pressed on unconcerned.

Though the old woman's ease gave her confidence, her stomach still clenched at the memory of the phantom. She knew most people considered such creatures nonsense, or at the very least unimportant. Eliška would have agreed a few days ago, but knew better now and believed in the real danger they must present for Babička Olga to be troubled by them. And yet, some deep, gnarled part of her mind was glad for the víla. Glad the small village around her wasn't the only real thing. Soaked in the sights and smells of the night, the jagged parts of her heart thrilled at the truth of a wide, wild world beyond her imagining. Even if such a world was beyond her understanding. She smiled against the shadows and opened her mouth to breathe deep. The air tasted of possibilities.

"Here we are." Babička pointed to a patch of shadowed greenery just off the path, her knobby fingers white as bone in the moonlight. "We shall be needing plenty of wild garlic to treat wounds and keep the festering away, and perhaps—" She paused, tipped her old head back to consult the stars. "Perhaps a bit more rosemary and juniper since Pán Simko cannot seem to keep his eyes away from young Dagmar, despite her betrothal to his son. She may need a warding off draught."

Eliška's eyes went wide in the gray night, but she held her voice in check. "Where should I begin?"

The old hedge witch, for she now knew the name to be true,

pointed off in the opposite direction. "Twist the stem and pull hard. You want all the garlic fibers for the most power."

"Yes, Babička," Eliška said and moved off to work, tucking away her mentor's words for another night. She felt sure she would need them. Though she still didn't know why Babička was revealing her secrets now, a warm bubble of pride swelled in Eliška's chest. The old healer trusted her, and that was no small thing.

Time passed. Eliška moved from task to task as directed, though she knew many of the requests before they were given. When she reached Babička's side once more, both women's baskets hung heavy with leaf and seed, root and fungus. A screen of clouds drifted over the moon, covering its nakedness as an owl hooted in the trees, unseen. Olga straightened as if in response and leaned on Eliška for support. Both women felt heavy with fatigue.

"Come, bird. My bones ache."

Eliška stood, stretching her cramped back and yawned. After rubbing the feeling back into her hands, she linked arms with Babička Olga and started for the road. With her back to the dark frieze of trees, unease clung to Eliška's shoulders like a cobweb. She couldn't help but imagine the white shadow peering at her through the canopy, calling her name, beckoning her with the withered, crooked finger of nightmares. Eliška took a deep breath and pushed the notion aside. The white shadow had not appeared, Babička had not spoken of it, and her memory of it would be enough to both terrify and delight her forever. She did not look back.

After being on their knees, the crone and the invalid moved slowly through the meadow toward the road. It was a good thing too, because they nearly stepped on the girl as it was. For all of Babička Olga's canniness, she didn't see the figure laying in the underbrush until they were on top of her. All three let out a startled cry as Eliška pulled the old woman back before both of them fell.

"Christ!" she hissed in surprise. "Are you well, Babička?" she said as the women steadied themselves.

"*Samozřejmě.* Of course," chided Babička before swatting her arm for the blasphemy. Then she leaned forward and clucked. "Now then. What have you done to yourself, *dieťa*?" the old woman whispered as the figure on the ground came into focus.

Caught in the briars and scratched bloody, a girl huddled wide-eyed and pink-nosed as a terrorized rabbit. Eliška, stunned into muteness, stared at the girl as if she had sprouted from the ground like an enormous milky mushroom.

The girl hesitated, her wild gaze swinging between Babička and Eliška and back again. "I fell," cooed the voice, thick with accent. A Viennese accent.

Eliška shot a glance at Olga, but the old woman held her pleated expression in place. If the healer noticed the stranger was Austrian, she didn't let on. Eliška tried to master her face and follow along.

"Be an easy thing to do when abroad at night," Babička Olga chattered, reaching for the girl's hand. "Gathering by moonlight as well perhaps? My apprentice and I find the best herbs for healing by moonlight."

Trusting her mentor in all things, Eliška held her tongue and stooped to untangle the girl's skirts from the thorns, pricking her own fingers in the process. The material was heavy and soft. Richly made. Eliška moved closer. The young woman was lovely behind the smudges of dirt. Plump and fair as a Sunday roll. Eliška pictured her own sharp, freckled nose and too wide mouth with regret. When she had finished freeing the girl's fine petticoats from the briars, the stranger pushed herself to standing.

Tall and buxom under the velvet cloak, the girl's face was a pale moon. "Gathering? No. I was just looking for... You mentioned herbs. Please. I need—I'm losing..."

Without warning, her wide face crumpled and the young woman doubled over in pain, a base moan slipping from her pretty mouth. As the young woman crouched, the foul tang of blood and waste bloomed around them. Eliška shuffled back in surprise, but didn't get far. Olga thrust her basket into Eliška's arms and grabbed her chin. Going still under the callused hands, Eliška tried to focus on Babička and not the moaning creature at their feet. The old woman's clouded eyes were lit with urgency.

"We cannot leave her here. Go. As quickly as your heart can take you. Set water to boil and find the peppermint. Begin a poultice of garlic and linseed." Olga glanced at the elegant stranger, now befouled and bleeding in the grass. Her pale hair spread out like a patch of snow on the dark grass. "Do not be seen. I will bring her soon," she added before bending to her patient.

Eliška spared the girl one more glance before tightening her grip on the basket. She wouldn't fail. "Yes, Babička," she said and pushed her burning limbs through the darkness.

⌒∽ↀ℃⌒

The street was quiet and empty, which didn't mean a thing. She knew, better than anyone save perhaps Babička, that the ears and eyes of the village were everywhere. It would be a miracle if no one saw her. But that's what the healer had asked, so Eliška prayed to the Blessed Virgin for cover as she crept through the meadow behind the houses along her street. If she was seen, she'd be questioned, and God only knew what atrocity could come from such exposure. Babička had good reason for discretion.

Eliška's heart roared dangerously in her ears as she stole along in the dark toward Babička's dilapidated back garden. Crouching in the grass, she scanned for a stray light or open window, but the row of homes was dark. Breathing as slowly as possible and crossing herself, she eased open the latch and hurried up to the door.

The old cat hissed at her intrusion, but Eliška knew the house like her own and quickly found a lamp. Her hands shook as she lit it. Light flared and the scent of burning oil mingled with the already pungent air of the cottage. She glanced cautiously out the curtained window. There would be no sign for some time, so she set about preparing what the healer had asked. She worked quickly, and when everything was ready, clasped her fingers together and sat by the stove, anxious. Questions about the wealthy Austrian flickered through her mind. Who was she? What was she doing in their woods? What would happen if she died in their care?

After thinking on it, the young woman's affliction seemed clear to Eliška—too much tansy or barberry root. Eliška knew little of such things, but suspected Babička Olga's knowledge to be vast. Healers who ushered babes into the world sometimes ushered them out. Father Timotej said this was a grievous sin, but she wondered what men truly knew of such things. Staring into the flickering hearth, Eliška knew in her heart Babička would do no harm—and if she did, there must be a tremendous reason. It was enough.

They were taking too long. Worry creased her brow as she checked the water on the stove and paced. Did they need her? What if the girl was too weak to walk? Frustrated with waiting, Eliška reached for her shawl when her gaze caught on a book resting against the leg of Babička's chair. Lamplight licked across the tattered spine, illuminating the title of a familiar volume. She froze. The hollowed-out book. Remembering the grimoire inside, Eliška bent to pick up the precious object. Excitement burst down her spine as she eased open the cover, worry eclipsed by curiosity. A small, leather notebook peeked out from within its papery nest.

Desire to leaf through the feathery pages and discover Babička's secrets for herself grabbed Eliška by the throat. Perhaps she didn't have to wait for the healer to reveal her craft at an infuriatingly slow pace, but could learn it for herself. Trailing a hungry finger down the worn cover, she noticed something sticking out from between the pages and eased open the book to the marked spot. Pressed close to the spine was a dried sprig of rosemary. The sharp, piney scent of the brittle needles wafted up as Eliška took in the single word scrawled at the top of the page—*víla*. Excitement curled in her belly and her eyes flew down the page, hungry for the scattered notes below, just as a soft cry sounded outside. Eliška jumped. Guilt flooded her face with heat, and she closed the book with a snap. There was no excuse for prying into her mentor's things without permission. It didn't stop her from wanting to do it again.

Moving to the back window, she peered into the darkness. Two shadowy figures, dark on dark, shuffled toward the house. Moving as quietly as possible, Eliška opened the door a crack and pressed her eye to the slit. A doorway full of light at this hour was a beacon for prying eyes.

"Babička?"

"Bird," came the healer's voice. "*Pomoc.* Help me get her inside."

After tucking the lantern into a corner, Eliška stepped out and took hold of the stranger's arm. She was a stately woman, with thick-bones and good hips for bearing children. If she could conceive after this. The stranger, as if reading Eliška's dark thoughts, clutched at her abdomen and whimpered. Tear-stained and shaking, the girl lurched through the door and onto the surgery table. Olga waddled in behind and shut out the night.

"*Ďakujem.* Now go home before your mother's worrying reaches her feet."

Eliška drew a deep breath through her mouth. "But I could help you."

"And help me you have, child. Now you must go." Babička ground out the command between wrinkled lips.

Eliška turned, but not before the hurt touched her face.

Babička must have seen it and softened. "Someday, I shall teach you all I know." She looked over her shoulder at the pathetic creature on the table, filthy skirts rucked up past her knees. The young woman was crying in soft, stifled sobs. Babička frowned. "All of it. But not tonight, bird. This work is for an old woman."

Eliška resented being sent away, but knew no good would come from her mother coming in search of them. With a frustrated sigh she kissed Olga's soft, pleated cheek and crept home under a blaze of silver starlight, the scent of blood and regret heavy in the air.

Eighteen
Albin

The day had been full of high, brilliant sunlight, and a faint breeze threaded through the long rows of vines carrying the steady songs of the harvesters on it. Beautiful. As Albin paused to catch his breath and ease a cramp in his back, he once again peered over the tops of the vibrant vines for the one thing missing from his day.

She was not there. Not that he'd expected to meet her in the fields necessarily. He wasn't completely devoid of the powers of observation and assumed whatever ailment turned Eliška's lips and fingertips indigo, made her brow sweat and her breath short, certainly kept her from the hard work of harvesting. And hard work it was, Albin thought, stretching for what seemed like the hundredth time. Blood oozed from a blister on his hand where the shear handle had worn a tidy hole in his palm. He flexed his fingers against the sting, wiping away the evidence of his softness. He had hoped to see her at the afternoon meal, but had not. A blight on an otherwise fulfilling day.

Albin watched the men and women in the fields, many of which were children actually, and saw them in a new light. Their bright clothes and rough hands spoke of lifetimes he'd never really understand. The fresh wounds on his hands made him wonder what happened when someone did get seriously injured. It must happen. The shears glinted like great fangs in the sunlight—they must have claimed more than grapes over the years. His father employed a physician at the castle, but did not know if these people for whom he would be responsible had access to a healer or apothecary at all. Albin examined his hand again as shame flushed hot in his neck. He'd never really considered their wellbeing before. And if he hadn't, how much more unaffected was his father?

"I'm just as much of a bastard as he is," Albin said aloud, and made a fist around this realization, determined to make inquiries about a village physician.

"There are several ways to take that statement. I hope I'm not the other bastard."

Albin looked up to see Miroslav, dirty and sweating, striding toward him. His friend's wide-brimmed hat cast a shadow across his face except for his prominent chin which was pink with sunburn.

"Of course you're a bastard, though not in every sense, I assume? But in this case, I was referring to my father, who, being a first-rate asshole, seems to have raised one as well." He lowered his voice to a whisper. "Do you think these people have any kind of physician or surgeon?"

Miro stopped a short distance from Albin, his shears tucked expertly into his belt. Vexingly, his friend didn't appear nearly as tired as he felt. Albin supposed weakness was a price of luxury and made a vow to himself not to get fat on his fortune.

Miroslav tipped his hat back revealing a smudge of dirt on his long nose. "A physician? I shouldn't think so." He gestured around to the poor farmers, herders, and merchants, but not unkindly. "How many physicians do you know who will take cheese or mending for payment? Money-grubbing charlatans, I say."

Albin chuckled at Miroslav's familiar distrust of anyone who wielded a leech, but didn't necessarily disagree. "You've got a point there. I just wondered what they do for the ailments this work undoubtedly brings." He held up his blistered hand as illustration. "Though I dare say they're somewhat hardier than myself."

Miroslav snorted in agreement and Albin swung a mock blow at him, which Miro blocked. "You and I both, sir." Then Miro scratched his chin in consideration. "I'm sure there's a healer in the village, though. A midwife. An apothecary perhaps. Those crones know more than they're given credit for."

Albin nodded. It only made sense that a village the size of Hrozno would have a healer, but he wondered if perhaps a surgeon wouldn't also be of use. His expression must have betrayed his thoughts, for he glanced up to find Miroslav eyeing him suspiciously.

"What?" Albin asked, his voice defensive. "Aren't you the one always reminding me of my cursed obligations?"

Miroslav held up his hands in surrender. His pink palms were creased with dirt. "Do not mistake my surprise, sir. I only wonder what has turned your attentions so close to home." It wasn't a question.

The two men stared at each other openly, in the frank way only complete strangers or intimate friends can. A moment passed. Then two. Albin looked away first. He cleared his throat; flexed his sore hands again.

"You may have the truth of it, I admit." Albin felt his ears burn with embarrassment as he gestured again to the massive expanse of field, the bent backs of the harvesters working to bring in the grapes while the relentless sun glinted off the trembling vines. For the first time, he felt a flicker of affection stir in his chest at the sight of the land. His land. "But you cannot deny it would benefit these folks to have more care, yes? Perhaps I should be somewhat less of a fop and aide them?"

"You could start by getting the fuck back to work. Do you think I hired you two assholes to stand around and gossip like a pair of shit-for-brains hens?" Pán Nagy bellowed from behind, and smacked Miroslav's hat from his head.

Albin bit the insides of his cheeks to keep from laughing at the rather apt description of them. Miroslav snatched his hat off the ground, grumbling quietly, but stood at attention slightly behind Albin's shoulder as if they were awaiting a military inspection. Albin clamped his jaws harder to strangle another chuckle as he realized it was quite possible the damned man had been a soldier. And would likely captain his militia should he ever need one.

"You think this is fucking funny?" The tall man sneered down into Albin's face, confirming Albin's suspicions about his military experience.

"No, sir," Albin said, casually elbowing Miroslav in the stomach to keep him from divesting them of their cover. "Forgive us, sir. I'm afraid I stopped because of my hand and asked my brother if he knew of a physician in the village?" Albin held up his hand for inspection. Thankfully, it was still bleeding.

The harvest master spat on the ground without so much as glancing at the hand. "Physician? For a few blisters?" He swatted his hand toward them as if shooing away a hornet. "You're the last damned pair of vagrants I ever hire. Get back to work."

"Yes, sir," Albin said and suppressed the urge to salute. He knew speaking again might get his nose broken by the foreman, but couldn't miss the chance to ask. "Is there a village physician? Would one be of use? I have a...cousin who may be able to offer his services for a small fee." Albin spoke quickly as he and Miroslav resumed cutting clusters of grapes. No need to further tempt the man's wrath with their idleness.

Albin braced for the rebuke, but it didn't come. Careful not to cut off his fingers, Albin ventured a look up and saw the harvest master examining him with hard, quizzical eyes. Albin turned back to the vine, his breath held tight in his throat.

"How small a fee?" Pán Nagy asked, his voice reed thin.

Albin straightened. He hadn't really expected the foreman to respond. "What do you pay your current healer? I'm sure his fee would be scant," he said, trying not to let his voice pitch higher with excitement.

"Babička Olga takes only what can be offered freely—and she's a damn fine healer, for a woman. Good as any physician." He pushed his hat back in an oddly defiant gesture, his mouth pinched in thought. "Though she is old as Methuselah and has chosen the invalid for her apprentice. The girl has wit and a spine, I'll say, but a waste of teaching that."

Albin sensed the man was rambling to himself more than anything, but didn't dare interrupt him. He shot a questioning glance at Miroslav who gave the faintest shrug of his shoulders.

"Does that mean a new physician would be of use to the village? If his price was reasonable and his practices sound, of course?" Albin tried to sound unconcerned with the man's reply.

The tall vineyard master sniffed aggressively and nodded. "I suppose so. Though he would have to pass both Father Timotej and the crone's inspection, you see? No small feat. It will take more than the word of an uppity harvester."

Albin smiled, feeling accomplished, and nodded at the foreman. "Of course. I think everyone will be pleased. I will speak with him once we return home and send him on his way when I can."

Pán Nagy ignored him before spitting at his feet again and striding off to badger some other unsuspecting harvester. The man whistled as he went.

Albin stared after him, then turned to Miroslav who had come up alongside him. "I like that man more every time I encounter him. What a bizarrely capital fellow. He would be great fun to take gambling."

Miroslav shook his head, but smiled. "You always did have the most appalling taste, sir."

Albin turned back to the vines, the sting of his hands a

pleasant reminder of honest labor and a lovely girl. "Present company included?" he asked and laughed when Miroslav snorted and turned back to work.

Nineteen
Eliška

The grass shivered underneath her and Eliška drank up the sensation, soaking it into her skin like an energizing elixir. She hadn't known if a second day in the meadow with Lajos would come, but it had, and she was determined to enjoy it, no matter how her chest ached and her hands tingled. No matter if every other soul they each loved would disapprove. After another day of harvesting, a few rows of lingering grapes needed to ripen on the vine and she would not argue with such a gift.

Weary from another sleepless night, Eliška had barely wrestled herself into the garden to work before a sunshine-bright whistle sounded from beyond the back fence. Lajos. Frantic with anticipation, she promised to meet him at the tree stump and pressed through her work. Though every muscle throbbed and her breath snagged in her throat, she would not be stopped. Not even by the warning memory of the bloodied and weeping noble girl in the woods. Somehow, Babička had secreted the mysterious young woman away in the night and would not speak of it.

"Yes, I know you promised to stay until after the festival," Eliška said from her spot in the shade. "But will you really? It seems your brother Otokar is anxious to be on his way." They had been talking of many things, but this one thing lay at the base of her mind, dense as an autumn mist. She put the question to Lajos teasingly, but could not help the asking of it. She needed to know if he intended to stay or not; even if the power of such needing frightened her.

From his place next to her, Lajos rolled to face her. The long meadow grass darted up around his head like a fairy crown. "Hell's hounds could not drag me away. Didn't you know? I thought for certain my impressive feat of strength the other day had proven my affection."

She swatted his arm even as her stomach tightened at his words. "You waste your flattery on me. But, in earnest, have I done something to offend your brother?" Eliška asked, embarrassed for caring. "I fear he disapproves even more than my matka is bound to."

She had never even spoken to Lajos's brother, but there was no need. His dark stare and tight jaw at yesterday's evening meal told her all she needed to know. Never had anyone unknown to her disapproved so much, and she was no stranger to being looked down upon. This mysterious brother's low opinion stung more than she liked to admit, and she wondered what Lajos had told him of her. If anything. Perhaps Otokar did not think her good enough. Strong enough. He would not be the first to think so. It was the very reason her disinterest in Radek stung her mother so much—no one else had ever pursued her. She was a guaranteed burden and the men of Hrozno already had their hands full.

The worry must have shown itself, because Lajos took her hand and gently rubbed his thumb along her wrist. She shivered, softening against him. Slowly, as if testing her reaction, he brought her wrist to his mouth and brushed his lips against the tender white skin. Blood thrummed against his touch and her stomach tightened, low and sharp.

"Do not fret over such things," Lajos said, pulling away with an inhale. "I apologize if my brother has been rude. It's just that —" He paused, and his sunny brow furrowed.

Eliška knew in her gut he was deciding whether or not to lie. She waited.

"Otokar has taken care of me for a long time. Been the one person who always gets me out of scrapes and sees that I keep my wits about me. Or tries at least." He laughed as if remembering something funny, and Eliška felt a startling jab of jealousy. She had no such memories with this man and hated it. She swallowed the bitter feeling, ashamed at the fickleness of her own desires.

"He wants to see me safe and settled, but does not always trust my judgement." Lajos's voice was light, meant to be reassuring, but she couldn't help but notice he kept his eyes on their linked hands now slick with sweat.

"Is that why he dislikes me? He doesn't trust I'm good enough for you?"

Lajos pressed his mouth flat. "Not precisely. Please do not let his dour face fool you," Lajos said, finally meeting her eyes with a crooked grin on his face even as he dodged her question. "I know he hasn't been amiable, but my brother has never willingly missed a celebration in his life." He nudged her playfully with his elbow. "We will attend the festival and have a merry time, even if Otokar prefers to skulk around the edges like a disapproving babka."

Eliška smiled through her irritation at this, for she knew a great deal about watchful, disapproving eyes. The mood lifted by the faintest degree, like the edge of a heavy shawl being pulled back. How could it not with Lajos's obvious devotion to his brother? Yet she was not quite ready to relent.

"Alright then. I will do my best to charm your protective brother and not take offense at his glowering." She leaned forward, bringing her face too close to his in the sunlight. His pupils tightened in the high light and she lost focus. She could swim in those pools of amber. Nearly dizzy with his beauty, she inhaled his scent—salt, sunshine, mint—and gathered her lingering strength. There was one more thing she needed to know.

"And after the festival? Will you go on to another town for work? Another harvest?" She didn't say 'Another girl,' but she didn't have to. Eliška watched as his dimples ducked in and out of sight, his hair glinting. Her mouth went dry with desire and fear.

Reaching out, Lajos toyed with an errant strand of her hair before tucking it behind her ear. She tensed as he brushed his fingertips against her cheek, then the soft hollow between ear and neck before letting it drop. His hands were warm and surprisingly smooth. His eyes darted between her mouth and her eyes. She knew they brimmed with questions he had yet to answer.

"I will not abandon you."

The words were meant to soothe, but Eliška couldn't fight down the swelling dread that filled her chest as his normally jovial face turned serious. "I will not," Lajos repeated, his voice vehement. "Though, in truth, I must leave for a time. There are affairs I must set to right."

With the admission, a ferocity she had not yet seen came over him, and he squeezed her hand tight, crushing the tender bones together. She didn't care. The pain was a reassuring anchor against the truth. He would leave. She suddenly felt small and stupid for expecting anything else. Of course she was not enough to make him stay.

"There are matters I must attend to with my family. My...our father is ill. No one else knows this and there are...arrangements to be made." Lajos took hold of her chin with one hand, the pad of his thumb pressing just under her bottom lip. He forced her face up. "But hear this, Eliška Ciernikova. You have my heart. I will come back for you. I will take care of you."

Eliška shivered under the warmth of his hands, every inch of her aware of him. Every fiber of her wanted to trust him fully; to revel in his declarations and affection, but she could not help notice he hadn't answered her question. Not directly. Despite the frantic hope surging through her body at his words, her face betrayed her doubts.

"You do not trust me." It was not a question, and Eliška did not contradict him. He dropped his hands and pushed himself up to sitting. "Nor do I blame you."

His touch was like fire against her ever-chilled skin, warming her, drawing her in and she desperately wanted to believe him. But back in some still small space of her mind, a jolt of panic coursed through her. She pushed the unwelcome feeling aside, but did not lean into him.

"I fear you will think me terribly suspicious. It is just we have had so little time..." She longed to press him for more information, but would not let herself hope too ardently. Nor would she expose her already tattered pride.

Lajos smiled, but kept his distance. "Never. It is to your credit you are hesitant to take my word." His words remained gentle as his voice hardened. Sharpened. "We have spoken of many things these last days. Things I hold close to my heart and perhaps to yours too, but neither of us can be sure the other speaks the truth, yes?"

Eliška startled at his choice of words. She longed to tell him that his coming was foretold to her—his appearance something more than chance. To admit her body held a dark secret and was little more than a draining hourglass. But would such knowledge frighten Lajos away? He seemed like nothing so much as a charming, joyful scamp who comes begging for crumbs and affection only to disappear without warning when another house puts out better rubbish. And part of her enjoyed that about him. Despite the meaningful things they'd told one another, Lajos spoke the truth: they did not know each other well.

"Your glass face betrays you," he said, pulling away. There was a determined set to his mouth. "Tell me what to do. Perhaps another feat of strength? A battle of wits?"

Giving in to his attempt to lighten the conversation, Eliška made a face and shook her head. "I think not. You've damaged your hands enough and I'm afraid you'll have an unfair advantage if we are to calculate sums or recite scripture."

"I see your point." Lajos gave her an exaggerated frown and scanned around. The late August sun shone on the meadow in which they lay, and she watched as his gaze snagged on a clump of wildflowers. He jumped up and darted away, returning with a handful of uprooted blossoms.

He plucked a single, creamy daisy from among the fresh throng in his hand and held it out. "Shall we play?" He arched a gold eyebrow. "Perhaps the Fates will help me win your trust."

"Don't." Her own command startled her. Eliška had never willingly played at romance before and did not know the rules of such flirtations as this. But what she did know unnerved her all the more. What he proposed was divining and playing with such things was unwise. But Lajos's gaze held guileless warmth, and she let go of her breath. "It's just—I've never done that before."

"Plucking petals from a flower?" Lajos smiled quizzically at her answer, but didn't seem to notice her unease. "Haven't you? I thought everyone enjoyed such diversions."

Eliška hesitated. Her focus shifted between the blossom held in Lajos's outstretched hand and his face, all dusty and sharp in the sunlight. One moment, she watched the corners of his mouth rise just enough to expose his dimples; the next, her eyes dropped to each papery petal quivering in invitation. Babička Olga had warned her not to ask questions she'd rather not know the answers to, but how could she not want to know the true nature of his affections? Could playing along really hurt?

"Are you afraid to find out?" Lajos strolled up and placed the flower in her hand.

The question was meant to tease. Eliška allowed the warm flush of pleasure to wash over her misgivings, burying them. Perhaps it was only a game after all and Babička's warning about divinations was overbearing.

Her fingers tingled where they touched. "Do you think me a coward?" She matched his smile. "Or are you just a spoiled boy who likes to trifle with girls?"

Lajos tipped his head back and laughed. "You are no coward." Then he leaned in so close, she smelled the yeast and wine on his breath. He fixed her with an intense, peculiar stare. "And I tease you not."

A tightening in her core pulled at Eliška as she lowered her gaze to the flower. Her hands shook. "He loves me."

The first petal fell.

"He loves me not."

The second petal fell.

"He loves me."

She stopped. Counted. Then the ground tilted as her vision blurred. The world had not shifted and yet Eliška felt herself shrink, her own petals plucked. She dropped the flower and gifted Lajos a false, jagged smile. "He loves me not."

Lajos gave a derisive chuckle and reached for her, oblivious to any alteration in her. "A trick I say! Now let it be my turn."

She tried not to believe the divination, but too long had she been in Babička Olga's tutelage to ignore such a sign. Distrust coiled around her heart. "You do not get a turn," she said and moved away from his honeyed touch.

The amusement dropped from his face. "Eliška, wait. Surely you would not put your hopes in the frailty of one bloom?" He reached for her, but she stepped farther away. "I only meant to ease your mind with play. I do care for you."

"I know you think it sport for children. Perhaps you are right, but Babička Olga says—"

"Babička Olga?" He crossed his arms over his chest, mouth tightening. "I know you love the old witch, but she has not seen the world as I have and cannot know—"

"Do not call her that." Eliška lifted her chin. "You know nothing of her or of what she knows. Perhaps it is only that your feelings are so small even the wildflowers cannot find them." The words were out of her mouth before she knew they were even in her mind, but she could not deny their truth any more than she could swallow them back down. She steeled herself against his response.

Lajos did not counter her accusation, but neither did he relent. "I do not think you childish." He stepped toward her again and succeeded in trapping her hands between his. "Nor do I wish to offend you. But I do not believe in peasant magic and fairy stories. I know only that I crave your company beyond reason and am not prepared to give you up so easily."

Her mouth tightened and she pulled away so he would not feel her trembling hands. It was as if he had spoken her own thoughts aloud to her, mirroring them. She dared not believe it. "Perhaps it is all a game. But believe me when I tell you this—I have no time for games."

"Eliška, please. Forgive me. I meant no harm," he said, his voice panicked. "I am a stranger to this place. Count my behavior as ignorance and not a lack of affection." He reached for her again, but did not grab. "I think of nothing but you. The way you laugh and throw my jokes back at me. How you speak about your work and wanting to see more of the world. I want all of it. I hardly sleep for dreaming of you."

She saw the frantic plea in his eyes, felt his dry fingers against her neck and cheeks as he drew close. She couldn't move. Didn't know if she wanted to.

"I want only you. I swear it," he said and pressed his mouth to hers.

Eliška gripped his shoulders to keep her balance, but it didn't help. Lajos dropped one hand to her waist and pulled her against him, his mouth and hands searching her in ways she didn't fully understand: hot, strong, pleading. Her insides tightened, burned, even as her mind went numb to everything but him. The pressure of his fingertips along her neck, the scrape of his teeth on her lips. His arms snaked around her. Tightened.

Lajos broke the kiss for breath, his face stamped with questions. Their eyes met, held. He did not try to kiss her again, though a hunger she both wanted and feared lit his face. Neither looked away as Eliška entwined her fingers in the hair against his neck and brought his face back down to meet hers.

"Eliška," he whispered against her mouth before gently licking into her. "You save me."

She smiled and tipped her head back as he trailed kisses down her neck. With her eyes open to the blinding sky-shine above, she crushed the offending flower underfoot. She did not care. Nor did she notice the shadow falling across them as they slipped to the ground until it was too late, his body pressing down on hers in ways that made her head spin, her breath hitch with pleasure.

The first kick glanced off Lajos's ribs, narrowly missing her. Eliška let out a shocked yelp as Lajos grunted from the blow and rolled away before leaping to his feet. Panic shot through Eliška as she frantically sat up only to see Radek lunge forward, smashing his fist into Lajos's face. Another scream, this one intentional, ripped through her as Lajos hit the ground. Blood and spittle sprayed as his beautiful face contorted in pain.

"*Prestaň!*" She scrambled off the ground and flew at Radek before he could take aim again, grabbing his shirt. "Stop it this moment, Radek!"

Radek whirled on her and took hold of both her arms, pulling her close. Hot with anger, he leaned down until they were nose to nose, his breath like dragon smoke in her face. "What in God's name do you think you're doing?"

Exactly what I want, she thought as indignation boiled up in her chest. "Nothing that concerns you," she hissed, meeting his scowl.

His already livid face darkened, his grip growing tighter, but

Eliška wasn't afraid of Radek any more than she was of the churlish dog at the end of the lane. She'd grown up with both. How could you fear someone who cried against your shoulder as a boy over his sick sister or pulled your braids during mass? No matter how thick his beard grew or how broad his shoulders, she saw nothing in Radek but a pestering, red-headed little fiend who smelled worse than the time he shat himself after eating spoiled goat.

She sucked in a breath through her teeth and straightened under his bruising grip. "Take your hands off me and go."

His mouth flattened, whitened, but he dropped his hands. "God forbid I touch your hand after courting you properly for months, but you would shame yourself with a stranger in the open air? After the care I've shown you?" He cast a baleful glance at Lajos who had regained his feet and faced them. Blood and dirt smeared his face.

"I owe you nothing." She jerked out of reach even as the blood rose to meet her tender skin. The aching blue stamp of his grip would be visible. "I never asked for your help."

Radek's nostrils flared. "But you took it anyway."

Eliška sucked in a breath as the truth found purchase. She had no reply. He was right, but she refused to bend any longer to a will not her own. "And if I had rejected you outright, what then? Would you have taken no as my answer? Or would you have stayed the same stubborn ass you've always been and lingered where you weren't wanted?"

Her words ripped through the space between them like arrows. As each barb found its mark, hurt spread across Radek's face. Eliška flinched, half expecting Radek to strike her as he leaned in and then sharply away. Perhaps he had expected to strike her, too.

"Be damned then, Eliška Ciernikova. Be. Damned," he said and stalked off through the woods.

She shook with rage and fright. Her heart thundered in her ears and her chest felt tight, her hands numb. She needed to calm herself. Closing her eyes, Eliška sat down hard and breathed deeply, flooding her system with oxygen.

In, out. In, out. In, out.

She was so focused on breathing, she didn't hear Lajos approach. When his hand fell on her shoulder, she startled and swung around, her hand raised to slap. He met her swing and wrapped bloody fingers around her wrist.

"Forgive me," Lajos said. Blood smeared the bottom half of his face, and his eyes were already starting to blacken. "It seems I am not even man enough to protect myself, let alone my love."

He let go of her and leaned away, his head bowed.

Eliška threw herself forward, wrapping her arms around him. Not caring if anyone saw, she buried her face in his neck and breathed in the sharp, warm smell of him. "I don't want protection. I want you."

Her voice hitched as he pulled her into his lap and rested his head against her hair. "Then it is fortunate for us both that you have the heart of a lioness."

She let out a long, ragged sigh and ignored the growing tightness in her chest. She hugged him tighter; breathed deeper before pulling back. His long, fine nose was definitely broken. "Come. Babička Olga shall tend to you."

Lajos tensed in her arms, and a new awareness of his body shot through her. He might not have fought off Radek, but every point of contact between them was smooth and firm, his body dense and warm beneath hers. Her focus blurred.

His mouth quirked up in one corner. "At the risk of you thinking me more of a coward—will she hate me as the tanner does? Old woman or not, I would rather avoid another beating today."

Coming back to her senses, Eliška regarded him. His tawny eyes shone out from his face, now mired with blood, like translucent river stones still full of mischief. He'd never been more inviting. She forced a smile and gingerly tucked a strand of golden hair behind his ear. "She'll tend to you like her child because she loves me as such."

Lajos's expression turned serious then and extracted himself from her grip. After finding his feet, he helped Eliška to hers. "Then lead the way, my dear. I am at your service and starting to get a wicked headache," he said and brushed a broken-lipped kiss across her cheek.

She took his hand and didn't wipe away the blood.

TWENTY
ALBIN

Albin couldn't say for certain whether the old woman was truly a witch, but something about the healer set his nerves on edge like a dog sensing danger. Her cloudy eyes seemed to see everything, and he of all people had much to lose if she truly did.

"What have you brought me today, bird? Another broken creature in need of mending?" the old woman said after opening the door to them. She squinted up at Albin, her tufted white eyebrows pinched with concern. Or suspicion.

Eliška had taken him through the woods to the back of the old healer's house, which was blessedly set apart at the end of the main lane leading into the village center.

"Not broken, Babička," said Eliška, her voice unusually timid. "Just a bit bruised." She took his hand then and faced the old woman, her chin lifted. "Will you help?"

It was no simple question and all three of them knew it. Lajos felt Eliška tense up next to him, her ever-chilled hand in his squeeze tighter. He didn't mind. The pressure gave him something to focus on instead of the throbbing pain in his face. Eliška was nervous and he knew then how much she loved the old woman, for the small, beautiful girl next to him had not been afraid of the loathsome tanner with his big red fists.

The old woman remained silent and watchful, her mind clearly unmade. Albin cleared his throat softly. "Good afternoon, grandmother. Please forgive me. I had an argument with another harvester and he took his revenge on me. Your friend here was kind enough to bring me to you for mercy."

Next to him, Eliška let out a long breath. He didn't know what it meant, but felt his own breath release next to hers. Babička Olga looked them up and down once more before pursing her wrinkled lips and nodding.

"Sit down at the table, boy. Touch nothing. Little bird is right —I love her too well to turn you away, though I'm a fool not to," she said and shuffled into the dark cottage.

He turned to Eliška for reassurance. The old witch had not sent them away, but her censuring gaze did nothing to quell his discomfort. But perhaps he deserved no such reassurances. Though he was the one beaten, deep in his heart he knew he deserved it. And so, it would seem, did Babička Olga. But if Eliška sensed any of this, she did not show it.

Instead, her beautiful too-wide mouth turned up in a cautious smile as she glanced up at him. He raised his eyebrows at her in question and she nodded, a smear of his blood still visible on her cheek.

"Thank you," she called softly and gestured for Albin to go inside.

He did, but not before licking his thumb and wiping her cheek. "You should not be sullied by me," he whispered, glancing inside to where the gray outline of the old woman stood by the stove. "I do not think grandmother would approve."

Eliška touched the place where he had wiped her cheek. Her lips parted as if about to speak.

"Shall my bones be ground to ash before you come inside? Has the boy no manners as well as no name?"

Eliška pulled him into the dark cottage. "Coming, Babička Olga."

Albin did not feel hopeful, but his nose throbbed and the drying blood on his lip had started to crack. He didn't know what the old woman planned to do, but hoped it would mend him enough to keep Miroslav from knifing the tanner in his sleep. Albin smiled at the thought of Miroslav's temper. His friend was more than willing to let Albin talk himself into a heap of mischief, but was often the first to come to blows. Albin flexed his tender hand, glad Miroslav had avoided this particular fight.

"This way, boy. Let me look at you." Babička Olga's sharp directions brought Albin back to the moment and he gave her his full attention. He sensed she would tolerate no less. The cottage was austere and run down, but something crackled in the corners, warming the place, like baking bread or the smell of cinnamon. He still didn't know if it was magic or knowledge, but he thought they might be the same thing.

Without further delay, he bent down to give her full access to his face. "Thank you, Babka. My name is Lajos." Then he took her wizen hand in his and kissed it, trying hard not to bleed on her.

The old witch threw back her head and laughed. "If you think that works on old women as well as young ones, you are right," she wheezed as she pulled away and set about her kitchen, gathering bowls and bottled from cupboards. Eliška fluttered at her side, anticipating the healer's every move.

Albin's face throbbed, but he smiled at the sight of his beautiful new acquaintance aiding with a practiced hand. While she so often seemed constrained and unsure of her movements, here she moved with grace and obvious knowledge. Unshackled. He knew that feeling; felt it himself on the bow of a ship or on an open road. Once again, Albin smiled against the darkening bruises and was pleased to be here, no matter the reason.

Babička was less pleased.

"Run afoul of a beast, did you?" she asked with a frown,

wiping his face and applying salve as no one had done since he'd been a child. She poked at his swollen eye socket. "Not broken, it seems. Good, good," she muttered and turned her attention to his hand.

Unsure how much to say, Albin quirked his good brow at Eliška. "Of a kind. I'm afraid I irritated it quite thoroughly."

Her smooth face pinched tight for several moments in consideration. Then she took a long, serrated breath and relaxed her expression. Albin had no idea what she was about to say.

"It was Radek. He discovered us talking in the glen." Eliška shot Albin a wide-eyed warning not to comment on her use of the word 'talking.'

He shot her a look back. Did she think him a complete fool?

The old woman made a rusty sound in the back of her throat, but did not pause her ministrations or say anything. Albin knew himself to be an ass but was not stupid enough to prove it here with another comment. This was clearly a conversation between the women. He watched with curiosity as Eliška fisted her small hands in frustration and walked the room. A dingy gray cat appeared from somewhere and rubbed against her ankles as she tried to move.

"You were right," Eliška said, wringing her hands in her apron. "I should have given him a direct answer a long time ago. It would have been kinder. To everyone. Now I don't think he'll believe I was never going to accept his hand."

She stopped then, and cast a hasty glance at him. Albin suspected she was trying to gauge his reaction to the knowledge that the red bear of a tanner was her suitor. He used his good eye to wink and felt a swell of pleasure rise up in his belly at the upward curl of her violet mouth. After all, he had not hounded Eliška, only admired her. It was she who had turned to him.

This knowledge filled him with satisfaction just as the old woman took hold of his nose and pulled. "Ouch! Son of a—" He stopped himself from cursing and sniffed loudly, half-choking on his own blood. "Thank you, Babka. Perhaps a warning next time?" he muttered, as the healer pressed a clean rag that smelled strongly of garlic into his hand.

"Hold this to your nose until the bleeding stops," she said without answering him and set a basin at his side. "Spit into this unless you want to vomit up the blood."

More embarrassed than he had been in some time, Albin flashed the healer a macabre smile only to wince against the swelling already taking hold of his jaw. For once, he could find nothing to say and sat docile, as the witch tended to him. What a fool he was and deserved every bit of this. Miroslav was going to laugh at him and then possibly beat Albin himself.

When he finally managed to cast another glance toward Eliška, her back was turned as she cleaned up after healer, replacing bottles and wiping tables and scrubbing his bloody rags. God what an oaf he was. But even the sight of her slim wrists and long neck, her tiny ears that stuck out just the slightest bit, made his loins tighten and his breath catch.

A loud, strangled-sounding cough sounded at his ear. Albin turned to find the witch mere inches from his face. Her milky eyes regarded him as he tried not to stare at the bristle of white whiskers sprouting from her chin. He nodded his head at her in deference for he was indeed thankful and recognized protective love when he saw it. "Thank you. I should not take up any more of your time."

"Where did you come from?"

He started to smile, grimaced instead, and pointed vaguely north. "Over the mountains."

The old woman continued to stare, her eyebrows crowded together like two wiry birds. Albin had the unpleasant suspicion she could see directly into his shallow heart. He'd met heads of state less intimidating and resisted the urge to squirm away from her. She might not be able to see well, but something told him she would perceive such discomfort with perfect clarity.

"But my brother and I have been traveling for so long, home

seems to be wherever we happen to rest our heads. We are quite fond of your village and are in no hurry to leave." He met Eliška's eyes over Babička's shoulder. She seemed as curious about his answers as the old woman. Damn him for digging his own grave of falsehoods ever deeper. Albin looked back at the healer, willing her to see his affection for her young friend if she believed nothing else.

The old woman leaned closer still, pushing his hair back from where it had fallen over his eyes. "I have seen your face before, though I cannot remember where. I have seen too many faces. I suppose it matters little."

She didn't smile at him, but put her gnarled hands on either side of his face and kissed his forehead. "Grandfather škriatok says you too will suffer. It would be best for you to go, now, before they come." Then she patted his cheek as if wishing him a good day and shuffled over to a chair by the stove.

Both shaken and calmed, Albin felt a sinking in his gut at the strange words and looked to Eliška for help. Her face was pale and still, but when she met his gaze, her eyes blazed, as unrelenting as his own. Whatever Babička Olga's words had meant, she wasn't giving up either. He held back a grimace and winked.

TWENTY-ONE
ELIŠKA

The untimely introduction between Babička and Lajos had gone better than she had expected. Not that her mentor hadn't pinched her face at Eliška's weak protests of innocence or believed for an instant Radek's beating of Lajos had been a misunderstanding. No one, least of all Eliška, took Olga Prochazkova for a fool. But Eliška wasn't ready to speak her hopes —or fears—about Lajos aloud and the old woman hadn't pushed. Eliška didn't like lying to her mentor. Her friend. But there were too many shared secrets between herself and Babička for Eliška to fear being betrayed. Of this at least, she was still sure. And her old friend had let her go home without a fuss, which was more than Eliška deserved.

Yet, even as she sat by the window with her embroidery that evening while Mamička hummed from the kitchen, a persistent, unnamed dread plucked at Eliška. Something was amiss. The wind whispered about it, passing the news from tree to tree in a low hiss. She didn't know if it was the presence of the white shadow or Lajos's arrival or something else entirely. Now that she'd begun to believe in some of Babička Olga's superstitions, there was no telling what this disturbance might be.

Her mind darted through childhood fears of a slouching, green-bearded leshy lumbering out of the woods toward her cottage or a small, shriveled butzemann sculking in the dark corners of the garden waiting to bite her ankles in the half-light. She shivered, feeling foolish. Despite what Eliška had seen in the woods that night, part of her remained doubtful. She didn't know if she could ever be as faithful as Babička, who never forgot to pray to her rosary or leave crusts of bread for her humble house škriatok. Perhaps, Eliška thought as she stared through the lace curtain toward the road, this was her problem. Unbelief.

Babička was always telling her to ask better questions and pay attention. Perhaps if Eliška believed more, she'd be ready to learn all the healer had to teach. Rolling her shoulders with newfound determination, she committed to doing what she could to earn the old woman's confidence. Until then she would mimic the old woman, copying wisdom until it was her own.

Imagining she was Babička Olga, Eliška inhaled until her lungs ached, closed her eyes, and bent her ear to the whispering wind. It was shocking how quickly her senses opened to the unseen things riding the air around her. The sounds, smells, sensations, yes, but more than that, the things beyond reason. She felt the texture of the spider's web in the corner; coolness from the shadow of a cloud that hadn't quite covered the setting sun yet. The sweet, resinous scent of herbs and the yearning thick inside her own house. What it all meant, she couldn't begin to guess and wondered what Babička would say. Did the healer always experience the world like this?

Eliška opened her eyes, pulling her senses back into her own body as a flower closes its petals, and tried to imagine all the things the old woman knew. How long had she been able to taste the air and smell intentions? Eliška couldn't imagine such a life, and yet a small thrill ran along her bones at the idea of one day being all that Babička was. No wonder the woman stooped—the weight of knowledge was no light thing.

Then Eliška caught her dark lips between her small teeth and bit down until she tasted the salt of her own blood. Fighting to swallow down an unexpected sob, she lifted her face to keep the pooling tears locked behind her lashes. She was a fool. No such life could ever be hers. Only old women lived in freedom, and she would never be old.

L ajos did not come. She shouldn't have expected he would. The remaining grapes needed harvesting, the fields to be cleared before the grape crushing and the festival. Still. Eliška had hoped and now suffered the familiar shadow side of hope—disappointment. Keen as a gutting blade, the edges of her broken expectation wedged themselves deep, and her lungs protested more than usual. The tingling weight stretched across her shoulders and down her arms, making every movement and deep breath a small victory.

It had been a long day. Unable to shake the queasy stomach and swimming head, she'd worked only a little on her embroidery while her mother was out. She would not risk degrading her one source of pride. If she could not even stitch properly, then delivering the aprons and bonnets she'd already finished was out of the question. Tomorrow, she told herself. Tomorrow when she felt stronger, though Eliška knew the evidence of her fatigue would not go unnoticed by her mother. Even as she'd yearned for a sight of Lajos, she dreaded the idea of him seeing her so weak. Cold sweat had poured from under her arms all day and she'd had to lie back down twice, her heart fluttering like an injured bird in her chest. A Bad Day, as Mamička called them.

Eliška shook her head as if trying to fling the bitter thought from herself. "You'd think I'd be used to it by now," she said with a heavy sigh to the small bird on the window ledge. It had landed earlier to hunt for beetles in the flowerbox and stayed, chirping aggressively at her every time she drew near. At the sound of her voice, the bespeckled creature ruffled its feathers and flew away.

"Traitor," Eliška said, her mood darkening by the moment. She brought the knife down harder than necessary on the end of a parsnip and the knife slipped, nearly cutting her, and clattered to the floor. The shock was enough to bring Eliška back to herself, though her blood hammered in her ears like the pounding of feet. As if on cue, she heard her mother's distinct tread on the road outside. Heard the garden gate creek open. Eliška grabbed the knife off the floor, rinsed it in a basin, and started on the root again, this time with more care.

Mamička rolled through the door like a sturdy wind. The air around her nearly crackled with energy and accomplishment as she smiled her greeting. Then her mother stopped, no doubt taking in the unfinished meal, the half-done embroidery discarded on the chest of drawers, the unswept floors. All pointed to Eliška's wan face and stooped shoulders, as clearly as an accusing finger. Eliška set the knife down just as her mother rushed over, the earlier air of triumphant energy already forgotten.

"You should have sent for me or Olga. How could you be so foolish?" Mamička said without preamble, pressing rough hands against Eliška's face, chest, hands.

Eliška reared back, her irritation a stoked flame. "Am in not on my feet? I'm not a child to be fretted over," she said, swallowing hard, voice tight. "Can you not trust my judgment for once?"

The words fell between them, hot as coals. Her mother's hands dropped and hung at her sides, motionless. Eliška wanted to regret her words. Her unkind tone. But she didn't. Couldn't. She had been pressed down and held aloft and stepped around and looked through for so long she could not stand another moment of it. Even if none of this was her mother's fault.

Mamička did not move, stunned into an unnatural stillness.

"I will call for Babička Olga if and when I see fit to." Eliška wiped her damp hands and took hold of the knife. Even as she gripped the blade, she could not muster the strength to hold back her words. "I am sorry Father died. I am sorry he gave me his weak heart, and I am sorry you are afraid." She started chopping again though her hands trembled. "But it is *my* life, and I will not spend it in bed."

Her mother didn't move at all. "I know you are not a child, Isha. I see how you chafe against my worry. That does not mean I will stand by and let you throw your life away. Do you even—" Mamička cut herself off, but she didn't have to finish for Eliška to know what her mother was about to say.

Eliška grimaced and carefully set down the knife. She was weary to her bones of this conversation. "I will always love you. This has nothing to do with my love for you."

As if she hadn't heard Eliška speak, her mother burst into motion and started unnecessarily tidying up the cottage. Slamming cupboards and straightening platters that did not need straightening. "Then for Christ's sake, why would you make yourself ill and not call for me? Or Babička at least? I know how you prefer her company to mine, but you could at least show me some respect."

Her mother slammed a final cupboard and whirled to face her still empty handed.

Eliška met her mother's stare. She didn't know what was more surprising: that her mother had cursed, or that she hadn't heard Eliška at all. Still. She took a deep breath. Tried again.

"I do not *make* myself ill, Mamička. I am ill. Every day. Some days are better than others, but I am never well and I never will be." Speaking the truth aloud burned like bile in her throat, but she pressed on. "So I will see to my own care if and when I decide to. Loving you has nothing to do with it."

Eliška braced for exasperation. Tears. Rage. She did not expect her mother to laugh.

"Nothing to do with it? Nothing?" Mamička asked with a hysterical brightness in her eyes.

Eliška stepped back.

"Are you so foolish as to think your health—your very life—has nothing to do with mine?" Her mother laughed again, the sound jagged, before prowling the cottage, shaking her head and wringing her hands. "Me, your mother. Who has cared for you on my own, never taking another husband who might not understand? Who would expect too much of you? Resent my care for you?"

Hot shame flooded Eliška, and she could not hold her mother's gaze.

"You say it is your life alone, but every disappointment you have suffered I have suffered too. So don't you dare say you have born this half-life alone," said Mamička, before trapping a sob with her hand.

At her mother's words, Eliška's anger slipped through her fingers and she stepped forward. "Please don't cry, Mamička. Please."

Then her mother's eyes, shining and hard in the low light, found hers. "You leave me no choice, Isha," she said under her breath.

Eliška froze as fresh dread crept down her back. "What do you mean, no choice?" she asked, voice thin with fear. "If this is about Radek, you know I cannot—"

"The festival." Her mother bit out the words. "I forbid it. You will stay inside and rest as you should until you have regained some of your strength. You push yourself too hard."

Eliška flew back as if slapped. Her head spun and her stomach dropped to her feet. Strong, familiar hands clamped onto her arms, irritating the bruises left by Radek, and Eliška slapped away her mother's offending help.

"You can't. I won't obey," she cried and scrambled into a nearby chair. She would hold herself upright if it killed her.

"Don't be a fool, child. It is for your own good. Radek will understand."

"No!" Eliška's voice broke as she truly shouted at her mother for the first time in many years. "It is for your good!" She jabbed an indigo-tipped finger at her mother. "You care only about what you want. What you would choose."

Now it was the older woman who pulled away as Eliška's words found their mark. Nostrils flared, her mother planted her hands on her hips. "Then you will risk your life for a party? You would rather become one of Babička's specters and be swept away by fiends than miss a dance?" Mamička hissed, her face scarlet with anger. "Can you see nothing beyond the tip of your own—"

"I'm going to die!" Eliška shrieked at her mother as she slapped her own heaving chest, her hands completely numb. "Can't you see? I will never give you grandchildren or harvest grapes or spin flax or lose my teeth no matter how much I rest. There is no *time*." She grabbed her mother's hand, begging her to understand, only to have it wrenched away in the wake of stunned silence.

Tears blurred Eliška's sight—she did not wish to hurt her mother. Only to make her see. "I love you, Mamička." The words caught in her throat, but she forced them out with a ragged sigh. "I'm not afraid of dying," she said, and slumped to her knees. "I'm afraid of not living."

Eliška pressed her face to her hands and wept. Mamička said nothing, but met Eliška on the ground and cradled her head in her lap, as if she were a child again. Lying there, she let her mother wipe her face and hum until their slushy breaths came and went in unison, a tide to their private sea.

TWENTY-TWO

ALBIN

It was time to leave. The last of the grapes had been collected and he and Miro had been in the village well over a week now. His bride and her caravan would certainly arrive any day and it was reckless to keep up this facade. Albin had thought on it all afternoon as he'd hauled water and set about scrubbing his and Miroslav's shirts and stockings which had gone stiff with sweat from the fields. Here, he found himself in the waning heat of the afternoon, Miroslav having gone to check traps.

But even as the press of his impending reality weighed heavily, he thought of little else save one thing: Eliška. Her fresh beauty and biting wit pleased him endlessly. Even as he scrubbed at the cloth, his hands already blistered from harvesting, he smiled. She was knowledgeable in things he knew nothing about and strong of mind, though her unnamed ailment plagued him. Eliška didn't speak of her twilight lips and fingers, and he knew enough not to ask a woman about what she does not wish to discuss. But her eyes burned with passion and held his long after another would have demurred. A kindred spirit stared out at him every time they were together. Time. It was exactly what he needed and the one thing he didn't have.

Thus, his torment grew. Should he tell her the truth of who he was? How? Damn this marriage, he thought for the thousandth time, and raked his soaking, stinging hands through his hair. The more Albin thought about his future, the more he wanted to rail against it. To take Eliška and leave the village forever, consequences be damned. With some luck and much stealth, he could line his coffers with enough ready money to get them into the East where his name would be unknown. He could change both of their fortunes. Make them partners in an adventure, away from estates and politics and expectation. Something deep in his gut told him she wouldn't object.

The stockings forgotten in the rusting tub, Albin started to pace as the plan solidified in his mind. Possibilities flew past and he grabbed wildly, not knowing which yet would prove useful. Only one truly sobering thought remained. Would she come away with him? He paused his frantic walk and closed his eyes. With the sun heavy on his head and the breeze cool at his neck, Albin recalled the persistence of her gaze and her lingering touch. The way her fingertips drifted over his palm. He did not think himself a fool to hope she wanted him with a similar passion.

"Yes. It could work," he said aloud as he paced, excited now to the point of agitation. "But I need more goddamn time."

"A shame, sir." Miroslav strode around the corner of the cottage, traps slung over his shoulder. "Since time is one thing not even you can buy." He was grubby from being in the woods, but clear-eyed and stone-faced as he took in the scene: the neglected chores, Albin talking to himself, his pacing.

Albin flushed guiltily. He knew how crazed he must look. "Damnit, man, why do you creep up on me? Do you enjoy watching me make a fool of myself?"

Miroslav did not take the bait.

"How long have you been spying anyway?" Albin grumped, snatching at a wet stocking.

Miro strolled over to Albin, his face unreadable. "Long enough to suspect you want more time to trounce around as the village dandy." He swung a small bag from over his broad back and dropped it at Albin's booted feet. "Grouse. Not fat enough really, but they'll keep our stomachs from gnawing at our backs for another night. The village meals are hearty, but one hot meal a day is wearing on my physique." He tipped his hat up and ran a forearm over his brow, smearing his freckled skin with earth. "You were right, you know."

Albin hadn't expected this and was momentarily startled out of this sour mood. "Oh? About what exactly?"

Miro squinted at him before gesturing around the shabby yard. Linus the mule, who had enjoyed a long, lazy holiday while the men worked the vineyard, brayed in apparent agreement from the rickety corral. Miro cracked a smile at the beast, but Albin was in no mood for a cheerful ass.

"All of this. I've enjoyed this nonsense more than expected. Even with you farting like a beast at night and chasing every skirt in the village."

Albin scoffed. "Not every skirt. And at least I don't snore like a dying swine."

Miroslav conceded the point with a tight smile. "But I must tell you, sir, I am looking forward to a sequence of proper meals." Miroslav leveled a pointed look at him then, all playfulness set aside. "At home. With your fiancée."

Albin eyed the sack puddled between them, but made no move to pick it up. "Actually, Miro, I'm glad you feel that way. I've discovered an opportunity. You are to leave tonight and go tell my father I've encountered a new enterprise and will be delayed somewhat in my return. But I will be back," he said, suddenly gripped with the need to be rid of his friend. He needed to find Eliška, discover the depth of her feelings, and begin plotting in earnest. Because Miroslav was right about one thing—Albin was out of time. Even as the thought settled around him, panic slithered down his spine. His jaw tightened. He was trapped.

Miroslav's expression was as cool and dark as the shadows falling across the pair. "You must truly think me a fool. Or a nuisance. Nothing more than an errand boy to be ordered about." Miroslav stepped forward, and despite the steel in his gaze, he raised his hand to Albin, beseechingly. "You cannot possibly be serious about this."

Albin avoided his friend's eyes. "I don't know what you're talking about. I simply need more time with the vintage and wish you to tell my father that I—"

"Don't. Lie." Miroslav's clipped words fell between them like stones. "At least have the decency to tell me the truth before sending me before your father. I have lied for you before and would do it again, but don't you dare think yourself above telling me the truth."

Chastised, but not cowed, Albin redoubled his resolve. "Fine. I'm resolved to stay and there's nothing you can say to persuade me otherwise."

Miroslav stepped closer still, his mouth twisted. "It's her, isn't it? The girl from the well. You've been seeing her." A vein jumped along his temple as he fisted his hand. "And here I thought you were bedding the tanner's sister from the pastry stall. I'd bet my best boots she had something to do with the beating you took, too. Game of cards, my ass."

Albin met his friend's eyes with a cold stare of his own.

"My God, I'm stupid." Miroslav made a derisive bark of a laugh and shook his head. "You cannot be serious, Bini! This truly was the worst—"

"I don't care what you think!" Albin shouted, surprising them both. He never spoke to Miroslav this way. Both men stared at each other as an unfamiliar chill crept between them like a foul mist. The wind started to rise, whipping through the yard and snatching at their clothes. The mule gave a panicked bray.

"Forgive me." Albin ran a hand through his hair, disheveling it. He shook with festering rage. With fear. With wanting. God, if only he could stop the wanting. Albin tried to calm himself. "Please, Miro. You must listen. I love her."

Miroslav scoffed, shaking his head in frustrated disbelief. "You hardly know her. That is not love."

"Listen!" he beseeched. "She's beautiful, yes, but she's bright and sad and kind and brave. You don't understand. I can't think or sleep. She's enthralled me and I have no wish to be saved. Please, I need more time to make a plan. To set things in motion before I speak to my father." He started to pace again, his legs eating up the ground around them seemingly without his command. "If you've ever been my friend, you'll do this. I beg of you. If I go back now and play the puppet for the rest of my days..." Albin turned away, gagged with spite for the life laid out before him. Everything in his being screamed if he did not free himself now, he would be shackled to his father's expectations and the political future of this place forever.

It was a privileged existence. He'd seen enough of village life the past week to know how easy his life was, but the price for such comfort was steep. Agency. Passion. Discovery. Freedom. The only things he'd ever truly wanted.

Miroslav's hand closed on Albin's shoulder, gently. Albin clenched his jaw, but did not pull away.

"Listen to me. She isn't good for you. Madness has grabbed hold of you. I know it to be more than the girl you seek, but you must leave before you do something you cannot take back. Yours isn't the only life at stake."

Albin jerked away from his friend's sobering touch. "I will not give over my life without a fight." The words seemed to spring from Albin's mouth without his consent.

Miroslav's voice was calm, but the pain on his face was evident. "Then you leave me no choice but to remove you from here myself."

The weight of Miro's intent slapped Albin across the face and he stumbled back. "She is the only thing for me now! I beg you not to betray me. In the name of our friendship and as your lord." Albin clenched his hands, pressing his fists to his eyes. He must make Miro understand. "You don't know what it's like. She's right in front of me and I can't—"

"Don't you dare." Miroslav straightened to his full, considerable height, his mouth white as bone. He did not quake with passion as Albin did, but stood frozen with rage.

Stunned by Miroslav's sudden ferocity, Albin leaned away, feeling quite sure his friend was about to strike him. He did not. Albin wished he would.

Finally, Miroslav spoke. "If you think I do not know what it's like to yearn with the deepest affection for someone irrevocably out of reach, then you are a far greater fool than even I imagined. Sir."

The words hit Albin in the chest like an ax as he saw Miroslav's stern face finally unmasked. The naked longing and fury in his friend's eyes nearly brought Albin to his knees.

"Miroslav—"

"Shut up," Miroslav hissed with unnatural animosity. "You can bemoan your lofty lot in life and lust after this girl to no end, but do not tell me I don't know what it's like to watch everything you love slip through your fingers." Miroslav bent close to him, his nostrils flared and eyes black. "To watch it flit away and be helpless to call it back. You have no goddamned idea."

It was too much. Too much truth coursing through him, between them, raw and jagged and hot, threatening to undo him completely. Albin hardened his heart against it. "Then help me escape."

Miroslav gave the wild, haunting laugh of a man gone mad. "No. My rightful lord or not, I will do no such thing. This charade is nothing less than a road to hell paved with the bodies of *your* people if you do not wed and secure even a tentative peace. We would both have to live with that." Miroslav turned and made for the cottage, grabbing his hat from the door post.

Albin's stomach boiled. This could not be happening.

"Miroslav! Damn you, man, get back here. I demand it. You call yourself my dearest companion, yet you abandon me now?"

Miroslav banged around gathering his things and did not stop. "You have abandoned yourself."

"No, I have found myself." Albin jabbed at his own chest. "Shaken off the lies poured out by my father, the empire, and every other fucking person who would control me. I finally have a chance to be free."

"You are lost!" Miroslav shouted back, his face dark with anger.

Albin panicked. Miroslav could not betray him to his father now. Could not. Desperation flashed through Albin like fire, twisting his words into weapons "I am lost? What about you, Miro? Still pretending to be a man when you're nothing more than a groveling sod."

The word sliced through Albin's tongue as it fell from his mouth. Never had he said such a thing. Never had he regretted anything more; would have swallowed coals to get the word back. Instead, he watched his own misery drive itself chest-deep into his dearest friend as completely as any blade. Silence fell over them, as unyielding as the whipping wind.

"Oh, Christ. Miroslav, please—" Albin sagged under the weight of his cruelty. Fell to his knees.

Miroslav didn't even stagger, only glared at Albin with utter contempt. "I will deliver this message to your father and then, no more. Ever." Miroslav pulled down his cap and strode into the woods.

"Miro. Miro!" Albin scrambled to his feet as if to follow. "Come back!" he choked, ready to throw himself to the ground and beg forgiveness.

Miroslav did not stop. He did not slow. He did not turn. He did not weep or rage or do anything but walk away.

Albin buried his face in his hands and wept. How could he have done such a thing? Miroslav had been his brother and now he was gone. Albin himself had made sure of it. As his world crashed around him, he knew he'd cut a wound in Miroslav that may never heal. Shame crowned him. Albin had known about Miroslav's preferences for years. He wasn't blind, nor had he ever cared. It had never mattered and never before had Albin been such a coward as to use it against him.

Mad with guilt, Albin climbed to his feet. Miroslav was gone. His father would send men to reclaim him once Miroslav delivered his message. Unless Miro lied for him, and Albin held out no hope of that. His betrothed would arrive soon—may already be nearing the village—and every real freedom in his life would end. Oh, his cage would be a gilded one for sure, but a cage nonetheless. His heart beat a pulpy rhythm as he grabbed a new bottle of brandy from inside the cabin and slid to the ground.

Leaning heavily against the wall, Albin uncorked the bottle with his teeth and took a long, desperate pull. Closing his eyes as the welcome burn seared down his throat, Albin didn't notice how the trees at the edge of the clearing shuddered violently even as the rest of the yard quieted. He didn't see the hazy outline of the woman crouched on a low branch, her kohl-blackened eyes squinting at him. Nor how her fur cloak blurred into the swirling winds, or sense her sharp smile through the veil as she watched him, waiting. Hungry.

Twenty-Three

Eliška

Sleep claimed her early after their argument and did not let her out of its welcome oblivion until the sun was high the next day. The rest had done her good, for as Eliška moved into the day her breath came more easily. Her hands ached less. Her stomach greeted the warm porridge with honey and strong tea with appreciation. But even as Eliška welcomed the momentary strength and knew that her mother was right—she was pushing her body too hard—she could not find the grace to admit such a thing aloud.

They danced around the silence. Mamička noisily rinsing and salting fresh butter in the kitchen while Eliška worked on the embroidery she had left unfinished yesterday. Neither spoke, but twice Eliška noticed the kitchen go quiet, and looked up to find her normally diligent mother staring off into the distance. More than once she opened her mouth to ask what was bothering her mother, but thought better of it. They were both worn out and Eliška decided to let her mother have her own memories, whatever they were.

This time, it was Eliška who left to venture out of the cottage for the day. Stepping out into the street, she was grateful to trade the confining walls for fresh air, though she hoped Lajos wouldn't call on the house in her absence. At the thought of him, she smiled despite herself. Perhaps her fate was changing, no matter what the petals said. With open lungs and a clear head, Eliška admired her hands, more rosy than blue today, curled around her basket of bonnets. She hadn't finished them all, but those she had completed would be worn proudly at the festival and lead to more requests for her work. Eliška pursed her lips and wondered if she pleased Mamička enough, she might relent about the festival. Then perhaps if Mamička met Lajos, Eliška could put her mind to rest about the future.

She smiled to herself as a giddiness she hadn't known since girlhood welled up from her belly. It happened every time she so much as thought of Lajos. The flood of joy made her head spin deliciously as if she'd had too much wine, and she regretted being such a hard judge on other girls in the village. Peers she'd not-so-secretly held in contempt for falling away from themselves for a man. She simply hadn't understood. Though she still had no intention of abandoning her crafts, Eliška stared at the dark road under her feet and felt a twinge of shame. She was the fool now.

But it was different, she thought. Lajos was different. Holding tight to her conviction and her basket of embroidery, Eliška walked slowly along with her face to the sun and the wind at her back. She was determined to let nothing spoil her day.

⁂

She had lingered too long while delivering her goods, but it was pleasant to feel mostly well for a change. It had pleased her to surprise people and accept the invitations for a cup of tea or slice of bread and cheese; to visit with her neighbors and listen to the children play and the grandmothers gossip. All too often, she refused these polite interactions in her rush to return home to rest.

Plus, Eliška wasn't above being proud of the clink of coins in her basket and smiled to herself for this small proof that she was useful.

She was still smiling to herself when she heard the carriages. The jingling harnesses, the clomping rhythm of hooves like stone against stone, and the gentle groan of wood caught her attention well before she saw them. As she neared the well, Eliška paused and listened with her whole body as Babička Olga had taught her. Every sense turned toward the road, waiting. The ashes only predicted one stranger, not many. Perhaps the sign had been wrong? She gripped her precious basket as the source of the noise came into view from around the bend in the trees where the road led out of the village.

"Definitely more than two," Eliška muttered as the elegant caravan drove steadily up the lane toward her. There were three of them, each coach a moving piece of art with their polished wood and velvet curtains. Eliška had seen fine coaches before. Occasionally, Baron Pálffy would visit during Christmas or after the harvest. She hadn't seen the son in years—not since the baroness died. She would never forget the first time she saw the velvet curtains of the late lady's coach. The deep blue of a winter twilight and made from cloth fit for a queen, Eliška had longed to touch them but knew such luxuries were beyond her reach.

These carriages were of a different style and continued quickly up the road. Too quickly. Everyone heard the commotion and came out to see, including Maria and her brood of children. Eliška's gaze fell on the open gate of their cottage. On the littlest boy and his kid goat. On the wheels of the coach as the goat startled and darted into the street. On the child who pulled away from his elder sister and ran after the goat.

Without thinking, she dropped her basket and ran, waving her arms wildly.

"Stop! Whoa!" she cried as she planted herself in front of the boy. The driver saw her and pulled the team up hard with a sharp command.

The horses stopped close enough for Eliška to see their foaming mouths and smell the sweat from their powerful bodies. Only a few feet from where the child sat holding his goat. Seeing her son treacherously close to the carriage's wheels, Maria let out a belated scream and ran. Scooping the boy and goat into her arms together, she ran back to the yard, crying and admonishing her son all the way.

Eliška couldn't speak—her heart squeezed in her chest trapping her breath. What felt like shards of ice spread down her arms, up her neck. She heaved a huge sigh, gulping air. Her head swam. She hadn't meant to endanger herself, but the boy hadn't moved and...

"What are you about, girl? Trying to get yourself killed?" The furious, nasal voice of the coach driver barked down at her, his cheeks and neck the color of new beets.

Eliška scowled up at him, anger pressing away her dizziness. "How dare you, sir? Did you not see the child?" She pointed toward Maria's house, her brood of offspring still pressed up against the fence, gaping at the scene. Boy, goat, and mother sat together in a heap on the front step.

The driver followed her hand, nervously puffed his cheeks, and went quiet as a new voice boomed from inside the coach.

"Why have we stopped? Have we arrived, Josef?" At this question, a bearded face appeared from behind the curtained window.

Disgust, hot and spitting, welled up in her. A child had nearly been run over. She could have been trampled and this was the occupant's only response? Her gaze met that of a red-faced man wearing an elaborate collar and a primly curled mustache. He motioned her to approach with fat, ringed fingers. She stepped toward him, her scowl firmly in place.

"You there, girl. Is something amiss?"

If the nobleman was taken aback by her bold stare, he didn't show it. Eliška was close enough to see his eyes. Though protruding and pale, they took the measure of her with mild concern.

"Yes, my lord. I'm afraid your driver nearly crushed a child." She lowered her eyes and cast them toward the family.

The nobleman followed her gaze. "Oh. Many pardons, miss."

Maria, solemn now, stood tall and nodded her head at the man who immediately turned his attention back to Eliška without changing his expression. Despite the fact her child had just nearly been trampled, it seemed there was nothing more to say.

"Shall we proceed, my lord?" asked the irritated driver.

Eliška listened as another voice spoke up from inside the carriage.

"What was that, dear? Oh, yes of course," said the nobleman, clearly responding to his unseen companion. "Uh, not just yet, Josef," he continued and motioned to Eliška. "You there. Is your cottage nearby? We are in need of refreshment."

Eliška kept her face carefully blank and nodded, even if the last person she wanted to serve at the moment was this nobleman and his careless driver. "Yes, my lord. My matka is there." She pointed toward her house, unwilling to say more.

"Excellent." He smiled and leaned back inside the coach. Eliška heard muffled voices, but could not make out the conversation. Then he leaned back out, his pointed mustache twitching as he spoke. "Be a good girl and inform your mother we wish to make a visit."

Lightheaded from the combined effects of the long afternoon and outrage, Eliška cast a look toward Maria. Only a few years older than herself, Maria had three children already and would likely have another on the way before long. She didn't need to anger a nobleman. Understanding passed between them and the young mother nodded her head, granting her consent to serve the careless man, before ushering her family inside. With another deep breath, Eliška turned a forced smile to the coach window.

"Of course, my lord. If you will follow me." With her hands pressed to her chest, she walked quickly to her cottage and stormed through the gate, not waiting to see if they followed.

"Mamička," Eliška hissed as she opened the door, the rush of the afternoon's events carrying her forward. "Hurry. A nobleman is at the door. He nearly ran over little Alexej in his coach and now seeks refreshments. I swear rich men have no shame."

Her mother looked up from the table where she was kneading bread. Normally sharp as obsidian, her gaze wavered. She smiled softly at Eliška. Too softly. She stormed further down the throat of the cottage and pressed her face into her mother's. The reek of wine was unmistakable.

"Sixteen years ago, Isha. Today. Did you know you have his eyes?" her mother slurred, though she kept kneading the bread with perfect rhythm. "Sixteen years."

Exasperation and pity swelled in Eliška, but she didn't have time for either. She heard the door of the coach close. They were coming.

"Listen to me. You have to get in bed. Now. Pretend to be ill." Eliška took her mother's hands and pulled her toward the bed. The fresh dough stuck to her fingers and matched the color of her mother's cheeks. She wouldn't have to pretend very hard.

"Don't let the dough fall. Ján's favorite," her mother said. She blinked her eyes wide and stumbled a little, but allowed herself to be led into the back of the cottage. "He said—he said." She paused and wavered on her feet. Eliška feared she would be sick, but instead her mother covered her hands with her face smearing dough into her always tidy hair. "To tell you..."

Panic gripped Eliška. No matter Pán Nagy's title, it was her mother who helped bring in the grapes and she could not be humiliated. "Please. You must get abed or we shall be ruined."

The swing of the gate startled them both. Her mother nodded and climbed into her cot just as a sharp rap came at the door.

"Yes, my lord. One moment," Eliška called while covering her mother with a blanket. Her chest started to tighten, but she drew in several quick breaths and moved to open the door.

There stood the most elegant trio she had ever seen: the fat nobleman, a thin matron with faded yellow hair, and the beautiful, moon-faced girl from the woods. She met Eliška's eyes for a moment and then dropped her gaze, petrified.

There was no mistaking the girl. Now dressed in a pale green damask gown with her hair delicately curled, the girl no longer smelled of blood and shit, but Eliška would have recognized her anywhere. Would have known that round face in a dream. The girl knew her too. Eliška could see it in the way she pinched her ribbon mouth tight; the way her summer sky eyes widened and her nostrils flared. A fat mouse in a trap could not have been more terrified.

She thinks I will betray her.

How sad, she thought, and wondered what kind of intrigues went on in the luxurious world of this girl's birth. Eliška knew little of life outside the village, but even she understood marbled halls, fine coaches, and velvet gowns didn't guard a heart. Here was the proof.

The girl stood tall, but wrung her hands pink and made an odd humming noise in her throat as if trying to swallow her distress. Eliška cocked her head in interest.

"Be still, Anja. Do not shame us in front of our hosts," the nobleman said, and showed his big teeth. The red flesh below his jaw wobbled as he spoke.

Eliška curtsied, her gaze escaping to the floor. "Forgive me, my lord, but I'm afraid my mother has taken ill. I would be happy to bring you refreshments, but am unable to offer you rest just now."

A stiff *humph* came from the bedecked matron. Ignoring her, Eliška shot a glance at the girl named Anja. Having forced her hands to be still and her voice silent, the girl's face remained ashen and her eyes glassy. Pity welled up in Eliška—she too knew about the betrayal of your own body.

"But if you would be so kind as to wait in your coach, I will fetch you something to eat and drink and find another home to welcome you."

"I suppose that will do if we must," said the nobleman.

Eliška stared hard, trying to catch the girl's eye while the lord and lady made their way stiffly back to their carriage.

Finally, Anja braved a look at her. Eliška quivered her head. *No, I won't tell.*

Anja's pink lips twitched up, not quite daring to smile. She squinted at Eliška, unsure. She held the young noblewoman's stare. Smiled.

"I see you have taken a fancy to the country beauty here, aye daughter?" boomed the still-unnamed nobleman. "Shall she keep you company?" He turned his whiskered face on Eliška and surveyed her as Babička Olga would a prized goat, before turning back to his daughter. "I consent," speaking as though he was pleasing them, though neither girl had requested such a situation. Oblivious to both young women's discomfort, he turned back to the coach as his wife eased herself inside with the help of the driver.

Unsure what to do, Eliška left the girl on the steps and went inside to gather refreshments. She stormed about a bit, thinking of her mother's precious bread and cheese going to feed the careless noble and his dismissive wife.

"Isha?" called her mother from the bed in the back.

With her tired arms full of bread, Eliška peeked around the stove at her mother. "I'm here, Mamička. Stay still for now."

Mother nodded weakly, her cheeks wet with tears.

Anger and sadness twisted Eliška's fluttering heart as she steadied herself with a few deep breaths. "I'll be back soon."

She went out the door without waiting for an answer. Lady Anja stood on the front steps, looking as out of place as a single rose in a patch of kitchen greens. Eliška remained quiet as she made her way to the coach. The driver opened the door as she handed the basket of sliced bread and cheese up to the couple.

"If you will permit me, sir, I'll go find a home to welcome you now," said Eliška, knowing exactly where she would take them. Let Pán and Pani Toth give over their time and chairs and wine to fawn over the wealthy pair. Alena and her sisters would never speak of anything else, but at least Mamička would be safe. Eliška needed to get back to her mother and apparently had the Lady Anja on her hands as well.

The matron gave a nod and a lethargic wave of her hand. Eliška was pleased to get away and started for Alena's house when the girl cleared her throat. She glanced back.

The velvet girl was twiddling her hands with discomfort again. "I wish to stretch my legs, Papa. May I accompany you to inquire after a place for us to rest?" She looked directly at Eliška for the first time.

Eliška sighed. There was only one possible answer. "Of course, my lady."

The father waved a lethargic hand towards his daughter. "I'm glad to see you feeling better after being unwell, my dear. I suppose it was a good thing the axle broke so you could rest another day. Still, best take Josef with you."

The girl offered a tight smile to her father as the coachman descended from his seat. The

aforementioned Josef did not look pleased to be sent on an errand and shot Eliška an annoyed glance just before the young noblewoman fell into step beside her. She rolled her eyes at him and turned her attention toward the road. She was going to need her wits for this and hadn't energy to spare.

The women wandered up the lane in silence. Thankfully, the coachman fell behind and seemed as uninterested in following them as they were in being followed. Though the harvesting was officially over, many villagers remained in the fields to collect the debris and aid in the washing and crushing, so the street was quiet. But not empty, and Eliška knew it was only a matter of time before someone approached them with open curiosity. She hoped the mysterious lady at her side would speak before then. Eliška didn't dare question her first. Thankfully, she didn't have to wait long. As soon as the coach was out of earshot, Lady Anja whispered, "You know me then?"

Eliška kept her own eyes at her feet. Not far from where they walked lay the woods where Babička Olga and herself had found this splendid creature. Eliška remembered the shame and terror on her face that night and turned to examine her in daylight. There was no doubt.

"Yes," Eliška said, though she wondered if she should plead ignorance instead. "And you are well now?"

Lady Anja shot her a sidelong glance. "Better. I wanted to know if you kept quiet because you didn't recognize me or because you are kind." A sad smile tugged at her pink lips. "I'm glad to see you are kind." Then she stopped and placed a soft hand on Eliška's wrist. "But I must ask, may I count on your continued kindness?"

Painfully aware of her own rough skin under the lady's touch, she met the stranger's stare. Seeing only pleading, Eliška nodded. "Yes, my lady."

"Anja, if you please. You must give me my Christian name after rendering me such a service." Her round eyes looked sincere, and Eliška nodded, though she had no intention of ever addressing her in such an informal way.

"And what are you called?"

"Eliška Ciernikova," she said, curling her fingers into fists. She wasn't uneasy under the young woman's gaze, but didn't want to expose herself completely either.

Lady Anja glanced around. "Well, friend Eliška, once we have situated my parents, would you be willing to render me one more favor?"

Eliška hesitated, though she knew there was no real choice. She would not blackmail the woman, and so must consider doing whatever it was she asked.

"Do not be frightened," she said, clearly reading Eliška's expression. "I only wish to see the old woman." Her eyes grew even rounder with pleading. "To thank her."

Eliška paused outside the wide, showy front gate of Pani Tothova's cottage, and sighed. She didn't like exposing Babička Olga to speculation any more than she already endured, but something about the lady's desperate expression moved Eliška and her heart softened toward the bloody girl in the woods.

"Be careful of these ones," she said, pointing to the Tothova's house. "They have wagging tongues. After, I will take you to see Babička Olga."

Lady Anja smiled radiantly before pushing through the gate herself.

Twenty-Four

Albin

"A drunkard. As expected."

The deep voice startled Albin awake and he immediately resented it. Head pounding, he blinked and squinted up at the towering shadow, instinctively hating it. Then the smell hit and his vision wobbled.

"Dear God," was all he managed before he rolled over and upended his stomach into the undergrowth next to him. Once he'd heaved himself empty, Albin spat and rocked back on his heels and glanced about. Even sick, Albin was aware of the green fronds brushing his thighs, the bright afternoon light slanting through the trees. Clearly, he'd wandered into the woods at some point last night in his drunken attempt to follow Miro. And damn if he hadn't passed out and slept away half the next day. He groaned as his head started to clear. Wiping his face, he looked back up at the offending shadow, careful not to breathe through his nose. "Radek Varga. Always a pleasure."

"You and your brother missed the field clearing and the crushing this morning. Pán Nagy sent me, in a cruel joke, to tell you he's docking your wages. Today was critical for the vintage.

Not that any of it ever mattered to a pair of tramps like you," the tanner said, before he spat on the ground next to Albin.

The money was of no importance, but Albin didn't care for the accusation that he was indifferent to the outcome of the vintage. Nothing could be further from the truth. He was intimately attached to this year's harvest and cared very much. He wanted it to turn out well, and not just for the price it would fetch. Radek might have been perceptive, and rightfully suspicious of him, but it didn't keep Albin from hating the man. His nose and ribs were still bruised and aching from the tanner's last attack, not to mention his pride.

Albin appraised the man who had blackened his eyes. Radek's bright hair and thick beard glowed orange in the offending light as if he were a hulking fox. Albin didn't care for another beating, though he deserved one. Fragments of the day before came back like flashes of a nightmare. Miroslav's accusations. His own vicious behavior. Stumbling through the forest, a bottle in hand. Blacking out when he could no longer numb his desperation any longer. The tanner was just another cog in the wheel of his misery. Blinking aggressively against a hammering headache, Albin wondered where exactly he was. He wasn't familiar enough with the woods to know off hand. Were his father's men searching for him already? Had Eliška been expecting him? But before he could attend to any of these problems, he needed to rid himself of the tanner.

"Pán Nagy runs the fields as he sees fit. We will not contest the wages," said Albin as he struggled to his feet. "But tell me this—what do you care what I do, Varga? You have been against us from the start." The world spun as he spoke, but his newly emptied stomach helped his sobriety as he faced the man who coveted his love's attentions. Albin could hate him for that alone. "I know you think me a villain, but I would have paid your sister back for the food. I'm quite invested in the well-being of the harvest, and I have no intention of harming her."

Chapter Twenty-Four

The tanner's eyes flashed as he scoffed and spat on the ground between them. "You think because I've lived my life in this village, I don't know your kind? Grifters who come and go with the wind of the season?" Radek crossed his big arms across his chest and gave a humorless laugh. "I'm not stupid. There's something amiss with you and I will find out what it is. Nothing good comes from vagrants and their stinking, self-serving hides."

Albin couldn't help but chuckle at this. "You don't know a thing about me and it drives you mad. Stinking hides on the other hand..."

Radek's eyes flashed, but he didn't move. In fact, nothing moved save for a whirring breeze in the underbrush. The sharp call of a bird. Then the tanner's unfashionable beard peeled back to reveal a sharp smile. "Don't tempt me, fop. Another beating would be too easy."

Albin showed his teeth in return before bowing deeply to the man. "As it happens, I am not so great a fool as you think. I would never taunt a man I cannot hope to overpower in a fight. But that is not the game we're playing, is it?" Albin started to walk shakily past the tanner, pretending to know where he was going. The woods still wobbled slightly from the drink, but he managed to keep his path straight. When he was sure he was out of easy reach, he looked back at the big tanner. "Though there are more ways to win a fight than with your fists."

Without waiting for a reply, Albin turned on his heels and walked away, a whistle on his lips. He half-expected a blow from behind, but it did not come. He forced himself on, determined not to turn around. The air smelled damp, and although the afternoon sun heated the floor of the woods, the light dimmed off and on as clouds gathered. He kept going, listening for Radek's heavy steps behind him, but there was only the faint rumble of thunder in the distance. A storm was brewing, and he could think of nothing more fitting.

Trudging toward the tree line—thank God he hadn't stumbled

farther in—Albin ran a shaking hand over his face and tried to think. But his mouth and brains felt like cotton and there seemed little he could do until he felt more like himself. Water, bread, and sleep he thought absently as he trudged on. Impulsively, he wondered where Miro was, but cut the thought off at the knees. No. He would not think of Miro. He did not deserve to ever think of Miroslav again. He was alone now. He deserved to be. There was only one thing worthy of thinking on now. Eliška. Perhaps if he succeeded in winning her affection and found a way to call off his engagement, this nightmare could be salvaged.

Twenty-Five
Eliška

"Take Josef with you, child, and do not spoil another gown," called Lady Anja's mother from inside the Tothova's large sitting room. "I do not expect there to be many replacements for you at the castle." Her shrewd gaze took in one of the finest homes in the village as she sniffed in displeasure. "It may take some time to order new things."

"*Natürlich, Mama*," Anja assured the grand woman, all the while inching away. Eliška had stayed silent throughout the conversations but couldn't help feeling an affinity for the fine girl. Perhaps there were some things riches didn't change.

Once outside the house, Lady Anja slipped something into the coachman's hand. He darted an appraising look toward Eliška before giving a faint nod. Satisfied, Lady Anja gestured for Eliška to join her. Cautiously resigned to this errand, she fell into step. Their feet hit the gravel road in stride, her in simple boots and Lady Anja in gleaming leather travel shoes. Josef gave them a lengthy head start.

"Are we free to seek out your healer now?" Lady Anja asked with nervous smile.

Eliška glanced at the man behind them. "Do you trust him?"

She watched the young noblewoman closely. Taking the lady to see Babička Olga was one thing; a spying servant was another.

Lady Anja gave her a small, but decisive smile. "I trust he wants to keep his position and knows who will line his purse with extra coins."

Eliška understood this motivation well and it was enough. "Then yes, though I must get back to my mother before long."

"I understand," said the young lady and linked arms familiarly with Eliška, impervious to the gawking stares of a few passersby.

The afternoon had worn away and the remaining harvesters were trickling back into town. Eliška was tempted to scan the passersby for Lajos, but couldn't bear the questioning stares already pointed at them, and so she kept her eyes carefully averted. Questions about the lady's condition and appearance in the forest rushed through Eliška's mind, but she kept quiet.

Lady Anja cleared her throat softly. "Your face betrays you, friend," the lady whispered and leaned down close, her perfume strong and sweet. "You have questions but are afraid to ask, yes? I know I would if our places were switched, but I'm afraid my memories of that night are blurred."

Eliška met her companion's gaze, but remained quiet.

"It's like remembering everything and nothing at the same time." Her voice held the jagged edges of shame. "Do you understand?" she asked, her sky eyes round and glassy with pleading.

Eliška did understand, all too well. She too remembered everything and nothing of many a night. Laying her hand atop the smooth whiteness of Lady Anja's, Eliška gave her a knowing nod. "Better than you know. This way. Babička Olga will be pleased to have you."

Lady Anja's smooth brow knit together in worry, but she held her shoulders straight, her chin high as if balancing a crown. It was the first time Eliška saw the noblewoman within, and not only the outer finery.

They found Babička Olga squatting in the garden muttering to herself. Her white hair hung loose today and streamed around her like a gnarled canopy. At the sight of the old woman, Anja hung back.

"All will be well," Eliška said, though how she did not know for certain.

Regaining her courage, Anja swept through the gate Eliška held open and they approached together.

"Babička. I have brought someone to see you." Eliška laid her hand on her friend's shoulder, though she suspected their presence in the garden was already known.

Babička Olga held out a papery hand. With a practiced move, Eliška helped her to her feet before the healer turned her head with owlish dexterity and stared at Anja.

To Lady Anja's credit, she approached Babička humbly and offered her assistance. "Shall I help you now, *Großmutter*?"

Anja's German flowed into the air like a warm breeze, and Eliška couldn't help but be drawn in. This noble girl was nothing like Eliška had suspected and she felt a stab of guilt over her assumptions.

Babička Olga tipped her head toward the lady before letting her eyes dart around. The old woman knew her business and lived without persecution because she was a gifted keeper of secrets. Satisfied they were alone, she leaned close to Anja. "Are you well, child? The bleeding has stopped? No fever?"

"I am well, *Großmutter*. Thanks to you," Anja replied and held the healer's hand. "And your apprentice." Lady Anja gestured gracefully to Eliška. "Who did not betray me and insisted the thanks be given to you."

Babička Olga nodded in approval and linked arms with Anja as if she were her own granddaughter instead of their future baroness.

"Eliška is a good girl," she said, her old voice full of affection. "She will be a great healer one day."

A billowing warmth rose up in Eliška's chest and took root in her heart where it had always belonged. *Yes*, thought Eliška. *I will be.* Then she followed Babička Olga and the lady into the old woman's disheveled cottage where the fat gray cat lay curled around itself in a wedge of sun and the air smelled of rosemary and remembrance.

"I fear you have tarried too long with an old woman," said Babička Olga after the three incongruous women had spent the better part of an hour drinking Olga's meager supply of tea and nibbling yesterday's bread and cheese.

"Yes, I'm afraid I should go before they come for me." Anja spoke with the easy power of one to whom little could happen. Even if they all knew differently.

Although Eliška genuinely liked the young noblewoman, she kept her reserve pulled tight around her, guarding herself from any impropriety. It would not do to have some stray word be taken as an offense. Babička, on the other hand, held nothing back. She probed and jested with the young noblewoman as if she were a beloved urchin off the street. The very old can get away with much.

"I will walk you back." Eliška rose to clean up.

"Thank you," said Lady Anja as she handed over her chipped teacup. "This has been—I'm quite grateful," she said, her voice quivering, before she pressed a hand to her mouth. Lady Anja choked back an audible sob.

"My lady?" asked Eliška, startled by the sudden display of emotion. She looked to her mentor for guidance, but the old woman had eyes only for the crying lady, her head cocked and curious.

"Forgive me," wheezed Lady Anja as she wiped her face. "It was only the one time and when I realized what happened, I was sick with fear. Desperate. If I had been found out—so much depends on my match—I nearly ruined—and my love—"

Once again, the lady choked on her words and heaved a shuddering sigh, struggling for mastery of herself.

Eliška sat back down and watched as Babička gathered the lady's hands in her own wizen ones, clucking softly at the girl's tears.

"Calm yourself, girl. Breathe. *Dýchat.*"

Lady Anja sucked in her quivering lips like a child and stared back at Babička. Eliška found herself breathing in rhythm with them until the air in the tiny cottage was charged with their peace and seemed to breathe itself. When all was still, Babička spoke again.

"It was a terrible thing, girl. All of it. But the danger has passed. Now you must let your mind and body grieve and then, move on."

Lady Anja's eyes filled again, but she held herself firmly in check this time and nodded at Babička. Eliška's throat burned at the sight.

"May I ask one more question, *Großmutter*?" Lady Anja asked, her accented voice thin but steady.

Babička smiled her gummy grin and nodded. "Of course, child."

Eliška found herself swallowing hard in anticipation. What more would come?

Lady Anja sat taller, visibly steeling herself for whatever answer Babička might give. "Will I still be able to bear children?" Her blue eyes pleaded. "I will be expected to give my betrothed an heir and if I—"

Babička raised a hand to stop her and sighed. "I cannot say, in truth. There are no answers. But I did the best I could do to keep you whole—God must handle the rest. Pray, take good care of yourself, eat well, and perhaps someday."

Anja nodded and wiped her nose. Eliška continued to tidy up as she slid a glance toward Babička. The old healer met her stare, milky eyes serious, though her scratchy voice remained cobweb-light.

"Now, my lady, if you will help an old woman to her feet, I shall make you a healing draught of red clover I think," said Babička Olga, and the lady hurried to offer her arm for support.

Eliška busied herself and tried not to intrude on their conversation. When the last cup was cleaned and hung on its hook, Eliška wiped her hands and tucked them behind her back. She did not need a healer to tell her the deep violet of her fingertips did not bode well.

"Yes, yes, child. I will tend you if you are so blessed. Though you must send a carriage. These old bones do not go uphill anymore." Babička cackled as she patted her knees with enough dexterity to bely her words.

Lady Anja smiled and nodded, now fully composed. "Anything for you."

Eliška raised her eyebrows at this, but said nothing. Babička Olga deserved all the praise, so she could not be jealous of whatever the lady had promised.

Then Eliška found herself under the lady's gaze, her pale eyes once again blue and clear. "Thank you for bringing me here, friend Eliška. Would you see me back?"

"Of course, my la—Anja," Eliška corrected as Anja arched a golden eyebrow at her in mock annoyance. Eliška couldn't help but smile back even as her chest started to ache.

Then, rising in a rustle of crisp petticoats, Anja turned and gave the old healer a brilliant smile and carefully pronounced, "*Dovidenia.* Until we meet again," before stooping to kiss Babička's pleated cheek.

Chapter Twenty-Five

"As you say, *holubica*," Babička answered and turned to Eliška.

Knowing she needed to hurry back to check on her mother and rest before she became faint, Eliška planted her own kiss on the top of Babička Olga's head and followed Lady Anja outside where the coachman was still waiting across the street and pretending not to notice people staring at him. The once glaring afternoon sky had clouded over, and a rough breeze darted about, but it was more invigorating than unpleasant now that the grapes were in. Eliška filled her lungs.

Without speaking, the young women made their way through the wild garden toward the street when Anja stopped short and grabbed her wrist. "Wait. I have something for you."

Eliška paused, curious. "That is not necessary. We did not offer our help for payment."

The young woman looked abashed at this, but pressed on. "I know. You and your mentor are true of heart, which is why I wish to give you this," she said and removed a pendant from around her neck. "I have no ready money, you see, and I do not mean to insult you." She paused then and held the necklace out to Eliška. "But I would have you know my gratitude."

Overwhelmed, Eliška took it carefully into her hands. The gold edges of the large disk swirled inward like little waves with blue, green, and yellow enamel flowers poking their blooms out from between each golden curve. And shining in the center sat a deep blue stone. Dark as twilight, the jewel found every trace of dim light and threw pale blue shadows across the ground like a splattering of paint. The long chain hung heavy from her hand, betraying its worth.

Eliška cleared her throat, her emotions stuck between awe and insult. "It's beautiful, but I can't accept this."

Lady Anja's smile tripped, then broadened into a full slice of white teeth. "I want you to have it," she said as if this solved everything. In her world, it did. "Perhaps you will wear it on your wedding day and spare me a kind thought?"

Eliška held it back out. "Truly, my lady. We are used to keeping sec—"

"Please," Anja cut in. "I must feel as if I've paid my debt." Gently, she took the necklace back from Eliška and this time placed it over her neck. Eliška let the pendant drop and savored the feel of the elegant gift between her breasts for a moment. The weight of it somehow soothed her limping heart. But a moment was all she could spare.

"Thank you. I'm grateful, but if you really want to thank me, then give the amount of coin this is worth to Babička Olga." Eliška lifted the gift off her neck and held it out to Lady Anja. "There's nothing I can do with this."

Lady Anja's rose-colored cheeks fell and Eliška wondered if the lady had ever been told no before. She thought likely not. But there was no anger on the lady's face. Only dismay. Eliška boldly took her hand. "Please do not think me ungrateful."

Lady Anja covered her hand with her own and smiled. "Your kind heart does you service." Then her smile widened, and her pale eyebrows shot up in excitement. "And for it, I shall insist you keep my gift"—she leaned in close to whisper—"and I shall secret enough coin to the healer to keep her comfortable the rest of her days once I am married."

Her breath hitched in her throat as the lady leaned away, a satisfied smirk on her bow mouth. Eliška couldn't keep her eyes from brimming. She didn't want to trust a noble, but everything in her yearned to believe the lady would not forget her promise once she was installed as their baroness. Riding that hope, a question she should not ask rose in her tight throat. "Do you swear it?"

If Lady Anja was taken aback by such a request, she didn't show it. In fact, she leaned in close to Eliška again, her eyes delighted as if they were sharing a sisterly pact. Perhaps they were.

"I swear it," said Anja and linked arms with Eliška just as the first peal of thunder stretched across the darkening sky.

"Isha." Her mother's voice cracked from the back of the cottage where she lay abed. "Water."

The afternoon rain had settled in cloaking the day in darkness. And though it was just after supper time, Eliška was bone tired. She wanted to be angry with her mother—she was angry—but some tender spot remained unprovoked by her mother's behavior. Mamička fought hard against the thirst that overtook her when father died, but sometimes it became too much to bear. Part of Eliška understood this. She knew what it meant to crave.

Eliška poured the cold water, spilling some onto the stove. The droplets hissed, then disappeared. She thought it was perhaps a good way to be extinguished. Better to burn up than drown slowly in grief like her mother.

"I'm here, Mamička," she said, moving to her side with a cup. The faint tang of sick still lingered in the back room and Eliška took a breath through her mouth. "Drink slowly."

Her mother wrapped her long, strong fingers around the cup in Eliška's hands and sipped. Then she trained her dark eyes on Eliška and her mouth crumpled. "Forgive me, Isha."

She kissed her mother's forehead and wiped the hair from her face. "Rest. I shall make you the draught Babička Olga recommended."

Now the obedient child, her mother nodded and held on to the cup as Eliška moved back to the stove to gather the dried herbs.

Lady Anja and the noble entourage were no doubt still hunkered down in the neighboring houses they had taken over as the rain drizzled on. She received word earlier from a messenger that, being disinclined to travel in the rain, Lady Anja had convinced her parents to stay on for the night in the hope of enjoying the upcoming harvest festivities. Eliška was surprised to find herself glad of it. Now the rain just had to stop.

Eliška took down the jars of necessary herbs and put water on to boil. Stoking the fire in the stove sent a breath of welcome warmth through the kitchen nook, and she shivered in its wake. Pulling her shawl tighter, she glanced out the window. Rivulets coursed down the road in front of the house and the trees swayed to the rhythm of the wind. But the bulk of the storm had passed leaving the night the drip and drizzle. She sent a selfish prayer up for a blazing morning sun, knowing it would be needed to dry out the square for the festival.

Despite her fatigue, Eliška thrilled at the idea. After the events of the day, she hoped Mamička would change her mind since by this time tomorrow, the whole village would be celebrating: eating, drinking, laughing, singing, dancing, fighting, kissing. Kissing.

Eliška blushed at the thought, but could not turn away from the memory of Lajos's lips on hers. How his fingertips went from gentle to urgent and then restrained again. Merely thinking on it made her belly burn, her heart stutter. *What must it be like to have even more*, she thought, and then shook her head against such an idea. Nothing good would come from Lajos's lips trailing across more than her hands, her face, her neck. Eliška closed her eyes, imagining being his and then started back to herself when the kettle started to whine. Ashamed of her unchecked thoughts, Eliška quickly set about preparing the tea for her mother. It was Mamička who needed her this time, and no matter how they fought, she would not turn away from her mother.

As Eliška ground the herbs, her mind wandered back and back, one thought snaking into another until she landed on her father. Her hands kept pace with the draught she was preparing, but her mind belonged to the single image of green eyes behind a smoke ring—and then her mother's lips, forever red with wine. Years had passed, Eliška remembered, with the wine on her mother's trembling lips. Years when Eliška curled up at the foot of Babička Olga's bed when her mother was deep in her drink. Then the harsh, ragged air about her when the drying out came. That's what Babička had called it—a drying out.

Eliška could still hear Babička's voice. See her pleated face dipped low to Eliška's, her scent of tallow, mushrooms, and age heavy about the old woman even then.

"Your mother has suffered a great loss," Babička had told her. "And has soaked her wounds long enough. Now we shall be the sun and dry out her sadness."

Eliška hadn't understood, but remembered the darkness in Babička's eyes as she took hold of Eliška's chin and tipped her blue-lipped face up. "You are her life now, bird. Take care with yourself."

Annoyance twitched like whiskers in Eliška's heart. She resented this responsibility, but could not help but wonder if their argument had pushed her mother too far. It had been some time since Mamička eased her grief with drink, and Eliška's guilt sprang up like a new shoot of grass, complete and swift. But she could not take back her words, and wasn't sure if she wanted to. Even now.

Removing the kettle, she poured the steaming water over the herbs and let the green, cleansing scent of them sweep over her. No, she did not regret speaking her heart, but neither would she punish her mother for her own cravings. With the steaming cup warm between her palms, Eliška moved toward her mother determined not to distress her, at least for tonight.

Twenty-Six

Albin

He had no memory of returning home, but home he most surely was. Albin found himself strolling through the halls of his ancestral castle. Trying not to panic, he kept moving, searching for a way to get out. Every candelabra, sconce, and chandelier glowed, the light reflecting off the polished wood and glass where garlands of greenery and hothouse flowers hung. Bejeweled men and women he didn't recognize swept up and down the halls and clustered in corners. Laughing and talking gaily, their faces flushed with wine and mirth as they turned to him in greeting, each displaying a wide, wolfish smile.

He moved to speak to them, to ask what the occasion was and locate his father, but felt pulled further down the wide corridor to the great hall where the double doors were flung wide. Couples whirled across the ballroom floor as if carried along by the strains of the music itself while the enormous hearth fire roared and cracked to its own rhythm. Dark shadows raced across the stone walls, and the air was thick with the scents of roasted meats and sweet breads, of Parisian perfumes and sweat. More confused than ever, Albin turned in a dizzying circle desperate to find a familiar face to explain what was going on. Then, suddenly, she was there: Eliška.

She appeared the way she first had—as if materializing out of the air in front of him. The loveliest of phantoms dressed simply in a blue gown, her soft brown hair loose down her back. His spirits rose as he stepped toward her only to have her pulled away, jerked backward as if on a string. Albin stopped, puzzled. The revelers around him didn't seem to notice and continued dancing. He tried again and Eliška was once more yanked away, this time her arms flung wide before dropping limp to her sides.

More cautiously, Albin stepped forward. Matching his gaze with her own full of longing, Eliška stretched her indigo mouth into a welcoming smile and reached for him. Rushing to her, Albin bit back a roar of frustration when Eliška jerked sideways and then spun around madly, always just out of reach. Her arms flailed, her head twisted back and forth so her long hair flew around her face. He opened his mouth to call her name, but no sound came out. Albin screamed again, silently, and rushed after her body as it danced manically around the room, weaving in and out of the elegant couples still waltzing as if they could not see her. All around him the dancers laughed and smiled, their gaping mouths red with wine.

Darting through the crowded room, Albin followed, straining to catch a glimpse of her blue dress. But she had disappeared. Despair rose sharply in him as he spun around, frantic, only to have Eliška appear in front of him again. Relieved, Albin reached out to grab hold of her lest she dart away again. He stopped. Her face had changed. Eliška's wide plum mouth had been painted into a tight red bow, her freckled nose powdered white, her amber lashes blackened. And a sense of dread crept up his back as beautiful Eliška's mouth dropped open at an unnatural angle and her meadow green eyes went doll black. He saw the strings attached to her arms and legs just before her marionette's body flew at him.

Albin sat up gasping for breath. Trembling all over, he blinked against the blackness as if to clear it away, but the room remained dark as pitch. He wiped a sobering hand over his face just as thunder clapped outside. Albin started and swore loudly before registering the beat of rain on the thatched roof; the howl of wind against the cottage shutters. The cottage. He was in the crofter's cottage, ripe with drink and filth, clearly having fallen back asleep after stumbling his way out of the woods.

Still unable to see anything, he groped around and found himself fully dressed on his cot. Cautiously, he swung his legs around and stood up. His head ached something fierce, but the darkness didn't spin. Nor did his stomach protest as he shuffled in the direction of the cold hearth. His throat ached with thirst and his mouth tasted of bile, but first things came first—fire. Once he'd coaxed a small flame from the embers, Albin made quick work of a pitcher of water blessedly still sitting on the table and the remains of a loaf of bread.

The storm continued outside as he sat shivering and miserable in front of the weak fire. What an ass he was. Glancing around the cottage for his cloak, Albin's gaze snagged on Miroslav's empty cot and he swallowed hard. Memories from the day before rose up and crashed over him, a surge of guilt nearly pulling him back under. The things he'd said. Miro's shattered expression. The tanner's accusations in the woods. Turning to the quivering flames, Albin stubbornly pushed them all away. No, he had to focus on the future now. There was no going back. Eliška was his destiny. She must be. He would woo her tomorrow at the harvest festival, and they would escape together for a life of adventure and passion. As he chewed the remaining crusts of bread, a plan solidified in his brain and his spirits lifted a bit.

Beyond the thick log walls, though the rain still fell hard, the thunder seemed to be drifting farther away, the wind running out of breath. Calming. Feeling more resolved and with a clearer head, Albin added a few more sticks of kindling to the hearth and stood up. Even in the damp chill of the cottage, he could clearly smell himself and had no intentions of whisking Eliška away while reeking like the swine he had behaved like.

He would do better and would start by bathing. But with no tub to wash in, only one option remained. Standing as close to the fire as possible without singeing his own ass, Albin stripped off all his closes and balled them up in his hands. Making sure not to let the fire blow out, he opened the door and strode into the storm. Shivering and shaking out his clothes and hair like a dog, he did not notice the peculiar patches of white swirling overhead as the rain rushed down his body, washing away the day.

TWENTY-SEVEN
ELIŠKA

estival day dawned thick as a dull knife, the air perfectly still. The bulk of the storm passed in the night leaving everything swollen and damp, the earth gorged on rain. There was an added softness in the air that curled the tips of her hair and made the wood squeak. It was a bad morning for Eliška. The kind when her head ached and her insides churned; when her heart felt like an over-fired clay jar in her chest, heavy and crumbling all at once. She shifted in the hard chair trying to ease her discomfort without moving too much. Mamička could not know. They had made their peace, but if her mother suspected she wasn't well, she'd hold fast to her threat and keep Eliška home from the festival. That couldn't happen. Eliška refused.

She hadn't seen Lajos since taking him to Babička Olga's, and had no way to know if he would keep his promise to stay for the harvest festival. The very marrow of her bones yearned to make it so, as if wishing hard enough could force her love's hand. But even she knew this to be foolish. He could disappear the way he'd arrived, like a dream. Eliška pushed the thought away. She would not believe his absence until she had no choice. No, she was going to the festival, the consequences be damned. And, perhaps, the charming wanderer would be true to his word and come for her. They could live in a tiny cottage with her training as a healer and him finding work. Perhaps he'd even take a position in the castle. Anything that kept him tucked into her arms each night.

But even as Eliška savored the daydream, dread washed over her like a cold wave of nausea. The Knowing, Babička Olga called it. The deep sense of truth a person gets in their belly when something isn't right. *'The heart will lie to itself,'* Babička said, *'but a body always knows the truth.'*

Nonsense, Eliška thought. Closing her eyes and senses against the feeling, she shifted in her chair again and firmly pushed the knowing away. It was just nervous excitement, and she didn't have time for worry. She must save her energy. But when Eliška opened her eyes, Mamička was eyeing her with a familiar, fretting expression.

No, no, no, no, thought Eliška and gave her mother a too-bright smile. Despite a kink in her neck, Eliška went perfectly still except for her hands, which picked up speed causing her thread to tangle. It was her mistake.

"I know you don't want me to ask, but how do you...you look..." Mamička didn't finish her sentence.

"I'm tired today," Eliška answered in truth. "I had a dream about the festival and it woke me too early. A good dream." She smiled a little at her mother then and went back to work as if nothing pained her at all.

Mamička, now fully recovered from the day before, wasn't convinced. "I know you have much to be angry with me over, but...your color is wrong. Does your head pain you? Chest? Let me see your fingers, Isha." She moved closer.

Eliška put on a smile and curled in her fingertips. Her nailbeds were the color of irises this morning. She wanted to bite life into her lips but didn't dare just then.

"No, Mamička. I feel fine, just tired from the...extra work yesterday. Walking to the Tothova's was a bit taxing. I promise to rest today instead of helping Babička Olga." Eliška hoped the truth of her promise to rest would soften the barbed reminder of her mother's drunkenness.

Concern waged against guilt in her mother's eyes. Eliška didn't dare hold her breath, but waited to see which emotion would win over her mother. When Mamička pinched her thin lips and let her stiff shoulders fall with a sigh, Eliška knew she'd won. Not even her mother would deny her this longed-for pleasure. Not after the last few days.

Her mother pointed a stern finger at Eliška. "No dancing," Mamička said, brows knit in worry. "Not even a *cardas*. I forbid it, Isha, and will tell Radek as much. I suspect he has been too busy in the fields to call, but I will make sure he knows tonight."

Eliška held herself still, her face impassive. Though her mother had noticed Radek's absence, she clearly did not know the reason and Eliška hoped to keep it that way. But damn her glass face, she could not keep her alarm from her expression. Thankfully, her mother misinterpreted her panic.

"I know you're disappointed," Mamička said with surprising gentleness. "I do. And it's a shame since you're such a natural dancer, but promise me you will not tire yourself." Impassioned, her mother came closer, grasping Eliška's cold, cold hands in her own. "Be content for once to watch and listen, yes? We will be together." She turned her pleading eyes on Eliška, demanding an oath. An oath Eliška knew in her heart she could not give.

"I swear to be careful. Just give me one dance. Please." The words slip out in a choked whisper. The naked pleading should have shamed her. It didn't. Not today. She felt no remorse at forcing her mother's hand. She wanted all of tonight. More than she wanted to see her father again. More than she wanted to learn Babička's crafts. Just one perfect night of passion and revelry and life was all she asked for. If her desperation was a reckless, clawing thing, so be it.

Her mother held firm. "Do not ask this of me, Isha. I worry for you so. I could not—" Mamička stood suddenly and turned away, but not before Eliška saw the spasm of fear cross her face, deepening the well-earned lines of her grief. Was fear always the price of such love?

Empathy gripped Eliška and she relented in word if not intention. "As you wish. I will be still and careful. Please don't be afraid. I only want to enjoy the night." If she had felt strong enough, she would have gone to her mother. They rarely embraced, but a yearning to wrap her arms around the only family she'd even truly known rose strong and sure in her. Instead, Eliška willed all her love into her face and smiled as the sun shines at noon.

Mamička looked over her shoulder and smiled back. Coming forward she touched Eliška's pale cheek, ran her strong fingers over her head and down her braid. The churning inside her stilled under her mother's hand. She hadn't been a child for a long time and even as her body and mind pined for things beyond the boundaries of these walls and the cage of her own body, she tipped her head into her mother's hand and felt safe.

"I feel as if I've been trapped in a fairy ring, dancing away my life. One day, you're a tiny girl, and the next moment, I see this lovely woman before me. What is a mother to do?"

Let me go, whispered a voice in Eliška's ear. She suspected it was her heart. But Eliška only lifted her head and smiled her most reassuring smile. "You have done everything you could, Mamička."

Her mother pressed her lips together and patted Eliška's cheek before moving back toward the stove. "I suppose I have little choice. Well then, I'll be back to change into my good *kroje* for the festival, but need to see to it the proper casks are tapped and the bunting gets hung in the square and..." her voice trailed off as she gestured broadly to the many tasks still undone.

"Are you sure..." Her mother's eyes rested on her again, worry and duty waring.

"Yes, Mamička. Truly. I am tired, but excited for tonight. I will finish my stitching and then start the bread. Go. You know they cannot do without you," she said, not above stroking her mother's ego to get her out the door.

"Well," said Mamička, as she smoothed her cap and brushed breadcrumbs from her apron. "Perhaps you're right. Would you like to wear my beads tonight?"

The Knowing gave a sharp twinge, but Eliška only brightened her expression and nodded. She'd never worn her mother's choker of milky beads before and recognized it as the peace offering it was. "I'd love to."

Mamička smiled.

Eliška felt a small, familiar thrill twist with guilt as her mother gathered her things and opened the door. When her mother paused in the doorway, she seemed little more than a familiar shadow against the bright outdoors. "Until tonight then, Isha."

"Until tonight," said Eliška as the door clicked close against her mother's retreating back.

TWENTY-EIGHT
ALBIN

The sun was setting in a splash of red and pink that glazed the bedecked square. Though the ground was still a bit soggy, the villagers had swept away most of the puddles and filled in the ruts. Dripping branches had been shaken out and festooned with colorful swags of bunting and flowers, while long tables from the harvest lunches once again groaned under the weight of food and drink. Even a few musicians had taken up residence by the well in preparation for the dancing. Clearly it would take more than a rainstorm to postpone the celebration of the vintage. From his hiding place at the edge of the woods, Albin could not have been more pleased. The scene was charming.

Clean, sober, and driven by a near painful lust, he crept along the outside of the village square scanning the crowd for any sign of her. Albin found himself sniffing the air in search of her scent—lavender, desperation, sweat—more like a beast in rut than a man love. He couldn't help it. He was aware of himself enough to know part of what drove him forward was grief. Shame. The tired, feckless boy in him longed to bury his face in a woman's neck and rest. To release the weight of his own privilege and cruelty and fall asleep thinking of nothing but her. Eliška. He hated himself for it, but couldn't press the longing down.

Carefully keeping to the shadows, Albin climbed atop a nearby stone and searched. Someone started playing a *dvojačka*, and the double shepherding flute's mournful howl mixed with the brighter sounds of the *koncovka* and the whine of the *ninera*, until music built and swirled as fast as the dancers hurrying to their places on the leveled dance floor. In a blur of red, green, white, and black, the dancers moved across the ground, their slapping feet and whoops of joy blasphemous to his aching heart and wicked tongue. Albin's throat squeezed at the simple beauty of it all, and he turned away hating them for it.

There. He spied her across the dance floor. Sitting on a low stool in the shadows and blessedly alone, she looked stunning. Small and bright and sharp; a priceless jewel whose worth only he truly perceived. Gratitude at her presence flooded his throat and he nearly shouted with relief. There was nothing left for him but her —no future he cared for outside of this moment. This passion. A sliver of guilt jabbed in his gut, but Albin pushed it aside. He'd tell her the truth. He would. Just not yet. He wanted this night to be unspoiled for both of them. Let the practicalities of his predicament wait one more day.

Albin leapt down from his stone perch and grabbed a cup of wine off the serving table. Downing it in one gulp, he picked up another and licked his lips. As the sweet heat of his father's wine hit his system, Albin started moving around the edges of merriment when a woman in a bright red gown blocked Eliška from view. He stopped short, sluicing wine over the cup and down his hand. The tall blonde had her back to him and was talking animatedly, while Eliška smiled up at the woman with what appeared to be genuine affection. He didn't need to see the woman's face to know she was noble. The wine in Albin's stomach sloshed as his limbs went cold. Carefully separated worlds were colliding, and there was nothing he could do but back away into the shadows, the wine forgotten and spreading across the ground in a dark stain.

Twenty-Nine

Eliška

She couldn't remember ever seeing the town square look so lovely. Twilight slid across the castle and soaked the woods, throwing everything into shadow. Though it was still early evening, every lantern and torch was lit and the dense air hung heavy with the smell of freshly crushed grapes and the spicy aromas of endless cooking.

Ribbons interwoven with sprays of wildflowers bedecked each doorway and draped into the streets where children chased and fought and danced in mimicry of the adults. Everyone, herself included, was scrubbed clean and dressed in their Sunday finest, ready for the long-awaited evening. She touched the strands of pale beads at her throat and smoothed a tingling hand over the bright apron of her best *kroje*. It had taken Eliška a long time to ready herself, but she'd been mostly pleased with her reflection in Mamička's small looking glass. Self-conscious now, she chewed at her dark lips.

Mamička had warily left Eliška sitting on a bench off to the side under strict orders not to dance and to send someone to fetch her from the food tables if necessary. Eliška had assured her mother she would, without the slightest intention to do so. Her head and neck still ached, and Lajos had yet to appear in the square as he'd promised, but Eliška held fast to her determination. She would enjoy this night no matter what.

"Eliška!"

She turned at the sound of her name and responded with a genuine smile when she saw Lady Anja approaching. The young woman's beauty was astounding. Her blonde hair was pulled back from her face with ringlets cascading around her soft shoulders. Her Viennese dress, though wildly formal for their village festival, was the most stunning gown Eliška had ever seen. The plush red fabric and full sleeves swayed and shone in the lingering sunset like a flame. Eliška felt small and plain even though her vest, skirt, and apron were jewel bright and intricately embroidered; her sleeves and cap edged with the finest lace in the village.

She curtsied politely and allowed Lady Anja to take her hand, feeling the strange, cold press of rings against her already aching fingers. But she didn't dare pull away from the excited young noble and felt a small thrill at the affection despite herself. She'd spent too many years as the object of village disdain not to feel a bit satisfied at the noblewoman's attention. Alena and her shallow friends would be simmering in pools of jealousy.

"Good evening, Lady Anja," Eliška said, drawing in close enough now to see the hand stitching on the lady's dress. Tiny golden leaves splayed across the neckline and sleeves added to the image of a dancing flame Eliška had first been struck with.

"It is a good evening indeed, is it not?" asked Lady Anja with a radiant smile.

"Your gown is very beautiful," Eliška blurted. She thought she should comment on the lady herself as well to avoid seeming rude, but it was the dress which took her breath away.

Lady Anja smiled with delight, her cheeks turning a lovely shade of pink. "Oh, do you like it? It was a gift from my father last

Christmastide. It is a bit out of style perhaps and too formal I'm afraid, but my other gowns have long sleeves and I thought it would be festive for today?"

Eliška was struck with the odd realization that the lady was seeking reassurance. The intonation of her voice quite clearly sought approval—from Eliška. *How odd*, Eliška thought, and found herself charmed even further by the young woman. What kind of noble cared if she looked well enough for a country harvest festival?

A good one.

Eliška steadied herself against the taller woman as Lady Anja wrinkled her brow with unease.

"Do not fret, my lady," said Eliška as she gave the warmest smile she could manage. "You are the most beautiful of all and sure to be crowned the Harvest Queen."

The lady pinkened further and leaned close. "You're too kind. And please call me Anja. I know it is forward, but we are in each other's confidences, no? You've been a friend to me, Eliška Ciernikova. I intend to be one back."

It was Eliška's turn to warm with pleasure, though she doubted her cheeks glowed as Anja's did. "Now it is you who are being too kind." Taking in the bedecked square and smiling faces, her heart calmed even though Lajos had not appeared. She was determined to enjoy herself. "In that case, would you like some wine...Anja?"

The lady's eyes sparkled with pleased mischief. "I thought you would never ask," she said and laughing, pulled them both toward the casks of wine as the musicians struck up a new tune and the flutes sang together in the growing dark.

She'd had too much wine, but couldn't seem to care since it dulled the ache in her chest. Eliška liked the bittersweet tang it left in her mouth, the bloom of warmth in her belly. Tipping her head back, she smiled in dreamy appreciation of the night. Everything seemed colored with a lurid brilliance. The music, dancers, and lanterns all blurred pleasantly and held a faint violet glow, as if infused with wine. The notion that they actually were infused with wine made her giggle, and for a moment, she felt more like a wild wine nymph than a sickly, blue-tinged girl from nowhere.

Next to her, Anja chuckled. "What are you smiling at now?"

Eliška turned toward her friend, who was noticeably less affected by the wine. Too happy to be self-conscious, Eliška gestured broadly to the revelry, her cheeks sore from smiling.

"Yes, it's a beautiful night. I'm glad to be here," Anja said, sipping her wine. As she did, the lamplight flashed against her bejeweled hand and Eliška was dazzled by the adornment.

"Your ring is striking, if I may be so bold?" Eliška had noticed the jewel earlier, but hadn't mentioned it. Now she couldn't keep from staring. Sitting on Anja's marriage finger, the stone glittered like a red egg in a nest of tiny white diamonds. While the pendant Eliška wore tucked under her dress was lovely, this ring was more extraordinary than anything she'd ever seen. A gem fit for royalty.

Lady Anja glanced at the stones on her hand as if they were embedded in a manacle. Eliška watched as the lady's well-controlled expression softened into quiet sadness, before quickly rearranging itself into a polite smile as she lifted her hand toward Eliška.

"Yes, it is. A gift from my fiancé," she said. And though her voice remained soft, Eliška heard the echo of anger in it. "I haven't worn it until tonight, but seeing as we will be announced soon my mother insisted."

Though she couldn't help but admire such a ring, Eliška knew something of that muted anger and it troubled her to think of the sweet noblewoman married off to the baron's reportedly hapless son. She leaned close to Anja's ear. "Will he be kind to you?"

Lady Anja slid her glaze toward Eliška and nodded. "I believe so. I've known him since childhood. We aren't close, but have written to one another on occasion and spent some time together as children." She paused then and lifted her regal chin. "I hope to be a fine couple."

Eliška, made bold by the wine and their easy companionship, pressed on. "But you do not love him?"

A bitter smile pressed itself onto the lady's pink mouth. "No, but I have seen where passionate love leads and have no wish to stumble down such a path again," she whispered so low Eliška hardly heard her.

Not knowing what to do but unwilling to let the lady believe her indifferent, Eliška reached out and gently squeezed her future baroness's other hand. Anja did not pull away.

"I will not be so foolish again," she said. "But we were often happy companions as children. Many years have passed, and I know we've both changed, but..." her voice trailed off as she slipped a delicate finger around one of her curls and pulled nervously. "Perhaps we can be so again."

Eliška considered this and was torn between admiration and pity. Why couldn't she be so content?

"Will it be enough?" The question came easily as she thought of Lajos: his golden hair and wicked smile, his wit and charm, the sensation of his hands and lips on her skin. She shivered, unable to imagine a life without such passion. A life with nothing more than companionship. It seemed unfair to have so little choice in the matter. But she wasn't surprised that wealth and nobility only made a girl more of a pawn. Eliška let out a shaking sigh. Suddenly, Radek's attention and her mother's tantrums seemed less of a burden.

Lady Anja smiled another sad smile and placed her ringed

hand over Eliška's. It was warm and slightly damp atop her dry, icy fingers.

"I hope so," she said, her voice lifting. "And who knows what time will bring, yes?"

Eliška smiled back as best she could, though she did not share the lady's airy confidence. She knew exactly what time would bring her. In that moment, Eliška knew she'd rather die than be stuck under the rutting body of Radek only to bear a babe she would never see grow. She stood up abruptly. Rudely, though she did not intend to be so.

"Forgive me, my—Anja. But it is getting late and there is someone I must find."

Lady Anja's pale eyebrows rose, but she released Eliška's hand. "Of course. On one condition: you must confide in me whom you are rushing off to meet." Then she grinned fully at Eliška, and she knew the lady wasn't vexed.

When Eliška didn't answer, the lady wrinkled her nose with pleasure and gave her a sly smile. "Come now. I see how it is and will be married off soon, so indulge me with your romance. Does he have a name?"

Eliška, who could never have confided in her own companions, returned the lady's smile and leaned in. "Lajos." More anxious than ever, she stepped back even as Lady Anja's mischievous smile broadened, her eyes twinkling.

The lady actually clapped her hands with excitement. "And is he handsome? Of good family? Romantic?"

Eliška cocked her head and blushed deeply. "He is the most handsome man I've ever seen but, in truth, I do not know about his family. He is here only for the harvest with his brother. But," she added quickly, "never have I met a more well-spoken or charming man." She knew how this sounded, was not deaf to the audacity of her own claims, but Eliška could not make herself care. He could be the son of swine, and she would not turn her back on Lajos.

Lady Anja's smile softened, but if she judged Eliška in her heart, she did not show it. "Well then, if he is worthy of you, then you must enjoy the night while it lasts."

Eliška curtsied deeply to her mistress before whirling around and flying swiftly into the night.

After leaving Anja, Eliška had carefully avoided her mother and Radek only to find herself engulfed in a merry circle of girls all admiring an elaborate flower crown. Woven together with every type of local bloom in shades of white and yellow, violet, pink, and red strung through with purple ribbons, it hung from a peg on the old belltower just outside the village square. Used to crown the Vintage Queen, Eliška had secretly coveted it since childhood, as had every other girl in the village, she was sure. This year's crown was even more beautiful than most, a vivid halo of blossoms, and Eliška found herself torn between yearning for it and shaming herself for caring. She would never be chosen. But it didn't stop her from imagining. Wanting.

There was no question as to who would be named this year's queen, and Eliška smiled through her longing at how lovely Lady Anja would be with the riotous crown pressed against her pale hair. The red flowers were the exact shade as her gown; the purple ribbons dark and lush as grapes. Just then the harvest horn sounded and Pán Nagy burst through the ring of girls to retrieve the flower crown. Behind him, with Alena simpering at her heels, was Anja.

Eliška moved swiftly into the shadows to rest and watched the stern harvest master crown the young noblewoman the Vintage Queen to delighted shouts. Eliška clapped from her perch outside the circle of revelers as the music started back up and Anja danced by with an overjoyed Vladimir on her arm. The boy looked ready to perish from pride.

No one noticed her in the background, least of all the festive dancers, but Eliška smiled anyway. Her head swam slightly, and her hands and feet ached, but she was happy for her new companion. The memory of Anja's befouled petticoats and tear-stained face the night in the woods proved wealth and nobility didn't guarantee happiness or safety. Through her envy, Eliška rejoiced for her new friend tonight.

But even as the celebration pitched higher, a sadness crept in. Lajos had not come, nor had she seen his tall, stern brother. She was not fool enough to think all men to be honest, but the burning in his eyes when he'd touched her had spoken of true affection, hadn't it? Surely the way he gazed at her held a grain of truth. As she thought on this, the divination from the petals leaped to mind. She shivered with a sudden chill and tried to push the warning away. The night was still young, and she would not dwell on the possibility of his falsehood. Not yet.

So she waited and watched until despair threatened to choke the very life from her fragile bones. Then, like a single candle flaring amid the darkening night, a presence slipped from the shadowy woods at her back and stood next to her. She didn't have to look as heat spread through her chest. Lajos held out a cup of wine, casually, as if he'd always been there. She took it, letting her fingers graze his.

"It seems the festival is a success," he said, lip curling slightly in what might have been amusement. Or derision. "I'm sorry to have missed it." He took her hand gently in his, entwining their fingers. "But I cannot say I regret having you all to myself."

Eliška's breath thrashed against the cage of her ribs with excitement. Her skin warmed under the pressure of Lajos's hand and she smiled. Leaned into his flattering words as a butterfly leans in for nectar. His petal lips parted, inviting her closer. He smelled of wine and sweat. She wanted to taste him again.

"I feared you wouldn't come," she said, her breath rasping with fatigue. "But you did." She sipped the wine for strength and licked her lips. Then she rose and stepped into his shadow. "I care for nothing else tonight."

Moonlight slanted through the trees, illuminating Lajos's smile. "Forgive me for inspiring doubt. I wanted only to be here. With you."

Eliška laced her free hand through his and met his hungry stare in the crisp white moonlight. His mouth found Eliška's and opened as if trying to swallow her whole. The dry cool feel of his lips and the pressure of his fingertips lit a flame low in her belly. She tightened around this new throbbing and leaned into him. Opened her mouth. He smelled and tasted so different from anyone she'd ever met. Not only of wine and bread, but like adventure and wanting. Escape and passion.

He released her hands and ran his up her arms, leaving goosebumps in his wake. One big hand found the back of her neck, the other her waist. In turn, Eliška grabbed hold of his arms to keep from falling, her head tipped back. Breaking the kiss for a moment, she opened her eyes and found Lajos's eyes watching her above their kiss. He looked ravenous. A man half-starved and it was her kiss he hungered for. An unfamiliar feeling filled her chest like a billowing sheet: power. Eliška—small, poor, frail—had power. Letting this knowledge expand into every crevice of her being, she smiled up at Lajos, drunk on his desire. He smiled back, dimples winking, and bent to kiss her again, but she stepped back.

"Where can we go?" she asked.

Lajos paused, tilting his head. "To be alone?"

Eliška nodded, the sail in her chest expanding further. She felt like she could fly. Lajos's jovial eyes went serious. She could smell his wanting mingling with her own, but a sudden unease grasped her. Had she misread him? Perhaps Lajos didn't want her in the same way. Then Lajos leaned in and kissed her again, slowly this time as if tasting her and her spine tingled. The gentleness of this kiss erased all thought or care.

"I know of a place," he said after leaning away. His voice still held a question. "If you are sure? You would not prefer to stay and watch the dancing?"

In answer, Eliška took hold of his hands, her head swimming with recklessness. "I have never been more sure of anything."

Lajos hesitated still, his hands trembling slightly in hers as he glanced around. They were totally alone. "Follow me," he whispered after a long moment, his eyes a wet shine in the moonlight.

Eliška sucked in as much cool air as her lungs would hold and followed, leaving the bright sounds of the festival behind her.

THIRTY
ALBIN

He hadn't planned for this. Dreamed of it, yes. Fantasized about what he'd do with her lovely body day if he ever had the honor to touch her since the moment he laid eyes on her. Despite it all, he hadn't intended to seduce Eliška. Feast on her violet mouth and fill her small, winged ears with tender words, and convince her to leave this place with him? Yes. But here she was walking beside him into the night, trusting him. Albin felt green and humbled as he squeezed her thin hand, praying like a heretic he wouldn't disappoint her.

He told Eliška he knew of a place, which was true. But the dense copse of trees was a half-remembered thing from his one disastrous childhood adventure with Miro, and he had no idea in what condition they'd find it. Albin recoiled from the memory and glanced at Eliška. She looked beautiful in her fine clothes, but paler than usual, as if the moonlight had entered her blood and lit her from within. A sense of unease flared in his mind, but he stamped it out. It had just been a long, strange week.

The wind picked up sharply, rattling the tell-tale aspen leaves he was looking for. His pulse spiked. "Almost there," he said to fill the heavy silence.

Eliška nodded, but she trembled in his grasp. Albin stopped and reached for her other hand, turning her to face him in the darkness. "Would you have me take you back?"

She didn't hesitate. "No. I'm just a bit tired." Her voice was breathy, and his stomach tightened at the sound.

"I can help with that," he said and scooped her into his arms. Eliška gave a startled little laugh as she clung to his shoulders. Then her face was right in front of him, eclipsing everything. She felt warm and soft in his arms. He pulled her close to his chest and her usual scents of lavender and salt mixed with the dark green smells of the woods. Moonlight struck the curve of her jaw, and he swallowed. "Is this alright?"

With her eyes wide and her lips slightly parted, Eliška nodded before resting her head on his shoulder. The tenderness of it unknotted something cinched tight inside him, and Albin let out a contented sigh. Then he pressed a kiss to the top of her head and stepped in among the ghostly trees.

Miraculously, it took only a few minutes to find what he'd been looking for. Several paces into the copse, the white trunks thinned leaving a small circle of ferns, which lay like a plush black carpet on the forest floor. Moonlight slid through the narrow trunks, but the woods around were still. They were alone.

"It isn't the kind of comfort I would like to give you, but what do you think?" he asked, setting Eliška on her feet.

Keeping a tight hold on his arms, she tipped her head back to take in the sweep of star-brightened sky overhead. Her mouth curved into a pleased smile. "It's wonderful," she said, but the expression changed as her gaze fell to him. Eliška chewed nervously at the corner of her bottom lip and Albin settled his hands around her waist, breath tight in his throat. The cool air between them hummed as his heart hammered.

"Don't be frightened. I will take care of you," Albin whispered and bent to her.

He pressed his mouth to the tip of her nose, her cheek, the

damp corner of her mouth, always gentle, coaxing, tasting, ready to savor every sweet inch of her. He held his desire tightly in check both for her innocence and for his own satisfaction. She was delicious and he wanted this to last. But Albin was not prepared for her hunger. Each time his lips avoided her mouth, she made a tiny, frustrated sound and tried to capture his.

With his arms firmly at her back, Albin nuzzled into her neck before gently sucking at the skin below her jaw. Eliška shivered and made the frustrated hum again. "Patience, darling," he murmured into her ear. "I must be gentle with you."

She jerked away and grabbed his face, forcing his eyes to hers. "No," Eliška said again. "I want more than your gentleness. I want your passion."

Albin's body blazed with longing when he saw the truth in her face. She wanted this and he would do as she bid. His mouth crashed to hers and he did not relent, did not slow, did not ask, but pressed every part of them together. Her mouth opened and she gave no resistance to his tongue, his teeth. Though she let him lead, his tiny lover gave back every ounce of passion he poured into her, fisting her cold hands in his hair and clinging to him as if to life itself.

With one hand clamped behind her neck, Albin filled his free hand with her breasts, lush for all her fragility and he nearly lost himself like a boy when she arched into him, the tips of her breasts hard against his palms.

"My God. Eliška," he rasped against her bruised mouth. "You'll destroy me. You're so fine it pains me."

"Please," she gasped into his mouth and bit his bottom lip. She tasted like wine. "Please." Her voice was thin, but insistent, and he would not disobey.

Easing them to the ground, he tried to be gentle; cradled her head and hips under his hands for he knew the earth would not forgive her tender flesh. But she writhed against him amid the swaying fronds and Albin fought to retain control. His cock ached and his mind blurred as he ran a hand under her skirts, trailing along the soft flesh of her thighs. The sharp jut of her hip fit perfectly into his palm.

Slowly, he dragged his hand to her center and Eliška gasped when his fingertips brushed between her legs. His own breath caught and his hand shook.

"Yes?" he asked, his voice a rasp.

She nodded, and he kissed her deeply as his fingers explored. When she moaned and arched against his hand, Albin went rigid with wanting. His head swam with her scent.

"If I must stop, tell me now, my love," Albin said through clenched teeth, his stillness a question.

She swallowed his words and pressed her hips up in a last command. Frantic with lust, Albin settled himself between her legs and freed himself from his breeches. She was soft and hot against his skin despite the cool, damp world around them.

"It may hurt at first," he warned, forcing himself to move with tenderness. "You must tell me if I am to stop."

"I'm not afraid," Eliška breathed and kissed his neck. "I want to feel everything."

Nodding, Albin slowly pressed inside and stole her breath with a long, hungry kiss.

⚬

After, Eliška smiled up at him through a sheen of tears that leaked down her glowing face. He kissed them away, trailing his mouth across her jaw and neck, the corners of her eyes and ears, always following the salty path.

"Forgive me, darling. I never want to hurt you," he said, unsure if she regretted her request that he not stop. She had gone very still, and he watched her closely, concerned.

"No. I feel perfect," she said with a deep, sated breath and curled her fingers into the hair at his nape.

Relief ran through Albin and he shivered, the cool air already drying the sweat from his brow. She was lying of course, but he didn't contradict her. She was braver than he would ever be. Selfishly, he wanted to keep her that way, if only in his mind. Brave and pure and his. He couldn't bear to break the spell.

She squirmed under him then and twin lines of concern appeared between her brows. He felt himself rising again. Christ, he thought. She could be the death of him if she wanted. He was mad for her. Needing a little space to think, Albin gently eased himself away from her hips. "Are you sure you're well, darling?"

"I'm...slick," Eliška whispered. Her voice betrayed her distress.

"Ah," he said, understanding her discomfort and kissed her forehead smooth. "Do not be frightened. That's perfectly normal, I'm afraid. Here. Let me help." As much as he hated to pull his body away, he eased back in the dark and grabbed the edge of his long shirt. He caught a last glimpse of her pale thighs and the dark smear of her sex before she pulled down her skirts. Albin smiled at her in the dark, his heart squeezing. Everything about her was pleasing. Even this timidity. Carefully, he reached out to help her smooth the white petticoat into place.

"I'm afraid I don't have a handkerchief, but this will help," he said and tore a strip of his shirt free. "Let me," he said, wiping his seed and her blood away as gently as possible. Eliška went still under his touch, but didn't pull away. Another girl might have been embarrassed, but his Eliška looked straight at him and smiled back through the dark.

When they finally rose, she took the soiled cloth from his hand. He didn't think she should be discovered with such a thing, but Eliška folded it carefully and tucked the visceral evidence of their joining deep into her bodice.

"I must go back," was all she said, her eyes glassy.

Albin didn't like the look of them, and kissed her hard against some nameless fear rising in his throat. But he did as she asked, and walked her to the edge of the woods, letting her go on alone at her insistence.

"It will be best. For tonight. Come for me tomorrow," she whispered against his final kiss before disappearing into the starlight, a ghostly outline of skirt moving among the trees toward the glow of the festival, which looked like nothing so much as a gathering of the fairies in the dark of night.

Guilt plucked at him like a cloud of tiny insects; insistent and bothersome. He should have denied her. Done something honorable for once. For even as Albin remembered the taste of her, he knew it was Eliška who would pay the price for their love. Albin knew this as surely as he knew everything—desire included—had a price. Especially for a woman.

It was a lesson his father had taught him well, at the expense of Albin's mother. His father's one redeeming quality was he had loved Albin's mother. Desired her so much he got her with child again and again even as she lost each to the bloody battle of the birthing room. All except Albin. When she finally bled away her life's blood after conceiving again, both husband and son mourned her hard in their own ways. But a small part of Albin couldn't help hating his father as he supposed fathers sometimes hate the children who take their wives in childbirth. Albin simply couldn't help himself.

But he had not been honorable and there was only one thing left to do. He would go home in the morning and speak with his father. If he renounced his inheritance, he would no longer be an eligible match and the engagement would be called off. Then he could broker a peace deal with their neighbors some other way. His fiancée would have no problem securing another husband.

Cloaked in the warm night air with the stars winking through the trees, Albin gave a heavy exhale and started up the road toward the castle. He could not let Eliška down.

THIRTY-ONE
ELIŠKA

It was not as she had expected, the hard-soft joining of their bodies. The blood, yes. Eliška knew something of this. Mumbled stories of wedding nights and hayloft trysts rustled older women's lips even when small ears were around. And the too-loud whispers of her married peers were inescapable. But Eliška discovered other things. Unexpected things done with teeth and tongue. The way he'd looked at her, questioning, and waited for her answer. The precious ache of opening. The frantic rhythm. The heat. The salt of Lajos's sweat on her lips and his breath, rough with tenderness as he whispered her name while he shuddered and bucked against her hips. It was on these memories, and not the burgeoning embarrassment of her new knowledge, that Eliška thought as she gingerly took her place back on a shadowed bench at the edge of the square.

Her neck ached and her stomach wobbled, but everything paled against the deep, pleasurable fire in her core. Dizzy and desperately in need of water, Eliška nonetheless smiled stupidly at the couples dancing by. She had yet to dance, but had also escaped the smothering attentions of her mother and Radek, a gift she did not take for granted. But the thought of both lit up her nerves—had she been missed?

Another part of her mind was fascinated with new understanding and bubbled over with questions she could not ask. Or could she? There was perhaps one person she could question about the act of love without fear. After all, she thought, rubbing at her arm as it began to ache, a girl did not find herself with an unwanted babe without having lain with a man. Gathering up her skirts and courage, Eliška picked her way through the crowd, her eyes searching for the young noblewoman dripping in ruby red and crowned with flowers.

As Eliška searched for Lady Anja, one thought kept rolling through her scattered thoughts—Mamička must not know until her and Lajos were betrothed. Then all things would be right, and she would have a love of her choosing and continue her work with Babička. Warmth surged through her at the idea, exaggerating the ache in her jaw. Pausing, Eliška looked around for something to drink before starting violently as a familiar form pushed into the center of the dance floor, scattering dancers like kicked pebbles.

"Stop the music! I have an announcement!" roared Radek Varga above the noise.

Everyone turned toward the tall tanner, his eyes and hair blazing in the light of the lanterns. Many shoot him baleful looks and protested the interruption. Most were deep into their cups and in no mood for civility. The festival was one of the few days Father Timotej turned a blind eye to such revelry and the villagers made the most of it.

"*Bud' ticho!* All of you!" he yelled, waving his arms at the musicians and cutting off the remaining dancers. "I have news which concerns the entire village."

At this, the grumbling crowd quieted down, their attention piqued by Radek's bold claim. Suddenly, a terrible, dizzying dread took hold of Eliška. She closed her eyes against it, begging she was wrong. He was going to call out her ruin in front of everyone. He must have seen her and Lajos sneak off and was taking his revenge. Her stomach rolled and she fought the urge to be sick.

"Get on with it then, Varga," shouted Pán Nagy. "You're wasting our time." Many around him nodded.

Eliška tilted her head trying to ease the ache in her neck, and fought the urge to flee as Radek scanned around, clearly looking for someone. She leaned back into the shadows, but it was too late. He'd seen her. His expression darkened in the firelight, his jaw muscles working. But his gaze moved past her without further acknowledgement, and she sagged with relief and fatigue. She needed to lie down.

Instead, he pointed to the opposite edge of the circle toward the road leading to the crofter's cottage. "Forgive me, friends. I would not interrupt this night if it were not important. But I have discovered something you must all hear," he said, his deep voice raised high over the hum of confusion. "We have deceivers in our midst. Liars. Thieves."

Muffled cries went up from the crowd and Radek sneered with pleasure. A cold shiver bloomed at the back of Eliška's neck and raced along her limbs like hungry vines seeking purchase. Was Radek talking about her and Lajos as she'd first feared? But the accusations didn't make sense. Even she would assent that Lajos was a flirt and secretive. And perhaps Radek considered Lajos the thief of her affection, though he had no right to. But a liar? Clearly his jealous mind had invented some story to humiliate her for not accepting him. Eliška, along with every set of eyes in the square, turned toward the empty road to which Radek pointed. Trembling with agitation, Eliška willed Lajos to appear and put an end to Radek's show.

"Get to the point, man!" came a shout.

Radek raised his hands as if blessing the crowd, and Eliška's stomach turned yet again. He was enjoying this.

"As you wish," he shouted and reached within his vest, pulling out a long, gleaming dagger. Eliška squinted to see it more clearly, but saw only a flash of gold and pale green stone. She could not make out any details, though it looked fine even at a distance.

"Nearly every year we have travelers come to work the harvest alongside us. Indeed, we depend on their strong backs and sure hands," Radek said, meeting the eyes of fellow harvesters around the circle. "But have you ever seen a stranger pair than the two who call themselves Lajos and Otokar?"

Murmurs of assent rippled around her as Eliška stepped free of the shadows, more confused than frightened now. What was Radek doing? She had little love for Otokar, but what could he have done to invoke this public shaming?

"Have you ever seen an older brother grovel before a second son in such a manner? Ever heard a peasant with finer speech?" He paused, looking around the tightening circle. "Or known one to carry such a blade as this? I found this in the crofter's cottage when I was sent to speak with them about missing the final day of harvesting only to find one gone and the other drunk." He held the elegant weapon aloft and a ripple of irritated confusion traveled over the crowd.

The wind started to rise.

Eliška stepped forward again, her heart beating wildly. Where was Lajos? He had to be here. She could not defend him alone. He must refute this nonsense.

"What of it?" someone shouted. "Does anyone here own that? If it was not stolen from us, why are we to care?"

Again, the mob thought in unison, and whispers of lost items fluttered around the circle.

"You miss the point, Pavol. As usual," Radek jeered to a smattering of laughter. "It is not what has been stolen."

Eliška, her body and mind reeling, started forward again, her blood surging at his presumption as he went on.

"But the fact is this weapon wasn't stolen at all! Friends, I believe we have had noblemen in our midst all along. Spying and degrading both themselves and us with their deceit."

Shouts of outrage and fear rose up from the crowd like smoke, choking Eliška as she followed Radek's gaze back toward the road where a lone figure had appeared out of the dark. Like a specter from a dream, Lajos stood against the blackness, taking in the scene before him. The firelight licked at his feet, but he stayed just beyond it, shadowed, his face unreadable in the distance.

"He appears!" Bellowed Radek in triumph. "Come and defend yourself if you will, though I do not think you'll have much to say. My lord."

Not real, not real, not real, Eliška thought over and again with each heartbeat as she pushed her way to the center of the crowd. Radek was wrong—he must be—and was about to ruin her life without the slightest care. If Lajos would not come forward to defend himself against this slander, then she would.

Before she could move, a strong hand clamped onto her arm and spun her around.

"Let go," hissed Eliška as Mamička's face came into focus in front of her.

"Isha, where have you been? What has happened?" her mother asked, her eyes wide with fear. A strand of silver hair blew free from her mother's bun, her face damp with sweat, and Eliška knew she wasn't the only one in distress.

"You must let me go, Mamička. You must!" With all her failing strength, she wrenched out of her mother's grasp and stumbled into full view. She could feel everyone's eyes slide over to her and then back to Radek and then over to Lajos again. At the sight of her, Lajos started forward, but Eliška looked at no one save Radek.

"Go back to your mother, Eliška," he said quietly. "This does not concern you."

"It most assuredly does concern me."

Radek's eyes flashed like a wounded animal before he turned his back on her. "Lajos!" he shouted, as his rival stepped closer. "If that is even your name. What say you? Are you a thief who takes what does not belong to him," Radek said, holding out the precious blade. "Or are you something else entirely?"

Eliška grabbed hold of Radek's sleeve, releasing his tanner's stench like a plague. "Stop it. This has nothing to do with him." She jammed a finger into his face. "You are angry at me. Jealous of the one thing refused you and now shame only yourself with these lies!" The words slid from Eliška's mouth like venom.

"He has poisoned your mind. You must listen to me. He is a liar," Radek said, trying to capture her hands in his as if they were tiny birds, strapped and startled. "A spy and a thief come to ruin us. He is not what he seems."

Eliška's head started to spin. "I must do no such thing. I have never been yours to command. Go to the devil, Radek Varga."

He did not budge, but stood stoic as a mountain towering over her, his brows furrowed like twin flames. Eliška heaved herself away from him as the circle of onlookers broke open next to them, spilling Anja's, her parents, and their entourage into their midst. The noble family's jewels winked like brilliantly colored eyes in the night.

"By God will someone tell me the meaning of all this?" the fat viscount bellowed. "Where is the music? Is this some sort of country farce? A crude lark?"

Eliška blinked as the villager's faces around them hardened at the insult. She couldn't help but think the man's fleshy pink face resembled that of a pig.

"It is no game, my lord," came Radek's cool, hard voice. "But a deception of the foulest kind. That man claims to be a lowly harvester traveling for work with his brother who is now curiously missing. Everything in his manner is peculiar."

Sweat broke out across her whole body as Lajos finally stepped forward. He looked as ravaged and desperate as she felt, and so beautiful it hurt. Dear God, why didn't he say anything?

Eliška watched Lajos closely, though her vision blurred with fatigue. He remained silent, though his expression blazed with defiance.

Radek pressed on. "Yet he carries a weapon fit for nobility." Radek held up a gleaming dagger with a pale green handle. "And drinks the rarest of our vintages." With his other hand, he produced an empty wine bottle from the bag slung across his shoulders. The Pálffy family crest was clearly visible.

Eliška's ears started to buzz, her reasoning lost in the terrible roar of outrage coming from the crowd. She looked around in horror. Everyone was mistaken. They had to be. Surely this was as the viscount said: a terrible jest. A cruel joke. Fire raced up and down Eliška's neck as she started toward Lajos only to freeze at the sound of a voice she had every reason to trust.

"Albin? Is it really you?"

All eyes turned toward the speaker. Lady Anja stepped forward from between her parents, her gaze trained on Lajos. "Why did you not send word you would be here?"

He did not meet her stare, his face stricken and pale. Eliška was close enough now to see

his eyes were red with tears, his lips pressed thin.

"Albin," Anja said again, her voice soft. She looked around them hesitantly. "Whatever has happened, we will make it right." The lady stepped closer, still speaking to Lajos who stared at the earth as if it might cave in under his feet. As if he prayed it would.

When Lajos didn't reply, Anja pressed her hand to her mouth in distress, revealing the enormous ruby ring sparkling on her finger.

Eliška went cold and very, very still, remembering her conversation with the young noble earlier. She was indeed engaged to be married to the heir of Castle Hrozno. Eliška's gaze trailed over to... Lajos?

Trembling all over, Eliška waded deeper into the center of the broken circle and felt every eye bore into her. With all the strength she could muster, Eliška made her voice bright, her smile frenzied and full of teeth. "Do not play, Lajos. Lady Anja has been most kind to me and you must stop this wicked tale. Tell them who you are." With her eyes fixed on Lajos, she waited.

He remained silent, with eyes roaming everywhere but at her. Panicked, Eliška boldly went to him and took hold of her beloved's tear-stained face, forcing him to meet her gaze. Her head whirled and her stomach clenched at the movement, but she didn't let go. His hands clasped tenderly around her wrists as he turned his head to kiss her palm. "Tell them they've made a mistake." Her demand boomed around the square like a drum. *Tell me*, she thought.

Tell me the truth.

Lajos finally met her pleading stare as his words drove through her, sharp as any blade. "I cannot. The tanner speaks the truth."

A cry of satisfaction erupted behind her, and she swayed.

"Eliška, please forgive me," Lajos whispered, still holding her wrists, his face a shattered mask. "I love you. I only wanted you."

She pulled away just as the cursed weapon that was his undoing landed with a thud on the ground at their feet. Its jade and gold hilt winked cruelly up at her and the world spun.

Lajos kicked the evidence of his deception away as if it were a snake before turning to the crowd, his face severe with emotion. "Hear me!" he roared, shocking the agitated crowd into silence. "I am most grieved to say that this foul tanner is not completely wrong." Now galvanized into movement, Lajos paced back and forth with barely controlled rage. "Rest assured that I am no thief," he hissed. "For a man cannot steal what is rightfully his."

At this, he stopped pacing, looked at Eliška with such ferocious longing she thought he might fall at her feet. Instead, he swallowed hard and turned away to face Anja. "But what *my betrothed* says is true. I am Albin Pálffy von Erdod, heir to Castle Hrozno and future baron of this estate. I must beg your forgiveness for my deception. I truly meant no harm." The crowd was silent.

Eliška couldn't breathe and clutched at her chest, wheezing.

From the corner of her eye, she saw Anja's beautiful face go white, her expression grave and unreadable as the moon. Then the man whom Eliška loved but could no longer name, pointed a trembling finger at her.

"This remarkable girl is innocent of blame. I am the villain." His voice broke, and even now her quaking arms reached out to comfort him.

And then Radek was between them, his strong back eclipsing her view of Lajos—Albin—as she stumbled away, her stomach churning. Hands Eliška did not recognize tried to steady her, but she pushed them away, frantic as an injured bird. She was dreaming. She must be dreaming for this could not be happening. Eliška clenched her fists, pressing her fingernails into her palms with violent force.

Wake up wake up wake up, she commanded herself as the weight of the village's eyes and her own shock pressed down on her aching head, back, chest, heart. She did not wake up.

Eliška shook her head and started to flee, then stopped, suddenly aware of a strange weight around her neck. She looked down. At the end of a gold chain, the blue jewel rested below her breasts like a small, calcified heart, the color of twilight. Her heart. She lurched forward at the thought, and it swung like a pendulum, *tick tocking* to the beat of her misery. Wrapping a tingling hand around the stone, she pulled the tainted gift over her head. The chain tangled in her hair, pulling strands from her braids as she spun around to face the crowd. Radek had moved aside, and she caught a glimpse of him standing between Mamička and Babička Olga, whom she hadn't seen yet. Her heart lurched at their tear-stained faces.

Eliška pulled her eyes away until they found Lajos—Albin— and she threw the necklace with all her might. He let it strike his chest and fall to the ground without flinching. His eyes bored into her, his mouth trembling.

Now, a familiar voice was calling to her, over and over, crying out her name, but she heard little over the rush of wind against her ears. The breeze rose again, sharpening, wrapping around her, pulling at her skirts and petticoats as if begging her to dance. She took a step, then another, as pain shot down her left arm. Eliška thought then of swaying gently in her lover's arms in the woods. Of the way he'd carried her into the meadow. Touched her with reverence. Her traitorous heart yearned to go back.

She shook her head against the thought and her foot struck something on the ground. Focusing hard, she saw the elegant, jade-handled dagger at her feet. She picked it up. The blade hung from her hand, heavy as sin. Gripping the smooth hilt, lifted the blade to the torchlight. Veins of gold raced through the steel shaft, flashing her haggard reflection back at her. Her bruised mouth and ashen face were nothing compared to her haunted eyes, bright and wild. She swung the blade toward the crowd, anchored by its weight.

Suddenly, strong hands came from behind and clamped onto her shoulders, pulling the blade from her weakened grip. It felt good to be held up by another's strength, but the stench of her captor turned her stomach and she struggled against him, scratching at the vile truth-bearer.

"Eliška." Her name slid from his mouth like a hiss. "Come to me and we will forget this night."

She opened her mouth to laugh, but could only wheeze at him, a vicious smile on her blue lips as she spun in his arms. The big tanner's eyes were soft with pleading, his jaw clenched. He threw the brilliant blade to the ground.

Eliška had no room for sympathy in her heart. "You did this, Radek," she said, speaking his name as if it were a slur. "Do not pretend to save me," she spat, her wavering gaze finding his. "You cared nothing for what I wanted. You thought only of yourself and your own desires."

"Then we are the same," he whispered. His hands fell away, and she dropped to her knees. Her throat ached with unshed tears, her chest on fire. She wanted only to slip into the earth, taking every betraying, greedy soul down along with her. But she hadn't the strength to move, and hung limp even as hands familiar as her own slipped around her. Cradled her.

"Isha, my girl. Get up. I'll take you home." Her mother's voice brushed against her cheek. "Your home, where you never have to leave if you don't want to. And we'll be happy together, just us. I swear on your father's grave. I will take care of you always."

Eliška turned her head and found her mother's face hanging over her own, a mask of terror. Eliška tried to smile against the fire behind her eyes. "I'm sorry, Mamička. I wanted more."

"Shhh," her mother cooed. She twined her strong arms around Eliška and pulled her to her feet. "Babička and I will take you home."

At these words, the Knowing she'd felt the day her father died filled Eliška and forced the frozen tears from her eyes. Her head swam as she kissed her mother's cheek, as slick with tears as her own. Eliška swallowed hard against the burning in her stomach.

She is coming home, woman.

The strange voice echoed through Eliška's skull coming both from within and outside of her mind. Eliška tried to turn her head, scanning the square for the unknown speaker.

This way. Come, sister.

Terrified, Eliška reared back, dangerously unsteady. She stumbled. Stopped. Shuffled further and stood swaying, a marionette on tangled strings. Eliška glanced around, dazed, but saw nothing that made sense. Her mother, a torch lit with terror; Lady Anja's white and startled. Faces she recognized but knew nothing of flecked her vision but could not hold her wavering gaze. Cold. She was so cold and yet her neck ached with fire. Pain pierced her chest. She kept touching it, surprised to find herself whole. Surely a blade had sliced open her heart. She felt ready to be cleaved in two.

"Bird?"

Eliška turned at the sound of her pet name. The healer held out her gnarled hands. She recognized her name, but the old woman's voice sounded far away as if coming from a great distance. Eliška started to move and then a white light flashed off to the side and she turned toward it, staring. The white shadow. Long and billowing, it didn't hold a shape, but rippled on the air. Eliška watched it. With her last moments of strength, she darted after it and the despairing cry of her old friend fluttered to the ground.

As Eliška followed the shadow around the square it grew denser, taking shape, and glimmered like a patch of snow. Tears blurred her sight as she stumbled along, forgetting the pain racing through her like fire. The sickness boiling in her belly. What did she care? She was a fool just as they'd all said. Naïve and wayward and stupid. Mad for wanting what was never for her.

She stopped. The shadow hung behind Lajos—Albin—crowning his head in a ghostly glory. The vile dagger, evidence of his betrayal, lay discarded at his feet. His golden face was a ruin. A hollowed-out gourd of falsehood. No matter his tears and wailing and reaching, she would not go to him. Now he, her enchanted lover, was more mirage than the thing behind him and she looked away as the splitting of her heart took hold.

The hewing ripped through her in a bolt of hot pain, and Eliška tasted salt and bile on her lips as she crumpled. The ground rushed up to welcome her home.

THIRTY-TWO

ALBIN

lbin knew it was over when he saw her hand limp on the ground beside her mother, its blue-tipped fingers perfectly, grotesquely still. He stepped closer and peered at her purple mouth, glazed eyes, befouled hair. Her breast did not rise. In an instant, the sweet creature had ceased to be herself and was now the shell of some small, felled creature lying on the damp earth. Bird indeed. But she was not a bird. She was his lover—a girl whom he had taken to his body that very night and then killed. Not with his own hands. No. But never in a hundred lifetimes would he forget the agony in her eyes when his deceit was exposed. He might as well have taken an ax to her breast.

Stunned silence swept across the square followed by gasps and sobs. Then the mother started to keen. A sharp buzzing filled his ears like the drone of insects and Albin began to shake. The trembling rattled up his frame until his knees gave way and he sank to the ground. Words would not form as he laced his fingers through his hair and pressed his forehead against the ground near her feet. Bile burned up his throat, and he retched violently.

Ohgodohgodohgodohgod spiraled through his mind, the only conscious thought until a new sound ripped through the roar of grief filling the air around him. Albin looked up, hands still clasped behind his head, mud and vomit falling from him. A large shape entered his line of sight, red and sulfurous as a demon. Albin blinked and the tall man solidified. Bent over the prostrate figure of Eliška's mother was Radek. The big man brushed gentle fingertips over the top of the older woman's head before turning wet, blazing eyes on Albin.

"You." The word sprayed from Radek's mouth like spittle as he stumbled forward. "You filthy swine. If you hadn't come here, like a deceiving snake, she might be alive!"

Albin struggled to his feet just before the tanner lunged, punching Albin with all his vast strength. He flew back and hit the ground like a stone. Air rushed from Albin's lungs as his side cracked under the impact. Pain shot up his jaw and through his skull. Stars burst behind his eyes. He coughed and spat before rolling over. Chest heaving, he fixed Radek with a bloodshot eye and nodded. So be it.

"You're right. But she still wouldn't have been yours," Albin wheezed and bared his bloody teeth like the wounded prey he was.

"Shut up, you goddamned bastard!" Radek roared, towering over Albin like a great ruddy bear. "Lord or no, I could kill you with my hands and laugh."

Albin cradled his side and waited for the attack. Gasping for breath through his cracked ribs, he didn't move. Beyond the big man's feet, he could see the body that used to be Eliška cradled in her mother's lap. The old witch's white head bent low, shaking with sobs he did not think her bones were strong enough to withstand. He closed his eyes, unable to watch. Death by beating was more than he deserved.

"What are you waiting for then, peasant?" Albin slurred at his rival as he kicked out at him, throwing dirt at Radek's feet. "She couldn't stand your stench or your company. Or were you too stupid to notice?"

Radek stared down at Albin with clenched fists, but did not strike.

Albin pressed on. "She preferred the crone's company to yours."

Still, the tanner did nothing more.

Furious and desperate, Albin drew a painful breath and hissed, "Did you know I had all of her? This very night. She was so sweet."

The taunt found its mark and the man's eyes went wide as a startled beast's only to fill with tears. Albin closed his eyes with relief and waited for the blows to come. Welcomed them. But the strikes did not come. He opened his eyes, ready to spur the wild man over the edge of his restraint, only for Radek to spit in Albin's face and back away. Goddamn the retched tanner, why wouldn't he end him already?

"I will not give you the satisfaction. It was you who came here with your lies," Radek ground out. "You who killed her." The big man's voice broke. "I may have driven her to you, yes. We will both live with that. But if you want death, find the courage to do it yourself." Running a bleeding hand over his face, the tanner turned away and sobbed.

Albin didn't know which was more terrifying, the man's fists or his tears, and scrambled up holding his side. Each breath ripped through him as he stumbled back to Eliška's limp body. Her mother clutched at it violently as if trying to reanimate her child. Eliška's head hung back, her smooth neck exposed.

He reached out, trembling and bloody. "Please. Please," he begged and knelt to touch her once more.

The woman whirled on him, rabid with grief. An inhuman noise left the mother's throat as she slapped him across the face and howled. "Get away from her!"

Albin held still and let her slap him again. And again. And again. Each lash sent a wave of pain through his head and he leaned in. Perhaps the mother would slit his throat, and they would be done with it.

The viscount stepped forward then, the first to move out of the frozen tableau of townspeople. "Madam!" he barked. "Control yourself. He is to be your lord after all." He grabbed her shoulders as several manservants rushed forward to intercede.

"Let her be!" Albin shouted. Still gasping for breath, he pushed the viscount's ringed fingers from the woman's shoulders. "Let her be."

"Albin. Albin, please," begged a shaking voice. Dazed from the blows, he turned to the sound. Perhaps this would be his release.

Anja's beautiful face, now red and streaked with weeping, stared back at him. She held out a hand to him. The scarlet stone flashed. She beckoned him to her. Cautiously. Her hands were open, but there was no mistaking the fear on her face. He choked back a sob and covered his face.

Eliška's mother continued to keen and thrash over the too-still body at their feet. Albin made himself look at her again. The corpse of the girl he had just made love to. For a second time, bile rose in his throat as he stared at her gaping eyes. It was too much. Turning from the evidence of his villainy, Albin swallowed and staggered back to his feet. Darkness bloomed across his senses as a single thought entered his mind: the dagger. He needed his dagger. He spun around, senseless of anything but finding it. There. The jade handle glinted at him from the edge of the crowd, and he rushed forward, nearly knocking a stunned onlooker to the ground. Albin grabbed hold of it, lifting it into the air, just as strong arms wrapped around him, staying his hand.

"Easy, Bini. That's not the way to fix this. Come away from this madness. You can do nothing here but cause more harm."

The sound of Miroslav's voice next to his ear held Albin upright as much as his friend's arms, now wrapped around him. Suddenly, the rage rushed out of him, leaving behind a bottomless well of shame he had no hope of escaping. The dagger dropped back to the ground at his feet, kicking up a cloud of dirt which the still gusting wind threw in his face. It drowned out every sound but the mother's wail.

"Do you see what I've done? What I am? You were right about everything," Albin wheezed and wept against his friend's neck.

"I know, goddamn you," Miroslav said, even as he stooped down so Albin could wrap an arm around his neck. "Now shut up and walk before they turn on you as they should."

"I killed her, Miro. I didn't mean to, but I did and oh God what I said to you—" Albin's voice cracked as he sucked in a sharp breath against the fire in his chest.

Miroslav did not pause, but Albin felt the slight hitch in his friend's step as he dragged him further away from the square.

"Not now. I'm getting you out of here before that tanner changes his mind and gets himself hung. Shut your mouth and walk. I have horses cobbled not far from here."

Unable to think even if he wanted to, Albin clung to Miroslav like a man on a cliff and allowed himself to be led. On and on through the winding woods he stumbled away from the village, away from the wailing at his back, bloodied both inside and out.

ACT TWO

After

VILA SONG I

The moon dips
its spooned edge into the river where the girl is

sinking

lifeless

before she had been
movement incarnate

Now
her crimson hair fans out, coral-like
mirroring the blood
blooming from her side
as her lover washes his hands in the cold, cold water

THIRTY-THREE

ELIŠKA

Eliška opened eyes that were not eyes and blinked. A filmy mist filled her vision as if she was staring into a dense fog. Frowning, she blinked again, trying to clear her sight, but the haze remained. She was dead. Somehow, she knew this. Her eyes were dead. She remembered closing them. Remembered her mother's face slick with tears hanging over her own, mouth agape in a silent, red cry. She remembered the clutch of Babička Olga's withered hand in hers, the blank horror on Lajos's—no, Albin's— pallid face just visible over her mother's shoulder. Remembered the hot pain cleaving her in two. Then, nothing. Wasn't that death?

She squeezed her eyes shut and opened them again, testing. Her body seemed to move at her command, though she felt noth- ing, not the ground beneath her nor the touch of fabric against her skin. Unable to see where she was, Eliška listened, but heard only the wind, rushing and swirling around her like an invisible tide.

Then a truly horrific possibility occurred to her: was she in a coffin? Alive? Had there been some kind of mistake? Panic flashed through Eliška hot as lightning and she sat up, half expecting to find herself confined. But her limbs obeyed with a languid grace, and she was suddenly sitting upright in a shroud of mist. Eliška rubbed her eyes this time, but the film continued to cloud her sight.

"'Tis the veil you see," an icy voice whispered from behind her.

Eliška sprang forward with unnatural ease and whirled to face the speaker before she gasped. Her feet weren't touching the ground. Terror twisted inside her like a choking bramble as a shadowy form solidified in front of her. Eliška flailed to get away, a soundless scream gurgling in her throat.

"Imagine your feet on the ground," the voice said. It came from the direction of the shadow. "Your mind's eye still works. Picture yourself standing and you will be."

Eliška continued to tremble mid-air as both the figure and the bizarre world around them clarified. Closing her eyes against things which could not be, she imagined herself standing on the ground and then she was. She expected to feel the shock of impact, but felt nothing at all. Not the bleached, rippling ground under her feet, nor the constant wind against her skin. It was then, standing in the glow of milky light emanating from everywhere and nowhere, Eliška understood two things: she was dead and awake outside of her body and standing in front of an ancient pagan warrior. Eliška stood transfixed. Not much older than herself, the woman was tall and bedecked with firs. Her lime-whitened hair hung in coils around her ashen face, and pale, kohl-blackened eyes stared at her, unblinking. She was the most fearsome creature Eliška had ever seen and a terror greater than death lodged in her gut. She was damned.

"Welcome, sister," said the woman in a voice as cold and treacherous as a mountain peak.

Eliška froze, her dead heart growing colder still. "Who are you?" she whispered, startling at the hollow, ricocheting sound of her own not-voice.

Then, without appearing to move, the woman was in front of

Eliška, her plated hair and heavy clothes rippling behind her as if underwater. Weightless.

"I am called Queen here, but once, my mother named me Jörd."

Eliška's not-eyes darted around for purchase on something that made sense. Perhaps she had not died at all, but was sick with fever, dreaming. She was still in a version of the village square after all; still wearing her clothes from the festival. She recognized the familiar buildings and street now, but saw them only dimly—through a veil—as the mighty woman had said. All around, the familiar landscape was leeched of color and life, leaving only the stain of shadow and memory. There was no sound. No other people. No movement save for a perpetual wind that stirred Eliška's insubstantial skirts and tangled hair. If this was death, then she had been sent to Hell.

"You have questions, but this place of betrayal has no answers." The woman called Jörd curled her lip at the shadow of the village and spat on the not-ground. "Come," she said, reaching out.

Eliška didn't move. Instead of taking the stranger's hand, she lifted her own and examined them. Other than being drained of color, they appeared solid. Familiar. Hers. Once again, dread lanced through her. She pressed her hands to her eyes as the desire to weep welled up, choking out the fear. But Eliška found no release, her mouth opening and closing in soundless grief. It seemed tears were a privilege reserved for the living.

Jörd huffed a bitter laugh. "You wasted your life on wanting what you could not have. Do not waste your death."

Then she took hold of Eliška's arm, her touch imperceptible. "You asked who am I, as if that truly mattered. What you should ask is *what are you now?*"

Before Eliška could respond, they were airborne. The gray, billowing world roared by in a silent blur that would have stolen Eliška's breath if she'd had any. It was difficult to decipher direction or landscape as they moved, so Eliška found herself violently shocked once again when the tunnel of wind around them ceased and she found herself standing on a vast plain unlike anything she'd ever seen. Tall, pale grass and a clean black sky stretched away in every direction, the horizon marred only by scraggly trees and a strange pair of spotted, long-necked beasts.

Though she could not feel the earth under her feet, Eliška knew she was looking at another shadowed part of the world just as she had her own. She tried to picture what it would have looked like in life, full of color. Even now, its beauty was unimaginable. Her heart broke all over again.

"Where are we?" Eliška's words echoed less here, as if there were no boundaries at all. As if this place of sky and grass was an endless world unto itself. Perhaps it was.

Jörd spread her arms wide, magnanimous. "The first place. We call it The Mother's Gut. The place of birth before either you or I came to be. It is where the first queen came to be and where we have all gathered since."

Eliška wrapped her arms around herself and tipped her head back as if to kiss the heavens which were not Heaven and never could be, before facing Jörd. "Why am I here?"

The warrior gave her a scythe-sharp smile. "To meet your sisters and brothers."

The wind broke open around them, a living thing with edges. Eliška peered into the gray world and gasped as a drove of ghostly figures emerged from the tall grass. Despite being drained of most color, the figures were startlingly unalike. Scores came forward at their matriarch's call and Eliška had never seen such a horde.

Some seemed of a time and place with herself, of similar dress and appearance. Many were ancients or natives; people Eliška could not have imagined. All were ashen versions of who they had been. Some carried the gruesome scars of their deaths with them—a slashed throat, a misshapen head, a twisted back. Eliška thought of her own body again. Hers, but not. She shivered, and pulled her hands into fists though her fingers no longer tingled or ached. In fact, she felt nothing of her body at all. Perhaps this was a small gift of death. Or a curse.

Eliška searched the myriad faces of the beings closest to her until a lone figure stepped forward. The girl was dressed in flowing silks that exposed one shoulder and part of her midriff. Her black hair flowed down her back and framed large, deep-set eyes. The only signs of her untimely death were wide, dark bruise around her neck. The gold hoop in her nose swung as she nodded to Eliška in greeting.

"Welcome, Sister. Do not be afraid. We were all reborn of heartbreak here and do not judge the dead."

The girl looked near her own age and was smiling, though Eliška couldn't imagine why. She could only stare as more figures, each different from herself, closed in. Her mind filled with a strange hum, like a ringing in her ears that ran through her whole being. Finally, Eliška formed the most logical question she could manage. "How do you speak my tongue?"

A second woman with nearly black skin and bright eyes, as well as shockingly bared breasts and a shaved head, approached Eliška. "Death has no language except itself. We are all of the same god in this godless place." As she spoke, the beaded collar encircling her neck danced.

Eliška's shiver solidified into complete stillness at the woman's words. She knew she hadn't been a good Catholic. In her heart she'd always preferred Olga's older traditions, but the idea that anywhere other than oblivion could be godless, and that she should inhabit such a place for daring to want more felt like the deepest kind of betrayal. Some small, tender part of her soul rebelled against the idea.

She swallowed her despair and turned to Jörd. "What do you want with me?"

No matter her many sins, Eliška knew in her once-heart she did not belong to this crowd of lost souls. She couldn't. She refused to believe in a God who would damn her for grasping at a fuller life, no matter how foolishly. For pushing against the boundaries of what she'd been taught, simply because she cared enough to search out the truth.

Jörd smiled, pleased Eliška had finally come to the point. "To give you a second chance, my child. You were betrayed. Snatched from life, as we all were," the woman said with a sweeping gesture toward the host of undulating figures. "At the hands of a selfish, violent lover. A betrayer. I saw you in the woods, child. Felt your ecstasy there. Your devastation in the square. I took pity so you might have another chance."

Eliška shook her head, frantic both to deny and understand. The ramification of what she was hearing—that she was now a víla like in one of Babička's stories—was overwhelming. "A chance at what?" Eliška asked, wanting to flee but having nowhere to go. "Another life? Is there a way to go back?"

A wicked smile stretched across the warrior's face. "Revenge. The chance to right the imbalance of power. To give back the death and betrayal unjustly given to you." She was in front of Eliška again, hovering just off the ground, her glacial eyes penetrating. "It is our right and duty. An obligation I now give to you by claiming you as one of our own."

Revenge. The strange, tempting idea immediately brought to mind Lajos's—Albin's—face flushed with shame and horror when Lady Anja had stepped forward. She remembered how he fell to his knees under the weight of his well-earned misery. Eliška had been a fool about much, but the regret covering her lover's face had been sincere. Even if their love had not.

Fear coursed through her. She did not know what to make of this strange gift, if that's what it was, or what would happen next. But Eliška knew in her not-heart, revenge was not something she longed for. She raised her head and met Jörd's gaze. "I'm sorry, Mother. Your mercy was misplaced. It...was an accident. Though he did deceive me as you saw," she whispered, unable to utter the words 'my death.'

A hiss slipped past the woman's curled lips. It was an ungentle sound, and Eliška instinctively pulled back in alarm. She could not feel or cry, but fear was still alive in this veiled place.

"You know nothing, child," she spat the words at Eliška before shooting up into the sprawling branches of the solitary tree beside them like a leaping cat. Lying languid on a branch, her long white legs hung free as she sank into the shadows. "You wish for mercy because your mind still believes it is just. You will change your mind, for there is no pain like the hands of your lover crushing your throat. No despair like the moment you know the dark smear of his traitorous face above the water is the last thing your mortal eyes will see."

Eliška started to speak, but before her words could take shape, the woman flew down from her perch and thrust both hands into Eliška's face. The woman's palm and fingers were covered with markings—staccato slashes that fanned across her skin like a tattoo. Eliška had heard of such things before, but never seen them. She leaned closer. Then the scent of resin and camphor hit her senses, and she met Jörd's eyes. "Rosemary?"

"My husband's last gift. A remembrance." She made a fist around the embedded needles and drifted backward. "A great hedge of the herb grew near the waters of a lake outside our village. After calling me to meet him there, we quarreled, and he beat me before dragging me to the shallows." Jörd curled her lip in disdain and made a noise that might have been a laugh. "I did not go quietly, and was quick enough to grab hold of the hedge, stripping the stalk before being overcome. They are the evidence of my fight."

Eliška went still under the spell of her story. It was all too easy to imagine. The powerful woman this creature once was, her pale face flushed with rage, her eyes livid with fear. Black water swallowing her whole as the lake filled her lungs, dragging her down.

CHAPTER THIRTY-THREE

Her life blood drifting up like liquid smoke. Eliška would not judge her rage.

Without appearing to move, the ghost woman was once again in front of Eliška, her face close enough to kiss. "Remember not the tender touch of your lover, child, but the cold finality of your death as he beds another. Embrace your bitterness. Let it rise up and sing. Only then will you find power to live as you wish. To be free."

Eliška turned away, but couldn't deny the seething in her heart at the thought of Albin—she would think his false name no more —married to another. To Lady Anja, the lustrous, steady moon to his sun, her strong heart pounding under her husband's touch. Everything Jörd said was true. Even so, she hesitated. "What if I do not wish to be as you are?"

At this many in the horde laughed, the sound echoing across the vast sky. Eliška faced the ghoulish company. A tiny, fair-haired girl in a rough woolen gown stepped forward. She looked far too young to be here. "You already are, sister," the víla girl said and smiled up at Eliška, her pale lips tight over sharp, young teeth.

Thirty-Four

Albin

Sprawled across a velvet chair in his study, Albin was drunk again. He'd briefly entertained the idea of remaining sober, but soon disregarded it. Again. It started weeks ago, when he'd first laid himself low with his father's finest vintage and later by the brandy when wine was no longer strong enough to dull his senses. The failure to remain sober was a relief. Now he could be alone and numb, the haunting of his shame dulled for a time, though he deserved no peace.

They—Anja, Miroslav, even Vater—had tried to console him at first. He would not have it as he deserved nothing but their rage. And rage they had. All three of them. But each was too good to hold his feet to the fire for too long. Pity dowsed the flames of their anger leaving little but contempt. Later, when he refused to tolerate any kindness, they left him alone. Then they began hiding the alcohol. But they were the only ones willing to defy the lord of the castle and his thirst would not be thwarted by a kitchen maid with instructions from the retired master.

Turning his head slowly so the room didn't spin too fast, Albin took in the gilded apartment: gleaming wood, massive carpets, priceless art, the tall expanse of glass. All this multiplied by dozens of rooms. Grand as it was, he knew a cage when he saw one and he'd damn well drink himself to death in it if he wanted. Besides, he mused as the ocher liquid sloshed in his goblet, they had received four casks of the brandy as a wedding present from Anja's family.

Wedding. Albin ran a shaking hand over his face as if to blot the event, if not the very word, from his memory. What he could remember of the day anyway. The whole affair had been a blur; another stain on Albin's conscience. Anja had gone to great lengths to acquit him of his guilt, though he knew she too grieved. But even perfunctory duty in the face of the havoc he'd wreaked was more than he could bear. He knew she didn't love him any more than he loved her, but she was far braver—willing to try. To be kind to one another and enjoy their future children knowing their union had brought stability to their homelands. She'd gone so far as offering to name their first daughter after—

He shifted and the brandy tilted, a golden sea tossed about between its shining shores. Albin stared at his hand: the cut crystal glass, the deadening alcohol, the neglected, ragged fingers of a murderer. For what? A chance to play at adventuring?

"Nothing but a fucking fool!" he cried in disgust and threw the glass across the room. It shattered against the stone wall, barely two hands away from where its match had met the same fate just over a month ago. Albin watched the dark patch on the rug spread, soaking into the fine fabric and started to laugh. He couldn't stop. Manically, Albin laughed until his still-tender sides ached and he slid to the floor, letting his head hit the rug with a thud.

The room spun wildly, but he didn't care. His plan was made. He would linger long enough to give Anja the children she wanted and then free her of himself in whatever manner would be least shocking. It was the only kind thing left to do. Her dowry would help stabilize the estate's finances—something his father hadn't told him was necessary until after Miroslav had dragged him home that awful night. Now that it was done, everyone would be better without him once there was an heir. He had no doubt the mother and old witch would dance on his grave when the time came. He didn't blame them, and wiped clumsily at the tears running into his ears.

"Goddammit, man, get up. Sir."

The familiar voice cut through his alcoholic haze. Albin let his hysterics die down to broken, sardonic gasps and opened his eyes. Miroslav's face wavered above him. Even Albin's inebriation could not hide the condition of his friend. Miroslav's dark eyes were sunken, his mouth drawn. Ever fastidious, his friend's cravat was loose, and his hair had grown overly long down his neck. Starting to feel nauseous, Albin closed his eyes again. He was worse than Midas. Worse than Medusa. Everything he touched came to ruin. Including his friend.

"Leave this place, Miro. Go and do not come back. I'm a goddamn pestilence and you know it," he said and groaned as he found himself being pulled to sitting.

"For once, do me the favor of shutting up, Bini. I'm taking you to your chambers."

"I shall stay here," Albin said and planted his hands firmly on either side of himself to keep from slumping over. Even he could hear the childish petulance in his voice, but didn't have any dignity left to care.

Miroslav looked down at him and Albin stared back as best he could. There was no anger in Miro's gaze, just a sad exhaustion. Anger would have been better. Disgust. Judgement would have given Albin something to rage against. Maybe then he could make Miroslav go for his own good. But what could he do with such pity?

"Well then," said Miroslav as he settled on the lush carpet next to Albin. "You force me to sit on the ground with you until you vomit or pass out."

"I shall not lose my drink," Albin countered, head swimming.

"I do believe you said such nonsense before. Do you remember how that went the last time?"

Albin scoffed and leaned back against the legs of the great chair. Miroslav followed suit, his legs stretching well past Albin's own. The sight brought something to Albin's mind; the faint inkling of a memory, the kind triggered by scent or sound. But what was it? Then Miroslav yawned and it came back to Albin like a hammer to the chest.

"We could have seen them, you know. The tall beasts of Africa." Albin tried to focus his stare across the room, but saw nothing beyond his visions of adventure. "We could have hunted beasts and followed silk roads east until the end of the world. Watched old masters carve jade and sailed across an ocean to the Americas. We could have—" Albin's voice broke off as he heaved onto the floor next to himself. Bile burned his throat and nose as the brandy left his stomach. He felt better immediately.

"I win," came Miroslav's stern voice.

Albin laughed until the sound cracked into a sob. Holding Albin's shoulders tight, Miroslav pulled him away from his own filth and pressed a cup of water into his hands. "Drink slowly or it shall come right back up to both of our disgust. Let me ring for Kveta. Poor thing. You owe that girl a tremendous increase in wages, sir."

"If you call me 'Sir' again I shall strike you. I am hardly worth my own name let alone your pleasantries."

"Before you try, shall we place a wager on that as well? I could use some extra coin now that I think of it," said Miroslav, pulling him to his feet. "And you must forgive me for saying so, but I shall call you whatever I damn well please. My lord."

Regretfully upright, Albin found himself clinging to Miroslav's long arms. "Fine. If I must move, get me to my chambers before Lady Anja finds me. I have grieved her enough."

"On that we can agree."

As they clumsily left the room, Miroslav rang for the maid

and they started down the long hall. Albin kept his eyes trained on the polished floors. The gilt-framed portraits and brocade draperies passed unseen, but he knew them all by heart. He stumbled and felt grateful his bed chambers were on the same floor as his office.

"You know," Miroslav said as they rounded a corner, "your lady grieves as well. She was fond of the girl so perhaps—"

"There is nothing you can say to make me hate myself less. Nor should you try. My wife may have been fond of...but she did not know her as I did. She was not responsible for..." Albin's head lolled to the side, and he was unable to speak.

"Your misery does nothing for anyone. What is done is done."

Albin planted a foot, stopping them. He peered into his friend's fatigued face. "Do you think I don't know that? I think on nothing else."

Miroslav stayed quiet for a long moment before whispering, "Then perhaps it's time you started."

Albin jerked his head away angrily and felt his stomach roll again. Finally, they made it to the grand chamber, which was blessedly empty. *Anja must be in her drawing room*, Albin thought and sighed with relief. After the first night of humiliating, all-but-forced consummation, Anja had avoided his bed chamber as much as possible. He didn't blame her.

"Here you are," said Miroslav as he propped Albin up against the carved bedpost.

With his stomach now devoid of alcohol, Albin's wits were clearing by the minute, and he pulled himself into bed, boots and all. As he lay staring at the brocade curtains, he knew there was something else he must say to Miro. Something long past time to say.

"Miro," he said and sensed his friend tense at the quiet sound of his name. "It would be better for you to leave me." Albin paused, fighting against the lump in his throat. "You are dearer to me than any other, but I cannot...care for you as you would want."

Rallying his nerve, Albin looked at his beloved friend then and blinked, his treacherous eyes burning.

Miroslav had gone very, very still. "Bini, you don't have to—"

"Yes, I do. Please. You deserve to know it's not because I've never...considered it. I have." Albin paused, squeezing his eyes shut against a wave of dizziness before forcing his focus back on Miro who stared down at him, face blank. With a deep breath, Albin pressed on. "Both of our lives would be simpler in many ways if we were companions in more ways. In all ways."

"Albin, this isn't—" Miro interjected.

"But I can't...I'm not..." Albin flailed, and he raked a hand over his face. "You deserve a true love. A much better one than I could be."

Terrified that he'd somehow made the whole thing worse, Albin closed his eyes in misery and fell silent. Until he felt Miro's long fingers smooth the damp hair off his forehead. Albin looked up.

"I know who you are, Bini," said Miroslav, his voice and touch tender. "And I know who you are not. You are my oldest and dearest friend, and I have contented myself with your friendship on purpose for some damnable reason."

Miro smiled sadly then and moved his hand down to cover Albin's. "I have no wish to torture myself." Miro's brows knit together briefly before he let out a long breath. Albin waited. He didn't move his hand away from Miro's.

"And I do not keep any false hope as I might have once. It is unfair to us both. So, I intend to seek companionship and pleasure whenever and wherever it can be found." Miro's eyes lanced down to Albin's in challenge.

Albin gave none, and Miroslav continued. "Even so, for some ghastly reason, I find myself happiest here. Still. With your ridiculous, selfish heart." He gestured around the room he'd seen so many times before. "This is my home too, after all, and I will keep to it. And to you for now."

Albin stared up at the brocade draperies around his bed. His head pounded, but he didn't care. It was the most forthright conversation they had ever had on the matter of Miroslav's affections and Albin found himself tremendously glad for it. His only regret now was the pain he would inflict on Miro when he took himself from this life. If only Albin could make his friend see he was better without him.

"However," Miroslav pressed on. "If the day comes when I see fit to seek my fortunes elsewhere," he thrust at look at Albin, "I shall expect your blessing."

Albin, fighting to keep his eyes open, nodded once and squeezed his friend's hand. "You've always had it and more," he said before closing his eyes.

The last thing Albin remembered before passing into oblivion, was the press of lips to his forehead and the crisp echo of steps walking away.

Vila Song II

Afterwards
more than anything
he remembered the smells of
woodsmoke and cardamom
also
the weight of his lover's hand on his
arm
cock
throat
pressing down
until the sharp burn of steel in his gut
became everything and
nothing
at all

THIRTY-FIVE
ELIŠKA

The ground flew past in a blur of treetops and mist. Eliška tried to enjoy it. Even through the muted tones of this existence, she admired the way the veil bent and fractured the light all around her, dappling the surface of dense jungle below. The world was stunning. Brilliant is a way that would have made her battered heart dance. Once. Now, she knew better. Though the exquisite beauty of the world was not lost on Eliška, she took little joy in it. There was no real freedom in this not-life. Only hunting. Only the dance.

Their hive traveled as far and fast as the wind moved to anywhere Jörd sensed their particular kind of despair and heartbreak. Human violence drew the víla in like carrion to a slaughter. The queen's long-dead soul fed on the fear of Betrayers, as she called them, and Eliška couldn't deny the dark pleasure that filled her like air when Jörd made them dance. Most Betrayers were guilty. Whatever her not-body was made of now felt the rage and passions of the living as their souls left their broken bodies. Eliška did not ask her queen where those souls went.

What Eliška hadn't expected was that not all their prey were deserving of such an end. Some were merely hapless souls who wandered into the wrong glade at night where Jörd was collecting a new sister or brother. Eliška did not delight in these deaths, though the infectious pull of the hive's hungry glee was impossible to resist. It hummed through her body like a strong wine—like the ecstasy she'd felt once. What would be the point in resisting when nothing mattered anymore?

Quite suddenly a soft, energetic hum traveled through her body, drawing her attention. A command. She hadn't understood what it meant the first time the sensation ran across her limbs, bullying her to move. Now, when her body dove in unison with the other víla around her, dipping down and down, spiraling through the low clouds toward a canopy of trees, she wasn't afraid. Shooting gracefully through the mists, Eliška alighted without impact on a great branch as the hive descended to rest, each of their bleached bodies clinging to the trees like a mass of giant butterflies.

Eliška surveyed the hive. She and several other familiar faces— she did not yet know many names—rested in the limbs of a jungle tree so vast its arms stretch wide as a castle wall, while vines thick as her own legs dripped down like black ribbons. Birds that must have been brilliantly colored beyond the veil, shrieked from wicked black beaks at the invasion and now watched warily from neighboring branches. Not knowing how long Jörd would want to lounge in this wild place, Eliška thought herself to sitting and leaned against the trunk of the giant tree. She missed the sensation of bark against her back, no doubt dank and rough. She remembered lying back in the grass with the sharp prickle against her skin. The way sunlight warmed her hair. Her throat tightened at the memories and she shepherded her thoughts elsewhere. It was pointless to remember.

Time had passed since her death, though she did not know how much, and she sometimes wondered if her not-life would always be like this—a nebulous string of fantastical new horizons and morbid deaths. She wasn't sure she cared to know. And although Eliška had grown stronger and more accustomed to this new existence, her new brothers and sisters remained mostly a mystery to her.

There was Sushma, who often sang in her first language as they flew, her elegant silks flowing behind her, and Fiadh, whose tiny frame and sharp teeth marked her as barely more than a child. Fiadh had a hungry look about her, but her bright laugh reminded Eliška of birdsong. Naeku, the woman with skin the color of coal who'd spoken to her on the first night, had a name for every tree the hive landed in. Eliška had heard many other names murmured while flying, though she did not know to whom they belonged.

She doubted she would ever know them all, for their horde was large and still growing. A new young man, Samuel, had been collected since her own rebirth, though she had not spoken to him. All she knew to do was offer a sad, lifeless smile when his pale eyes went wide with fright. Eliška did her best not to stare at the wound to his gut. Pondering how it had been inflicted made a shudder run through her not-body.

But the víla she saw most often was one brother in particular who always seemed nearby. Almost as if he was watching her. He was a tall, lean man with light brown skin, a tidy black beard, and dark eyes. He seemed older than herself, though still young, and she remembered being surprised by his presence at first. It had never occurred to her in life that men could be used and betrayed, too. But there was much she did not know about the world she had once lived in, or about this veiled in-between place.

As if called by her thought of him, the man with the kind, sad smile descended to the branch where Eliška was roosting. He had never come this close before and tended to keep himself somewhat apart in general. She had grown used to the varying appearances of the other víla, but she was interested to see him close up. He was quite handsome and wore a long white tunic with loose trousers underneath. A patterned cloth wrapped around his head and trailed over one wide shoulder like a bold swing of hair. He wore leather sandals and Eliška wondered what it must have been like to live with your feet exposed to earth and sun. If he noticed her appraising him, he didn't show it. Instead, he dipped his head to her in greeting and smiled, his teeth a splash of white above his beard.

"Peace be upon you, little sister," he said in a voice warm as fresh bread.

"Good evening," Eliška answered automatically before looking around. The veil shifted and rippled, making it difficult to tell dawn from dusk, or if the weather was fair or foul. "If it can be called that."

The man squinted out at the foggy expanse of the veil. "Yes. I believe you are correct. Evening. Or soon to be," he said with the surety of long experience.

Eliška followed his gaze, unable to make out any indicators of night or day. "Can you really tell? Or are you teasing me?"

The man smiled at her skeptical expression and pointed off to his right. Eliška looked closely and noticed a small, slightly brighter patch near the horizon amid the darker shade of the sky.

"The sun? It's setting?" she guessed, delighted by this new information.

Her new companion nodded. "Adjusting to the veil takes time, but you will learn to see the world again. Not as it was, of course, but as something more than a shadow. I would not tease about such a thing." His voice was somewhat formal despite his gentle demeanor.

She knew he meant to be comforting, but his words had the opposite effect on Eliška. A sadness she couldn't explain swept over her and she nodded, but couldn't find anything to say back. All her life she'd longed for the strength and freedom to go where she pleased, and now that she had it, she couldn't even tell day from night. The unfairness of it made her want to rage.

He didn't press, but nodded at her and touched his forehead. "I am called Ahmed. I had other names a long time ago, but Ahmed suffices now. Here."

His voice held such devastating sadness, something in Eliška's not-heart broke loose. She knew by the tightening in her throat, she would have cried if she were able.

"My name is Eliška." She couldn't bring herself to utter her family name. So she fought for a smile and handed it over to him. It was all she had. "May I ask where...where you were from? Before." She stumbled and immediately regretted saying anything. She did not know if, or how, to speak about their lives before their deaths. She shook her head in frustration. "Forgive me. Perhaps I shouldn't—"

Ahmed held up a hand to stop her. He smiled kindly again, and steepled his hands under his chin for a moment as if in Christian prayer. "Do not fret. I am not offended, though you are right to be cautious." He gestured with his large hand to the other members of the hive, all reclining in various states of rest. "Not all our brothers and sisters welcome such questions about the past. Even our unfeeling bodies cannot erase the pain of memory."

Eliška nodded in understanding. "Of course."

"It had many names, my home. It was a land very different than yours. A place of vast dunes and huge cities. Wide rivers and harsh mountains. So beautiful." His face went soft then, nearly wistful, his smile gone. "I loved my home, though it was not always a simple place."

Eliška watched Ahmed carefully, and though she did not understand his meaning, she saw her own unhappiness and longing carved into the delicate lines around dark his eyes. Perhaps there was something else beyond betrayal she and her new family had in common: longing. Grief.

"But already I have said too much and you not enough,"

Ahmed said as he reclined onto his elbow. "Tell me of yourself, Eliška. Tell me of your home."

Eliška didn't yet know if such a human thing as friendship could exist in this half-place of flying and hunting, but decided having a companion was worth the risk. So, she did her best to follow his lead and began to speak of Hrozno.

THIRTY-SIX

ALBIN

His wife was the most beautiful woman in the room. She glowed like a winter moon. Her icy blue gown matched her eyes, and her golden curls cascaded across her pale shoulders. Anja smiled with genuine warmth at each guest and played her part to perfection. Albin could hardly look at her without waves of nausea lapping at his ankles, a relentless surf of guilt. Anja was keeping up her end of the marriage bargain, while Albin shut himself away, soaking his wretched heart in drink.

He surveyed the room over the edge of his glass. No one paid him any attention. Oh, he knew there were furtive stares and barely contained whispers among his many guests, but they didn't dare challenge him directly. People kept their distance, pretending the situation—his perpetual drunkenness—was normal. He supposed it was, actually, and Albin required little else but to be left alone. He wished only to drink and die, leaving this farce of a marriage behind so Anja might be free. It was the least he could do with himself.

The room tilted slightly as Albin craned his head around. Miroslav had to be here somewhere. He was sure of it. The blasted man had hardly let him out of his sight since that night. Albin dropped the thought as if it was a glowing coal and looked the other direction. There. He would have recognized Miroslav's unruly hair and fine waistcoat anywhere. Miroslav was conversing in an animated fashion with that blasted merchant from Kosice. The reedy man had arrived nearly a week ago and refused to leave until he had a decision from Albin about the new prices of his wine.

Albin scowled and signaled to a servant. His glass was nearly empty. The damned man. Albin's father had answered the man's letters addressed to Albin when he was bound to his chambers while recovering. It was an unexpected kindness, Albin admitted. But since Father had officially made Albin acting baron upon his marriage to Anja, the merchant would not rest until he had reassurance on the wine contract from Albin himself.

Which he could not bring himself to give on principal alone. He tipped back his newly filled glass, enjoying the dry bite as it slid down his throat. Let all these vultures grow accustomed to dealing with someone else. He wanted no part in the running of the estate and never had. And if he was being honest, a festering part of him wanted his father to suffer as he did. To share in the guilt Albin could not bear on his own.

He observed Miroslav again, struck with a thought. His friend, though low born, had always moved more smoothly through these circles than himself. Perhaps he would make Miroslav his heir if Anja didn't conceive soon—there was no other family with a rightful claim to the place and if he died without naming an heir, then he supposed the emperor would gift the estate away. Even he didn't want that to happen.

Just then, the door across from him burst open with an undignified bang and a small boy rushed in. He was dressed in dark blue short pants and an overly ruffed shirt that made Albin smile even in his bitter, inebriated state. The child's face was red and streaked with tears, but brightened as his small wet eyes fell upon a woman near the window. She had a soft figure and plain, kind face, though the jewels on her neck were extravagant for an afternoon gathering.

A young, flustered nursemaid came rushing in, but the boy was already pulling at his mother's skirts whose face lit with radiant concern as she bent down to her child. The domestic scene unfolded off to the side, but Albin was rivetted, his eyes filling shamefully at the adoration on display between the mother and son. What a beast he'd become. Not so long ago he'd wanted only one thing—to honor the memory of his mother. To be a good husband and a father, though his nature strained against the confines of such things. He wanted, above all else, to be different than his own father. And now, as he watched the elegant woman address the needs of her son and lead him back to the nursery with the apologetic nursemaid following behind, he knew he'd failed completely.

Full of self-hatred and excellent wine, Albin gave a hysterical laugh which drew the attention of the room. Polite conversations died away as all eyes either turned toward him or scattered to the corners. Albin lifted his glass in a toast. "To mothers," he said. "God bless their souls for putting up with sons."

A pained, polite echo went through the room until Miroslav burst out laughing, drawing the attention to himself. "Here, here, my lord, though I do think my mother could hardly have done better with me." A relieved twitter of laughter spattered the air and Albin watched Anja sweep into the center of the room, picking up Miroslav's saving thread. "And on such an amusing note, I do believe cakes and port are being served in the drawing room, so if you all would make your way down, my lord and I shall meet you shortly."

Albin watched in shame-filled mystification as Miroslav took up the charge and teasingly led the way out of the room as Anja smiled beautifully to each as they exited. When the last guest made their way through the gilt-edged door, Anja turned to him, her lovely face a sheet of ice.

Chapter Thirty-Six

"Will you all please excuse us for a moment," she said without inflection.

Servants scattered. The door closed behind them with a gentle *click* and Albin smiled in anticipation of a berating. She faced him in all her livid beauty, eyeing him closely as one does a wounded animal. Something like resignation crossed her face as she let her sloping shoulders and décolletage fall. He could not have agreed with her assessment of him more.

"You must stop this, Albin. This torment of us all. It will not take us back."

Anja spoke with such tender care, it made him loath himself all the more. He deserved nothing. Certainly not his wife, who carried the weight of humiliation as well as his grief and scandal. She did not cave under it as he did.

"Punishing myself is all the good there is left for me to do." Albin leaned back in the mahogany chair and cradled his aching head as her scent drifted toward him. Their chambers were connected by a discrete doorway, but he had never spent time in her room. It smelled of sandalwood and Parisian perfume, of powders and flowers from the grounds and only served to whet his longing for *her* scent—lavender, sweat, wanting. Albin rubbed his face and shook the thought away.

"That is a selfish lie and you know it," Anja said, standing over him now. They were of a height with one another, and had been since before he'd left for university. She used to tease him about it, but he never minded. Of all the things he was ashamed of, his average stature wasn't one of them.

"You aren't the only one who's made mistakes, you know." Her voice caught. "Terrible mistakes that hurt you and those you love. Do not pretend to be the only one who suffers."

At this, Albin looked her full in the face for the first time in weeks. Her beauty felt like a punishment. "Unless you deceived and then inadvertently killed your innocent lover, then I don't think our mistakes have much in common, Anja." He seethed.

But she did not move away from his bitterness, only closer. With exquisite precision, Anja leaned into his face, demanding his attention, before slapping him hard across the face. Albin's head whipped to the side, but the back of the tall chair held him steady. He wouldn't have moved anyway and felt a surge of relief at the sting of her strike. Finally. Something he deserved. Something he could accept.

"Yes, you deceived and made love to a sick girl whose heart could not bear the strain. Only God can forgive you for that. But do not think for a second you're the only one who has ever caused pain and lived to tell of it." Her nostrils flared, and her chin quivered as she turned from him. "You are not the only one who knows of regret."

Albin couldn't move. His head felt thick and the buttons on the back of Anja's dress blurred, but he'd heard her words. And though he did not know exactly of what she spoke, he saw the sorrow in her eyes. Unsteadily, he pushed himself to standing. Anja turned to face him, her head held high and defiant, as if waiting for his reproach. He would not give it. Broken down, lying, seducing, drunkards should not throw stones.

Instead, he gently grasped her elbow, both to steady himself and to offer some solace.

"We are a desperate pair, wife. What are we to do with ourselves?" He raised his hand to her soft white cheek, his heart breaking all over again for the quiet misery she carried with her while he stumbled about, caring nothing for his reputation. Even as it pertained to Anja.

He'd expected her to pull away or strike him again. Wouldn't have blamed her if she had. She did not. As they stood together, their battered hearts beating out a rhythm of guilt, Anja tilted her cheek into his hand. Albin watched as she closed her eyes; let out a shuddering breath, her lips parted in a small act of release. Here was a beautiful woman he'd known all his life. His better in every way. If only he could have been content.

"We may not have been each other's choice, but we must keep to each other now, Albin." She blinked her eyes open, but did not lift her cheek from his palm. A tear leaked onto his hand. It was the first tender thing he'd been aware of in a month.

Albin felt his mouth twitch in what might have passed for a smile, though it did not reach his ruined heart. "You would be better to leave me, you know. To ensconce yourself comfortably somewhere far from here. Anywhere. I will keep you in the comfort you deserve and will not call you to my side," he said, pulling away. Despite her hope, he feared there was no stopping his cancerous presence.

A fierceness he'd never seen swept across her lovely face. "Are you still so blind to think I have a choice in this matter?" she spat the words at him, in a shock of anger. "That I, a woman, ever had a choice? In anything? Are you so blinded by your own misery that you believe *you* are the only one bound to a fate you never wanted?"

Albin stared at her, searching his heart.

"At least you are a man and own what is called yours." Anja lifted her chin at this and moved toward the door. "We may be unwilling companions in this life, you and I, but do not forget who holds the keys to every door." Anja spared him one long, sorry gaze and swept out of the room.

With blurred eyes and a burning throat, Albin drained his glass and followed her.

VILA SONG III

She did not hear her lover come in over the
Monsoon pouring down from the black sky
a great inverted mountain crashing
covering the sound of her
howl strangled until she
lay on the damp
floor a limp
doll and her
spirit leapt
into the
jungle
free

Thirty-Seven

The hive did not linger in the jungle for long. Eliška suspected it was too quiet there. Too remote. There were few Betrayers to be found, and the living beasts became more and more agitated at their death-reeking presence. So before the sun could set once more, the víla rose into the sky at the call of Jörd and soared off to another hunting ground like the great flock of carrion they were. Ahmed did not leave her side as they flew, but just before landing, he'd touched his brow in a wordless farewell as was his custom and disappeared among the hive. Eliška did not protest, though his company and sympathetic ear had been a gift, even for one day.

When they landed among the treetops of a great wood turned amber with the first touches of autumn, Eliška recoiled. She knew these trees. The veil could not disguise everything. She wanted to rub her eyes out of habit but knew it would do no good. Ahmed had told her it would take a while to adjust. The concerning part was how long 'a while' was to ghosts.

Crouching high in a great elm not far from Babička Olga's gathering grounds, Eliška took in her surroundings. The familiar scent of her old forest filled her memory. She wrapped her arms around her knees and ached to be away from this sad place. She wondered why Jörd would bring them back here. She had seen the other side of the world and knew there to be enough heartbreak to drown them all forever. Yet, her new mother had circled back to the woods of Hrozno. Eliška shuddered to think why, and wanted to fold in on herself. It wasn't fair, she thought. Had her foolish wants in life really been foul enough to deserve this half-death? This unholy yearning?

The skeletal leaves rattled against her ears and she shivered. She didn't want to be here. Her only solace now was the beauty of distant lands and her freedom of movement. It was not lost on her that only in death had her body found its power. Its own twisted vitality. Eliška scowled at the thought before noise below drew her attention. Her new brothers and sisters were murmuring amongst themselves about something happening below. She fisted her hands at her sides and ignored the rising din. Eliška knew that sound. They were hunting. Even as her not-body clung to the tree, she felt the thrill of the chase rising in her, unbidden. She longed to press it down even as her consciousness burned with thirst.

The wild cries from below her perch swelled. She closed her eyes and remembered being told that such mysterious banshee screams at night were just the wind. She knew better now. Surely the víla had been hunting then, too. The first time Eliška watched her companions swoop from the air and terrorize a man, she wanted to stop up her ears to the victim's pitiful pleas for mercy, but there was no escape. For him or for herself. Jörd's voice penetrated her mind and compelled her.

Look, the voice whispered and she obeyed. Eliška resisted at first, but the mindless tug of the mob resurrected something inside her. It tasted like blood, metallic and salty. Rage. Wild, unrepentant rage. Swept along on the víla's vengeful tide, she could no more resist the pull in her veins than the current of a powerful river. Dropping from her perch, Eliška felt her mind roll back, shifting into a deeper, more primitive state as she drifted down to the hunt, compelled by invisible strings.

Then, through the whipping winds below, a cry pierced her awareness. She froze midair. Listened. The cry came again, swept up to her with the stench of ammonia and animal flesh. She hissed through her clenched teeth. She knew of only one living man who smelled so much like death.

Radek.

Eliška darted through the woods, following the sounds of the hunt. Trees she knew intimately in life whipped passed her until she landed in a clearing that carried the sharp tang of damp bracken and leaf mold, woodsmoke and manure. All around her the air rippled with the glimmering shadows of her brothers and sisters, swirling and darting through the darkness in a devilish dance. She hung back, not wanting to confirm who writhed in the center of the storm.

"Join us, child." Jörd's voice slid to her from across the meadow. "This one's special."

Eliška felt her not-body drift forward and through the sweep of specters she saw him—her once upon a time suitor. Radek's amber eyes bulged in fear as he moved with the jerky, gracelessness of an animal caught in a trap. The big man hung midair, chest heaving for breath as sweat dripped from his body. Eliška knew it was only the beginning. Crazed with Jörd's bloodpull for revenge, the víla flocked around him, pressing in and then pulling away in a choreographed rhythm made perfect by unknown years of practice. The quivering outlines of the creatures faded in and out of focus as Eliška struggled to keep her eyes on Radek. She felt the unnatural desire to feed rise and flood her mind, choking as nettles.

"Come, sister," Fiadh called over the conjured wind. "He's for you."

The tiny víla's uncanny grin practically split her pale face in two, and Eliška saw a glimpse of the beast inside them all. The one beaten down. Broken. Rejected, unloved, betrayed, and murdered, now fed by centuries of Jörd's lust for revenge. Eliška's wind began to swirl around her, rising with the dull roar of outrage. And she remembered. Recalled all the times Radek had pressured her; tried to buy her affection and then bully his way into her heart. The buzzing in her limbs grew as she remembered Radek's bruising grip, the dark triumph in his eyes when he threw her lover's dagger to the ground at her feet. His refusal to listen to her.

Eliška let go. As the rage filled her soul and the winds of death whipped across her face, thrilling her, she felt her eyes roll back and her heart darken. With every hurt fresh in her mouth, Eliška fell in with her new family as if entranced. Like a great flock of birds, they dove and rolled, circled back, and pushed Radek further than a human body could go. On and on they danced through the night until the proud tanner was ragged as a flax doll. Stumbling through the woods on bloody feet, his face was the mask of a man damned. And when Radek's last breath slipped past his broken teeth, it was Eliška who flung it into the void.

⁌◦⁍

The tanner's big body lay on the muddy bank of the river, bruised and wretched. Slowly, like an animal coming back to its master, Eliška's hackles fell. Her blood no longer boiled and her eyes fell back into place. Her not-breath slowed and she stared at her hands. She didn't recognize them. Even as she flexed and moved the memory of her most capable tools, she couldn't believe they were hers. Hands that had brought beauty and wellness in life, now brought death. There was no denying the smell of violence now coated her skin as completely as the stink of the tannery had clung to Radek. She peered at his clouded eyes, his battered body. She had allowed this to happen. No, she had reveled in it. She was a monster now, in truth. A white shadow. A thing of nightmares. A víla.

Eliška hid her not-hands behind her back. The putrid smell filling her senses was not that of vindicated power no matter what Jörd said. It was shame. The thought swirled with dizzying speed through her mind as she replayed the hunt. Jörd called it a dance of retribution for those who had been wronged, but a hunt it most surely was.

She didn't know if Radek had recognized her, but there was no denying how his soul had felt in her hands. She'd sensed his fear. The bitterness of his own heartache, the anger at her rejection, and the sorrow at her death. All had flowed through her for an instant and she knew the stench left behind was her fault. No, she thought. Not completely. If he hadn't been such a boar. If he hadn't pushed and pursued and deceived—

She stopped. Radek hadn't deceived her. He'd tried to tell her the truth, even if for the wrong reasons. Though he'd had no right to disregard her wishes in life, he had not been the one to truly harm her. Selfish as he'd been, Radek had wanted her for herself and nothing more. She hadn't liked him, and wouldn't have been a good wife. But he hadn't deserved to die. If Eliška could have conjured tears, she would have drowned herself in them now. If only she'd had the strength to resist her own bitter heart, perhaps Radek would have survived. Perhaps the people who loved her wouldn't have to die.

THIRTY-EIGHT

ALBIN

Dear God, he'd never wanted a drink so bad in his life. Abstinence of any kind had never been a strength of Albin's, a fact which had never been more painfully obvious than in the past month. Not only was he a fool, a coward, and a cad, but a drunk as well. Another darker, more sinister word rose to the surface of his mind, but he plunged it back down into the murky depths. Not today. Today he was going to do better and admitting his most heinous crime would not help keep his need for a drink at bay.

But damn his own soul, he was still going to have to be the lord of the estate until he could find a way for everything to pass to Anja legally, with or without the presence of a male heir. He must try to make amends. If for no other reason than to ease the burden Anja and the rest of his household would bear. She did not deserve to be despised as he did. The fault of this tragedy was his alone and though he knew there was no way to assuage the damage he'd done, atonement was long overdue.

Though the breeze was cool—too cool for September—he pulled at his collar, trying not to gag against the knotted scarf at his throat, and glanced at the man sitting in the wagon next to him holding the reins. The Austrian physician was of middle age and rather soft around the center, but had a sharp nose, keen eyes, and a mild voice. All spoke of his competence and good nature. At least that's what Albin observed when the man had been recommended to him. While he expected to be stoned upon sight once they entered Hrozno, he held out the smallest flame of hope the wagon loaded with new harvesting supplies and the monthly installment of the physician would perhaps, in time, lessen the hatred.

Then the mother's eyes rose up in his mind in accusation, just as they did every single time he found a shred of peace. A peace he did not deserve. Albin fought down another gag and ran a trembling hand over his face. His heart quaked at the thought of facing her. But face her he must. Which said nothing of the uncanny Babička Olga, whose spotted, papery hands he could still feel on his bruised cheeks. He shivered at the memory, a condemned man.

Eliš—she—had insisted he not call the grandmother a witch, but Albin knew better. Had felt the truth in his gut the first time the old woman laid her milky eyes on him and looked directly into his shallow heart. Whatever connection she had cast or unearthed in the touching of her capable hands had stayed with him, plaguing every dream and waking nightmare which was his life now. Though the rational part of him feared the physical and emotional violence of the mother, his stomach twisted even tighter at the deep, probing understanding of Babička Olga. Distracted by his own impending doom and precarious sobriety, Albin startled when the physician cleared his throat with great intention.

"Forgive me, my lord, but there appears to be a disturbance ahead," the man said in an unconcerned, matter of fact way.

Damn men of science, Albin thought as he reined in his self-loathing and followed the physician's gaze. Albin steeled himself.

"*Danke schön*, Herr Wagner," Albin said and fought down a rising wave of panic at the sight of so many people clustered along the side of the road. They were still outside the boundary of the village, but only just. Another curve in the road would reveal the first cottages as the path widened into the central square and the well.

A few people were gesturing and shouting, while others pointed off toward the right where the tree line kissed the road. Albin recognized several of them from the harvest and yanked at his cravat, pulling it from his neck. "Goddamn this thing," he swore, which earned him a sidelong glance from the unruffled physician who was still driving the wagon forward.

"Indeed. Always hated those things myself. Perhaps we should investigate, my lord? See what the trouble is?" Herr Wagner said politely, though there was no way the men could avoid them anyhow. The wagon couldn't pass with so many people clogging the road.

The last thing Albin wanted was, in fact, to prolong this visit in any way, but nodded to the physician. "Very well."

"As you wish, my lord," the physician said as if stopping to investigate had been Albin's idea instead of his own. Albin ignored the man's pandering and took a gulp of air, savoring the cold bite deep in his chest. He would meet whatever chaos this visit delivered.

They pulled the wagon up alongside the crowd just as several men plunged into the tree line, calling out to one another as they moved downhill toward the river bank below. A woman who stood back from the scene with her hand pressed to her mouth in concern noticed them first. "My lords," she greeted and dipped into a curtsey.

"What seems to be the trouble, madam?" Herr Wagner greeted.

Albin remained silent, his neck burning with shame as he watched the woman squint at him, register his identity, and whip her attention to Herr Wagner. Albin lowered his head further.

"A b-body," she stuttered. "There's a body by the river at the bottom of the hill."

"A body?" the physician echoed in shock, and no sooner had

he spoken than shouts erupted from the direction of the river below.

Albin felt his heart seize and his head swim, but he didn't move until Herr Wagner pushed the reins into his hands. "If you would, my lord," he said before hefting himself out of the driver's seat with surprising nimbleness and heading toward the commotion. Albin clutched at the cold leather reins as his heart raced. That left Albin with the woman who recognized him. He didn't know her name, but had seen her in the fields with her husband and a grown son. She was tall and sturdy-looking with dark, graying hair and a long nose. Gathering his courage, he met her stare. Hastily she dropped her gaze, but not before he saw the condemnation in it.

"Please," he said, and held out a hand in peace. "I do not deserve your manners. But I'd be grateful if you held the wagon for a moment so I may go with my companion?" He pointed into the back. "They are for you—the village."

The woman pushed at a loose strand of hair as she faced him. She glared openly, and he let her, before she gave a small nod and moved to take the reins from him.

"You have my gratitude, madam," he said as he slid down from the wagon. Picking his way quickly down the steep hillside dense with trees took focus, and it gave Albin something else to think on other than the scene awaiting him. Both the body—whoever the poor soul was—and the men he'd have to face.

Following the path of churned up soil and undergrowth the villagers had made, it didn't take long for the woods to clear enough for Albin to make out bits of the river below. Then he heard the buzz of tense voices over the babbling of the water, and followed the sound until he saw them hunched over staring at a spot on the shore.

Stumbling out of the woods and onto the rocky riverbed, Albin watched all heads snap toward him in unison. The conversation stopped. Heads turned away as quickly as they'd looked up.

No one spoke except Herr Wagner who, upon seeing Albin, straightened out of his crouched position and gestured to Albin. "It's a damnable shame, my lord—oh pardon me, good sirs—" the physician rambled as he approached, stepping around the five men who were now as still as Albin. "These fine men have identified the poor fellow." Wagner turned back to the body, which was still mostly obscured by the men standing around it. "There's, ah, significant damage to the cranium and face. Looks as if he might have fallen from a great height, but I can't imagine from where unless he was brought here from somewhere else." Herr Wagner shook his head. "Do you think we should offer to carry the body back, my lord?"

Albin hadn't moved since he'd stepped foot on the embankment and ignored the doctor's question. His stomach roiled with as he stared at the body, which was clearly a large man on his back, though Albin could not see the face. Water lapped grotesquely at the body's right side and Albin wondered how long it had been there. Trying not to vomit, he forced himself to face the men. They deserved more than he was capable of giving, but at the very least he would hold himself together in the face of their shock and loss. "My condolences on...another...loss...for your village. I'm so sorry. Do you know him?" Albin managed to get out.

A young man stationed nearby during the harvesting was the only one willing to so much as look at him. The youth's long, tanned face was pinched with anger. "See for yourself. My lord." The young villager spat Albin's title back at him and stepped aside, revealing the head of the body.

Albin felt the blood drain from his face as he stared down at a half-crushed face that still displayed the fox red beard of Radek Varga.

VILA SONG IV

Her small right foot
bare and blooded from running
Away
Away
Away

Across the green black grass
slick and cool as a
snake is the last thing
she sees

Before the shadow that smells of him appears
And
She
Falls

Through a pit of air
she descends to the
rocks
below

Thirty-Nine

Eliška

The hive left Radek's body on the riverbank and retreated to the cover of the treetops upstream. The living would come soon, and Eliška had no desire to see them. Ahmed hovered nearby as he had since their meeting in the jungle. There was an ease to his presence that reminded her of Babička Olga. Eliška didn't know whether to push the painful memory of her mentor aside or cling to it for comfort. Watching Ahmed's head covering billow down his back as he sat quietly, she wondered at the possibility of honesty. She did not yet know if real friendship could exist in such a state as theirs, but decided to try. A question lay heavy on her mind, and there was no one else she dared ask.

She drifted closer to Ahmed. "May I ask you a question? About being like...this?" She gestured down the length of her semi-transparent appearance.

Ahmed cocked his head in thought before turning to face her. "If it is within my power to answer, then of course. What troubles you?"

She took a deep not-breath. "Is it possible to choose not to hunt?"

The hope-sharp words slipped past her teeth before she could stop herself. She bit her bottom lip and waited. Had she misunderstood Ahmed's kindness? If he was loyal only to Jörd and took offense to her question, she didn't know what would happen to her. Was it possible to die twice? Or would she be cast out to wander alone for eternity? So far Eliška knew only one thing was for certain on this side of the veil—Jörd's command.

Ahmed's warm gaze slid sharply past her, his head jerking in warning. "Follow me at a distance," he whispered and thought himself languidly to a huge elm tree, now bright yellow with dying, a short distance from the bulk of the hive.

Unsure how to take this response, Eliška rested on her branch a while longer, toying with her not-hair before following in a roundabout manner. When he finally came into sight through the golden leaves, she drifted toward him and perched on a great limb at a respectable distance.

"You speak of the bloodpull, yes?" Ahmed whispered.

"I think so," Eliška said, still caught off guard by his hesitation. "Is that what you call the feeling inside when we..." she trailed off, not wanting to speak the words aloud.

Ahmed nodded and rubbed a long-fingered hand against his bearded chin as she'd seen him do before when he seemed to be thinking. "I believe it is possible in theory, but a difficult task." He looked across the hazy expanse of the veiled horizon and then back at her, a sad smile pressed to his mouth. "I have seen it done only once," he said, his eyes grave. "Do not underestimate the strength of Jörd's bloodpull. To break such a hold would be very dangerous and take the heart of a lion."

Eliška wilted. If there was one thing she did not possess—even in death—it was strength. Frustrated tears yearned to fall, but of course they did not. At her obvious distress, Ahmed leaned in. He looked at her, hard.

"Are you a lion, little one?"

Eliška stared back, knowing her face told its own tale. She broke her gaze and watched the undulating ground far beneath their feet. "If you had known me in life, you would not have to ask such a thing." She'd been nothing but a sick, stubborn girl foolish enough to think she'd been loved and desperate for a taste of freedom. And now it seemed her weakness would doom her even in death.

"But I did," Ahmed said.

Eliška's head snapped back up as she eyed him with disbelief. "I saw only Jörd in the woods and when I...awoke. Surely you jest?"

Ahmed's mouth quirked in amusement. "Hardly ever, in truth. I'm afraid I was often accused of being a mirthless even in life." Around them, the trees quivered in the breeze of their ungodly breath, and he shifted as if uncomfortable. Eliška assumed this was a remnant of human habit as their not-bodies felt nothing.

"I'm afraid I speak only the truth about this." His brow creased then as his expression once again turned serious. Mournful even. "I saw you near the end. Before Jörd came to claim you. We—"

Ahmed paused as if searching for what to say. "We had been watching for some time." He stopped again as if unsure how to go on, tasting his words before speaking them. "She has been hunting for a long, long time. Her senses are honed, and she often perceives things which have yet to occur. So we waited." He whispered the last word, and Eliška had the sense he was trying not to alarm her. She nearly smiled at his consideration. As if the past could hurt her now.

Eliška let her mind wander back to the last week of her first life, realizing now there was so much more happening than a single white shadow under a full moon—and Babička Olga had suspected it. Babička. The name seeped through her being, aching like a bruise, and Eliška's mouth filled with regret. She swallowed it down out of human habit and turned to Ahmed.

"I saw her once. In life. My mentor and I were gathering at night. Babička tried to banish her." Eliška thought back to that night. To the hearth's foretelling of a stranger. She still didn't know who, exactly, the prophecy had meant, but it didn't matter now. She'd been meant to stay away from all who came to the village and hadn't listened. There was no going back. "None of that matters anymore, does it?"

Ahmed didn't answer, but offered a sad smile of under-standing.

Eliška did not know what made her trust this brother so freely, but trust him she did and asked yet another question she'd been curious about for some time. "If you had known what was going to happen to you," she asked carefully, "would you have done things differently in life? Would you take back what got you here?"

If Ahmed thought her questions foolish, he didn't let it show. He just met her eyes and rubbed his beard again in consideration. "A wise question. But one I think each heart can only answer for itself. As for me..." his words trailed off, and Eliška suspected he was remembering his own end, something he hadn't been willing to share with her. It did not seem to upset him though, and she wondered how long ago he had died. Who he had loved. Then his sudden, brilliant smile caught her off guard. In an instant, Ahmed changed from solemn and almost intimidating to so handsome it nearly stole her not-breath.

"It was a fine thing to live and love, wasn't it?" he asked, turning the question back on her. "I do not know if I could have resisted the call of passion, even knowing what was to come. To be ecstatic is to be alive, is it not?"

Eliška didn't know what to say, but thought she understood. If she could go back, would she do as Mamička said? Stay inside, stay calm, stop gathering, never dance, ignore a beautiful lying baron and marry Radek? Even now, the answer was obvious. She would not. Could not.

"But this," he said, now referring to themselves as Eliška had. "It has its advantages. As does being at peace. Or so I imagine."

Eliška nodded, and tried to lay aside her disquiet and admire being in the top of a mighty tree. Suddenly another, more troubling question struck, and she hoped he would indulge her one last time.

"Ahmed, what happened? To the one who resisted?" she whispered, sensing it was something not to be spoken of lightly.

His eyes slid around them before answering. He leaned so close that the wind of his not-breath touched her ear. "She was destroyed for her rebellion."

Eliška had not been expecting that, though she should not have been surprised. Jörd made no mystery of who she was. "Tell me. Please."

He lowered his voice even further, as if expecting someone to set upon them. "We may speak of longing for peace, but dying twice is not pleasant. Jörd carries a blade given to her by the First Mother, which can end even this existence."

Eliška didn't know what she'd expected him to say, but felt crestfallen at his answer all the same. Had she thought resistance would be easy? And to what end would it serve to not hunt? It wasn't as if there was any other life waiting for her. She cleared her eternally empty throat. "So we carry on as we are. If you have never resisted, then there can be no hope for me."

Ahmed hummed in thought. "Perhaps. Perhaps not. For I have never even dared to try. You are already the braver of us for asking the question." Then Ahmed thought himself into the air next to the branch and bowed deeply to her, a gentle expression in his eyes. "Hope is a flame, little one. Some flames destroy. Some sustain. Both are a light to see by." With that, he drifted away to join the others, leaving her feeling more alone than she had since her last breath.

Alone perhaps, but not entirely hopeless. As she perched high among the rattling leaves, an idea smoldered to life. A dangerous, tenuous idea. She didn't know if it was even possible, but she had to try. Revolted with her own part in Radek's death, Eliška fought against the despair boiling inside her. She knew giving herself over to the bloodpull would get easier and easier until she no longer saw the inhumanity of it and was as vicious as many of her brothers and sisters in death. This last thought filled her with a new dread. She had already lost her life. Of that there was no doubt or solution. But to lose what little humanity remained in her undead soul would be intolerable. She would not have it. She didn't know if Ahmed was right about dying twice or not, but she did know carrying out this revenge over and over and over was no way to live. Even if you were already dead.

If ghosts could have sweat, Eliška had no doubt she'd be drenched. Anxiety like she'd rarely even known in life churned inside her as she slipped away from the hive. The veil shimmered brighter, sharper here as she flew through the trees and she guessed it was daylight. After Ahmed had taught her to distinguish day from night, Eliška noticed that Jörd and many of the older víla went still during the daytime. Not to sleep—spirits required none. But into a kind of brief dormancy she was racing against.

Pushing aside the thought, Eliška turned all her attention to the graying wood of the cottage door in front of her. She could just make out the erratic rows of herbs and cabbages, the lace curtains fluttering in dark windows, and the fat cat curled up on the back step. Even without its color, Eliška would have known that cat anywhere. She'd found her way to Babička Olga's. Fighting the desperate hope roaring through her, Eliška thought herself toward the house.

But no sooner had Eliška drifted up to the back step then the cat leapt to its feet. Arched and spitting, it growled low in its throat and shot a paw out toward her. Startled into movement, Eliška didn't pause to think as she passed through the wall. The tightly stacked and sealed logs slid through her as if she didn't exist. Which she supposed was true in a way. Refusing to dwell on this, Eliška blinked against the veil and peered into the dark hollow of Babička's cottage. When she saw her, Eliška's dead heart ached.

Babička Olga, more disheveled and wan than ever, sat in her chair by the stove and snored. Her white hair was a wild crown around her uncovered head and though the house was in order and a thick shawl sat across the old woman's shoulders, she seemed smaller. Shrunken. Choking on dry tears, Eliška drifted forward, landing at the feet of her beloved mentor. But there was no time for self-loathing or pity. She came here for answers.

An idea formed, and for once, Eliška thanked God in heaven that Babička hadn't swept. The dust and ash were thick by the hearth, and though she didn't know how she would do it, she had to communicate. But how? Quickly, Eliška spied a wooden spoon left out on the surgery table. She went to it. Gathering all her might, she tried to wrap her not-fingers around the spoon. Her fingers slipped over and through the handle as if it were made of water. As if she was made of water. As if she were nothing. She didn't have time for this.

Frustrated at her lack of control, Eliška slumped by the stove and exhaled dramatically. And saw the curtain across from her move as if blown by a draft. Her not-stomach fluttered. Thinking herself upright, she moved closer to the curtain. Seen through the veil, the lace looked more like a sheet of splintered ice than fabric. Carefully, Eliška imagined filling her lungs with air, more air than her living body could have possibly held, and blew. The curtains flew up, wildly, and the broom leaning against the wall fell with a sharp *clang*.

Eliška froze even as a wave of excitement rushed through her, its own riotous wind. Not daring to move, she watched Babička Olga out of the tail of her eye. The old healer stirred in her chair and blinked her owl eyes open. With her gnarled hands resting atop her soft belly, the old woman yawned and farted briefly before looking around more fully awake. Then, Babička's eyes fell on the broom lying near her feet.

"What's this?" she asked the air as if expecting it to reply. "If They think this is the way to get me to sweep, They're wrong," Babička muttered as she bent to pick up the broom.

Eliška knew she must act now. Once more, she filled her not-lungs with the thought of air and blew hard. Dust flew up from the floor and whirled around her old friend's ankles. The wisps of hair around her lined face shook like cobwebs in a rough, unnatural breeze. Babička stirred, her attention fixed on nothing before she lifted her old chin and stared straight at Eliška. Babička Olga sat back up, the broom forgotten. Eliška had never seen her beloved friend and mentor, the grandmother of her heart, look frightened before, but an expression she'd never seen crossed the old woman's face as she stared into the space where Eliška crouched. Olga Prochazkova was afraid.

"Why are you here?" Babička asked the air, her voice thin but firm.

Eliška thought fast. Puckering her lips as if to whistle, she blew a ribbon of conjured air across the floor. Slowly, she imagined the exact route of the air and watched in satisfied shock as the air did as she bade it, cutting lines through the ash as if pressed with her finger.

Babička pushed herself to standing and leaned carefully forward, her eyes wide, and watched as Eliška carved her message in ash on the hearthstone.

"*Pomóc*. Help." Babička Olga read the word aloud, her wrinkled lips pinched before falling back into the chair with a groan. Her milky eyes filled with tears as a small cry fell from her wrinkled mouth before she pressed a hand to it. And she knew Babička understood.

"Merciful God in heaven. My darling girl. Tell me how to help, bird. Tell me quick."

Eliška wanted to fall into her friend's arms and weep, but knew she was beyond such comforts. This would have to be enough. And the healer was right—she must hurry. Jörd's call could come at any moment. She mustered every bit of her control and dragged her breath through the ash again.

"How Stop Víla"

Babička squinted at the poorly scribed words, her face hard as a gravestone. Then, once again, the old woman stared straight at her, though Eliška knew she wasn't clearly visible.

"The white shadow?" Babička asked, her face still stern.

In answer, Eliška blew softly against Babička's cheek. It was the closest she could get to a kiss. The old healer lifted a gnarled, spotted hand to her face in response as if cradling the touch.

"It is as I feared then," Babička said as she pressed herself up and hurried to the bookshelf.

Eliška knew which volume she would pull down. With deft fingers that belied her great age and sadness, Babička removed the book within a book and began flipping the tattered pages. Eliška hovered close by and let her gentle breeze ruffle Babička's shawl.

"Still impatient, I see," Babička muttered without raising her eyes from the book and Eliška felt her not-mouth peel back in a smile as she stirred the air more to tug at the old woman's shirts.

"Enough. Am I to get this done or not?" scolded Babička, and Eliška quieted her wind until the healer uttered a long, low whistle and tapped her ragged nail on a passage. "Come." She gestured as if expecting Eliška to simply peer over her shoulder. "Look."

So she did just that, surprised to discover her not-self could still make out and understand the words scrawled across the yellowing pages of the book. Then it was Eliška's turn to let out a surprised whistle and the hearth fire danced in her wind.

"Yes, you see then?" Babička said before turning to stare blindly at the space where Eliška hovered. "You understand?"

Gratitude and grief warred in her not-heart, threatening to pull her under, but Eliška could only blow another gentle kiss toward her mentor. Wisps of white hair fluttered around her pleated cheeks, and the old woman offered up a wobbly smile.

But Eliška couldn't leave yet. There was one more thing she had to know. With great care, she turned her attention back to the dusty floor and carved one final word.

"Mamička," the old woman breathed, and tears filled her filmy eyes. "Yes, I will tell your matka, bird. She suffers, yes, but is strong. She will survive. She has told me she will survive for you. Now go in peace and may it be." Then she crossed herself and held her hand out in benediction to the air. Eliška went completely still.

"I pray for you always," Babička said, her eyes glassy. "Do not be afraid, child. You are loved. You are mine and you are your mother's. You belong to God still. You are a child of this world still. Now go. Free yourself as you could not in this world. Be happy. Live."

Without taking her eyes off Babička Olga's face, Eliška felt a strength she'd never known in life fill her to overflowing as she thought herself through the ceiling. The last thing she saw before flying into the blinding brilliance of the day was a tiny, wrinkled man no bigger than the old cat with a thick beard and huge eyes, looking up at her from inside the hearth. A smile split her face. Babička had been right about everything. Eliška waved at the house's grandfather, and the old škriatok raised his wrinkled hand to her in farewell.

FORTY

ALBIN

As Albin trudged along the empty road, light from the full moon cast a slash of pale shadow across his path. He didn't know whether to be grateful for the added light, or terrified moreover. There was an unearthly quality to the light. An uncanniness. Albin stepped around it, keeping to the darkness when he could. He had no desire to be caught creeping away from the crofter's cottage where the physician slept in the middle of the night.

Many hours had passed since the tanner's body had been discovered, but to Albin it felt like days. Though the body had been brutalized, the injuries didn't make sense. Herr Wagner could not say the exact cause of death. No evidence of drowning. No way he could have inflicted such wounds on himself, but no obvious signs of foul play. Only his ravaged feet gave any clue to his demise. The man looked like he had walked near to death in a matter of hours and flung himself from a treetop. A magistrate would likely be called in, unless Wagner could pronounce it suicide. It was, Albin knew all too well, a possibility.

Albin shuddered under his heavy cloak thinking on the shriveled appearance of the man. As if the life had been sucked out of him, leaving only a wizened shell of the once mighty Radek Varga. Albin still hated the man. Even death could not quench his bitterness toward Radek. Perhaps if the bastard had not been so wild with jealousy—

Albin stopped the thought. He could despise Radek for his jealous claim on Eliška, for shocking her heart. But it was himself who had deceived her. Himself who'd broken her heart and caused her death. Albin would not let himself forget it on the very night he approached her grave in penitence. He had not dared attend the funeral. Anja insisted on sending an enormous bouquet of flowers —purple hyacinth—though God knows how she found them, and providing an extravagant meal for the village. Albin knew she meant well, but was not surprised when he overheard the kitchen staff talking of the food going uneaten, the flowers scattered in the river. He didn't blame them. He'd spit in his own face if he could.

But he would not fail in this. Albin tightened his grip around the flowers in his hand, savoring the bite of their thorns. He squeezed harder; leaned into the pain until blood wet his palm, the rusty scent mixing with the heady sweetness of the white roses. A small, welcome sacrifice.

With his other hand, he held the small lantern aloft as he entered the clearing. The lamplight beamed all around and cut the graying moonlight. He waded forward in the shallow pool of light as the ground started to curve upward. The hill was gentle, but he walked carefully, unsure of his footing. He'd never been to the village cemetery before. His mother had been buried in the family crypt in the castle, so he didn't know the way. Vague instructions from a terrified groom back at the castle were his only guide, a reality which shamed him. He didn't even know where the people who grew and produced his family's wine were buried. With the moon nearing its midnight peak, Albin crested the grassy hill and found what he'd come to see.

The village graveyard was small and tightly packed, but tidy, quite like Hrozno itself. Guarded by a low iron fence, the rows of modest headstones were uniform and straight, all gray thumbprints against the black earth. As Albin approached, the quiet night air shifted, kicking up around his great coat and causing the gate to moan. He stopped just short of the cemetery threshold, fisted his hands around his offering once again, and whispered her name, trembling.

"Eliška?" His voice trembled into the night as if expecting her to answer. Albin started to sweat in earnest despite the chilled air and entered the hallowed ground to search for her resting place. If she rested at all. He couldn't help but remember the pale shadow he'd seen in the woods that day. Or the way she'd darted around the square as if chasing a ghost on that last, terrible night. Albin told himself he was above believing in peasant superstitions, but it was a lie.

The headstones stretched before him like a ripple of gray water. Carefully, Albin waded in. It was not a good night to disrespect the dead. He'd been sober for three days and though his eyes and mind were clear, his whole body ached for a drink. He clenched his hand tighter around the thorns, focusing on the pain. Anything to ease the yearning for oblivion. He'd given his solemn word to both Anja and Miroslav that he would stop, and he would not break yet another promise. He did not deserve redemption. But he would use whatever strength remained to give them a second chance. As Albin curved around old plots, he focused on the sting of his palm and the burning in his throat to keep himself steady.

Most of the stones were as old and weathered as their owners. Generations of bones lay under his feet and he had a sudden, violent fear a macabre hand would burst forth from its tomb and drag him under. He shuddered at the thought, but did not imagine himself fighting. It would be a just sentence. Even as the thought drifted in, he knew Anja and Miroslav deserved better, just as Eliška had. He had dishonored her. He had dishonored himself. He would spend the rest of his life, however long that was, trying to repent for it by keeping Anja, Miroslav, and the entire estate and village secure and prosperous.

But first, he must pay his respects and face whatever fate brought his way.

"Eliška," he called again, listening irrationally for any sign of his lover's ghost. There was only the wind. Determined, he lifted his lantern higher and continued his walk of penitence, searching row by row for the stone he'd come to find. It didn't take long. Though the older part of the cemetery was vast, the new graves were thankfully few. When he rounded the end of the last row, the last plot was unmistakable. The stone cross glowed white in the moonlight and stood tall in the churned earth at its base. A spray of newly picked wildflowers covered the mound like one of Eliška's embroidered shawls.

He clutched his chest and heaved a great, shuddering breath. His hands shook with want of drink, but he held firm to his resolve and approached the cross, each step tender. As if to steel himself, Albin held the bouquet of flowers over his heart as he stopped in front of the grave. Moonlight kicked off the white stone and high-lighted every groove and edge, shadow and plain. He dared not touch it, but knelt before the mound and splayed the flowers across the earth. Albin took another deep, rattling breath and the white petals swam before his eyes. But no matter how the tears burned the back of his throat, he would not weep—he deserved no such release. Swallowing the burning grief, he bent his head in penitence.

"I won't ask your forgiveness," he whispered to the night, "because I deserve no pardon." Then Albin lifted his head to the moon. It hung fat and white above Eliška's stone cross and he liked to think her closer to the moon than moldering deep in the earth. "But I would do anything to take it all back so you might live."

The wind rose up around him in a sudden gale and his gut clenched in panic. Steadying himself against the unnatural elements, Albin struggled to his feet as he swallowed down bile.

Somehow, he'd expected this. Wanted it. Better to face her wrath and be done with it than drink himself into oblivion and further shame his family. He shivered with terror as the wind buffeted him, but he did not run. Then the air stilled and the sky above the grave started to glimmer and shift, dancing like a reflection on water. Heart beating too fast and his guts tightening in dread, Albin blanched and swayed, but never took his eyes from the white shadow looming overhead.

Vila Song V

In the distance
   the drums beat, beat,
   beat their hypnotic rhythm
   careless of the woman who has become
   no more
   her shadowdark skin still
   warm as Death swoops in,
   talons bared, and snatches up
   her breath
   her heart-drum silenced
   by his hand

FORTY-ONE

ELIŠKA

She thought she'd gotten away with visiting Babička. For it was some time after Eliška returned to the trees where her hive rested before she felt the weight of eyes on her back. She couldn't say what alerted her. There was no rising hair on her neck or tingling skin. But as she lounged among the rugged, sprawling branches of a great oak, she suddenly knew she was being watched. Closing her not-eyes to steel herself, Eliška turned already certain of who she'd see. There was Jörd, artfully hidden among the once-scarlet leaves; a great, pale cat waiting to pounce. Her furs and braids swayed in her never-ending wind as her kohl-blackened eyes mixed with the shadows of falling darkness. Night had come to the veil, but darkness did not obscure the view of her queen.

Eliška bowed respectfully to Jörd, who stared at her without blinking. "Great Mother," she said, not wanting to invite conversation but was afraid to stay silent. She wished Ahmed was with her. He had a way of steering conversations and putting everyone at ease. But he was not here, and Eliška must deal with her queen alone.

Jörd nodded at the greeting, her eyes never wavering from Eliška's face. Then the Queen of the Víla smiled a wide, knowing smile and Eliška went very, very still.

"You're not the first to stray," the víla said. "Far from it. Even I wander alone from time to time. It is a pleasure of this second-life." Then Jörd leaned out of her hiding spot at an unearthly angle and emerged from the leaves. "You should have thought to tell me you wished to visit the old witch. I would hate to lose track of such a young sister."

Eliška wasn't sure what she had expected, but it wasn't this. She dropped her gaze and played the part of the scolded child she knew so well. "Forgive me. I feared you would be angry. I did not wish to displease you." Eliška wrung her not-hands and did her best to look contrite even as her dead heart raced. "I only wished to see my Babička. To make sure she was well." She fixed her gaze on the queen. "I did not get to say goodbye after he betrayed me."

Now Jörd was in front of her, floating in the darkness, her gaze flat as a she-bear. "Yes. We have all been robbed of such things." Then, a smirk touched Jörd's split lips and her head cocked in cruel amusement.

Eliška shivered.

"I have watched him, you know," Jörd whispered with almost maniacal glee. "He suffers, as he should." She floated around Eliška as she spoke, a shimmering beast without edges. Eliška wanted to twist into herself, to avoid her new mother at all costs, but she held her place in the tree, and did not pull away. Jörd either didn't notice Eliška's disquiet or did not care.

"He calls for you this very night. Do you not hear him?" Jörd crooned, her voice a sinuous rope encircling Eliška's mind. "Shall we greet him together? What a shame it would be for your lover to follow his competitor into death without laying his lying eyes on you one...last...time." Jörd drew out her words as she came close to Eliška, her eyes the shocking blue of deep ice. "To know it was you who returned his suffering back to him. He longs for it as he should," she said, as she wrapped a hand around Eliška's wrist and yanked her into the air.

Eliška didn't struggle even as panic flooded her like ice water. She wasn't prepared to test her resolve to resist Jörd's violence so soon, but knew she would find no mercy, no reprieve from her queen. So Eliška raced across the sky until she heard *him* calling out her name in a cry of despair over the roar of víla winds.

At Jörd's release of her, Eliška crashed to a halt mid-air and saw nothing but the white face of the moon and gray waves of the veil rippling around her. But some sense older and deeper than sight told her exactly where she was. Dread pooled in her stomach like bile.

Peering hard through the veil, Eliška saw him. Albin stood in front of a delicate stone cross—her cross—transfixed by Jörd hanging in the air above him. Her furs undulated against the dark night, and she looked every bit the ghoul she was. Albin was ravaged. A shell of himself. But Eliška's not-eyes drifted from his beautiful, sunken face to the riot of drying wildflowers and the mass of white roses strewn across her grave. And though this not-body could no longer feel, warmth seemed to fill her. A lightness that had nothing to do with her form. She had not been forgotten. She was grieved. Missed. Perhaps—perhaps Albin *had* cared for her, even if it hadn't been enough. A smile tugged at her mouth and her belly lit with resolve. A lioness she would be.

FORTY-TWO
ALBIN

She appeared. Faintly at first as if in a dream, but then more solidly, and his stomach dropped like a stone through water. For it was not Eliška's restless spirit he gazed upon, but a being from the distant past. A warrior woman with writhing white ropes of hair, painted eyes; more beautiful and terrifying than any living being he'd ever seen. Because living she most certainly was not.

"Great Mother." His voice came out in a whimper. "Do you have her?" He held his hands up in a sign of surrender, though the dark stare of the phantom told him she had no need for it. He was nothing more than a fly in her web. "Do you have Eliška?"

The warrior woman smiled then. A languid, fatal smile and Albin went to his knees as a fear reserved for the night terrors of a child roared through him.

"Welcome, man," the creature said from behind her teeth, and Albin couldn't tell if the voice came from inside his head or from the very night itself. "My children and I have been waiting for you."

Albin froze, eyes wide, as the not-woman descended further

toward him. He stopped breathing, blinked as cold sweat ran into his eyes. The ragged, billowing shadow solidified further, tightening in on itself, until he could make out tufts of matted hair along the furs trailing from her shoulders, the bulk of her more like a great northern bear than a demon woman. Perhaps they were the same.

"I've come to see her. To beg forgiveness." The words slipped out even as his breath seized in his throat. He wanted to gulp back the confession, afraid of the wrath it would bring, but he could not deny the truth of it. He longed to see Eliška. Even now. He felt desperate to see her for himself and knew he would be content with nothing less. No matter what form she took. He *had* wanted her—body, mind, soul. That wasn't a lie and death couldn't change it. But she had never been meant for him, and that was the true haunting.

The phantom woman brought her nearly translucent face close to Albin's. And like a bird before a viper, he could do nothing but drown in the pits of her icy eyes, frozen, as every hair on his body stood up.

"Yes, she is here," the creature said, stretching her broken lips into a scythe-sharp smile. "A new, precious sister sent straight to us by you. I took pity on her. Chose her when you did not." She drifted around him causing Albin to crane his neck to keep her floating form in view. The demon woman let a thin laugh as he lurched to his feet.

"Do not despair. Yet. You will see your once-lover before the end of this night," she said, the cold voice echoing through his head.

Albin was petrified. Then, as if on command, his racing heart slowed, his already weak limbs went limp, and his voice turned to stone. The cold fear of every nightmare made flesh rushed through him as the not-woman put out her hand—a ragged hand embedded with needles that smelled of rosemary and remembrance. She placed it on his head.

"But first, you must dance," she commanded.

He did.

FORTY-THREE

ELIŠKA

Jörd called it a dance, but just like so many other things in this in-between place, it was a macabre mockery of the dancing Eliška longed for in life. Move Albin did—endlessly. But there was no grace in his flailing limbs. No joy. Only obvious pain and panic as Jörd wielded his body through the air like a broken marionette. Time was a blur and ceased to exist, minutes melting into hours as Eliška watched from a distance, her not-body battling for control of itself against the bloodpull.

Scraped bloody from being flung through trees and bashed against the ground, Albin's body heaved and twisted both under his own exhausting effort and Jörd's command. If he fought, Eliška couldn't tell, though the deep shadows around his eyes and the pallor of his unusually thin face told her enough. Grief had ravaged him, and he would not fight. A dark, twisted root of triumph shot through her as she took in his battered visage. He deserved this. Part of her agreed with Jörd and took pleasure in his suffering. But even as the root of revenge sought good soil in her heart, she remembered the aftermath of murdering Radek and her mouth soured. No. She would not delight in this and turned toward the cloud of víla swirling around him.

Over and over again she pushed the tempting pain of her betrayal aside and focused on the veil between herself and Albin. At the thought of his true name, she nearly lost control. Her rage coursed through her like poison spiked with Jörd's magic sway, willing her to surrender to the bloodpull. She resisted and held tight to the knowledge both Ahmed and Babička Olga had given her. It had to be enough.

Eliška redoubled her efforts to pierce the veil as Albin flew back in a gust of unholy wind stirred by her companions. He struck a tree trunk with a sickening crack and fell to the ground. His discarded lantern lay on its side near her burial mound, still lit and faintly smoking. She drifted closer, slowly. She did not want to draw her queen's attention. Not yet.

Albin's tawny eyes, already clouded with fatigue, bulged as he searched for his attackers. But the fiends—her undead siblings— remained hidden from him. Bright blood trickled from the corner of his mouth, mingling with profuse sweat. The passage of time was unsteady on her side of the veil, and she did not know how much time she had to act. She needed to go faster.

His vulnerability seemed to excite Fiadh in particular and she darted forward. Eliška held the dead air in her lungs and watched as the tiny, pale víla bent close to Albin. Sensing the unseen danger, Albin jerked his head away. Struggling to his feet with the great tree at his back, he drew his dagger.

"Eliška! Eliška, if you're there, I'm sorry. I'm so goddamned sorry," he sobbed to the wind. His voice was a web of anguish, fear, and remorse, as smothering to her rage as water poured over hot ash. Compassion for the foolish boy—for that is how he looked now—swelled in Eliška even as Fiadh cackled and whipped dirt into his bloodshot eyes with a gust of her wind.

Suddenly, Jörd appeared before her, vivid eyes boring into Eliška's. "Child. He foolishly calls for you to absolve his guilt." She spoke without emotion as if her words were irrefutable. They were. "Shall we give the betrayer his due?" she crooned.

Eliška met Jörd's baleful stare and then looked back at Albin. She could smell him; the stench of his sweat, blood, and fear brought two rival feelings into her dead heart. The first was this: Albin deserved to die as she had. Heartbroken and humiliated. Ashamed of one's own desires and the stupid things they drive people to do. While this feeling seared its way through Eliška, igniting the bloodpull in her, another thought rose to the surface of her burning mind and cooled it. Soothed. Banked the fire in her blood instead of feeding it. And the other thought was this: mercy. To sever the still-knotted tether between them not by demanding his death, but by granting him life. Demanding better of him. To hold a hand over Albin and let him go. Absolution as the ultimate revenge.

The truth of this stirred in Eliška's breast something the ire she'd felt for Radek never could. Sending a silent thanks to Babička and a prayer for strength, Eliška turned back to Jörd. "No." The word fell like a hammer. "Let him go."

Jörd's bright eyes widened, and she laughed. "Let him go?" She pressed her strong hands against Eliška's cheeks before she could fly away. "Do you think yourself the first of our kind to resist? Self-righteous in your moral piety?"

Eliška pulled back, but Jörd's fingers clamped around her skull, staying her retreat. Without her consent or thought, Eliška found herself pulled into Jörd's wind and rising higher off the ground. New fears rolled through her not-body as the veiled graveyard fell away.

"Because you are not special. You are just like the rest of us—destined to restore the balance," Jörd said once they were alone in the sky. "You owe this existence to me. I am your mother now. Your Queen. And I have brought you a gift. You should be grateful!"

Every echo of humanity remaining in Eliška's spirit rose to the surface as she watched Jörd bare her teeth. Peace washed over her and a knowing took hold. For the first time since her death, Eliška felt like herself.

"You are not my mother or my teacher or my baroness. I had those, and they were everything good and whole that you are not. I will not be grateful for your gift is nothing but control." Eliška wrapped her own hands around the Víla Queen's wrists. "Let me go."

Jörd let out a catlike hiss and Eliška suddenly found herself rushing back to the ground, face pressed into the ever-rippling earth. Shocked at being moved like a puppet by Jörd's power, she willed herself into the trees but wasn't quick enough. In an instant, Fiadh and Naeku had her pinned to the ground, their hands and minds intent on holding her still no matter how her not-body thrashed. Eliška turned her head as Jörd approached. The veil trembled under the warrior's booted feet.

But rage at Jörd's arrogance and cruelty roared up in her heart like a great wind and stomped out her fear.

"Is this how you treat your siblings?" Eliška spat. "Your children? Do you have no command except through terror and force?"

Jörd stopped in front of Eliška's face and bent close. Her large eyes, pale as a winter sky, rimmed in kohl glared at Eliška, even as she was held down by the other víla.

"Your mercy is a weakness. A blight. I shall not have it," hissed Jörd as she pulled a crude dagger from within her fur cloak. The blade was black as jet beads and glistened strangely through the veil, the handle bone-white. Eliška only had time to fill her not-lungs and scream for Albin to run before Jörd raised the glittering blade above her wild white locks and brought it down.

⁊∾◑∾◐∾⁊

Eliška flinched, her last thought a vague wondering if it would hurt to die twice. But when the dull thud of impact reached her not-ears, she felt nothing.

"No!" shrieked Fiadh, her grip loosening as if knocked loose.

Eliška's eyes flew open, her head turning to sounds of struggle and her mouth fell open at the sight before her. Ahmed. Sweet Ahmed was fighting Jörd. Shocked at their brother's rebellion, Fiadh and Naeku lost focus on holding Eliška to the ground. Taking advantage of their neglect, Eliška willed herself away, escaping into the trees. Her sister víla barely noticed and did not pursue her.

Hidden high in the canopy, Eliška gasped and ducked vicariously, her eyes never leaving the pair as Jörd and Ahmed exchanged blows in a flurry of movement around the cemetery. Jörd struck again and again with the ghostly dagger, and Ahmed dodged and parried her advances with incredible speed and a long staff of wood.

Eliška's dead heart leapt every time Ahmed evaded Jörd's strikes, but she knew the price her friend would pay for stopping his queen's attack on her. Watching Ahmed fight, Eliška vibrated with a gratitude so intense, it chased away the very last fragments of her fear. She would not let Ahmed's risk be in vain.

Glancing away from the tumbling forms of Ahmed and Jörd, Eliška's eyes fell on Albin where he lay a short distance from the battle. He didn't move. A pallor had taken over his golden flesh and sweat poured unnaturally from his pores. She could smell him from up in the tree. He was dying. Or would be very soon without help. Most of the hive was frozen with inaction, their attention wrapped on their queen, but a few víla started drifting toward Albin, clearly drawn by the taste of his despair.

Eliška's attention was torn until a cry of outrage she never expected to hear rose up against the night. In an instant, Eliška was at Ahmed's side where he stood at the edge of the graveyard. Jörd lay on the ground a good distance off, momentarily stunned.

Though she had been a shield maiden in life, Ahmed's size and strength had served him, and they were well matched.

"Ahmed," Eliška whispered and laid a hand on his arm. He had never permitted her touch before, but reached over to cover her hand with his own. Eliška wished violently she could feel it—warm and strong like it must have been when he lived. "What have you done? She will kill you too now. You should flee."

He looked at her then, his eyes as gentle as ever. "I have made my choice, little lion. Go make yours. Fly," he said before turning to where Jörd stirred. "Get him away from here. I can hold her until sunrise. She will retreat then. After that, it is in Allah's hands." His handsome face was impervious, though the muscles of his jaw worked as he watched his opponent, never once blinking.

Eliška watched, transfixed, as their brothers and sisters in death drifted to the ground around them in stunned silence. She felt the weight of their eyes. Their anger. From long habit Eliška took a deep, desperate breath. "You don't have to do this. You owe me nothing."

Nostrils flared, he glanced at her, his wide mouth grim. "I do not act only for you, but for myself. If it were possible, I would go back and make the choice you are making now." He whipped his attention back to Jörd as she rose from her stupor. Ahmed spoke quickly. "It was an accident. *Ya Hayati* did not mean to cause me harm; I saw it in her soul as it swept through me when I helped Jörd work her revenge." His eyes, still trained on their queen burned with despair. "A worm in my heart could not consume me more than that regret. I do not fear this next death."

His voice was jagged and Eliška knew if creatures like themselves were capable of tears, Ahmed would have wept himself dry decades ago. Jörd rose in the distance, and Eliška fisted her hand in his robe, tensing for battle.

"Come with me," Eliška begged. "We can leave them. We shall make our own existence." She gestured to the seething swarm of víla around them, all in the grips of Jörd's venomous blood pull for revenge. They were both in danger, which grew every moment. But Ahmed shook his head, a sad smile peeking around his beard.

"No, sister. It is time I faced my maker—both the white demon and the Creator—but for you, I give this last gift." He drew something from within his robes and handed it to her. Stunned, Eliška looked down at Jörd's dagger. More ancient even than the queen herself, it hummed in her hands. She had forgotten the weight of touch. He had disarmed her. "The old witch was right. We burn." It was the last thing Ahmed said before launching himself at Jörd.

Eliška cried out in protest, but Ahmed was once again locked in battle. She stared at the weapon in her hand, her mind a flurry of questions. Feeling like a traitor to her only friend, she lifted herself into the trees as Ahmed and Jörd thrashed. They moved in a blur of light and dark shadows, their blows falling too fast to see. But Eliška felt the battle in every fiber of whatever being she still had and knew from the transfixed expressions of the other víla's faces, they did too. Who they were hoping would prevail was another matter altogether.

Seconds that felt like hours passed as Eliška watched her only friend risk his existence to give her a chance. She could wait no longer. Redoubling her grip on the ghost dagger, she willed herself closer. Ahmed and Jörd spun and thrust and beat at each other, so Eliška was careful to keep Jörd in front of her. She longed to do as Ahmed said—take Albin and fly. But she would not betray this gift of friendship and needed to act fast. Floating above the battling specters, Eliška gripped the blade and dove, aiming for Jörd's twisted locks of hair.

She was still midair when a blow knocked her back. Tumbling like a leaf, Eliška fell to the ground, stunned, though she still clung to the blade. There was no pain, just a deep ringing through her whole body that echoed in her not-ears as if she were hollow. Perhaps she was. Then the pale face of Fiadh appeared in front of her, the young girl's tiny mouth pulled into a jagged grin. "Going somewhere, sister?" she said, and in a blur of movement fisted her ragged fingertips in Eliška's hair.

"You don't have to do this. Be this," hissed Eliška, wrapping her free hand around the ferocious little víla's ruined one, breaking her grasp.

Fiadh laughed. "I already told you, fool. We *are* this. There is no way back to life. There is no salvation. There is only power and vengeance. Embrace it." She flew at Eliška then, her mouth wide and obscene as if she were going to bite her.

Eliška did not think, only acted, and watched as the girl's livid mouth closed, her gaping eyes widen even more. Together, their eyes drifted down to find Eliška's hand around the hilt of the cursed dagger buried deep in Fiadh's gut. A shocked silence fell from the scattered horde around them before Fiadh pulled herself away. Eliška still clutched Ahmed's dagger. A dark shadow spread like an ink blot across the small víla's center.

Fiadh looked up from the wound as it seeped wider and wider. "You should not have done that," she said and flew at Eliška once more.

Shocked at what she'd done, Eliška frantically willed herself away, beginning a strange chase among the trees. As seconds passed and Fiadh closed in, Eliška flung her senses out in a wild search for Albin's heartbeat. To her astonishment, her not-body obeyed and cast a wide net of knowing that echoed back to her from the trees just as it had in life. Her mind anticipated each movement of Ahmed and Jörd's battle, felt Albin's agony on the ground, sensed her víla sister a breath away from her back, ready to strike. Diving for the ground, Eliška flattened herself against the trunk of a large tree, dagger in hand. It took only seconds. Tiny, fierce Fiadh appeared beside her and lunged. Every fiber in Eliška screamed to fly away, but she caught a handful of the girl's already shorn hair as the víla wrapped her fingers around Eliška's neck. Lifting both arms with all her might, Eliška brought the blade down and cut away a fistful of pale hair. A few of the strands drifted down like thistle down caught on a spring breeze.

Fiadh froze, stunned, but Eliška did not pause. She wrenched free and flew faster than ever back to the cemetery where Albin's lantern still lay, desperate to see if what Ahmed and Babička Olga said was true. Dropping from the sky next to Albin, now abandoned by the hive who were following Jörd and Ahmed, Eliška carefully blew open the latched door containing the guttering spark and dropped Fiadh's shorn hairs in. The tired flame flared up, eating the ghostly particles with a sizzle. An acrid scent filled Eliška's nostrils just as Fiadh landed close by, her ghostly visage nearly black with not-blood.

The víla stopped. Her outstretched hand went limp as cracks snaked up the long-dead girl's fine skin and her ruined fingertips started to crumble. Eliška gasped, floated backward, and watched as Fiadh puckered her small lips in surprise and breathed out a last silent breath before melting into ash.

⁂

The collective shriek of the hive rolled through Eliška before her not-ears heard the rushing of their raised voices like a great wind. As if he heard it too, Albin flinched next to her, his glassy eyes open and roaming in a panic. Her heart squeezed at the sight of him. So anguished and yet still looking for her. She stared at him with longing—to comfort him, to punish. But there was no time to linger with him. Not yet. She whirled to face the rush of wind coming toward them, some unholy instinct for survival triggered. This must be finished.

Jörd rushed at her like a spear, with Ahmed at her heels and the hive fanned out behind them; a billowing sail of the souls. Eliška took in the dark smudge across Ahmed's arm and the black smear of Jörd's mouth and knew both were wounded. Anger and gratitude swelled through her, quelling the fear as she gripped the stolen dagger and drifted in front of Albin. She could do this. She would do this. For herself. For Albin. For all of them.

Jörd stopped dead in front of Eliška, her face a shadowed flame. "I did not think you so stupid as this, child. To turn against your own kind. To give up your existence for a *mortal betrayer!*" She spat the last words at Eliška in a spray of not-blood.

Eliška didn't move. "The only thing I have given up is the desire to follow you." She didn't dare break eye contact with Jörd, but sensed the other víla clustering around them, forming a huge circle of phantoms, like a ring of mist. Ahmed hovered just behind Jörd, his face holding an expression she couldn't read. And right behind him, Eliška noticed a riot of black hair and the bright swing of jewelry. Sushma. Eliška didn't know what brought the sister so close, but there was no time to warn Ahmed if she was a threat. Jörd was upon her.

"Since you are too weak to claim my generous gift," Jörd hissed, her teeth black as she pointed to Albin on the ground, "I will take him for myself. But first—" The Víla Queen jerked her head, and Eliška watched as Sushma seized Ahmed by his wounded arm and clamped a ringed hand around his throat. Pulling him close, Sushma hissed something low in his ear. He grimaced but did not struggle as she expected him to.

Fear for her friend and Albin lanced through her. So with her dead heart thrashing inside her chest, Eliška coiled tight as a snake preparing to strike.

Jörd gave a languid smile and raised her gnarled hands like claws. "I told you. There is only power—either you take it or it takes you."

No sooner had the words left the queen's mouth than two sets of hands grabbed Jörd from behind and whipped her body around with her head thrust back at an unnatural angle—Ahmed and Sushma had their queen by the arms and throat. Eliška lunged. Grabbing a handful of the pale, matted hair, she brought the dagger down and slashed at it. Tangled strands came away like white ropes and then Eliška was flying for the lantern, not-heart pounding, racing toward the tiny flame of hope.

Roars buffeted the walls of her mind and the bloodpull flashed through her veins stronger than ever, wild and seductive, but Eliška did not stop and flung the hair inside the lantern. The flickering light leapt high, devouring the ghostly strands in seconds. A vicious cry erupted in the darkness and Eliška whirled just as the mighty Jörd, Queen of the Víla, shattered like an ember and was swept away in a final dance of ecstasy and ash on the dying breath of her own wind.

FORTY-FOUR
ALBIN

He'd expected to die. Welcomed it as his just end and had let out a macabre sigh of relief when the wind rose like a hurricane from the clear black sky. And when the chalky shadows dropped from the trees and swept him into the dance, he did not resist their siren's pull. He'd sensed Eliška even then; caught the faintest, most inexplicable scent of lavender and desperation amid the gale, confirming his most hellish fears. He'd damned her. His selfishness and lust had not only harmed his best friend and his wife, but condemned his sweet lover to a restless death. There was no consequence he did not deserve.

Though unable to control his limbs, Albin maintained some faculty of mind and sobbed aloud at his new certainty, unable to keep the grief from spilling out. As his body thrashed under the control of phantom hands like a giant marionette, he felt his instinct to survive take over. The body was a difficult animal to defeat. He fought against his impulses, pressed them down, beat his instinct to resist into submission even as the víla mastered him in a violent haze of mist. Minutes blurred into hours as sweat poured from his skin, muscles aching, lungs burning. Even as pain roared through his body, Albin remained determined. It would be over before the sun rose and part of him was glad of it. He would endure whatever came.

It would be easier this way, he told himself as he faded in and out of sense. Being taken as an act of justice instead of making Anja and Miroslav suffer his slow demise. Or his own violent hand. As if in response to this thought, Albin's head struck something cold and hard. Darkness spotted his vision, but he savored the chill of stone against his flushed, aching skin. As pain and light burst behind his eyes, he regretted only one thing: not having fathered a child. A daughter, whom he would name his heir so she'd never suffer the indignity of being married off as a pawn as Anja had been. Never face entrapment and desperation as he had. Never feel imprisoned by circumstance like his precious Eliška. No. His daughter would have been strong and beautiful and good like her mother, and he would have given her any life she pleased to atone for the one he'd so carelessly taken. If only it could be so.

Night air stung and soothed his wounds in turn as his body seized, shaking like a sapling before a gale as a red haze descended over his consciousness. Clouded with burning fatigue and pain, his insides rolling with sickness, Albin pressed the words from his broken lips.

"Take me already," he begged the air, and was rewarded with the request as his body was once again tossed into the sky. Night wind rusted past and there was a vein of joy laced through the terror he hadn't felt since he was a boy. A jagged sound escaped his broken mouth at the thought. Then, as if dropped from a great high—he'd lost awareness of his body in space—Albin crashed back to the ground, his breath pressed from his chest. He lay there, trembling like a fish, his lips cracked and swollen. Slowly, his hazy vision trained on his dropped lantern. One pane of glass was cracked, but the tiny flame trembled against the darkness, not yet snuffed out. Just before the world went black, he felt a cooling breeze scented with lavender drift across his body and he turned willingly toward the sweetness of death.

Forty-Five

Eliška, Ahmed, and Sushma stared at each other, the silence heavy. A few víla started to wail, but none approached them. Every face seemed caught between shock and relief. Many were blinking and looking around as if only just now finding themselves awake. Eliška shivered at what such a thing might mean. Ahmed drifted forward and Sushma just after. Eliška was startled at her sudden presence, but did not fear her. Whatever her motivation, the beautiful víla had proven herself a friend and Eliška was in no position to ask questions. Ahmed held his injured arm, but the wound had not spread and he seemed otherwise unharmed.

"Well done, little lioness," he said before offering her a soft smile.

Uncomfortable with the praise, Eliška held out the blade to him. "I owe you my life." She glanced at Sushma. "And you."

Her newest ally dipped her head in acknowledgement. "We have seen enough death to last many lifetimes." She eyed Eliška ruefully, but seemed content with whatever she saw. "I have no wish to follow another queen of death. Perhaps you will bring something new? Something more?" she challenged before turning to rejoin the host around them.

Ahmed touched his brow and took the blade back from her, tucking it into his belt. "It is I who owes you. Now go to him and make your peace," he said, gesturing to Albin's motionless body. Eliška turned toward her own grave where he lay.

With the stench of burnt hair still heavy on the wind, she flew to Albin praying she was not too late. Alighting beside him, she took in his glazed eyes and bloodied limbs. Smelled the rancid stench of sweat and vomit. She didn't have to open up her senses far to know he would dehydrate soon or be filled with fever and there would be no way to stop it. He would die.

A knot tightened in her core. He deserved this ruin. Had earned it with his recklessness and lust. She knew that. But the anguished expression in Albin's golden eyes, now clouded with pain, told her he knew it as well. Hadn't she too been reckless? Then, as she had done in life, Eliška opened her not-senses and let in his presence. She listened to his heart thunder to the point of exhaustion, his stomach squeeze with terror. She watched his pores open to sweat, his blood press against his skin in violet bruises, his muscles bind up. She inhaled his stink—he smelled not only of fear and blood and pain, but of something darker. A scent she knew well—shame.

He was no lord in this place. No high-handed master. He was nothing but a wretched animal seeking atonement and he would not fight her. He was broken now, as she had been, and here for her taking. Even after defeating Jörd, she considered it. Imagined the delight of tasting his soul as it drifted past her on its way to oblivion. But the echo of Radek's demise and the longing and affection she'd once felt for the man in front of her sang through her blood. She was stronger than she knew—had always been stronger—and held herself back.

Ahmed came to stand beside her. He gazed down at Albin and then over at Eliška, his eyes soft and dark, without judgement.

CHAPTER FORTY-FIVE

Eliška couldn't bring herself to smile, but was glad of his presence. She didn't have to wonder what her companion would do. He was good and brave. Perhaps she could be too.

With a phantom heart full of second life, Eliška leaned close to the man she had yearned for and forgave him. She unhooked the talons of Albin's heart from hers and opened her hands to release him. She became his better for doing so.

"Go," she said against his ear, her wind stirring the crushed rose petals beneath his head. "Live. Be better. Care for Lady Anja as she deserves. I will take what existence I have left and forget you." Then Eliška blew a kiss to his dimpled cheek one last time and rose over him. "*Zbohom.* Farewell," she whispered before drifting toward the treetops as the horizon turned pink with sunrise. Behind her, a swarm of unearthly figures fell in behind their new queen, exalted and free in her power.

FORTY-SIX

ALBIN

There was a noise. A voice. Someone was calling his name. These details registered in Albin's mind long before he could make sense of them—or decide how to respond. So he did the only thing he could do—lay still and tried to die.

"Goddamnit, you jackass, wake up."

He was surprised to hear Miroslav's voice so close. He nearly thought it was real. Without thinking, Albin rolled his head toward the sound and opened his mouth in automatic rebuttal, but of course he said nothing. Dead men didn't talk.

"Oh, thank God," came a softer voice. One of velvet and chiming bells.

Albin knew himself to be in Hell and thought the voices of his beloved friends a particularly apt punishment. He wanted to lean closer—breathe them into his aching lungs—and bask in a momentary comfort no matter their tormenting function.

Then someone grabbed his shoulders and hoisted him to sitting, his head lolling violently side to side and then tipped back as water spilled down his face. The icy burn of it going up his nose and the sting of fresh wounds brought him fully awake. Though it didn't feel possible, Albin blinked his eyes and found himself sitting on the ground with Miroslav and Anja leaning over him, each silhouetted against the rising sun at their backs, their faces grim with worry. In no possible universe could this be real.

"Albin? Can you hear us? Can you speak?" Anja's normally patient voice rising in desperation brought the realization of his survival into full relief. He was still alive.

A ragged groan he didn't recognize escaped his parched lips and he blinked rapidly against the shock. "You...you shouldn't be here. Not safe."

Miroslav wiped a shaking hand across his own pallid face. Deep bruises hung under his friend's tired eyes, and his jaw was shadowed with stubble. "Don't be stupid. We thought we'd lost you. What would possess you to—"

Albin watched as understanding flooded his friend's face. Shaking his head, Miro froze as his gaze snagged on something nearby and held fast to it. Albin followed his friend's stare and saw his own blood drying on the crushed stems of Eliška's flowers, now scattered wildly across the graveyard like skiffs of snow. Miro pinned him with dark, livid eyes.

"Not now, Miroslav. There will be time to scold later," Anja said, pressing a flask of water to his lips. "Drink."

Albin tried to obey and sipped the water. "I had to know," he rasped, clutching to Anja's hand. "If she was here." He sat up fully now and wiped a battered hand across his face. His clothes were filthy and bloodstained. He'd lost his boots somewhere and both his hands and feet were filthy and bloodied. His shirt stuck to him painfully. He looked like he'd been dragged across the ground and through the treetops for hours on end...only to remember he had been. "Christ," he choked out into his hand.

Just then, another figure hurried forward, puffing with exertion. Albin squinted painfully as Herr Wagner came into focus, medical bag in hand. The man looked like he'd run from the cottage. "I'm here! Don't move him yet," barked the physician.

"Just rest," Anja said as she took Albin's hand. "You don't have to talk now, Albin. We need to get you home."

Albin took another slow sip from the flask. If he didn't say it all now, he might never have the courage. It didn't matter if they believed him or not. "I saw her. She's...something else now." His throat tightened as his eyes filled. "I damned her to that existence, and she saved me anyway. Saved me from...them." He shook his head as if to clear it, but only felt the ache sharpen.

Herr Wagner was now squatting in front of Albin trying to examine him, but Albin didn't care. Nor did he care about the look Miro and Anja exchanged. Let them think he'd gone mad. Perhaps he had.

"I don't know why she did it." Albin's ravaged voice cracked as tears leaked down his face. "And I do not know why you both stay. I don't deserve your forgiveness," he said and waved the physician off.

Anja stooped close, but didn't offer comfort. "And yet, here we are," she said, taking in the shattered lantern, the scorched ground. She turned to the physician. "Can we move him?"

"I believe so," Herr Wagner replied as if only Lady Anja was present. "The quicker I can conduct a proper examination the better."

Albin watched the physician's boots back away. Then Anja took Albin's face in her hands and made him look at her. She was heartbreakingly beautiful and furious and far cleverer than he would ever be. He would try to see her as she was. For herself. Eliška would want that.

"I knew her, too. She was kind and brave and already dying." She stared at him then, her eyes somehow both sharp and fair. "I don't know what passed here, but we," she glanced up affectionately at Miroslav, "have made our choice. It's time for you to make yours. Come home to your family and live a whole life." Her mouth tightened with a deep sadness. "Or leave and do not come back."

Miroslav made a wounded noise, but did not protest. Albin leaned into the waves of pain rocking his body. As the dawn swam white and gold behind his companions, he began to shake and cramp, the exhaustion of his body taking hold. With his last effort, he stretched out a hand and felt Miro's strong grasp in return.

"Please," he whispered as the world tilted. "Help me. I will be better. I swear it." Then he was being lifted up and carried. The world swung back and forth and he feared he would be sick again just as he found himself settled in a pile of straw. The wounds on his back protested, but he didn't care. Moments later, Albin felt the straw below him lurch with movement and he realized he was in the back of a wagon, staring up at the lavender sky. They were taking him home. Albin heaved a ragged sob of gratitude.

Then he saw it. The form drifting above him like a puff of glimmering smoke. Tears leaked from Albin's eyes into his ears and blood seeped from his cracked lips as he smiled at the veiled creature above him, bright as a moonbeam. "Thank you," he breathed up to her. And he would have sworn she smiled back before floating up and disappearing into the breaking dawn.

EPILOGUE

She watched them from the uppermost limbs of a great pine. Sunlight shone on their blonde heads and warmed their young skin, sweet as ripe apricots. She could smell it. The toddling girl and small boy wove in and out of her sight, but it would not do to go closer. Children, still closer to beasts, sensed things beyond the veil though they were rarely believed by anyone except the very old. Already, the little boy squinted up into the tree, curious. Sensing. While their nurse sat nearby sewing and noticed nothing.

She never stayed long. Yet every harvest, when the grapes ripened and the shadows shifted toward autumn, she felt called back. Her brothers and sisters advised against it. They were not wrong. But the air here tasted of memory, and she enjoyed watching these small creatures breathe—listening to their blood pump and the stamping of their tiny feet made her feel almost alive.

The tiny girl stumbled then, falling on her belly and letting out a piercing howl of indignation. Almost immediately, strong, fleshy arms scooped her up and cooed over her imaginary wounds. Kissed her sticky cheeks. But the child would not be thwarted in her desire for a good scream and so carried on. Once-Eliška smiled, willing the girl to use her fierce lungs while she may.

It took the boy mere seconds to act. With the nurse occupied, he slipped behind the large trunk, dimples flashing in his round cheeks. Flinging his little head from side to side, he darted into the meadow, face alight with the joy of escape. Once-Eliška smiled wide, a bright crescent among the branches. Though both children favored their mother in appearance with their pale hair and round faces, this was clearly a boy after his father's heart. A traveler.

So she watched the boy of wonder and mischief dart about the meadow, terrorizing butterflies, picking flowers, and smelling the wild wind. Eliška's wind. In a moment of her own mischief, she sent down a breeze to ruffle the boy's hair. He flinched. The living could not see her if she didn't wish it. The veil secured her existence. Mostly. But the boy's large, amber eyes trained toward the tree where she perched, his little head cocked in curiosity.

Moving along the breeze, Once-Eliška thought herself to the child's side. The small boy froze, sensing her presence, but did not seem afraid. He only stared at the spot where Once-Eliška appeared as a white shadow, a glimmer of sunlight, on the grass next to him. Then she used her wind to pluck a flower from the space between them and dropped the offering into his hand, already outstretched as if awaiting her gift. He closed his tender fingers around the white petals and laughed. Once-Eliška smiled before she soared away, her heart beating strong as great wings on the wind of the world.

THE END

Acknowledgments

Any thanks given here will be incomplete because there are so many of you who've kept both me and this sad, strange little book on the metaphorical tracks for many years. Please know I did my best to remember you all.

Much gratitude to Ramona Mihai for her eagle-eyed editorial work and making it look like I know how to use commas. Huge thanks to Andy Payne Design for the exquisite cover. Fortune favored me the day I found your beautiful work.

Special thanks to Amanda Adam for her invaluable feedback on the Slovakian language and culture. Any remaining mistakes are entirely my own. Starla DeKruyf came through yet again with her expert formatting. Giant heart-hands to my virtual mutuals Brittney Arena, Jen DeLuca, Sarah T. Dubb, Kathleen Glasgow, Erin Hahn, JoAnna Illingworth, Paulette Kennedy, Cassie Miller, and Mara Moody—your encouragement means more than you know.

Huge thanks to the Tucson Author Alliance. I deeply appreciate your inclusion, guidance, and cheerleading. Here's to helping each other make all our wildest author dreams come true!

While writing often requires solitude, a writing life needn't. Forever grateful to C.B. Bernard, Erin A. Craig, Hester Fox, and Caroline Elle Murphy for not only reading early drafts, but for being in my corner from the beginning. You, my darlings, help make me and my words better. To my Book Club Friends, I couldn't have picked a better group to share my reading life with. Special thanks to Aileen Bell for fixing my homophones, and Lisa Powers for checking my German.

Many thanks to all the librarians, independent bookstores,

bookstagrammers, and readers who support indie authors. You build and maintain havens for joy and new ideas in a treacherous world, and I'm deeply grateful for your work. Special shoutout to Stacks Book Club, Stardust Books, and Mostly Books for taking a gamble on little ol' me.

Last but never least, thank you to my incredibly supportive family who remind me that love and grace are always the answer. To Jeremy for his patience and willingness to be my wingman. And to Sophia and Violet who will forever and always be my Best Thing.

About the Author

Jeanne can't remember a time when she wasn't in love with both stories and dancing. After earning a BA in English Literature and Creative Writing from the University of Arizona, Jeanne worked as a bookseller, assistant magazine editor, and elementary school reading tutor. She spent her childhood studying classical ballet and has been mesmerized by *Giselle* for as long as she can remember. An eclectic reader, admirer of sunsets, and connoisseur of dairy-free lattes, Jeanne lives outside Tucson with her husband, daughters, and a rescue mutt named Patrick.

www.ingramcontent.com/pod-product-compliance
Lightning Source LLC
Chambersburg PA
CBHW020241010826
48973CB00006B/1609